CLARE SAGER

For anyone who's ever been told they were too much.
For everyone who's ever mistrusted themselves.

Well-behaved women seldom make history.

— LAUREL THATCHER ULRICH

PUNISHMENT

At the bow of the ship's boat, Vice stood and surveyed the island she'd chosen. A hill rose at its centre, and a slender stream carved a line through the rainforest, so they'd have fresh water. Sun beat upon the curve of a white sandy beach. If they were smart, they'd light a signal fire there, attract the attention of some passing ship.

If they weren't, they'd die.

There were plenty of ways to die on an island like this. Scorched by the sun. Thirst. Starvation. Poisoned by a tasty-looking manchineel. Or the simple violence of one-time colleagues turned competition for food and water.

"Why do you listen to those animals?" The former captain's gruff voice rose behind her.

She sighed and rolled her eyes, turning to him.

He huddled in the boat with his surviving crew. Even torn, his blue coat, so like a Navy uniform, must have been baking in this sun, but he kept it on. Maybe he was clinging to some sense of order. The fifteen men around him eyed her from beneath lowered eyebrows, mouths set, some with bloodied noses or cut foreheads.

Between them, ten of *The Morrigan's* crew sat at the oars, backs to her. Beyond, at the little craft's tiller, Perry raised her eyebrows at Vice, a grin making her teeth flash bright against her sun-beaten skin. She was enjoying this almost as much as Vice. It wasn't every day you got to maroon the officers of a slave ship.

"*Those animals*?" Vice said, shaking her head. "*Tsk, tsk*, captain. That's exactly why you're in this mess."

"I'm in this mess because you're a pirate, but I thought even the notorious Lady Vice would put the wellbeing of her own countrymen above some foreign slaves."

"My *own countrymen* understand Albion outlawed slavery centuries ago. My *own countrymen* understand that owning another person is an affront to the fae, and they'd never court such disaster as pissing them off so bloody royally. The moment you took slaves on your ship, you ceased to be Albionic, in my book."

Never mind the fact it was plain *wrong* to claim to own another person—the way he spoke, he'd never understand that. She stood over him, looking down at his miserable face. "And away with your damn scruples flew any leniency I might have shown you for the sake of our shared country."

The muscles in his jaw rippled, seething.

This might require some intervention.

With a breath, she opened her fae-blooded gift to the rolling sea beneath them. The tide pushed its way towards the small island. A current drifted across the shore. Further out, beyond their ship, *The Morrigan*, anchored a hundred feet away, a stronger current streamed northwest.

The sea was an extension of her, or rather she an extension of it—it was far larger, far older, far more than her, just another creature in its domain.

Lips thinning, nostrils flaring, the former captain surged towards her.

How predictable.

Bracing, she pulled on the current, stilling it for a second. The boat jolted, and the former captain stumbled, landing on his knees and the fists he'd intended for her.

"Oh, please do"—she drew her fae-worked pistol and aimed at his head—"please give me an excuse to splatter your brains all over your crewmates." She pressed the muzzle into his forehead and smiled. She wouldn't shoot an unarmed man, but *he* didn't need to know that.

Chest heaving, he glared up at her. His shoulders slumped, and he sank back in place with the rest of his men.

"Pity." She returned the pistol to its holster and hurried along the current. It was light work to move the little boat, and the sooner they were rid of this lot, the better.

A few minutes later, thanks to her gift and the rowers, they bumped against the sandy beach.

Vice jumped out, sighing at the cool water on her feet and legs, the rightness of the sea's touch. With a firm grip, she held the boat steady and jerked her head towards the island. "This is your stop, gents. Get off my boat."

The slave ship's officers exchanged glances, then looked at her, the rowers, then Perry. Yes, they outnumbered the pirates sixteen to twelve, but they'd be damn fools to try anything unarmed.

Maybe they needed a reminder. She narrowed her eyes at Perry and gave a little nod.

As Perry rose, her pale blond hair fought to escape its plait, swishing in the wind. That, combined with her broad cheekbones and air of calm, gave her the look of a Varangian queen, despite her diminutive height. She lifted her chin. "Get out, dogs!"

The officers jumped at her throaty voice right behind them. As they looked over their shoulders, she drew her cutlass. The steel glinted as coldly as her eyes.

The pirates stood and brandished their oars like boarding pikes. Vice drew her pistol for good measure, waving them off the boat.

The officers scrambled out, splashing into the water, casting fearful glances between the pirates.

"Much obliged," Vice said, smiling her most winning smile as she bowed with a flourish. Perry threw them a duffle bag of supplies and waved.

Vice nodded in approval. Whatever the law might say, she wasn't a monster—she'd packed rope, a few tools, and canteens of fresh water to give the men a chance to live. Who knew? Maybe they'd see the error of their ways.

And maybe she'd grow gills to go with her sea magic.

Still, these men had bought and sold people. The fae would disown them, and that was punishment enough. Elusive as the fair folk were, without their favour, who knew what bad luck might find these fools? They were damned.

The longboat crew turned the vessel around, angling back towards deeper water as the former captain and his officers splashed to shore. Soaked breeches dragging her down, Vice clambered into the boat and resumed her spot at the bow.

The Morrigan bobbed gently in the waves, awaiting their return. Alongside, the slave ship, a pot-bellied brig, pitched to and fro.

She sighed. This little excursion to maroon the officers had made her almost a captain, albeit of the longboat, but once they were back on *The Morrigan*, she'd be under Captain FitzRoy once more. Not literally—they'd stopped doing that months and months ago—but she was under his command, and that was enough to chafe. She wanted to set her own course, to—

"You might have taken our ship," the former slaver captain bellowed across the waves, "but the days of Lady Vice are numbered!"

She scoffed. Everyone's days were numbered. Some just had fewer than others.

Smiling brightly, she turned and waved. "Not as numbered as yours, marooned dog!"

"Enjoy it while you can." Even from this distance, his eyes smouldered with hatred. "The price on your head is one thousand guineas. Maybe your crew should hand you over themselves."

She stuck a finger up at the slavers, before turning and grinning at Perry. "A thousand? That's more than doubled. I'm going up in the world."

Chuckling, Perry shook her head and adjusted the tiller.

Pulling her tricorne hat low against the harsh sun, Vice fixed her gaze on *The Morrigan*. With a bounty like that, someone had realised her worth.

Shame not everyone did.

Pursing her lips, she pushed their boat through the waves a little faster than necessary, the effort burning her muscles and making her stomach growl.

It had been her idea to chase the brig into the wind where it would be slowed, and she'd led the boarding party. She knew how to catch a prize and captain a ship, damn it.

Maybe now FitzRoy would realise that and finally grant her the captaincy he'd promised.

Maybe that pot-bellied brig, ugly and clumsy as it was, would be hers.

VENATRIX

It was a week's work to get the fat brig repaired and disguised—ready for sale, *not* for Vice's captaincy. But at least she'd managed to persuade FitzRoy to split the proceeds with the men and women who'd been enslaved.

Up in the shrouds, her sigh mingled with the breeze as they pulled into Port Royal's harbour, skirting as far from Fort Boudicca's guns as possible. She'd helped trim the sails to bring them in slowly and prepare for anchor. Now she wrapped one arm around a line and leant out, fingers reaching for the wide sky.

Beyond the ships docked at numerous wharves, the city rose. Stone, brick, and timber buildings housed taverns, brothels, craftsfolk, tradesmen, warehouses, workshops, cooperages, and the homes of rich and poor alike. As its three forts and barracks suggested, the city was a stronghold for the Albionic Navy. Perry said this had once been a pirate haven like Nassau, but now Port Royal had, for the most part, gone legit.

As they drew closer, the bustle of voices and work joined the constant *shush* of the sea. The shrill cries of parrots pierced the air as they flew between palm trees and nests tucked into the stonework of waterfront towers. Distant music drifted from somewhere—most likely one of the *many* taverns.

Legit didn't necessarily mean *boring*.

Maybe she'd get some time on shore leave for a spot of fun.

That was assuming their disguise as *The Three* rather than *The Morrigan* held long enough to let them stay...

She scanned the ships already here, watching for old enemies to avoid or potential targets they might follow out when they left.

The slaver brig bobbed behind, its fat hull just as slow and stiff as she'd expected. She almost felt sorry for Bricus running it. The first mate had a contingent from *The Morrigan* plus the former slaves, so plenty of hands, but the thing looked uncontrollable.

Much as she hated to admit it, FitzRoy was right—it was no pirate vessel. He'd promised they'd take a fast, sleek creature for her to captain. Something fine and low profiled with—

"Ooh." The sound breathed out of her.

A small ship sat in dock. She was three masted and shaped like a frigate with raised decks to fore and aft, but at only ninety feet long she was far smaller than any frigate Vice had seen. She wasn't much bigger than a schooner, and a touch shorter than *The Morrigan*.

At that size and fully rigged with such a sleek hull, she'd be fast. Eleven knots, maybe more? And that was without any help from Vice's gift driving the current onward. What was this beauty's name?

She leant further into the wind, lifting her spyglass, just one foot and one hand keeping her tethered to the shrouds.

On the hull painted in gold, *Venatrix*. Huntress.

Oh, Lords and Ladies. Something like *that*. That was a ship of beauty. A perfect vessel for piracy.

A perfect vessel for *her*.

How had she even thought of captaining that slaver brig when something like the *Venatrix* existed?

Skin buzzing with excitement, she tucked the spyglass away and hurried down the shrouds. She jumped the last few feet to the deck and compressed into a low landing.

Perry pulled up short as Vice blocked her path. She narrowed her eyes, lips pursed to one side—her withering look, as Vice liked to call it. "What's got you so excited?"

"Did you see that—that"—what to call it?—"I suppose it's a miniature frigate? The *Venatrix*." She grabbed Perry's shoulder and pulled her to the rail, pointing to her intended. "Isn't he gorgeous? I think it's love."

Perry snorted and pulled the spyglass from her. "You, talking of love? Never thought I'd see the day." She scanned the ship, a sound of approval in her throat. "He cuts a mighty fine line, I'll give you that. You could fall in love with a worse fellow."

Vice fished in her pocket for a cashew nut and tossed one in her mouth, munching as she watched the moored ship.

There had to be a way they could take the *Venatrix*. FitzRoy could be persuaded, surely. He'd been prickly recently—something had soured his mood, maybe the continued elusiveness of Drake's treasure, maybe something else. Maybe it was the fact he wasn't laying anyone currently, since their liaison had ended half a year ago.

Maybe she could use her feminine wiles to persuade him—he had to be susceptible after such a long drought.

"What're you grinning at?" Perry nudged her in the belly with the spyglass, releasing it into her grasp.

"If we take that ship"—another nut in her hand, she gestured to the *Venatrix*—"the Captain will have to give it to me." The slaver wasn't suitable for piracy, but the *Venatrix*? "It's perfect—the start of FitzRoy's own fleet." She flashed a grin and popped the cashew in her mouth.

"Hmm." The skin around Perry's eyes crinkled, and she looked away to the *Venatrix* again. "You want to captain it? You think you're ready?"

Chewing, Vice frowned and searched Perry's profile. What did she mean by that? "Of course I'm ready. I'm brave, bold, clever—my idea to chase the brig into the wind worked like a charm, didn't it?"

"But what if it hadn't worked? What was your back-up plan?"

She laughed and clapped Perry on the shoulder. "Back-up plans are for people without confidence in their first plans. And for people who can't command the waves." She winked and glanced down at the froth forming against their hull as they glided into place between a wharf and a tall brigantine.

She didn't really command it, not any more than a person commanded their arm to rise and fall. Command was what one person did to another. It was for things that were separate. She and the sea were one.

"Anyway," she said, putting her arm around Perry's shoulder and squeezing her close, "FitzRoy's been promising me long enough, we just haven't found the right ship, yet. Well, if that isn't the right ship, then I don't know what is."

It was going to be hers, she could feel it in the tides.

"But you don't know the first thing about it, about whose it is. I thought you didn't like attacking the Queen's ships—it has a whiff of the Navy about it to me."

"Here's Barrels, let's find out. Ahoy!" She waved at the pot-bellied docker, throwing him a broad smile and then one of *The Morrigan's* mooring lines.

Glancing up, he barely caught the line in time but smiled back anyway. "Nearly got me, miss." He touched his forelock as if he didn't know her, but used the gesture to wink without anyone else on the bustling docks seeing.

Miss. That meant there were people around he didn't trust. If he'd called her Vice, it would have been around port within an hour that Lady Vice, notorious pirate, was here.

And in a place like Port Royal, not every pair of ears was friendly. Here, they had to operate in disguise as a merchantman —they'd covered half *The Morrigan's* gunports and name and had raised their white sails, rather than the black.

The Morrigan eased into place, and Vice helped Perry and Saba with the gangway, with Barrels securing the other end. She was first up there, striding across to the jetty, Perry not far behind.

"Here, Barrels"—she sidled next to him as he coiled the spare line with an expert twist, tattooed knuckles flexing—"what do you know about that small frigate over there, the *Venatrix*?"

He straightened from his work, rubbing his brow. "Ah, well." He glanced left and right, then ushered her and Perry away from his colleagues. "That's something I was going to warn you about."

Perry frowned and leant towards him.

Vice scoffed. "Warn? Too late for that, I'm afraid—I'm already in love."

"Not with that ship, I hope—she's a pirate hunter."

"Huh." A pirate hunter's vessel. Low profile, swift, well armed. Made sense. And would make taking her all the sweeter. "Well, that just makes things more interesting."

"Not interesting, Vice, *dangerous*," Barrels murmured. "The hunter's here for you."

"Who's here for my sea witch?" the captain's low voice behind her cut through their hush.

She turned and smiled up at him.

Despite the pallor from too many days shut in his cabin, FitzRoy cut a fine figure in the sleek black coat he saved for visiting shore. The gold braid and brass buttons gleamed in the sun. His hazel eyes narrowed at her, red around the edges but just as intense as always. A flicker of a smirk pulled at the corner of his shapely mouth. "Vice"—one eyebrow rose—"what *have* you been up to?" There was a tease in his tone, like someone telling off a wayward lover.

She licked her lips and swallowed, heartbeat speeding. She might not have rolled with him recently, but he was still a damned handsome man. And that tone...

"There's a pirate hunter in dock, Captain," Perry muttered, arms folded, turning to Vice with a low-key version of her withering look. "And he's here for her."

Vice lifted her chin, hands on hips. A pirate hunter here for her. That would make Fitz see—she was enough for the Navy to send someone after her, surely she was enough to be a captain.

"Come all the way from Albion. He's meeting with the governor after her ball tonight," Barrels chimed in.

Fitz glowered, mouth flat, brow creasing. "And he's come for Vice specifically, not her captain?"

She raised her hands and shrugged, helpless. It wasn't her fault people liked telling tales of a woman pirate, who was also a sea witch, more than they did of her captain.

And it wasn't his fault, either. It was the fae blood. Even those only blessed by the fair folk—the fae-touched—possessed a charm that was difficult to resist.

For FitzRoy, the last straw had been the songs about her when they'd last returned to Albion six months ago. *The Song of the Pirate Queen*, especially. They'd argued, and he hadn't touched her since. Even with her fae charm.

Those folk singing and telling tales weren't her fault, but

hopefully she could steer it to her advantage. The more stories they told, the more likely she'd win her own captaincy. He couldn't keep her cooped up under his command forever, and the sooner he set her free, the sooner she'd stop overshadowing him.

At least that was the theory. She was starting to have doubts...

She gave him an apologetic smile before looking sidelong at Barrels. "The governor's ball tonight—I take it that'll be up at her mansion." If she could sneak in, she might be able to find out something about this pirate hunter. And if she knew something of him, of his weaknesses, then she'd have the upper hand in stealing his pretty ship.

Barrels nodded.

"And the hunter's going?"

"Aye, she's invited him—reckon she wants to dangle her daughter in front of him like some prize."

Perry canted her head. "What are you plotting, Vice?"

"Reconnaissance." For her eventual capture of the *Venatrix*, yes, but also for her own curiosity. Who was this man who'd sailed all the way from Albion for the chance to catch her? He had to be an optimistic fool to believe he'd succeed. But, Lords and Ladies, he'd chosen a tempting lure to dangle in front of her.

"No, you can't be—"

"I can. If this man's after me, then by extension he's after *The Morrigan*, so it's best we know about him, isn't it, Captain?" She looked up at him from lowered lashes.

"Something, at least," he conceded with a tilt of his shoulders.

"And I'm the best person for the job, considering..." She swallowed, and her smile grew tight for a second.

That girl was long dead, her past a distant memory, but she still knew how to summon her manners when necessary. Etiquette couldn't have changed in three years. A nagging discomfort tickled the back of her throat.

She took a quick breath. "Considering my background."

There, that was the closest she'd venture towards saying it. No way would she mention that foolish girl Lady Avice Ferrers. As far as the world was concerned, she was dead. Only Perry, Fitz, and those who'd served on *The Morrigan* three years ago knew she'd become Lady Vice—and they all knew to keep quiet about it.

Urgh, enough wincing at the embarrassment of Avice Ferrers. She was a pirate now, tough and free of a little girl's stupid ideas.

She lifted her chin, pulling back her shoulders.

Fitz tilted his head, mouth pouting as it did when he was thoughtful.

Perry's lips pursed. As quartermaster, she had no say in this decision unless the Captain asked, but Vice knew what she'd say if asked. *No. Too reckless.*

Sweet fae Lords and Ladies, she loved Perry dearly—she was her closest friend, practically family—but that woman did love to say the word *reckless* a lot. Everything was *reckless* in her book. Or at least everything Vice wanted to do.

Vice eyed Fitz—still thinking. If she could persuade him before he asked for Perry's input...

With a light brush of her fingers, she flicked away an imagined spot of dust from his shoulder. That would push his sartorial buttons. "Besides, we took that chest of fancy ladies' clothes from the brig last week. Would be a shame to let it all go to waste."

His brows flashed up, and his gaze flowed down her. He had to be picturing her in full stays and gown, hair brushed and curled and dressed. Gods, when had been the last time she'd done that? Surely not since they'd snuck into that masked ball together. And all night he'd strutted like a duke who owned a particularly beautiful sabrecat and showed it off on a diamond-studded leash.

Her captain wasn't easily led by his loins, but he did enjoy possessing the finer things in life. And, as he'd once told her, *a true lady in a fine gown is one of the finest things a man may possess.*

"Very well, Vice." He rubbed a lock of her hair between thumb and fingertips. "Just try not to get in trouble."

Oh, she intended to.

HUNTING THE HUNTSMAN

There was something about a man in uniform. Especially one who wore it so well.

Vice watched his profile sidelong as she poured a glass of punch. He was perhaps a couple of years older than her with mid-brown hair that was short at the sides and long and thick on top, swept back as if he'd run his fingers through it. It was nothing special, except that it framed a remarkably handsome face, all angled jaw accentuated by trimmed sideburns and high cheekbones.

Tall and broad in shoulder and chest, he stood imposing by the ballroom's high windows, peering out, apparently more interested in the world outside.

She couldn't blame him. Just like back in Albion, the people here were hypocrites more interested in gowns and etiquette than anything *real*.

"Oh, won't you look at those spills on the tablecloth," a grey-haired lady said at her shoulder. "What *are* they teaching girls these days?"

Maybe something more interesting than how to pour punch without spilling it? Vice flashed the woman a brief smile. "Quite." To avoid having to say any more, she sipped her drink.

He was still there, still absorbed by something outside.

Vice had been here an hour and heard no word of the pirate hunter. But maybe this wouldn't be a wasted trip. Men on shore leave could be persuaded to take a tumble before returning to weeks and weeks at sea without sight of a woman.

His fingers curved around a little punch glass, making his hands look almost comically large in comparison.

Large hands, powerful shoulders that didn't need epaulettes to exaggerate them, and long, lean legs. He would make an excellent candidate, now the Captain was off the boil.

The lady at her shoulder was saying something about *a gentlewoman's education* and now paused, expecting an answer.

Vice rolled her eyes. "Excuse me." She didn't spare the lady a look before sauntering towards the uniformed man.

To be invited here, he was some sort of officer. She hadn't bothered to learn all the silly little details that marked a man as lieutenant, commodore, or captain. Whatever his rank, he might let slip some useful information about ships in the area, naval movements, this pirate hunter...

Men could be very talkative between the sheets.

Just what was he looking at? She circled behind, peering past him through the window. Ah, the harbour.

"Keeping an eye on your ship?" she murmured, not quite in his ear.

He didn't jump, but he straightened slowly and turned towards her, brows raised in controlled lines.

Damn, even better face-on. His grey eyes surveyed her and what had looked like such unremarkable hair gleamed in the last rays of sunlight slanting through the window. This angle also revealed a pure white shock at the parting above his left eye. Below that, just crossing into the edge of his eyebrow, a scar traced a silvery line. What was that from?

And double-damn, a lady wasn't *supposed* to approach a man like this. She could deal with that, but she *also* wasn't meant to just address him out of nowhere without so much as a title. She was out of practice.

She added, far too late, "Ser."

Her naval gent cleared his throat, gaze falling to the floor. "I'm afraid so, madam." His eyes wrinkled in a charming wince. "I apologise, I'm afraid it's been some time since I've been in polite society and it's left me more at home on board a vessel than in a ballroom."

She couldn't blame him. The place was so stuffy, not helped by all the layers of clothing *polite society* demanded. Three petticoats, an overskirt, a chemise, stays, and then an open-fronted gown pulled on over all that and buttoned from bust to waist.

The soft voices of ladies and gentlemen drifted around the huge room—Lords and Ladies, they spoke so quietly, it was eerie. Glasses clinked occasionally, and a pianoforte sat unplayed. But there was no other sound. Not the groaning of timber or the shushing of waves or the whip of sails. Even her legs felt uncertain without the rolling deck beneath her feet.

Down in the bay, it was all movement. The gentle bob of ships at anchor, flags flapping, and the hive of activity—men and a few women at work, all with purpose. The people in here just milled about doing... *nothing*.

She sighed. "Ballrooms are so still, aren't they?"

His head cocked, and those steel-grey eyes narrowed for an instant as if he were confused by her comment.

Shrugging, she drank a cool mouthful of sweet punch. At least they had cold drinks here, though gods knew where they got the ice from.

He was still giving her that odd look as if she were something puzzling he'd found wrapped around an anchor. She swept her glass to indicate the room. "No creaking planks, no snap and furl of sail, no touch of salty breeze or spray, no sun on your skin."

The faintest of controlled smiles touched his lips.

What would they feel like if she touched them with hers? He wore no wedding ring, not that that always stopped sailors far from home, but with a little luck, it would make him more susceptible to her advances.

"Have you sailed much, madam?"

She laughed. What a question to ask a pirate. But she wasn't meant to be a pirate in here. She was a *lady*. "Only here from Albion. My family was terribly seasick the whole time." Just like *he'd* been all those years ago. He'd complained, and even when he'd stopped throwing up, he'd moaned and groaned in their bunk.

Lords and Ladies, how had she ever imagined they were a good match? The poor man dragged halfway across the world by her foolishness.

Blinking, she shook off his spectre. "But I found it most... exhilarating."

"Exhilarating?" The officer raised an eyebrow, the rest of his face still. Gods, did the Navy teach men to drill their facial expressions as well as everything else? "There aren't many young ladies who'd think that of cramped life on a boat for weeks and weeks." He glanced out towards the bay, but those steel eyes quickly returned to her. "Your family? So, your husband or parents or...?"

Checking if she was married or under the protection of a wealthy father. Ah, so he *was* interested. Excellent.

She smirked. "My aunt and cousins. My husband died some

years ago." That bit was true—the best lies came from a seed of truth, after all. And being a widow said she was available and had no virginity to fret over losing. "Oh, I *am* sorry, here I am having leapt upon you in your moment of solitude without so much as an introduction." With a little luck, she'd be leaping on him later, literally. "Lady Lyons."

His name. Technically it was hers since she'd ceased being a Ferrers when they'd married, but it had never felt like her own.

Maybe that had been her subconscious trying to warn her childish self. Their little game of romance was doomed from the start. She should have listened, rather than playing the idealist.

Ah well, that was an age ago. At least he'd been a better choice than the pathetic Villiers boy Papa had betrothed her to.

"Captain Knigh Blackwood," the officer said with a stiff bow. "My condolences for your loss."

"A pleasure, ser." She bowed in return. "And it was long ago, but thank you."

As she straightened, a beautiful blond lady in a lilac gown stopped in her tracks at the edge of the ballroom. Her eyes widened, and her mouth fell open, just for a second before she clamped it shut again, almost the picture of ladylike restraint.

Oh dear, with that hair and the delicate features, she had to be Governor deLacy's daughter. Hadn't Barrels said deLacy would be dangling her as a carrot before the officers?

The woman stiffened, glared at Vice, and spun on her heel, stalking away into the crowd.

Bad luck, Miss deLacy—*this* officer was taken.

With a feline smile, Vice slid her gaze back to said officer. "So, Captain Blackwood, what brings you to the shores of Xaymaca?"

"A woman."

Blast. She angled her head in question, and his cheeks flushed.

"Not in the way you might imagine. She's a pirate—perhaps you've heard of her. Even back in Albion, she's rather notorious."

Her throat constricted with the threat of a laugh. Oh, this was just too—

"They call her Lady Vice."

Of course they did.

He cleared his throat. "Though I'd wager that isn't her real name."

She scoffed and drained the rest of her punch. "You're the pirate hunter." She'd come to find him, hadn't she?

Damn the gods *and* the Lords and Ladies, they had sent her a truly tempting huntsman.

BLACKWOOD

Knigh Blackwood eyed Lady Lyons as she finished her drink, gulping the last mouthfuls in a most unladylike way.

An odd woman. Alluring with her wide eyes and easy smile. And yet she was far more forward than society allowed. Perhaps she was from Lunden. He'd heard the ladies there enjoyed a different lifestyle to those in the country—and as a widow, albeit a young one, she had the independence unmarried ladies didn't. Maybe that was it.

She'd said other strange things, though. She knew ships, she knew the sea. Her bright turquoise eyes, the colour of the clear, shallow waters around the island, had lit up when she'd spoken about the movement on a ship compared to the dull, deathly existence inside ballrooms. Life on board didn't agree with many ladies.

Something about the pink gown was incongruous. Her hair had been pinned up in a style that showed off her high cheekbones, pointed chin, and the bare skin of her neck. The deep aquamarine of her teardrop-shaped earrings and necklace set off her tanned complexion. With that dark hair and bright eyes, she'd suit vibrant colours. So why choose a pale pink when she'd made every other choice about her appearance so expertly?

She raised her eyebrows at him, their arch impish.

Damn, he was staring. He dragged his gaze away and lifted the glass to his lips. Empty.

Get a grip, Knigh.

He cleared his throat. What had she said? There'd been something strange about that, too. "*The* pirate hunter?"

"Oh!" She stiffened, mouth open for a second as if he'd forced her on the back foot. "I—I'd heard that a dashing young man was going to save us all from the clutches of that *wicked* Lady Vice." Again, with that effortless smile—how could someone be so easy with their expressions? "I'd just assumed the *dashing* part was an exaggeration."

Definitely flirting with him. Even he wasn't fool enough to miss that. Well, she'd have better luck with his colleagues.

And yet he didn't want to send her in their direction. They could relax and frequently did so in the arms of women in this port or that. But that was for men who could afford to give in to the whims of a moment.

Ah, that was what her smile was. Her whole manner, in fact. She was *relaxed*. Despite what she said about the stillness of ballrooms, she had this uninhibited air, as if she were utterly at ease with herself. Even her flirtation had no self-consciousness to it.

His heart ached with envy.

Her gaze had grown distant, and now her head cocked as a slow grin spread over her full lips. She chuckled and beckoned him closer. "Listen," she murmured, jerking her head over her shoulder, towards the table of canapés and punch bowls.

"... poor tablecloth! More spills," a short, grey-haired lady said to a younger woman beside her. "What *are* they teaching girls these days?"

Lady Lyons laughed. Not a giggle behind her hand but a full-on laugh. "She said exactly the same thing not ten minutes ago." Sticking her nose in the air, she went on, "What *are* they teaching girls these days?"

Despite himself, the corner of his mouth twitched.

She shook her head. "I think she's waiting there to say it to everyone who comes close."

"Well, at least we're a safe distance from her trap."

A footman closed in on the punch-pouring-obsessed lady and murmured in her ear. Behind him, a lieutenant Knigh didn't recognise sidled closer—perhaps a potential suitor for the younger woman. The punch-lady's eyes widened, and she herded her companion away.

"You know," Lady Lyons said, fanning herself with her hand, gaze flicking back to Knigh from somewhere over his shoulder, "it's rather stuffy in here and I appear to have forgotten my fan. How silly of me."

One-handed, she tugged on the window, but it didn't budge. Another pull, her neck and shoulder cording, but still nothing. "I'm feeling quite faint." Her chest heaved against her stays, the swell of her bust inviting above her neckline. "Would you perhaps oblige me, Captain?" The easy smile was gone now, leaving her expression as strained as the seams of her gown when she'd yanked at the window.

Poor woman, she must have been overheating—ladies *did* wear a prodigious number of layers. Unusual that she was so muscular. Though it wasn't uncommon for ladies to take up fencing practice in recent years.

"Of course." He handed her his empty glass, leaving both his hands free, and heaved the window up.

Fresh, salty air swept in and Lady Lyons huffed a relieved sigh. She gulped deep breaths, then smiled, all confidence once again. She thrust both empty glasses at him so decisively, he accepted them without thought. Sitting on the windowsill, she peered down. "Not too far," she muttered. "Oh, a creeper. Excellent."

Gods, she wasn't about to jump, was she? Staring left and right, he put the glasses on the windowsill.

Other blue and gold uniforms approached from all directions. The Governor's daughter, Miss deLacy, strode towards them, delicate nostrils flaring.

"Madam," Knigh said, taking half a step towards Lady Lyons, "are you—"

"Thank you *so* much, Captain Blackwood." Lady Lyons flashed him a broad grin, all teeth and glittering eyes, before winking, gathering her skirts, and scooting off the windowsill and out.

"Lady Lyons!" He grabbed for her, but his fingertips just grazed smooth silk. When he thrust his head out the window, instead of finding her bleeding, broken on the ground, he spotted her just below. She clambered down the woody branches of a climbing plant, swift as any sailor on the shrouds.

What in the world was she doing?

"That's my gown," Miss deLacy cried, drawing up beside him.

Officers reached the other windows and flung them open, hands reaching for their sides where there were no pistols—this was a ball after all.

"Your gown?" He frowned at her, then back out the window. Lady Lyons had reached the ground and was sprinting away into the gardens, skirts pulled up around her knees. "I don't—"

"Captain Blackwood," the Governor's low voice sounded from his other side, "I thought you were here to capture Lady Vice, not mind her punch glass for her." Her blond eyebrows and full lips sat flat, the picture of displeasure.

"Lady Vice?" What was she talking about? That couldn't be—

"That was a *very* expensive gown we ordered from Lunden," Governor deLacy said, voice level and low like a bosun about to give a raw recruit a good dressing down. "The ship bringing it was due in at the beginning of the week, but never appeared. Its captain was brought in today after *quite* an ordeal."

As Lady Lyons disappeared into the undergrowth, Miss deLacy glowered out the window, the expression out of place on her fine features. Once the pink satin had gone, she turned that glower upon him. Nothing about the look felt delicate. "He told a terrible tale about being marooned by *Lady Vice*."

Her mother crossed her arms. "Whom *you* just helped escape."

Knigh's throat clenched as his stomach turned. His hands tightened into fists, knuckles aching.

Oh, gods. Lady Lyons was Lady Vice.

VICTORY

"Perry, you should have seen him—poor thing had no idea what was going on." Vice threw back her head and laughed again. She was aboard *The Morrigan,* pacing her friend's small cabin.

Her skin still tingled with excitement—no, not tingled, *buzzed.* "I wish I could have stayed to see when he realised who I was. I bet that would have broken his expressionless mask. Gods, it would have been too much."

Perry was sitting on her bunk, arms folded. She raised an eyebrow, but the corner of her mouth quirked, spoiling the effect of disapproval. "Good thing you didn't. However much he was under the spell of your charm, I doubt he'd have hesitated to grab the notorious Lady Vice. Particularly not as she'd delivered herself so neatly into his lap." Her mouth flattened, and she cocked her head.

Beside her, Barnacle, the ship's cat, lay curled up. She opened one green eye at Perry, then closed it with a huff. The little grey cat was always on Vice's side.

"Oh, I wasn't in his lap—more's the pity." She grinned and winked, shrugging off the pink satin gown.

Now *that* would have been an achievement—bedding the very pirate hunter sent after her. And one so very handsome. Those shoulders, that chest, that *height*—at close to six feet herself, thanks to the fae blood, she was taller than a lot of men. Knigh Blackwood stood a good few inches past that, almost dwarfing her. Yes, he was a fine specimen.

"I would ask if he was good-looking, but your expression says it all." Perry sighed, shaking her head. "Besides the fact he's got a pretty face, did you learn anything actually useful on your mission?"

Vice looked up from untying her petticoats. "What?"

"You know—the whole reason you took the risk of going up there? To get information about this pirate hunter. I can't see that his looks are going to help us evade him."

"Oh, *that*"—Vice waved a hand and let the first petticoat fall—"well, he was easy to fool, I know that much. And"—that impressive figure straining against his dress uniform—she cleared her throat—"I wouldn't want to face him one-on-one in a fair fight, so let's not do that, right?"

Huffing, Perry stooped and grabbed the discarded clothes. "I don't think you understand, so I'm going to split this out into simpler terms and ask again. You risked your life by going up to the Governor's mansion—a building *full* of naval officers—while there's a sizeable bounty on your head, when deLacy has seen you and knows full-well what you look like—"

"Ah"—Vice raised a hand and dropped the last of the petticoats—"she knows what I look like as a *pirate*." She hooked her toe into the petticoat and kicked it up to her hand, brandishing it with a grin. "She's never seen me in the *lady* getup."

"That's still a risk—"

"A calculated one."

Perry cleared her throat. "You risked all that and went and spoke to the very pirate hunter who's here to capture you and make you see justice. Need I remind you, Albion's idea of justice for piracy involves an appointment with the hangman?" With strong, calloused hands, she turned Vice around and pulled the bow securing the stiff stays. "He's undoubtedly seen sketches of you and read descriptions."

Vice shrugged, breath easing from her chest into her belly as the stays loosened. She'd been wearing gloves, so there'd been no way he'd have seen the scar on her palm, and that was her most recognisable feature.

"You did all this," Perry went on, the cord whipping in her hands as she pulled it from the eyelets, "and your great insight is that he's a strong young man in his prime who's easily fooled by a pretty face? I'd call that an achievement if not for the fact it describes half the bloody Navy."

Vice examined her nails, cleaning a smear of leaf-green from under one. That wasn't *everything*. Perry was selling her short. "You missed out the bit where I wore Miss deLacy's stolen gown in front of her at the very ball she'd bought it for."

"Vice!" Perry said with such a forceful yank on the cord, Vice stumbled.

"Look, Perry"—she spread her hands to placate her—"all I'm saying is that he was stunningly easy to trick. I have no concerns whatsoever that he'll be any trouble to us unless we do something spectacularly stupid and let him get the upper hand. Even then, I'd put my money on us over him." She shrugged. "Gods, I'd even bet we could take the ship from under his feet before he caught on."

And what a pretty ship it was. Prime rover gear, that. She pulled the stays off, leaving just a chemise.

A vessel like that would serve her well. "Hmm."

"*Ay-viss*," Perry said slowly, drawing out the two syllables.

Avice. It shot through her, as sure as a pistol at point-blank range. Vice grimaced and clenched her jaw. "Don't say that name."

"Sometimes it's the only way to get through to you."

Vice turned, folding her arms and scowling. But she couldn't keep the expression in place, not with the idea of taking the *Venatrix* burrowing through her mind.

Perry narrowed her eyes. "What are you thinking? Whatever it is—*no*. Definitely not."

"Lucky for me, it isn't up to you." She gave Perry a broad grin and scratched Barnacle behind the ear. The cat purred her approval. "And I have ways to make the Captain agree."

"It's not fair of you to use your fae charm on him, and you know it."

"It's not like I can turn it off and on—it just *is*." She waved her hand vaguely. Perry worried too much about *everything*. "It'll be fine. It benefits him, anyway. Hells, it benefits everyone, including you."

Lips pursed, Perry folded her arms—the picture of unconvinced. "And how do you figure that out? What exactly *is* it you want to persuade him of?"

"If we take the *Venatrix*, he gets me out from underfoot—no more overshadowing him in the stories, no more songs about the 'Pirate Queen', *I* get a ship of my own, and—"

Perry burst into an incredulous scoff. "You want to take the *Venatrix*, a pirate hunter? Are you—gods, you're not even joking, are you?"

"What? Why not?"

"Pirate hunter. The clue's in the name."

"*Ha!* He's nothing to worry about—didn't you just hear me say how easily fooled he was?"

Inhaling slowly, Perry closed her eyes and pinched the bridge of her nose. "He won't be a second time—he must have done something impressive to make captain at such a young age. And to be stationed out here, not even under an admiral's fleet. He can't be an idiot. And besides, he's seen you now—you won't be able to get close to him like that again."

"Then I'll just come up with a plan that doesn't require it." Vice shrugged and shed the chemise, the last of Miss deLacy's layers. Sighing, she pulled on fitted breeches and a shirt with billowing sleeves. Thank the gods for that—normal clothes.

And Perry had fallen silent—double thanks. Maybe she'd realised her worry was unwarranted.

When she turned, Perry stood by the door, hands on hips.

Vice winced. Maybe not. Definite lecture incoming in three, two—

"You're seriously willing to wager other people's lives on this?" Perry's voice was low. "This pirate hunter has come halfway across the world after you. I asked around the docks—he has a reputation. Well-paid, they say—do you know what kind of pirate hunter is well paid?" Her chin jutted.

Whatever Vice said, Perry was about to tell her. She lifted one shoulder—let her have her fun explaining. Who was she to come between Perry and a good lecture?

Perry widened her eyes. "A good one. When he goes after a bounty, he gets it. Because he's clever—don't say it." She lifted her hands. "I know you tricked him into a drink with you, and I bet you wish you'd bedded him, too, just to add to your tweak of his nose, but you caught him unawares. From what they say, he's cunning—as sneaky as one of us. You only got one over on him because he didn't even realise he was playing your game yet." She leant against the door, folding her arms. "Out on the high seas—it'll be *his* game, and he'll be alert all the while. Our best course of action will be to stay well away."

"Where's the fun in that?" Vice muttered, folding her arms.

"*Fun?*" Perry stared at her, but instead of continuing with a half-shouted rant, she sighed and covered her face. "That's what you really think, isn't it? People's lives could be at stake if we go after a pirate hunter's vessel and all you see is the challenge, the *fun*, the chance to get a pretty ship."

Vice frowned, swallowing. Somehow those softer words hurt far more than any of the times Perry had raised her voice. "*And* my captaincy, which he's been promising me for almost a year now—don't forget that."

That was far more than just fun. It was freedom for her and whoever else ended up in her crew, hopefully, Perry. That was the most important thing—the *only* important thing.

Sometimes FitzRoy's decisions were downright unfair. His refusal to grant her the promised captaincy was a case in point.

But not only that. He was so obsessed with Drake's treasure, he'd pull them out of port to follow a lead before the crew had even had a proper chance to enjoy themselves and Perry had restocked the ship.

And even when his decisions were sound, they were exactly that—*his*. He chose where they went, what prizes they chased, who occupied which positions in the crew, when they stopped at port and for how long, what the rules were on board.

When she had her own ship, she wouldn't have to rely on his decisions, his whims, or... *him.*

Perry rubbed her face and let her hands drop. "And is your captaincy worth other people's lives?"

"Perry," she said, rolling her eyes, "no one's going to die. I do the risky parts, you know that. I always do."

Because what did it matter? She could die doing something apparently safe, like eating a bad batch of mussels. Any of them could die tomorrow doing the simplest task—even something that didn't seem dangerous. At least higher risks had the possibility of higher rewards.

"If something happens to me, it happens." She shrugged.

"And what about if something happens to you, and others—fools that they are—come running after you to help? Then what?"

Vice scoffed. They should know she'd be fine. She didn't need anyone chasing after her, *saving* her—she hadn't needed that in a long time. When she'd been young and stupid enough to believe she needed rescuing, the gods had taught her just how much of a foolish notion that was.

Her thumb ran over the smooth opal ring on her left hand. She clenched her jaw for a second. "Then make sure they don't come after me. I can look after myself."

Perry opened her mouth as if to reply but instead just sighed, shoulders sagging. "I give up." She flung her hands in the air and stepped away from the door. "I'm not going to be able to change your mind. Go and speak to the Captain, then, see if you can get him on board with your ridiculous plan."

Victory.

Grinning, Vice pulled on her boots. *"Thank you."* She leapt up and gave Perry a rough hug. "Ah, you know I'll take you with me when I get my ship."

A low sound came from Perry's throat, almost a growl, but her arms fastened around Vice and she squeezed back. "I have the worst luck, it seems."

"Ouch." Vice chuckled and pulled away. In an instant, Barnacle leapt up and draped over her shoulders. "You'd miss me if I left you."

Perry sighed, shaking her head. “Can’t live with you, can’t live without.”

Laughing, Vice clapped Perry on the back and opened the door. “You could,” she said from the doorway, “it just wouldn’t be nearly as interesting.”

IN THE TIDES

That woman. Knigh clenched jaw and fist until they both ached. How hadn't he realised he was speaking to a pirate? And that particular pirate?

Shortly after the Arawakéan Union invited the nations of Europa to trade, the surge in piracy had begun. Being smart, the Union had soon made it clear to Europa that the pirates were their problem to deal with. And for the past two years, Knigh had dealt with it rather effectively.

Now Lady Vice had made him look like a novice.

Glowering, he continued his stomp around the docks. His uniform—or perhaps his expression—sent men out of his path with salutes or bowed heads.

He'd arrived at first light as the wharves woke to get information about her—where she'd docked, when she'd left, where she was going. That was assuming she *had* left. There had been no sign of her or *The Morrigan* when he'd ridden here from the Governor's mansion last night. Still, it had been dark, and Port

Royal had berths for over a hundred vessels, plus anchorage in the harbour for dozens more.

Watching for a ship of that name was no guarantee anyway —*The Morrigan* could be here incognito, gun ports disguised. He had to give it to Vice and her captain: all the reports suggested they were cunning.

He bit back a sigh. Searching so many vessels would be quite the task, and if she had left, it would delay his pursuit. Not to mention the fact that holding all these ships in dock for a day on the chance she *might* be on board wouldn't win him any allies. If it turned out she'd already gone, it could be downright embarrassing for the Navy and, by extension, troublesome for him.

Asking the dockers hadn't been much help—either they knew nothing about Lady Vice or were damn good liars. Both were entirely possible.

Smoothing his expression, he scanned the ships at rest, bobbing in the ebb tide.

Ebb? Wait—

He pulled out his pocket watch. Six o'clock. The high tide wasn't meant to be until seven. From the way the water had dropped in the past hour, he'd have guessed there'd been a high tide recently.

He crouched by one of the wharf's timber posts. Wet almost to the algae-coated high tide line. The sea was too calm to have lapped up that high.

Rocking back on his heels, he scanned the port again. Had there somehow been an *extra* high tide? But—no, that just wasn't possible. The tides were caused by the moon, and the moon didn't just change its orbit on a whim.

Strange. Very strange.

There had to be some other explanation, perhaps—

A burly docker hauled crates at the end of the wharf. The

crawling starburst of a scar on his jaw, from gunshot or the edge of an explosion, was familiar.

"Here, Smith, isn't it?" Knigh rose, dusting off his hands.

The man's head jerked in his direction, and he nodded. "Aye, ser." He snapped a neat salute—former Navy, most likely.

Knigh circled to him swiftly.

The docker's eyes widened. "All's well with your ship, ser—I've been keeping an eye on it as you asked." He nodded again, body bending too, almost making it a bow.

"Yes, yes, excellent—thank you. It's not that I'm here about."

The man visibly relaxed a fraction. "Oh?"

"You might have heard by now—the infamous pirate Lady Vice was here last night."

His bristly brows shot up. "A pirate? Right under the Navy's nose, ser?"

Thank you for the reminder. Knigh clenched his jaw, nostrils flaring for a second before he cleared his throat. "I'm afraid so. Did you see anything unusual late last night or early this morning?"

Smith rubbed his whiskered cheeks. "Nothing that stands out, ser. Apologies."

"What about a woman roughly so tall"—he lifted one hand to his eye level—"dark hair"—he cleared his throat—"easy on the eye."

Smith's eyes widened slowly, his brows rising. "Oh, *her?* And you reckon that's Lady Vice?" He shook his head with an apologetic wince. "Sorry, ser, of course you do. Well, I suppose it might be. Quite a few merchant ships take women in their crews these days, though, not just the pirates, so she wouldn't've stuck out to most of us, ser. Only really remember her because—well, as you said, her face is uncommon pretty, ser, if you don't mind me saying such about a pirate."

Knigh scoffed softly and shook his head. "You wouldn't be the first to notice." *Or to be distracted by it.* He'd let a ballroom and a pretty face lower his guard. Well, he wouldn't make that mistake again.

But it hadn't only been that, had it? There was this disarming honesty to her—*apparent* honesty, anyway. She'd been lying through her teeth the whole time.

Lady Lyons—*ha!*

Although... she did call herself *Lady* Vice. He'd always assumed it was a piratical affectation—they so often liked to elevate themselves. But perhaps it wasn't. She'd passed herself off as a lady so easily—her accent and manners had both been excellent if a little forward. Maybe she had some experience amongst the gentry. She must have had some sort of life before piracy. Who had she been? Someone of consequence?

Exhaling, Smith's gaze went into the distance. "I didn't have nothing to do with them loading, ser, but I saw Barrels speaking to the lady when she arrived yesterday. He's over there—maybe he knows something, ser."

Hope flared in Knigh's chest, bright and warm in the cool morning air. If he could get a lead right away, he might even manage a capture within a day or two. That would undoubtedly silence any comments from the Governor or anyone else who'd seen him sharing a drink with Lady Vice.

He thanked Smith and strode straight for the pot-bellied man he'd called Barrels.

With a swift greeting, he got the niceties out the way before asking about Lady Vice. Like the others, he claimed ignorance, although a flicker of a reaction laced his movements—a shift in stance, a twitch of the eyebrows, a thumb pressing to his lips.

Could be nerves—speaking to an officer had that effect on some dock workers—but then again, it could be the sign of a lie. Time to probe deeper.

"Yesterday, you were seen speaking to a tall young woman, dark hair, pretty. Do you remember her?" If he didn't, he'd have to be blind or a damn fool.

"Oh, her? Aye, ser. Very pretty and tall, ser."

"Where is she? What ship did she come in on?"

"I'm afraid they've gone, ser."

Knigh huffed. It had been too much to hope they were still in dock. "Gone where?"

Barrels shrugged, hands open. "Afraid I don't know, ser. So—er—you think she could be that pirate lass?"

"I'm sure of it." He gave the man a flat look.

"Well," Barrels said, shaking his head a few times too many, "I wouldn't know anything about any of that."

Knigh gave a narrow smile. "Oh, but I think you do."

"I—no—I—"

"Mr Barrels, let's not waste anyone's time here." He raised an eyebrow. "As you're no doubt aware, I'm a pirate hunter of the Queen's Navy. This Lady Vice is a pirate. And you—well, you strike me as a good man, a hard worker, honest, always stayed the right side of the law. Correct?"

The docker's gaze dropped, and he nodded. "Aye, ser."

"While this so-called Lady Vice, well, she kills people for a living—on a daily basis, I dare say. Thinks nothing of it, just poof." He flicked his fingers into the air, then let them clench slowly into a fist. "*I* am also here to do a job. Occasionally I kill, but I prefer not to. Mostly I capture criminals and return them to Albion to face the Queen's justice."

Knigh drew a long breath and let his gaze fall on Barrels—the man stared, rapt. "As a pirate hunter," Knigh went on softly, "I have more powers than your average ship's captain. I can have a man arrested, Navy or not. Strapped in irons. Locked up. Gods, I'm sure I could even have them throw away the key. Imagine it lost somewhere in Davy Jones' Locker—just a tiny little key sinking in the vastness of the ocean never to be seen again. Now, I'd rather not do that—you seem a good sort—but as I said, I have a job to do." Plus a mother, brother, and sister relying on him to earn that bounty. "And you—*you* can help me, Mr Barrels."

The docker's mouth hung open, and he blinked suddenly as if waking from a stupor. He swallowed, a crease between his brows as he met Knigh's eye. "How, ser?"

"Tell me what you know about Lady Vice and her ship."

"I don't know nothing about her, ser—just that she's a pirate, ser. Just the normal things that everyone knows." He swallowed again, forehead gleaming.

Knigh patted him on the shoulder; it might have been friendly if it hadn't been such a calculated manoeuvre. "I've been away from Arawaké a while, maybe I'm behind on the latest news—tell me what exactly 'everyone knows'." He cocked his head and unleashed his smile.

He tended to keep a distance from, well, *everyone*, but sometimes a little warmth, even superficial, could go a long way. And being fae-touched came with a distinct advantage when it came to turning on the charm.

The docker's shoulders instantly lowered, and the tension around his jaw slackened. Slowly, the corners of his mouth turned up, just a touch. He glanced around, eyes flashing, furtive. "Let's see... Well, she's a pretty lass, as you said"—he ticked the piece of information off on one finger—"and a pirate." Another finger. "But I hear she always offers quarter, so..." He blinked, and his gaze snapped to Knigh as if he realised he was painting a pirate in glowing terms to a pirate hunter.

With a gruff clearing of his throat, Barrels went on, frowning: "Think her ship's *The Morrigan*, captained by a man named Fitz-Roy. Everyone says she's his right-hand woman."

When Barrels drifted into silence, Knigh clenched his jaw against an exasperated sigh. That was all information he already knew. If he could find out a bit more about her ship or captain, maybe that would give a clue about their destination from here. He forced another smile in place. "What about FitzRoy? What sort of reputation does he have? Any favourite haunts?"

The man's mouth screwed up. "Wouldn't know about that, ser. He's meant to be"—he lifted one shoulder and glanced around again—"let's say a bit less *reasonable* than the lady—so I hear. And if he gets a sniff of anything about Drake, he can get downright violent." His shudder suggested he had experience of that.

"Drake?" Knigh cocked his head. Surely not—"As in, *Ser Francis Drake?"* What did a long-dead privateer have to do with anything?

"Aye, ser. You've heard the stories about his treasure, surely? Everyone knows FitzRoy's obsessed with it—reckons he'll find it one day." Barrels scoffed and quite rightly—most people of sound mind had given up on it a century ago. "Well, he hasn't found it in all the years he's been around these parts." Sighing, he shrugged. "But then some men need their obsessions, don't they?"

Knigh blinked, a genuine smile easing into place. "Yes. Yes, they do." And obsession pushed men to make mistakes, like chasing every clue they came across. "Thank you, Mr Barrels, you've been a great help." He held out two silver crowns and nodded. It was possibly more than he should give, and it came out of his own pocket, not the Navy's—they didn't hold with bribes. But it was nothing compared to the bounty he'd get when he delivered Lady Vice to the authorities back home. "A great help indeed."

He had to catch up with her and get a message to his contact, first. Turning from Barrels, he took a deep breath and mastered his expression. Control. He didn't have her yet.

But he did have a plan starting to form...

All he needed was a rumour of a clue to Drake's treasure that led to a quiet spot somewhere he could lie in wait. Somewhere with shallow reefs where they wouldn't realise they were stuck until he sailed into view, blocking their exit.

Oh, yes, that would work nicely. He kept the smile under control, but his fingers drummed on his thighs as he walked back to his ship, his step much lighter than his earlier stomp and the sea air salty and sweet with impending victory.

He stroked his chin. Perhaps he could manufacture a fake clue. It could come in useful as a prop, and he could plant it somewhere. But the main stratagem would be the whispers luring her in.

It would be a simple matter to spread word around local gossips at the main ports. Sailors and dockers were a talkative lot. They'd do the rest for him, telling all and sundry about this rumoured clue to Drake's treasure. When FitzRoy took the bait and followed the fake lead, Knigh would spring his trap.

Why sail all over Arawaké searching for Lady Vice, when he could make her come to him?

RUMOUR

"Bugger."

Vice collapsed the spyglass and glanced towards the familiar ship again. Yes, the sails, that sleek hull, even the Albionic flag fluttering—definitely the *Venatrix*. "Gods damn it."

For the past few weeks, Vice and *The Morrigan* had criss-crossed the Arawakéan Sea, stalking and taking ships and cargo. That had left them with ill-gotten gains to sell off and a need to take on food and fresh water. Kayracou Port was the best bet in the area. The island walked a thin line between serving both legitimate shipping and pirates, so long as the latter pretended to be the former.

Even better, when they'd arrived earlier today, her friend and occasional lover, a docker named Sam had reported some interesting news. And this time it wasn't just more tall tales about ships with mysterious flags. Oh no, this was far juicier. The *Venatrix* had been seen a week ago anchored on a nearby island, the crew on shore *digging*.

Why on earth would a pirate hunter be digging? Unless he had a whiff of treasure even better than the bounty on her head...

As soon as he heard of it, Fitz had wasted no time in ordering all but a skeleton crew to gather information from every loose-lipped lubber in Kayracou Port.

The man was obsessed.

The rumours that had come back were mixed. Some put a clue to Drake's treasure in the possession of Captain Blackwood. Others said Blackwood had searched but not found anything. Others said he was merely interested in taking the riches for himself. Whatever the truth, Fitz had stewed in his cabin ever since.

Was Blackwood here now because he'd found something? Or was it just because this was the nearest major port and he needed provisions?

Either way, Perry, Bricus, and most of the crew had now gone off carousing, and she was stuck on watch duty, the *Venatrix's* fine lines making her heart leap.

That ship was meant to be hers, damn it.

Sighing, she thrust the spyglass into its case at her belt and paced the deck, absently scratching Barnacle under the chin. This was a friendly port—even if FitzRoy agreed to go after the *Venatrix,* he'd never open fire here and risk neighbouring ships, the wharves and taverns, *and* Kayracou's goodwill.

Fingers itching to *do something*, she yanked out the glass again and watched the *Venatrix*. They'd anchored, sails stowed. A flurry of movement suggested they were lowering their boat to come ashore. Scanning left and right, she groaned—where they'd anchored, every ship leaving would have to pass within yards of their hull.

The Morrigan was again disguised as merchantman *The Three* but that disguise was only designed to fool a cursory glance, *not* close inspection by a pirate hunter. After she'd tweaked Blackwood's nose in Port Royal, Perry had driven it into her that he'd be on full alert. He knew what to look for—he'd notice the outline of their closed gunports.

If he recognised *The Morrigan* as they passed to port, they'd be in the prime location to take a full broadside from his—she squinted into the spyglass—*ten* guns.

"Bollocks." And she'd have to hide as he'd probably recognise her, too. "Bollocks!"

The dozen hands left on watch looked up from their game of dice, surprise and query on their faces. Even Barnacle leapt off her shoulder and turned to give a sharp *miaow* of irritation for ruining her favourite spot.

"Sorry, little goblin-cat," Vice muttered.

Putting the glass away once more, she puffed out her cheeks and approached her crewmates. "Hunter out at the harbour mouth," she muttered. "Make sure our name and gunports are covered and don't even *think* the words Morrigan, Vice, or FitzRoy."

Saba rose, dark eyes alert, face calm. "Aye, *ma'am*." Her teeth gleamed bright against her jasper-brown skin as she grinned, one eyebrow quirking at calling her something so formal. Tossing her long braid over her shoulder, she set to work, and the others rushed to follow, game abandoned.

Eyes narrowed, Vice surveyed the rest of the harbour. Several ships bobbed between her and the *Venatrix*—they were hidden well enough for now.

But she still had to report this to the captain and Perry. No doubt they'd find some way it was her fault.

Vice sighed and squared her shoulders before making for FitzRoy's cabin.

Then again, could this be an opportunity? With a little sneaking, she could disable the *Venatrix*. A few lines cut here, a couple of knots hopelessly tangled there, and they wouldn't be able to set sail. *The Morrigan* would be able to slip by without pursuit.

Plus, if she could raise the tide just a little earlier, say half an hour, then Blackwood's crew wouldn't even be on alert. Why be on watch, cannon loaded when no smart captain would be leaving port for another half hour?

It would only take a few hours. Perry and the Captain wouldn't even need to know until she came back victorious. Instead of reporting a problem, she'd present them with a solution already executed and tied in a bow. FitzRoy did *love* a gift. And the more points she could score with him, the more likely he was to finally give her that captaincy.

Smiling, she backed away from the door and diverted her course.

"Tonight," she said, sidling up to Saba, "cover for me. If anyone asks—I snuck off with one of the lads from the *Firefly*."

Saba looked up from her work. "And where will you be?"

"With one of the lads from the *Firefly*."

"You're going"—she glanced towards the *Venatrix*—"Vice, don't. Perry will have your guts for garters." Her dark eyes gleamed in a pointed look.

"Only if I fail. Besides, she'll have to catch me first to pull them out." Vice flashed a grin.

"I can't—"

"You can, and you will. It'll only take an hour or so."

Saba sighed through her nose and lifted one shoulder. "Fine, but you be careful—that's a Navy ship, they run differently to us—they'll have a proper watch on deck."

"Noted." Chest pounding, Vice saluted and backed away to her cabin, gaze still on the *Venatrix*.

QUIET WORK

A few hours later, once the bright colours of sunset had faded and the sky was ink-dark and full of stars, Vice crept out into the night. She wore dark clothes and daggers. This wasn't a job for pistols, far too loud, but she felt their absence keenly, and her hand kept going to the empty spot at her belt.

It would be fine—no one would see her anyway, so there was no need for weapons. Sneak in, slip out, job done.

She circled around to the wharf nearest the *Venatrix*, passing through dark alleys between warehouses, and skirting the scant lamplight.

Pausing, she scanned the area. No guards—this was a good spot.

She eased into the dark water. It was cool but bearable, and any discomfort was offset by the welcome rightness of being in the sea. She swam slowly, taking a sweeping route across the few hundred feet to the *Venatrix*, the lap of waves covering her muted sloshing.

Once she was close to the starboard side, furthest from the wharves, she shifted to only kicking below the surface, making no sound as she passed into the ship's shadow.

Lords and Ladies, if she wasn't an even prettier prospect close-up. The planks of the hull had been hewn smooth and flush, all butted together and painted black until it almost looked like one piece.

Just above the waterline, the hull gleamed, metallic. Copper-sheathed. That must have cost a pretty penny. Then again, the Navy could afford it, and she'd heard how much it helped with speed and avoided the need to careen so regularly.

Now she was closer, a couple of male voices in soft conversation drifted across the water.

Moving slowly to avoid splashing, she scaled the *Venatrix's* hull. Here at starboard, she was in shadow, and once she reached the shrouds, she'd just appear a deeper shadow in the darkness. If she climbed up the port side, she'd end up silhouetted against the distant lights of the town, and even a careless watchman would spot her right away.

Foot over foot, hand over hand, the motion of climbing came easily after all these years, and her muscles sang with the movement, despite the weight and chill of her wet clothes.

This was what she needed—action. This was what had been missing in that former life—'ladylike' had no room for climbing or night swimming. Hells, 'ladylike' had no room for anything she did now.

Grinning, she climbed up onto the foremast's ratlines—she'd sweep fore to aft, so methodical even Perry would approve. Eight men dotted the deck—the night watch—but they all looked towards the wharves, backs to her. After all, who'd be approaching from the open sea?

The creak of ropes under her hands and feet merged into the

chorus of a ship at rest—the breeze, flexing timbers, the sighing sea. Still, Vice breathed as quietly as she could with the exertion of climbing aloft. The night air cooled her wet clothes and the sweat forming on her brow.

Almost there.

Her heart thundered as she passed twenty feet above the heads of the men on watch. Their lamps on the forecastle shone, almost as distant and small as stars from up here. And then she planted her hands on the yard and clambered onto the footropes.

So far, so good.

Up here the slight bob of the deck on the near-still water felt like a swell, but she'd developed the sea legs for this long ago. Within seconds, she side-stepped across to the first roband that lashed the foresail to the yard.

It was a shame to do anything to damage such a fine ship, but the sails could be lashed in place again easily, no permanent damage done. Although her best attempts at persuading the Captain to agree to capture the *Venatrix* had only received a non-committal response, that didn't mean she'd *never* have the vessel.

"Now," she whispered, patting the yard before drawing her knife, "this is only temporary, my lovely. I'll take good care of you when you're mine."

The whisper of steel sawing against rope made her grimace—it felt loud to her straining ears, but it wouldn't be heard from deck.

Currently, the sail was folded and stowed on top of the yard. If she cut all the robands as well as the lashing at the corners, when the *Venatrix's* crew went to set sail, it would just flap from the bottom edge, held up by only a handful of lines. Completely useless.

Now—she looked up another twenty feet to the fore topsail

on the next yard and the topgallant above that—if that were to *somehow* happen to every sail on the ship, he'd be stuck.

Grinning at the thought, she went back to work.

HANGING JUST BELOW THE RAIL, Vice leant back to look up at her handiwork. Although you couldn't tell from here, all sails on the fore and main masts were now detached from the yards, save from the lines holding them stowed. A typical hand going about their duties, untying those lines to unfurl the sails wouldn't ever think to look in the exact spots where she'd left the cut ends tucked away.

She could leave the spanker—he wouldn't get far with that alone. That left just the mizzen top to sabotage. Her gaze drifted down the mizzenmast to the raised quarterdeck, housing the captain's quarters.

If Blackwood *did* have a clue to Drake's treasure, that's where he'd be keeping it.

And she was here now. It would be rude not to at least have a look.

With those lamps and the watch on deck, it would be easiest to sneak into the captain's quarters through the stern windows. She could just climb around, slip through a window—it was warm enough that he'd leave one open for ventilation.

It took no time to scurry up the mizzenmast shrouds and sabotage the mizzen top, but on the way down she had to pause above one guard's eye level as he made a circuit of the deck. When he passed without raising the alarm, she exhaled and continued below the rail.

At last, her feet landed on the narrow ledge that the shrouds fastened into. Hands tight on the final stretch of line, she took the opportunity to pause and catch her breath. Her arms were warm now and—

Footsteps.

One of the watch on another circuit, no doubt.

Ears straining, she shuffled aft on the ledge. She made no noise—he wouldn't hear. She nodded to herself and took a long breath.

This next stretch was tricky—she needed to drop down, so her hands were on this ledge and her feet... well, there would be nowhere for them to go. The hull might give her bare toes a tiny amount of grip, but there were no real footholds.

Then, with her weight on her hands, she needed to reach aft and grab the carved moulding around a small, fixed window, climb across that and around the corner to the stern.

Shaking her arms out, she nodded.

She could do it.

With another deep breath, she crouched, gripped the ledge, and let her feet drop. For a heart-pounding moment, they swung, the sudden weight dragging on her arms, but she gritted her teeth and tucked her legs in, gaining control.

Biting her lip, she released the ledge with her left hand and reached across to the window. It was only a foot and a half, maybe two, but with her entire weight hanging on her right arm, it felt like leagues.

She huffed out what was meant to be a soft breath, but it came out as a grunt, just as her fingers closed on the moulded window frame.

Bollocks.

The footsteps came closer.

She stilled, feet braced, arms burning. If she moved, she might make more noise.

At least it was still dark—wait, no, was that lighter sky to the east? Damnation, what time was it? Surely it wasn't approaching dawn already. She swallowed, palms slicking with sweat, hair on the back of her neck prickling. That was always a warning, some gift of her fae blood.

If that man—his footsteps still sounded, steady, approaching—if he looked over the rail, he'd see her right away. There was no cover here.

The dagger at her hip was suddenly a leaden weight. She'd killed before, yes, but they were people who'd been given a chance to surrender and hadn't taken it. They'd made the decision to defend their ship and its cargo with their lives. When they faced her, they had weapons in their hands and *knew* they were in a fight.

This was some poor sod who'd signed up to the Navy and whose bad luck had put him on watch tonight. He was just taking a stroll around deck, investigating that grunt he'd heard.

Gods, her arms burned.

She gritted her teeth, pulse roaring in her ears.

A hand landed on the rail three feet above her head.

Eyes widening, she stared at the thick fingers, the short fingernails, the dirt beneath them.

Go away!

Actually, *that* she could do—or make him do.

Holding her breath, she let her feet hang and her awareness spread. The sea at night, cooler, fuller, thick with tiny creatures.

She swallowed. Focus. Those organisms weren't relevant right now. She needed—

Booted feet shuffled on deck near her head.

It had to be now.

The curved hull of the *Venatrix* sat light in the water—huge to her, but insignificant against the vast ocean—and just the other side, if she could push a wave...

A splash sounded from port.

Sudden steps—the man turning?—and a questioning sound. "What the—"

Clomping footsteps, fast, but fading to port. Shadows on the mast shifted—he must have taken one of the lamps to peer over the side.

Releasing her breath, she sagged, closing her eyes for a second. Thank the gods, the Lords, and the Ladies.

Her arms really were on fire when she continued her climb around the *Venatrix*. She passed the fixed window, then reached for the gilded carvings decorating the corner to stern. A last, straining burn on her arms, then she left the window, feet scrabbling and finally tucking into a spot above a curled oak leaf.

Squeezing her eyes shut, she took deep draughts of air, careful this time not to grunt. It was quiet to port, then the footsteps started up again, slowly walking fore.

Oh, Lords. That was close.

It took a minute to manoeuvre around the corner, level with the sash windows to the captain's cabin. This was another tricky spot, angling out over the water and making her calves and biceps burn.

She needed to get inside as quickly as possible before she dropped into the water.

Most likely, he had an office or a dining room and a separate space for sleeping. That's what someone had said these naval vessels had for the captain, just like she now occupied what had once been Fitz's office and he'd retreated to just one room that served as bed-chamber.

She peered in.

Darkness. She squinted past her reflection in the glass—was that the dim outline of a desk and chair? And, further in, to one side... a low shape. A bunk?

Damn, just one room... but it looked unoccupied. Maybe he was sleeping ashore, or maybe he was one of those on deck—she hadn't got a look at their faces.

Gripping a carved scroll above one window, she wedged her feet into the corners and let go with her right hand. The other arm shook—she must have been climbing for almost an hour now.

"Come on, my lovely," she whispered and pulled at the window.

Without a sound, it lifted open.

Seemed the *Venatrix* liked a little sweet-talk. Well, when she came back to claim her, she'd gladly give her all the sweet talk she wanted. Grinning, she patted the windowsill like it was a well-behaved sabrecat and slipped inside.

She landed in a crouch, low and silent. Blinking, she caught her breath and let her eyes adjust to the deeper darkness inside. Her fae blood helped her see better than most people in the dark, but it still took a moment to acclimatise.

Her initial search didn't turn up much of interest. Logs, books, neatly rolled charts, compass and sextant stowed in boxes alongside. Drawers of carefully folded clothes, a desk with inkwell, copper-nibbed pen, and blotting paper lined up ready for use.

Bloody Navy lot—they'd line up pebbles on a beach if they could.

When she rifled through papers in the little shelves at the back of the writing desk, a cylindrical leather case slid out. At first, she thought it a spyglass case, but it was far too small for that. The tan leather was cracked, and when she lifted it, it weighed little.

A scroll case? It had to be. And scrolls were old. Her heartbeat sped. She turned it over in her hands—this leather looked—

A drake, embossed on the surface. She angled it to catch the scant light, but yes—wings, two legs, curling tail. Definitely a drake. A little crude in execution but it had probably been made centuries ago and would have been knocked about over the years.

Letting out a huff that was almost a laugh, she clutched the case to her chest. This was it—a clue to Drake's treasure. She bit her lip to hold back any more noise and bounced on the balls of her feet before tucking the case into her shirt—as long as she didn't go upside down, it would be secure there.

Heart racing, she shoved the other papers back where she'd found them. Everything was in its place, and Blackwood would never know she'd been here.

Grinning at the door leading out to the deck, she saluted. He'd never even imagine she'd been this close.

Vice climbed back out the window and eased it shut behind her. Her muscles' earlier complaints were forgotten, erased by the excitement thrumming through her veins as she climbed around to starboard.

Blackwood's ship disabled, *and* a clue to Drake's treasure—even Perry would have to admit this was a great coup. And Fitz would surely grant her request to capture the *Venatrix* the next time they encountered them out on open water. She'd proven her ability to take charge, devise and execute a successful plan, and deal with a problem decisively. What more could they possibly want from a captain?

She bit the inside of her cheek—it was that or laughing out loud with excitement, and this really wasn't the place, dangling off the side of a Royal Navy pirate hunting vessel. With a couple of deep breaths, she calmed herself and climbed down the hull.

No sound of alarm. A job well done.

Vice paused above the glinting water and clenched the scroll case in her teeth before easing in and swimming away.

The next time she saw the *Venatrix*, she'd take it as her own.

SETTING SAIL

"Port, Captain," the watch shouted. "*The Morrigan*."

Knigh's head snapped up. He'd had a tip-off she was nearby, but this early? A thrill ran through him. If they came into port not realising he was here, he'd be able to close off the harbour entrance, trapping them within. His mouth twitched with a suppressed grin. She thought she'd got one over on him—well this would certainly show her. Who knew the notorious Lady Vice would be so easy to capture? Perhaps he wouldn't need those distasteful contacts after all.

He strode to port, nodding to his first lieutenant. "Stand by for my orders, Munroe."

The early morning sun glistened on the waves. From the docks, *The Morrigan* came, cutting through the water smoothly. Already in port? Damn—they must have been better disguised than he'd realised.

Gripping the rail, he turned his head slightly to shout to his men but kept his eyes fixed on the approaching ship. "Weigh anchor, make sail!"

Munroe relayed the orders, and in moments the shouts had rippled to the furthest reaches of the ship, together with men hurrying to anchor and aloft to obey.

Knigh narrowed his eyes—how was *The Morrigan* moving at such speed? The tide wasn't even meant to be high enough yet for ships to pass so easily, but here she came and—

Her. At *The Morrigan's* rail, dark hair long and loose in the wind—Vice. Unlike last time he'd seen her, she wore a red frock coat, braid and buttons glinting. Ostentatious, fitted well over her waist and bust—she liked to show off. She'd passed off as a lady and yet here, leaning on the rail, dressed as a sailor, she looked... *herself.*

Her eyebrows flashed up, and she grinned broadly. "Captain Blackwood," she called, waving. "Lovely morning, isn't it?"

His jaw popped with tension. Not just a show-off—cocky with it.

Behind her, *The Morrigan's* crew leered at him from their stations. None of them seemed in much hurry.

"Ready port guns," he bellowed, eyes fixed on her. Not that he could fire in harbour, not without risking others, but she'd hear the command, and it eased his irritation a touch to be doing *something.*

Almost level with him now, Vice pulled out a pocket watch, making a show of opening and looking at it. "Hope I've not woken you too early, Captain." She slipped the watch away and stretched, giving a theatrical yawn.

That bloody woman. A growl sounded low in his throat, and before he knew what he was doing, the smooth butt of his pistol was in his hand. He pulled back the cock, straightened his arm, and took aim over her shoulder.

Just a warning shot. He needed to take her in alive, after all.

She needed to face justice, and those fools who sang songs about her needed to *see* her hang for her crimes.

He squeezed the trigger. Smoke plumed and the *crack* echoed around the harbour.

Eyes wide, she ducked, glancing over her shoulder where the shot had sailed, clear of her by a foot, and—

And she laughed. *Laughed.*

Wild Hunt take her—who the hells *laughed* at someone shooting at them? And, gods, what a laugh—she tossed her head back and even from here, her eyes shone brightly.

Heart pounding the searing rage through his body, Knigh ground his teeth.

Why the hells weren't they moving? Gods, he needed to get a hold of himself. He swallowed and took two long breaths. In. Out. In. Out.

Unlocking his jaw, he cleared his throat. He was captain, he needed to maintain control. Lords and Ladies knew he couldn't afford to lose his head, not like last time. Never again.

He blinked. *Focus, Knigh.* What was the state of his ship? He hadn't heard the sails unfurling yet, and they'd had plenty of time. They'd drilled this—he ran a tight ship, and they could be ready in four minutes thirty-two seconds.

"Munroe, what the devil's taking so long with those sails?"

As if in response, the flap of canvas sounded. He blew out a relieved breath—they'd be after her quickly enough, and as soon as they were out of port, they'd be able to fire on her safely. That would teach—

The sound was wrong—that wasn't a sail catching the wind.

Voices rose in dismay.

"What the—" He turned in time to see all three mainmast sails fall, detached from their yards, so they just fluttered uselessly from their buntlines. Then the foremast sails, too. "How

—" His heart clenched, stealing his breath with a moment's pain. The mizzen topsail followed suit. Only the spanker, staysail, and flying jib remained, and they wouldn't get the *Venatrix* anywhere.

It wasn't possible. He was so careful, his crew well-disciplined. Sails didn't just come untied from the yardarm.

Unless...

When he turned to *The Morrigan*, Vice was grinning, eyes glinting, unsurprised. She passed just yards away and gave a little mocking bow, hair tangling in the breeze that carried her ship unerringly out of port. The same breeze blew his own sails across the deck as the crew ran to gather them together.

She had done this. Somehow. She must have snuck on board after they arrived yesterday, sabotaged the sails, and then left, all without raising the alarm. What kind of lunatic pirate boarded a naval vessel?

She winked, lifted her hand to her lips and blew him a slow kiss.

His skin burned. He'd only wanted to catch her for the handsome bounty but now...

Barking hoarse orders, he gripped the rail, knuckles aching and white.

Now, she'd made it personal.

THE CLUE

Lifting her chin, Vice held out the scroll case. She smiled at Fitz and the way his hand shook as he reached for the clue. His eyes shone with greed, desire, excitement—who knew? Maybe all three.

Much as she hated to admit it, breezing past Knigh Blackwood had been mildly disappointing. Not the execution—watching the sails flop to the deck... Lords, that was a moment she'd carry to the grave. No, that wasn't the disappointment—it was his face. He'd watched the sails fall, he'd stared at her, and his brows had lowered in what was *almost* a frown, but...

But there hadn't been that profound look of shock and horror and the realisation she'd got one over on him that she'd been hoping for. He schooled his expressions far too well for that. Prick.

So, yes, that had been a disappointment. But this, Fitz's gaze roving between her and the case, the lick of his lips in anticipation before he took it—this almost made up for it.

They stood in his cabin, on either side of the dining table that occupied the centre of the room. Morning light streamed through the stern windows, glinting off, well *a lot* of gilt work. The carved moulding around the windows. A small chest on a side table. The lion feet of the side table. The frame of the large mirror over his bed. Even the finials of the bedposts. Then there were the gilded candlesticks, the huge oval platter in the middle of the table, and the chandelier twinkling above.

Despite the excesses, the golden light, thick patterned rug under her feet, and red velvet drapes around the bed made the space almost cosy. She knew from experience that bed was a soft and warm place on a cold night.

Things between them had been tense for a while now—the stories and songs about her didn't help. A member of crew wasn't meant to outshine her captain in the tales of victory and adventure. No doubt that was why he'd stopped having her in that cosy bed of his. It was probably also why he'd delayed offering the captaincy he'd promised.

Well, she wasn't going to try and rekindle their relationship, but he was on the hook for her captaincy now. If this didn't win his favour, nothing would, short of handing over Drake's treasure on a platter.

"What is it?" He examined the case, fingers caressing the embossed drake.

She shrugged, lifting her hands. "I don't know—I thought you'd want to be the first to see it." More ingratiation—not that she needed it. She could have shed her clothes and offered herself on a plate to do *anything* he wished, and he wouldn't have looked up from that cracked old leather.

Even her fae charm was nothing compared to a clue to Drake's treasure.

"Open it, then." She nodded at the case, clenching and unclenching her hands. The hairs of her arms stood on end. Her skin tingled.

Fine, so he wasn't the only one excited. Not opening it had almost killed her, but the look on his face made it worth it—lips slightly parted, cheeks flushed. She'd seen it before, but they'd been wearing a lot less clothing at the time.

His throat bobbed in a slow swallow, and he twisted open the case, his thick, long fingers surprisingly gentle—reverent, almost.

There was a whisper of paper as he pulled out a scroll. So, she'd guessed right. Light, creamy paper, thick and smooth—good quality. She held her breath as he unrolled it. Although it was tatty at the edges, it was in surprisingly good condition.

He bent over the desk, holding it flat, brows lowering as he scanned it. "I don't—it's nonsense."

Her chest jumped. "What?" No, surely—

She rounded the desk, crowding next to him to see the scroll clearly. A string of letters, no spaces, all upper case, no *U*'s. She clutched her stomach and exhaled, shoulder rubbing his. "Not nonsense—Latium, written the old way." Thank the gods for that. "They didn't always use spaces between words in inscriptions, sometimes they'd put dots, but not normally spaces." With a reassuring smile, she patted his hand—his skin was hot as if he burned to read it for himself.

"Then what does it say?"

"Let's see..." She weighted the top of the scroll. "*I, Admiral Drake*"—she frowned, he'd only ever been a Vice Admiral, but maybe he'd been looking to exaggerate his position—"*have no treasure*—what? *And only a fool would still be looking for it after two centuries.*" Her mouth dried, but she kept reading, voice rasping on the words. "*Silver. Gold. Rubies. None of it for you, madam Lyons.*" Her breaths came hard and quick, flame burning up her back, her neck, over her cheeks.

"No. It can't be..." Blackwood had written this. She'd climbed all over his ship, risked entering his cabin for an insulting letter. "That bastard," she breathed.

At her side, FitzRoy shook, a strangled noise coming from his throat. Slowly, he turned to her, face contorting until it didn't even look like him anymore.

Without meaning to, she backed away a step.

"*Only a fool*," he growled, grabbing her arm and yanking her close. "Your hunter's calling me a fool." His breath blew across her face as he bared his teeth. His fingers bit into her flesh, and he tried to give her a shake, but she tensed her arm against it.

"Get your damn hands off me, Fitz," she growled back. "He's not my—"

"He's here for *you*. And you were the one stupid enough to fall for his trick. I should leave you to him."

"How *dare* you? The number of times I've saved this ship." She shook, body thrumming like the energy in storm clouds right before a lightning strike. If he didn't—"I *said*, get your hands off me." She wrenched herself from his grip.

He showed his teeth again, more sneer than smile. "Perry said it was too convenient the ship sent after us had a clue to Drake's treasure—she was right. And you'd have known it if you had her sense. How could you let yourself be tricked by a Jack tar?" He shook his head, nostrils flaring.

Blackwood had got one over on her, and now FitzRoy wanted to give her up to him? Prick. She thrust her face into his. "In case you'd forgotten, I'm the only reason we slipped past him out of Kayracou—*I* tricked *him*. Without any help from you or Perry."

"He was only there because of you."

"Yes," she spat, "because without me, you're not worth chasing."

Oh, gods.

She'd said it.

Her mouth fell open as if she could suck the words back in, but all that passed her lips was air, bursting in harsh breaths.

He froze. He wasn't even breathing. Dark eyes bright, he glared at her, every visible inch of him rigid. A vein throbbed in his throat beside corded muscle.

Silence hummed between them.

Slowly, his chest rose, and he lifted himself to his full height. His shoulders squared like he was a sailor readying himself for inspection, but it was she who came under scrutiny as his gaze trailed her from head to toe. "You think you'll be a great captain," he said, voice soft as distant cannon fire, "but you are a child. A rash child, with power she shouldn't have, who needs someone to direct her before she drops herself into hot waters."

His stillness made her bite her tongue. That quiet voice was far worse than any time he'd shouted. She'd certainly never seen him *this* angry.

He shook his head. "No one will follow you because you'll only lead them to death."

Her face burned as his words settled in her mind. A child? She gritted her teeth. What a bastard. And lead them to death—what the hells did *that* mean?

"Avice Ferrers."

Her nostrils flared at the name, but she held her tongue—it had already run away with her enough.

His eyes narrowed. "You are not fit to lead. You will never be captain."

The words struck her, pushing her half a step back. Was he—no, he couldn't be taking back his promise. He was just pissed off. Royally pissed off. That was all.

And maybe it was her fault—his being pissed off, not this business with the clue.

She shouldn't have said what she did—it irked him enough

that she was the one they sang about back in Albion, but to *say* it? To acknowledge it out loud?

It had always been a silent spectre in the room. If they didn't talk about it, it couldn't hurt them.

But now she'd said the words.

He'd driven her to it, though. Lords, she could wring his bloody neck.

She clenched her hands until the knuckles ached and the nails threatened to split her palms. She needed to get out of here before she said anything to piss him off even more.

And he needed to cool off. Once he did, he'd come around, and they'd pretend this whole conversation never happened.

He'd promised her a captaincy with witnesses—Perry and Saba and at least a dozen others. Eventually, he'd grant it to her. In the meantime, it'd be best if she gave him some space.

Still, she couldn't let him think he was right.

Lifting her chin, she gave him a withering look Perry would've been proud of and stalked out, slamming the door.

A PRIZE

Arm looped through the shrouds, Vice closed her eyes, letting the breeze, the spray, the sun rush through her hair. Beneath her, beneath *The Morrigan,* the sea breathed its rhythm, pushing them onwards under her direction.

Opening her eyes, she smiled at the prize she'd spotted half an hour ago. It had been a week since her fight with the Captain, and they'd continued in a cool, professional manner. She'd spent more time than necessary on watch from the main top. That's how she'd spotted this merchantman with its fat belly. It was positioned perfectly to allow *The Morrigan* to approach with the lowering sun at her back, covering their approach with its dazzling glare.

Rather than go to FitzRoy directly, she'd reported it to Perry—a schooner, just eight guns, and more full of cargo than crew. Vice let her propose the rich, easy target.

Vice urged the currents, the winds behind their sails, eager to be in battle or on the receiving end of a surrender. Either way, once they took the prize, Perry would be honest and reveal her involvement—she'd be loath to take credit that wasn't due. It would go some way to repairing the Captain's opinion.

Call it a peace offering.

They swiftly closed in on the schooner, her gift holding the merchant ship dead in the water near a hilly island as surely as it pushed *The Morrigan* onwards.

Below, on the main deck that stretched from bow to quarter-deck, her crewmates armed themselves. Bricus doled out pistols, rifles, pikes, and sabres, his dark beard split in a jolly grin. The gunner teams readied the port cannons.

Vice touched the grips of her sabre and dagger, then each of her three mismatched fae-worked pistols—all there, all solid, all prepared. Her body sparked with anticipation. Better for everyone if they surrendered, but she was ready if they didn't.

As *The Morrigan* shifted to starboard, she scurried down the shrouds, one eye on their new course, adding a touch here and there to help them turn to the best angle as they prepared to unleash a full broadside.

On deck, the atmosphere buzzed—they'd raised the black, and the merchants hadn't answered by striking their own flag or raising the white, either of which would give their surrender.

There would be cannon fire.

After the first round, they'd get another chance to give in—most took that offer, suddenly keen to avoid a further barrage.

Orders sounded from the deck as the gunning teams made final preparations.

Her heart pounded as she nodded to Saba, Lizzy, Wynn, Effie, and Aedan—her usual team. They gathered around her by the foremast, nostrils flaring, some grinning fiercely, others grim-faced.

"They're damn fools for not giving in," Saba muttered, handing Vice her rifle from the rack.

Vice shrugged, running her fingertips over the breechloader. Fae-worked, like her pistols, it could be stored ready to fire and resisted damp conditions better than the flintlocks. Naturally, they were hideously expensive. And of course, Vice hadn't paid a penny for it.

Loaded, ready to fire, and the leather case at her waist carried more of the reusable cartridges, charged and prepared to swap in at speed.

She nodded and snorted. "Some think they can escape, others think we're more bluster than blow. Maybe these think they can beat us. Whatever the reason, let's show them they're wrong." She grinned at each member of her team before fixing her attention on the schooner—from here she could read its name painted in white, *Veritas*.

Its deck crawled with activity, though from here the people were just figures, their faces indistinguishable.

She turned *The Morrigan's* course a degree to starboard, each adjustment a tiny drain on her energy. Still, they were now perfectly aligned, and the shout rippled across the gunnery teams.

With the down-pitch of the wave, she held her breath, then the up-pitch and—

Cannons boomed, the sound filling her, vibrating through the ship's hull.

Chinking, chain-shot spun towards the *Veritas's* masts.

Sails split and rigging tore apart, the ropes' frayed ends whipping away in the wind. One mast threw out a burst of splinters as it took a glancing blow. Around Vice, her people cheered.

Thick white smoke rose between *The Morrigan* and the *Veritas*, the taste of it like charcoal and sulphur.

Vice squinted through, watching the flag.

Even if they'd thought the way their ship sat dead in the water, becalmed was just a strange quirk of the weather, surely now they had to see they were no match for *The Morrigan*. They certainly wouldn't outrun her with damaged sails.

But instead of lifting a white a flag of surrender, an orange flare rose from the *Veritas's* deck.

Blue eyes on the bright spark of light, Aedan's straw-blond eyebrows lowered. "What the—"

Then as the *Veritas* pitched, angling upwards, light flashed along its hull, followed by smoke and the thunder of cannon.

Vice's eyes widened, and her fingers splayed as she reached her awareness back into the waves. Bracing against the foremast, she turned *The Morrigan* as swiftly as she dared. The ship groaned alarmingly, and she eased off a touch. Each foot of movement strained against her muscles and nibbled at her strength.

Shouts and oaths rose as the crew stumbled with the sudden movement. Crewmates had to catch each other. Some fell, skinning their knees on the deck.

But they presented a smaller target to the *Veritas*, so when the chain shot whistled overhead, it only tore holes in two sails and missed their masts entirely.

Vice huffed out a breath, muscles sagging after the exertion.

"You'll tear the bloody ship apart," Perry shouted, eyes wide as she pushed herself up from the rail several feet away.

Frowning, Vice shook her head. "I'd never!" She wasn't stupid. Perry knew that.

"Perry," FitzRoy bellowed from aft, clinging to the mainmast shrouds to stay upright from Vice's mad spin of the ship, "I thought you said eight guns." His brows were fixed in a fierce line, low over his dark eyes. "I make sixteen."

Bollocks.

"Sorry, Captain," Perry said, expression contrite and drawn as she lowered her gaze, "my mistake."

It was only once he'd looked away that she shot Vice a look, brows contracting, head angling in query.

Wincing, Vice lifted her hands and mouthed *sorry*. She must have missed some of their ports in her hurry. But she'd stopped most of them hitting, so no harm done.

"Wild Hunt damn it," FitzRoy bellowed, "slow us down."

They were hurtling right at the *Veritas*, far too fast to just butt into her to board. At this speed, they'd damage both ships.

Bugger. Vice gritted her teeth and yanked on the current and stilled the wind. *The Morrigan's* sails fell slack at once. Sweat broke on her brow as she fought to slow them enough to just knock the *Veritas* ready for boarding.

With much swearing, the crew again had to brace against her rough treatment of the ship.

"Bloody hells, Vice," Aedan grunted as he grabbed the foremast. The tattoos across his knuckles read *HOLD*. His other arm looped around her, keeping her tight to his muscular body, so she didn't fall.

The ship held steady, speed corrected, and Vice's shoulders eased as she huffed out a breath, sinking against him. "Thanks, Aedan," she muttered, patting his hand as he released her. "All steady, Captain," she shouted over her shoulder.

Catching her breath, she nodded to her team. "Rifles, ladies and gent."

Bracing one shoulder against the mast, she raised her fae-worked rifle, pulled back the cock, and peered along the barrel. Movement in her periphery told her others did the same, but the rest of the world faded. She even retreated from the sea surging beneath.

On the *Veritas*, men lifted their own weapons, but their wide eyes and gaping mouths said they weren't used to battle, maybe weren't even used to firing guns.

Wild Hunt damn it, why hadn't they surrendered?

A lick of movement behind one of the men. What was that? Then it flashed into view again—a whip. This wasn't their choice. She trailed her aim to the source of that lash—a broad-shouldered man with a cruel mouth.

A much better target.

She exhaled and squeezed the trigger.

A *crack* split the air, throwing the butt against her shoulder as smoke rose.

From here she couldn't see the blood, but she knew it was there from the way he jerked, head snapping back, and fell from sight.

The men he'd whipped stared over their shoulders, weapons lowering. Confusion, fear, relief—whatever it was, it would keep them busy at least until *The Morrigan* was close enough to board.

Flicking open the breach block on her rifle, Vice narrowed her eyes at the smoky water between them and the *Veritas*. No time for a second shot. She slid the gun in the rack.

"Brace!" The shout went up, echoed by others across *The Morrigan*.

Cries of dismay rose from the *Veritas*, drifting across the smoke-shrouded water.

Ducking behind the rail's cover, Vice hurried fore. She reached the bow an instant before the impact pitched through both ships, locking them together, rocking the crews, sending lines and sails lashing. Down on one knee, she clung to the rail until the deck steadied. Taking a deep breath, she drew her pistol and rose.

VERITAS

Smoke and spray, cries and groaning timber filled the air with sound and scent and texture. *The Morrigan's* bowsprit was tangled with the *Veritas's* lines—not ideal, but Vice could board now. If she could target the captain and anyone else forcing these men to fight, they'd surrender before too much blood was shed.

Trusting instinct, she raised her pistol. The antlered head of the hart that decorated the handle peeked over her hand, and for a fraction of a second, her sister's green eyes flashed into view. Heart sore, she squeezed the trigger—the whirr of clockwork, then a flash, a puff of smoke, the jolt of recoil, and a *crack*.

Another man, his own gun aimed at her, gaped, then fell.

"See you over there, ladies and gent," she called to her team, surging forward with a fierce grin. Either they were with her, or they weren't—she was going. She returned that pistol to its holster and in one movement drew the second pistol with her left hand and her sabre with her right.

Muscles springing, she leapt to the bowsprit, across the water, and onto the *Veritas*.

Scanning the deck, she spotted a thick knot of men and, at its centre, the captain and presumably his first mate. The way the men closest to them lifted their sabres higher with glances over their shoulders said they were the ones behind the attempt to resist *The Morrigan*.

Take them down, and the battle would be over.

With steel clashing, a shot from her second pistol, and her team at her side, it didn't take long to work her way towards them. Where she could, she clubbed heads with the butt of a pistol or the hilt of her sword, but by the time she reached the last row of men, her blade wasn't clean.

"Stand down, gents," she cried, voice ringing as clear as her blade as she parried a clumsy attack, "and you'll live to tell the tale of facing Lady Vice."

Shared glances, wide eyes—they hadn't realised what ship they faced.

"Come on, lads," Saba huffed, "surrender."

"Don't listen to the she-devils," the captain growled, "they seek to tempt you with their wicked bodies, their wicked tongues, their wicked wiles."

"That's a lot of *wicked*." Kicking a short man in the belly, Vice scoffed. "I'd be more worried about our sabres than any of that."

Lip lifted in a sneer, the captain shoved the poor man forward. "Kill the bitch."

"Fine." Vice sidestepped, and Aedan slammed his tattooed fist into the man's face, dropping him to the deck, groaning. "How about *I* kill the bitch?" She drew her third and final pistol, levelled it, and shot the captain clean between the eyes.

He blinked, red trickling down his face before his features slackened and he fell.

The breath heaved in Vice's chest. Enough blood for today. She surveyed the men still ringed around the first mate, some staring at her, others at their late captain.

Just give in.

Mingled cries of dismay, relief, and celebration rose—the latter not only from *The Morrigan's* crew.

She swallowed, meeting the blue gaze of the *Veritas's* first mate. *Please. End this.*

He bared his teeth with a yellow gleam.

Steel clanged on the deck as a young man near her team, little more than a boy, dropped his sabre. "I surrender." He stared up at her, fear, hope, desperation in his dark eyes.

Her heart twisted—the poor kid, had he been press-ganged into this? She'd heard it sometimes happened outside the Navy. Giving him a half-smile, she nodded. *Good lad.*

More steel rang across the *Veritas* as, one-by-one, the rest of the crew surrendered until only the first mate held a weapon.

Waving those who'd surrendered out of the way, Vice cocked her head at him. "What'll it be? Is this cargo, this ship *really* worth your life?"

Raising his chin, he stared at her, eyes narrowing as if sizing her up. To fight or just to work out whether she'd be true to her word, she wasn't sure, but he'd be a damn fool to lift that blade alone.

Slowly, his chest rose, tension inching across his body.

No, surely, he wasn't going to fight? Vice shifted her grip on her sabre and the weight on her feet, ready to spring forward to meet his blade if he went for one of her crewmates.

Eyes lowering, he huffed and threw his sabre to the deck, shoulders slumping.

There was only the whisper of the wind, the sigh of waves, and the flap of torn canvas.

Then the cheers erupted.

Thank the gods for that. Lowering her blade, Vice nodded at the first mate. "Good choice," she said, but it was swallowed up by the roar of voices.

It was over. She turned, scanning the path back to *The Morrigan* as the cheers faded. Despite their smiles and raised fists, a few of their crew were bloodied—cuts on shoulders, bleeding noses, split lips, but nothing worse. They all still stood.

The relief burst through her in a laugh, and she waved at Perry, near the *Veritas's* rail. Surely, she'd forgive her earlier misjudgement about the number of guns.

"Interesting manoeuvring," Perry called.

Grinning, Vice lifted her hands. "Not my finest performance, no, but we won, didn't we?"

Perry pursed her lips, but her eyes sparkled in the low sun. Then her gaze drifted over Vice's shoulder, and her face dropped.

"Perry?" Vice swallowed. "What's—"

Before she finished turning, a shout rose: "Sails!"

TAKEN ABACK

Rifle in one hand, Knigh stood on the quarterdeck of the *Venatrix*, gaze fixed on *The Morrigan* and *Veritas* locked together. The pirate vessel formed a T with the merchant, bowsprit tangled with foremast, as though the pirates had rammed their victim.

Other than dissipating smoke and flicking sails, though, it was all so still. Frowning, he yanked his spyglass from its holster and lifted it to his eye.

No one on deck of either ship. No one living, anyway—a few bodies lay on the *Veritas*. She had taken damage to mast and sail, too. *The Morrigan* looked in a far better state, just a couple of tears to the canvas.

Narrowing his eyes, he stowed the spyglass. What could have happened to clear the decks of both ships? Had the battle somehow ended up on a lower deck? He exhaled through his nose. That didn't seem likely—he'd never heard of fighting belowdecks while abovedecks was *empty*. And there was no sound of clashing blades or gunfire. No sign of men in the water, either.

"Take us in, Mr Munroe," he said, scratching the back of his neck. Perhaps the ships were in trouble—one could be taking on water, and the crews were belowdecks out of sight trying to save themselves. But surely a team would be up here trying to untangle the pair, so they wouldn't both be dragged down.

He wrinkled his nose. Something was off.

Still, it was his job to investigate, and he needed to get to Vice and her captain.

"Nice and easy, if you will." He nodded to Munroe. "Broach *The Morrigan*." Her crew had to be hiding belowdecks, perhaps thinking to stage an ambush—well, he'd present them with the smallest target for their cannon if that was their plan. Plus, it might bring him closer to FitzRoy more quickly, wherever he was hiding.

Knigh's message couldn't be trusted to anyone else—he needed a private audience with the captain and to get that, it looked like he'd have to lead a boarding party. "I want all port guns ready to fire."

The lieutenant saluted and relayed the order.

Knigh lifted his rifle as they approached the merchantman, ready to cock it and take aim the instant he spotted danger.

But both ships remained eerily silent.

His stomach knotted. The *Veritas* was meant to have signalled once the pirates came within range, then surrender. No one was supposed to get killed. Was the deck empty because they'd all died?

Nostrils flaring, his throat clenched. He couldn't be responsible for so many deaths—not this time. He squeezed his rifle until it creaked.

"There'll be some other explanation," he whispered.

"Pardon, Captain?" Munroe blinked and looked at him.

Knigh drew a quick breath and gave him a curt nod. "You have the *Venatrix*, Mr Munroe. I'll be leading the boarding party."

A momentary widening of the eyes was the lieutenant's only reaction, betraying his surprise at the odd instruction. Still, within a breath, he'd smoothed his face and saluted. "Aye, Captain."

Good man. He understood pirate hunters sometimes had to employ unorthodox practices.

Striding fore, Knigh nodded at the detachment of marines standing to attention on the main deck. "Half of you with me, gentlemen."

Their second lieutenant saluted and split the unit with a few brief orders, before sending ten with Knigh.

Efficient. That's what he liked about the man.

By the time they reached the bow, the *Venatrix* was drawing to a halt. She bobbed into position touching *The Morrigan's* port side, aft of all her sails to avoid getting tangled. From above, the three ships would have formed an imperfect U-shape.

Despite the tension thrumming through his body, there was no attack as he set foot on *The Morrigan*—all was as he'd observed.

Far too still.

Forming around him, the marines exchanged glances, too well-disciplined to air their concerns, but he could see it in their eyes.

They didn't like this any more than he did.

"Search the ship. I want Vice and I want her alive." If he captured her here, there'd be no need to deal with his contact. That would certainly be preferable—pirates made poor allies.

With a hand signal, he summoned the remaining marines. Two men at his side, he approached the two doors leading to rooms below the quarterdeck, one of them presumably the captain's cabin. The marines checked one door, he the other. Garish decor with an excessive amount of gold decoration and *a chandelier*—Lords and Ladies!

But there was no one inside.

He kept his face expressionless—it wouldn't do for the men to see him unsettled—but inside, the wrongness seethed.

As a child, he'd once seen a barrel of eels at the village market, their flesh twisting, slippery, dark. The sight of them in constant movement had haunted his nightmares for years. Now, it felt like those eels writhed under his skin.

"Ser," a man called from the stairs that led belowdecks, and Knigh strode over, raising his eyebrows in question. "We thought you'd want to see this."

Knigh glanced around—if he went down there... He narrowed his eyes. The pirates could have put something here to lure him and his men into the bowels of *The Morrigan*. Into a trap. "What is it?"

"The crew of the *Veritas*, ser. It looks like they're bound and gagged in the hold, ser."

"What? Here?" The *Veritas's* men on *The Morrigan*? Then were *The Morrigan's* crew—

Boom. Boom. Boom.

The unmistakable report of cannon.

On instinct, Knigh ducked, but *The Morrigan* rolled steadily with the ocean's heave—nothing struck her. That meant—

He ran to the rail, rifle raised.

The *Venatrix* rocked, holes in her sails, the top of the mizzenmast creaking, falling, crashing. With a splash, it dropped into the sea, lines breaking and whipping.

Smoke rose from the *Veritas's* starboard guns.

"To me," he bellowed as the pieces fell into place. Vice, FitzRoy, and the rest of their crew were on the *Veritas*. From there, they'd fired a full broadside into the *Venatrix*, while she'd sat there presenting the largest possible target.

And they'd done it while his forces were divided between two ships.

As if his realisation were the cue, every hatch and door on the *Veritas* flew open. Pirates poured out, led by an all-too-familiar red-coated woman who grinned fiercely.

Hells and damnation.

CONTROL

Knigh gritted his teeth, parrying another sabre swipe—it was undisciplined but powerful. *The Morrigan's* crew had already faced one battle, and he'd expected them to be tired, but perhaps their victory had buoyed morale.

Clenching his jaw, he caught another blow, sending the bald pirate off balance. With a kick, he sent the man splashing overboard. Better if he didn't kill too many of *The Morrigan's* crew—he didn't want ill will spoiling the next phase of his plan.

In the gap left by his opponent, he caught a glimpse of that red coat. Vice fought with a kind of lethal abandon, brows lowered fiercely, attacks imperfect, technically chaotic, but swift and unerringly on-target.

After she'd mocked him at Kayracou, he'd have expected her to laugh and pose her way through a fight, relishing in her opponents' defeat, their blood on her blade. But that expression, jaw set, a focused frown, mouth in a grim line—it was far more serious than he'd ever thought her capable of.

Back in Albion, most of his colleagues thought her little more than a figurehead—pretty and inspiring, but ultimately there for show.

The slash she dealt the marine facing her was anything but *for show*. And she led a boarding party—the group around her clearly looked to her for direction. His fellow officers were sorely mistaken.

Frown tight on his face, Knigh twitched away from a clumsy thrust, threw it wide with his own blade, and punched the pirate. Blood burst down the man's face, and he backed away, clutching his nose.

Shaking his head, Knigh scanned his surroundings again. Half the marines had formed up with him, the other half faced Vice, and the pirates gathered around her.

Damn it, he needed to end this—with his forces divided between *The Morrigan* and the *Venatrix*, he was losing men. Hells, the pirates might even be winning.

It wasn't meant to go like this. The plan was to overpower *The Morrigan* by force of numbers and superior training, gain their surrender. Then he'd use his code phrase to make himself known to his contact, and get an audience with FitzRoy. Then he'd execute the next phase to capture Vice and bring her to justice.

Growling, he punched another pirate and shoved him overboard.

Growling? Gods, no. He had to maintain control.

This was just another battle—it wasn't personal. He couldn't give in to his fury, not again. Swallowing, he straightened his back, pulling his muscles into one drill position, then another.

Discipline, procedure, drills.

Deep breaths filled his nose with the sharp smell of sweat and the metallic tang of blood, and most importantly, they brought a cooling calm over him.

He nodded. Much better.

That flash of red caught his eye through the melee again. Vice slammed her sabre's knuckle-bow into a marine's face and kicked him away, then glanced aft.

Narrowing his eyes, Knigh followed her gaze to a tall man, black-haired, his black coat even more ostentatious than Vice's. He had to be FitzRoy.

That would end this.

"To me, marines." Not checking they followed, Knigh started fighting his way towards the pirate captain. "FitzRoy," he shouted into the clash of blades. Still nothing—he must not have heard.

He shouldered one pirate, then another, out of the way, using his superior size to shove them with ease. His muscles rejoiced at the rough treatment, at the flex and jar of impact.

He could just let go, let the rage burning in his belly free...

Tightening his grip on his sabre, he shook his head. It would be easy in the moment, yes, but he knew better than that, he knew where it would lead. He had to be stronger.

Voice hoarse, he called the man's name again. The pirates nearest gave him wary looks, but FitzRoy didn't respond, and he wasn't even sure which man was his contact. For all he knew, the fellow could be dead.

Lords and Ladies, he hadn't even considered that. Then his plan would be dead in the water.

Teeth gritted, he pushed on—he needed to get through to FitzRoy.

Fifteen feet away now—even with the cries and clamour of battle, he'd have to hear.

"FitzRoy."

Red and gold closed in from starboard at speed.

"Parley," he bellowed, pushing towards the pirate captain. "Parley, FitzRoy."

But a body blocked his path—Vice, her sabre outstretched, tip inches from his chest. "Parley?" She snorted. "Pirate hunters don't parley."

Knigh's heart pounded. So close. He took half a step forward.

Vice bared her teeth and lifted the sword to his throat, only an inch from his flesh. Her eyes burned into him.

Odd—the colour looked different from when they'd met at Port Royal. A bright cerulean blue rather than clear turquoise.

She narrowed them. "That's close enough."

He kept his arms wide, lowered, non-threatening. Still, the tension thrumming through her lean arms, her muscular legs, and her glowering expression said she would cut him down.

Wild Hunt, surely even the notorious Lady Vice wouldn't kill a man asking for parley.

She wouldn't if her captain ordered her to stand down.

Knigh lifted his chin. "FitzRoy."

FitzRoy went still and turned, a frown etched between his eyebrows, dark gaze cool upon Knigh. That stillness radiated until the pirates and marines closest backed away from each other. Their blades were still raised, but they shared confused looks rather than blows.

Swallowing, Knigh took a deep breath. Gods, please let this work. "Elizabeth sends her regards."

FitzRoy's brows shot up, and his eyes widened. He recognised the phrase and a squat man at his side reacted in the same way—that had to be his contact.

Vice gave a pert smile. "And Davy Jones sends his, Blackwood." Gaze still on him, she lifted her chin to one side. "Captain, shall I send him to the seafloor with the other bottom feeders?"

FitzRoy cocked his head, calculation unmistakable on his face.

Knigh's stomach plummeted, but he kept his expression impassive. Lords, he'd miscalculated.

Was FitzRoy actually considering letting Vice kill him?

MISCALCULATION

The back of Vice's neck prickled. Jaw clenched, she stared at Blackwood, but he ignored her and watched the Captain, expression unreadable.

Arrogant bastard.

What was taking FitzRoy so long? He just needed to give her the go-ahead, and she'd rid them of this troublesome pirate hunter. It would be a shame to damage such a fine specimen, but he'd tried to trick them—to trick *her*. That flare from the *Veritas* must have been a signal for the *Venatrix*, bringing them circling out from behind the island.

Her lip twitched. Nice try, but she was the one who tricked people around here, as proved by the success of her idea to hide *The Morrigan's* crew on the *Veritas*.

If only she'd been able to see his expression when the supposedly friendly ship opened fire! But his eyes had widened a little when she'd led the charge—when it came to Knigh Blackwood, that would have to do.

Her gaze drifted over to the *Venatrix*. They'd aimed well—just a damaged mast and sails, things that could be repaired quickly, then she could be on her way with her ship.

Her ship. Captaincy, at last.

After she'd executed this plan, FitzRoy would have to admit she'd make a good captain, his earlier anger forgotten.

And not captain of just any ship—captain of the *Venatrix*. Her chest swelled, warm and full.

"Vice," FitzRoy called.

Smiling sweetly at Blackwood, she stood a little taller. Lords and Ladies, she was ready for this.

"Stand down."

She blinked.

Blackwood's grey eyes flicked to her, and his eyebrows rose fractionally in expectation.

"Captain"—sword still pointed at Blackwood, she turned to FitzRoy—"what—"

"I said, stand down, my dear."

"*My dear?*" she spluttered. Like she was some meddlesome wife who needed pacifying. She stared at him, but he just nodded. He actually wanted her to stand down.

Blackwood cleared his throat, and she spun upon him.

He held his sword wide, unthreatening. "If I may?" He lifted his other hand slowly. "I'm just reaching into my pocket."

"Vice." The low warning in FitzRoy's voice was unmistakable.

What the hells was going on? Had Fitz gone soft? Shaking her head, she lowered her blade without sheathing it and watched Blackwood pull sealed papers from his pocket.

"Captain FitzRoy," he said in a voice that carried, "I've come to offer a letter of marque signed by Her Majesty Queen Elizabeth IV."

Oh, that was brilliant. Even better than a pirate hunter calling for parley. She'd been trying for three years to persuade FitzRoy to turn privateer, and for three years he'd refused. This would be no different.

She snorted. "Good luck with that."

"What an interesting proposal, Captain Blackwood," FitzRoy said. "I assume you'll have your men stand down if I ask mine to do the same, then we can go and discuss this in my cabin."

Discuss this? "FitzRoy"—she whirled on her heel—"what the devil do—"

"I assume you meant to say *Captain*." He gave her a flat look, mouth a straight line.

Urgh, he wanted to make an impression in front of these Navy men, in front of *Captain* Blackwood. Nostrils flaring, she forced a smile in place. "Apologies, *Captain*."

"Quite forgiven, Vice." He spread his hands in a magnanimous gesture. "I imagine the heat of battle made you forget yourself."

She gritted her teeth, cheeks tense—her smile probably looked more like a grimace.

"Now, Captain Blackwood," FitzRoy stepped to one side and gestured for the pirate hunter to join him, "let us retire."

"But—Captain"—she fell in beside Blackwood, trying to outpace him but his long legs let him keep up without effort.

"Yes, Miss Vice?" He turned to her.

"Not you," she hissed. "Captain FitzRoy, with all respect"—inwardly she cringed, but he couldn't say she wasn't playing along with his wishes, however stupid they were—"I don't like this. This man's Navy through and through and, even worse, he's a pirate hunter. What if this is just a ploy to get you alone?"

FitzRoy scoffed and shook his head. "Ah, my dear, what an imagination you have."

She ground her teeth. If he called her *my dear* one more time...

One corner of FitzRoy's mouth rose in an odd smile that didn't meet his eyes. "Despite the insult you do him, I'm sure Captain

Blackwood will be happy to surrender his weapons to you. As a gesture of goodwill, I'll do the same." He unbuckled his sword belt and bandolier and passed both to the nearest marine.

The rest of *The Morrigan's* crew and the *Venatrix's* men sheathed their weapons.

"Only too glad to oblige," Blackwood said, flashing her a showy smile that seemed so out of place on him it irritated her almost as much as Fitz calling her *my dear*. "Miss Vice."

His grey eyes stayed on her while he flicked his belt buckle open.

Something about the way he did that, maybe the slowness, maybe the eye contact, made her face heat. It was far too much like a lover beginning to undress.

She swallowed and clenched her jaw. *Bastard.* He had to be doing that deliberately. After all, she'd flirted with him at that ball before she'd known who he was. She'd made her attraction to him clear.

Unblinking, she stared back, trying to look bored, and held out her hands to accept the polished sabre and matching dagger.

Still at that maddening speed, he removed a bandolier with a pair of Navy issue flintlock pistols. He handed those over, fingers brushing the inside of her wrist as he did so.

That was unnecessary.

So, he wanted to play games. *Fine.*

She thrust his guns and blades into Aedan's tattooed hands. "Just a second, Captain," she said, raising her hands and blocking Blackwood's path. "In the interest of maintaining goodwill, allow me to demonstrate to the crew you're not hiding any further weapons."

Smiling sweetly, she stepped into his space. Although the air was cooling as the sun touched the horizon, heat radiated from him. It warmed her skin as though they were already touching.

Despite his usual mask of neutrality and controlled, subtle expressions, his eyes widened, and he sucked in a quick breath. He didn't step away, but he swayed backwards as if he longed to escape.

Good, he was bothered. Taste of his own medicine and all that.

At such close quarters, her nose filled with the smell of soap, worn leather, and—was that cinnamon? She fought the near-irresistible urge to breathe deeply and check. There was also something masculine, raw in the scent—the tang of sweat, the hard work of battle.

With a quick exhale, she tried to blow his smell from her nose. She had work to do.

Her hands landed on his shoulders first—firm, broad, warm. Just as she'd imagined. Not that she'd imagined how he'd feel. Definitely not. She cleared her throat and frowned at him.

His chest stilled at her touch—he had to be holding his breath. So, the disciplined Navy man *could* feel something, he just fought to control, to hide it all.

Oh, this was going to be fun.

She ran her hands down his arms. No sign of straps holding further weapons, even when she patted his forearms—she'd seen people hide daggers up their sleeves. Deliberately, she paused once she'd withdrawn her hands and he sagged, the movement so minute she'd never have noticed it from a respectable distance. However, this was *not* a respectable distance.

He was relieved, thinking she was done with him.

Poor boy. But he'd brought this on himself.

Eyes locked with his, she placed her hands on his chest. A low sound like far, far distant thunder rumbled through him, so soft no one else could have heard it.

But she did hear it and felt it vibrate under her hands, and she saw his pupils blow wide, darkening his gaze.

The uncomfortable feeling they were lovers hit her again. That's where she'd seen that look before, and this was precisely where she'd place her hands as she mounted a man and claimed him as her own. Her heart pounded, and her throat, her belly, her core throbbed in response.

She was meant to be searching him, not seducing him.

Wild Hunt take her, she had misjudged. Badly.

Fighting to keep her expression flat like his so often was, she lightened her touch—that made it safer. Her fingertips lowered over the planes of his chest. No sign of weapons, but damn it, he filled his clothes well—there was no padding to give him that fine shape.

Again, with such a subtle movement she wouldn't have noticed if she hadn't *felt* it, he pressed into her touch, forcing the hard lines of his muscles against her palms.

Heat flooded her, and she snatched her hands away.

The corner of his mouth rose, eyes flashing in triumph.

What a prick.

Bloody hells, why had she thought *that* word? That was precisely the problem right now. It had been far, *far* too long, that was all this meant. Her body and its needs were betraying her mind and its dislike of this arrogant, up-tight Navy automaton.

Gritting her teeth, she made herself touch him again, hands sliding quickly down his sides, his hips, the outsides of his well-muscled thighs, and into the tops of his boots.

No weapons. Fine.

Straightening, she arched an eyebrow. She could check his inner thighs, a blade could be hidden there, and it was damn tempting to try and get *a rise* out of him as it were—from the speed of his breaths and the heat in his gaze, he couldn't be far off hardness.

But—but, no. She shook her head; that was enough torture for both of them.

There was one more thing, though.

Leaning close, she ran her hands up and down his back. Her breasts brushed his chest, sending unwelcome sensation streaking through her body and forcing her to bite her lip.

It was a small victory to hear his breath hitch.

She smiled and turned her mouth to his ear. "If you call me 'Miss Vice' ever again, I'll cut out your tongue with your own dagger. Got it?"

She released him and swayed back but didn't leave his space, chin raised in question.

He moistened his lips and swallowed slowly. "Yes, madam," he murmured.

Nodding, she backed off. "He's clear," she announced, voice hoarse.

"Glad to see you doing *such* a thorough job, Vice," FitzRoy said with a rictus smile before whirling and striding to his cabin.

Blackwood gave her a heavy look, just a second too long for comfort before he followed FitzRoy.

"WILL you *please* stop pacing and give me a hand?"

Arms folded, Vice blinked and looked up at Perry untangling *The Morrigan's* lines from the *Veritas*. She shook her head and rubbed her face. "Sorry," she muttered and climbed up. "I just"—she checked none of the crew was too close—"I don't like it." Sitting astride the bowsprit, she pulled herself along, closing in on the points where it was tangled with the *Veritas*.

"See, I wasn't so sure." Perry's voice was full of arched eyebrow.

"What's that supposed to mean?"

"You look pissed as all hells about the Captain agreeing to speak to this Blackwood but..."

Vice paused, wrapping her legs around and turning to narrow her eyes at Perry. "But *what?*"

Perry cleared her throat and refused to meet her gaze, seemingly absorbed in separating the lines in her hands. "Well, you took your time patting down the man. When I said it sounded like he was good-looking, you could have told me that was an understatement. If I'd known, I'd have rouged my lips before meeting him." She glanced up with a smirk, fingers still working the lines by touch. "I can't blame you for enjoying it so much. Find him packing anything interesting?"

Vice scoffed and rolled her eyes before sliding along to the first of the snags. She wasn't *that* affected by the whole thing. The rough hemp under her fingers was familiar and categorically nonsexual. Lips pursed, she let it consume her physical attention. "While you're distracted by a pretty face, *I'm* far more concerned about the fact those two are holed up in FitzRoy's cabin deciding all our fates."

With a shrug, Perry's gaze returned to her work. "And Bricus."

First rope untangled, Vice dropped it and turned to Perry, open-mouthed. "*What?*"

"Bricus is in there, too. Captain summoned him not long after they shut themselves away."

"What the hells? And you're fine with this?" Prickling irritation shot down her neck and across her shoulders. "You're the quartermaster—*you* should be in there." What was FitzRoy thinking? Did he not give a damn what Perry thought? Much as Bricus was a cheery first mate, Perry was more important to the ship's running than him.

"His ship, his choice."

"That's the problem." Arms straining after two battles and all that use of her gift, Vice heaved herself to her feet. "And he needs telling." She balanced her way back along the bowsprit and hopped down next to her friend.

Perry jumped, eyes wide when she looked up. "Wait, what are you doing? Leave him be, Vice." A line formed between her brows. "Have you eaten since the fight, since your..." She wriggled her fingers.

"I'm going to tell him since it looks like no one else will." She strode aft, Perry dropping her work and hurrying after. "And as for whether I've eaten, I don't see what that's got to do with anything."

"Because your gift burns through energy, leaving you tired and hungry, and when you're hungry, you're tetchy as a sabrecat with a toothache."

"That's patently untrue."

"See, and you use longer words, a *lady's* words when you get like that."

Vice grunted and strode along the deck. Her crewmates were already mopping up the blood and hauling fresh canvas to repair the holes from the *Veritas's* chain shot, chatting as they worked. A handful of men and women on all sides had died, and six bodies lay, already wrapped in their hammocks waiting for their burial at sea.

Vice shuddered at the sight of stiff canvas shrouding the unmistakable shapes, and she rubbed her opal ring.

Lizzy, who was sewing shut one of the hammocks, glanced up. Her brows lifted, and she gave a sad smile, pitying.

Clenching her hands, Vice forced her pace steady and lifted

her chin. She was fine. That sight didn't affect her at all. Everyone died. Some sooner, some later, but everyone ended up wrapped in canvas or wood and chucked in the sea or shovelled under mud. Everyone.

All the more reason not to rely on them.

Eyes forward, she took a deep breath that shook in her throat.

She was five paces from FitzRoy's cabin door when it swung open, and the man himself emerged, a feline smile in place. He stepped to one side, letting Blackwood stand alongside him, face neutral.

So neither of them had murdered each other. Surprising.

"Gents, ladies, good folk of *The Morrigan*," FitzRoy bellowed, gaze skimming the crew as they paused in their work. Despite her proximity, his eyes skipped over Vice. "It gives me *almost* the very greatest pleasure"—he paused and grinned, winking at Saba nearby—"to tell you I've accepted Captain Blackwood's offer. As of today, we're all pardoned by the Queen herself and are her very own privateers."

"Huh." The sound fell from her a split second before the crew cheered and clapped for the second time today. Privateers? And all thanks to this pirate-hunting *stranger*, rather than her own attempts for the past three years.

FitzRoy finally looked at her as if to say, *Well?*

Nodding, she clapped and smiled. With a half-laugh of confusion, she glanced at Blackwood. How on earth had he persuaded FitzRoy?

Shrugging, she threw her head back and cheered with the last of her crewmates. Whatever he'd done to secure FitzRoy's agreement, she should just be glad about the result, since it was what she'd wanted for so long. The Queen had been good to her, and although it was years since she'd seen her, years since she'd even been alive as far as the Queen knew, it hadn't faded.

Vice clapped Perry on the shoulder and grinned. Her other hand went to the small pin hidden under the collar of her shirt, its shape familiar from long years of wear. She didn't have to look at it to see the crowned drake—the red enamel was bright in her mind, the ruby eyes sparkled, the tiny pearls in the crown glistened, as vivid as the day the Queen had given it to her.

No more danger of attacking the Queen's ships. Now they'd help resist her enemies.

Vice snorted again. Never thought she'd see the day.

After that pleasant surprise, the crew finished tidying and repairing *The Morrigan*, and disentangled the three ships. As part of the deal, new weapons were brought over from the *Venatrix*—extra pistols and rifles, which Vice helped stow. They weren't fae-worked, but they were in good working order. Maybe that was what had sweetened the deal.

By the time the sun was just a thin orange sliver on the horizon, everyone was back on their own ships, and *The Morrigan* set sail.

Vice stood at the stern rail, watching the *Venatrix* silhouetted against the dying sunset. She sighed, heart dropping. Being a privateer made taking that ship strictly off-limits, probably forever. It was a pretty dream while it lasted.

They could take a Hesperian vessel instead, though it'd be hard to find something as swift and sleek. She bit her lip.

Still, she'd got her wish to ally *The Morrigan* with the Queen. Plus, leaving the *Venatrix* in their wake meant she'd got the insufferably disciplined Captain Blackwood off her back.

Silver linings and all that.

She watched the shrinking shape of the *Venatrix*, munching roasted cocoplum seeds from the pouch Perry had pressed into her hands with an order to "Bloody eat something, woman."

Vice chuckled to herself. Fine, so maybe she was feeling a little better now she'd eaten.

"Madam." The voice came from behind, setting the hairs on the back of her neck on end. "I understand you can show me to my new cabin."

Blackwood?

SPACE

Blood burning its way through her body, Vice clenched her hands into useless fists.

The Captain had given her cabin to Blackwood. He'd actually gone and done it.

She'd argued—Wild Hunt, she'd bloody argued, but he was adamant. The deal to turn legit privateer not *quite* of the Queen's Navy meant bringing aboard a representative.

Standing in the same spot as when she'd given him the fake clue, FitzRoy lifted his open hands. "As such, he requires an appropriate cabin, and if it wasn't yours, it would be mine."

And that wasn't going to happen.

She clenched her jaw, then huffed. "You didn't even kick me out when..." She stopped short, nostrils flaring and threw a quick look at Blackwood who stood impassively beside her.

She didn't talk about *then*, and she certainly wasn't going to mention Evered in front of *him*.

A flicker of a frown that looked worryingly like genuine

concern crossed FitzRoy's face. "Vice, I'm not *kicking you out* now. Perry's already agreed to share her berth with you, and I'm sure Mr Blackwood will allow you to access his cabin to fetch your belongings."

His cabin. Just like that, decision made. Vice ground her teeth.

Blackwood folded his arms, fingers resting on the biceps she now knew the feel of. Was that a deliberate flex or—but, no, the overly-smooth smile he gave was fixed on FitzRoy rather than her. "*Captain* Blackwood is only too happy to allow Miss—*madam* to enter and gather any belongings she may need."

FitzRoy stared at the other man, unblinking, then smiled coolly. "Indeed."

Ha, maybe he was regretting letting Blackwood on the ship after all. Well, he had no one to blame but himself—she'd tried to warn him.

"Vice," he said, dark gaze sliding to her before finally blinking, "is there anything else?"

Dismissed. She had no say in this.

"Fine, but you owe me. What we spoke about—"

Nodding, he raised a hand. "Of course. Some fine Hesperian galleon or—no, a frigate for you, I think, yes?"

She cocked her head. That was easy. Too easy. She threw a sidelong look at Blackwood, but he gave no response. No surprise there. Cold fish.

Still, part of their remit as privateers would include the license to take cargo from Albion's enemies, destroy their ships... or take them. And any vessel they took would need a captain.

It might not be the *Venatrix*, but it would be hers.

"A frigate. A fast one." She nodded, flashed him a smile, and swept out. "Come on, Blackwood," she threw over her shoulder, "I'll show you *my* cabin."

Striding back into the night air, Vice scowled at the handful of crewmates nearby who met her gaze, all frozen in looks of surprise. News of her being evicted from her cabin must have burned through the ship like wildfire. Pursing her lips, she lifted one shoulder, confirming the gossip.

Without checking whether Blackwood followed, she threw the door to her cabin open and swept her hand towards it theatrically. "Your cabin awaits, *ser*."

"Thank you," he murmured, ducking past her with a nod.

"A pirate hunter thanking a pirate." She scoffed and followed him inside, slamming the door. "Wonders will truly never cease."

He strode to the stern windows, looking out into the night. Maybe he was saying goodbye to the *Venatrix* himself. "Thanking a *privateer*, you mean." Taking a deep breath, he threw all the windows open.

Was he trying to say she smelled? Cheeky bastard. "You don't smell so sweet yourself," she muttered and lit the lamp that hung from the ceiling.

Stomping about the room, she grabbed the duffle bag from her sea chest and threw it on her bunk.

The space had always been plenty big enough, but with him here, it felt suddenly crowded. He had to duck to walk under the lamp, and his shoulders blotted out her view of the darkening violet sky through the stern windows.

"So," he said, back still to her, "if not Miss Vice, what *am* I to call you?"

"Vice. Or Lady Vice, if you're feeling formal."

He scoffed, a faint misting of breath hitting the window. "I refuse to call you such a ridiculous name as *Vice*."

She shot upright. "What's wrong with it?"

"*Clearly* you have a real name." He leant on the window frame, long fingers tanned dark against the white-painted wood. "No one in the world would call a child *Vice*."

That was true, but she wasn't Avice Ferrers anymore. That girl was gone, and so were Papa's claims over her, including betrothal to that boy he'd chosen. Papa, Knighton Villiers—she was dead to them and good riddance. Being parted from Mama, Nanny Alder, and her sister gave the thought a sour note, but if that was the price she had to pay for freedom, so be it. Besides, one day she'd return and keep her promise to Mama.

One day.

Frowning, she stripped her blankets and sheets from the bed, rolling them up and packing them. "*I* call myself Vice, that's all that matters."

"I'm sure I'll come up with something."

Lords, was he flirting? She paused, reaching into her sea chest.

"I"—he turned from the window and let out a quick breath. "Well, that's a lot of books."

"I'm sure you've seen more"—she shoved a handful of clothes in the duffle—"you officer types all come from the nobility, don't you?" The home of hypocrisy.

"You didn't seem entirely out of place in a ballroom yourself. Say, are these all yours or—"

"Yes, they're mine." When she turned, he stood at the shelves that lined the partition between her cabin and the Captain's, a book in his hands. "I may be a pirate—*privateer*, but I can read, you know." She snatched the book and returned it to the shelf.

"Oh, I don't doubt it." Rubbing his fingertips, he turned slowly. His grey eyes glinted as he took in every detail of her cabin.

It made her itch. This was all hers. No one came in here, it was *her* space. She clenched her hands then shook them out.

The sooner she was packed, the sooner she'd be out of here and away from him.

Trying her best to ignore him, even when she had to inch past his too-big form, she gathered the essentials. Hand mirror and a little bottle of perfume Perry had gifted her for her birthday. More clothes from the drawers, including her few nice chemises—all sheer silk and fine lace. Who knew what this lonely naval officer would do with a woman's underwear if left unattended?

That made her chuckle to herself.

"*Barnacle?*" He stood by the bunk, holding up the red broadcloth cushion she'd made from fabric left over from her coat. "I've never seen a lady take to embroidering the names of sea creatures before." He stared from the cushion to her, one eyebrow raised, corner of his mouth lifted.

Oh, yes, very bloody amusing. Somehow *this* was enough to make him wear an actual facial expression?

She threw him a withering look. "Don't touch my things." She rescued the cushion from his grasp and placed it back on the bed. "Barnacle is *obviously* the ship's cat."

"Oh, *obviously*. So, what's this? A tribute to him in all his feline glory?"

"*Her* feline glory, actually. She likes to sleep in here, and if you don't let her in, she'll just scratch at the door all night until you do. So, good luck with that."

Enough of him. This would do—if she needed anything else, she'd come back for it another time. She grabbed the duffle, and when she straightened, throwing it over one shoulder, he hadn't backed away, leaving their bodies much too close for comfort.

Again, that heat radiated from him, more appealing now night had fallen and the air had grown chilly after the heat of battle.

No, *not* appealing. Nothing about him was appealing. He was Navy to the core—no doubt he'd start arranging things in *her* cabin the moment she was gone, aligning it all, setting things at perfect right angles.

And yet her breath sped along with her heart rate. He stared at her lips where they'd parted entirely without her intention.

She clamped her mouth shut.

Wild Hunt damn him, this had truly backfired. She would never have pulled that stunt with the weapons check if she'd known he'd be staying on board. It had been too long since she'd felt a lover's arms, lips—or anything else for that matter—and touching him had sent her spinning off course, dizzy as a teenage girl.

Worse, FitzRoy was so possessive, even though they'd stopped bunking together, that there was no way she could satisfy her need with someone else in the crew. Not without winning them a tough time from him—Aedan had learned that lesson the hard way.

"Well, anyway," she said, voice coming out strangled, "Barnacle doesn't like anyone but me, so I'm sure she won't bother *you*, Navy boy." She backed away, calves slamming into the low edge of her sea chest, making her wince. "She's far smarter than FitzRoy—whatever you did to persuade him to trust you won't work on her. And *I* don't trust you, either."

His back and shoulders straightened, squared, just like the ridiculous desk in his cabin on the *Venatrix*, all hint of flirtation and informality snuffed out. "An excellent position, madam. I suggest you maintain it."

"Oh, don't you worry, I will." She shoved the door open and gave him a sardonic smile. "Enjoy sleeping with the cat—she likes having her belly rubbed."

Barnacle *hated* having her belly rubbed by anyone other than Vice. She'd scratch the man's hands to ribbons.

Vice bit back a laugh and left, slamming the door in her wake.

It was a wonder her skin didn't sizzle in the night air, it was so hot. She sank against the door and huffed out a long breath.

Gods, please say Captain Knigh Blackwood's presence on *The Morrigan* was only temporary while they gained the Navy's trust. If it went on too long, there was a good chance either she or he wouldn't survive.

ADJUSTMENT

It was worse than Vice had feared.

Far, far worse.

Scratching Barnacle's chin, she watched Blackwood doing—

"What *is* he doing?" she whispered to the cat.

Wynn and Effie stood at his side, heads bowed, looking at a short length of rope in his hands.

Knots? A bloody Navy officer thought he could waltz on deck and show the pirate sisters how to tie knots? She laughed, the sound somewhere between amused and frustrated.

This was the third time in a week she'd spotted him *changing things*. Yesterday, he'd raised a query with Perry about the efficient stowing of hammocks. His second day aboard, she'd watched as he'd checked and adjusted every single spare line on the ship. He'd coiled it afresh, tying a new hitch, and hanging it up, perfectly neat.

FitzRoy had let him on the ship *and* given him her cabin, but interfering with the crew was taking liberties. He might still have the title *Captain*, but he wasn't *The Morrigan's* captain. He wasn't even really part of the crew—Perry had told her that part of the deal meant he wasn't to take part in any attacks since this wasn't officially a Navy ship. He was only here to observe.

He crossed his hands and twisted the rope, then lifted it for Wynn and Effie to see.

Well, *that* wasn't only observing.

Folding her arms, she sidled over behind Blackwood. She'd tell him and—

Even better—FitzRoy was approaching, a small frown in place as he watched.

She wouldn't have to tell him anything.

Barnacle leapt off her shoulder and trotted over to Blackwood.

Vice glared after her. "What the—"

The little beast flopped over and stared up at him, green eyes wide.

Oh, he was in for a nasty surprise. *Clever kitty.*

Sure enough, he crouched and reached for Barnacle's fluffy white tummy—a trap.

Hook line and sinker. She'd tear him to—

Except she didn't. Vice blinked as Blackwood rubbed the little cat's belly.

And the little minx purred.

Traitor.

Fine. Well, Fitz wouldn't be so easily won over. She huffed and jerked her chin, indicating Navy boy's little knot-tying lesson.

"Blackwood," FitzRoy said, tone clipped, "if you'd oblige me." He gestured towards his cabin and turned, not checking whether Blackwood followed. "And you, Vice," he called over his shoulder.

What? Her, too? What had she done? Unless it was to report on all his interference.

She entered FitzRoy's cabin a pace behind Blackwood and

nodded. "Captain." If Blackwood was about to get a dressing down, she didn't want to put herself in the line of fire, too. Even if that did mean playing along with FitzRoy's ridiculous desire to seem important in front of Navy boy.

FitzRoy lifted his chin, level gaze falling on Blackwood in a way that made up for the fact he was a few inches shorter. "What were you doing with my crew members, Blackwood?"

"Demonstrating the correct method for making a gasket coil hitch. They're more secure than bight coil hitches, which I noticed were employed throughout *The Morrigan*."

So it wasn't just to look neat. At least as far as Blackwood was concerned, the hitch he'd used was more fit for purpose.

FitzRoy's jaw ratcheted a notch tighter.

Knigh tilted his head, lifting one shoulder. "Regardless of which is more effective, the bights had been started incorrectly, *FitzRoy*."

Vice's eyes widened, and she shot him a look. His face was impassive as always—wait, no, there was a slight narrowing of his eyes. He knew exactly what he was doing, dropping Fitz's title just as Fitz had dropped his. Two captains on a ship, of course it was bound to lead to a power play.

Good, maybe that would work in her favour—let Fitz direct his irritation at Blackwood, and she'd look great in comparison.

Fitz's nostrils flared. "And yesterday you spoke to my quartermaster about a matter of ship management, also, didn't you?"

"I did."

Vice cleared her throat. "And you asked about the powder storage the other day."

Tension knotted in Fitz's jaw. "And why are you making these alterations to *my* ship?"

"Because they were incorrect."

Vice snorted. "It can't be that wrong—*The Morrigan's* still afloat and thriving, and this is how we've always done things."

He surveyed her, grey eyes coolly amused. "That's the problem."

She bristled, and Fitz mirrored her, back erect, hands clenching.

Blackwood appeared unmoved. He went on, "Your methods were less effective, and, in the case of the black powder, I had concerns they might be dangerous."

"Then you take it to the Captain," she bit out. It couldn't have been that dangerous, the ship hadn't exactly exploded. "Chain of command and all that. Isn't that what you have—what you bloody *worship* in the Navy?"

"You mean you have some sense of order on this—"

"On this *what?*" Fitz's voice was low, sending a chill down Vice's back.

Great, that was all she needed, Fitz in a rage. Irritated was one thing, but if he lost his temper...

Blackwood swallowed and cleared his throat softly. He must have realised he'd stepped close to the line. "I'd heard pirate crews prided themselves on having no hierarchy, on living in a kind of" —he waved his hand through the air in a gesture far too loose for him—"anarchic chaos."

"Does my ship look like an example of chaos to you?"

For long seconds, Blackwood looked back at Fitz. His chest rose and fell as if he were about to reply, but no words came.

Dear gods, answer him, man.

Fitz worked his jaw, a sure sign of building fury. If Blackwood didn't speak soon, he'd blow, just as dangerous as gunpowder. Gods only knew what Fitz would do then.

She coughed softly and patted her chest, calling the attention of both men to her—anything to break the painful tension hanging between them. Eyes wide, she stared at Blackwood, willing him to speak.

"*The Morrigan* is a sound vessel."

Marginally better than nothing. She exhaled.

With an audible *pop*, Fitz pulled his teeth apart. "Quite."

This could still go badly. "Blackwood," she said—gods, where was she going with this? "Didn't I hear you telling Perry yesterday what a good state of repair the sails were in?" It was almost true—Perry told her he'd said *something* positive about their canvas when he'd made the suggestion about the hammocks.

"Very kind of you." Fitz's tone was frigid, but he didn't sound like murder was imminent anymore.

She swallowed and forced a stiff smile.

"Blackwood," Fitz went on, "I'm sure it must be... *challenging* for you adapting to live aboard a pi—*privateering* vessel and one where you're *not captain*. However, I trust I won't need to remind you again that this is my crew."

Blackwood folded his arms. "I'm sure you won't."

"Very good." He rested his hands on the table, leaning towards them. "Now, Vice, I'm sure it will help our friend here appreciate his *altered* position if you were to take him ashore with you tomorrow."

A strangled sound came from her throat. "Ashore?" Tomorrow they'd arrive at Nassau. That was her chance to explore the latest happenings in town, arrange the best deals with the local stores for Perry's cargo manifest, and even pick up items for her crewmates. "But I always go alone." And life aboard, much as she loved it, afforded barely any time alone now she didn't have her own cabin.

"Well"—he smiled but it didn't reach his eyes—"you can have a little company this time, can't you? I can carry your shopping."

She stared at him. She blinked. Exhaling through her nose, she shook her head. Did he think she was picking out a new gown or decorating the guest wing?

Fitz cleared his throat. "I'm sure Vice will appreciate any assistance, won't you?" He waved his hand. "And take your time. I'll make sure Perry gives you a little something extra to spend."

Take your time. She sighed. This wasn't about her—he just wanted Blackwood off the ship, away from him *and* his crew. And much as he'd couched it with a question, it wasn't a request.

"Aye, Captain," she said, backing towards the door. "Well, I'd best go and check over the list with Perry, make sure we haven't missed anything." Perry never missed an item from the cargo, but Vice needed to get out of here and no way was she asking for permission to leave like some Navy lackey. "Excuse me, gentlemen."

NASSAU

"A lovely day for a walk, isn't it?" Knigh tried a pleasant smile as he sidled up to Vice while she waited for the gangway to be slid into place.

So this was the infamous Nassau. A long stretch of brilliant green-blue water lay between chaotic wharves and a low sandy island that sheltered the harbour.

Past the wharves, the town—well, it looked like most small towns that had sprung up in Arawaké. Since the local island nations had invited foreign powers to the trading table, offering parcels of land to found settlements, dozens littered the islands. Nassau could almost be any one of them. True, there was no sign of soldiers and more buildings were timber than stone or brick, but the same could be said for a lot of the younger, smaller towns in the area.

Knigh's eyebrows rose. Not what he was expecting, especially after Perry's warnings.

He brushed down the front of his waistcoat. He'd followed the advice she'd given him and swapped his uniform for neutral civilian clothing—leather boots, plain breeches, a simple white shirt and cravat, and a waistcoat. On the one hand, it felt inappropriate to be about to walk ashore without full coat and uniform. But on the other, the linen shirt let the breeze breathe through to cool his skin. And with the sun so fierce, that breeze was welcome.

She'd advised him well. Ahead, the wharves and streets crawled with precisely the people he'd spent the past two years chasing down. Setting foot here in Navy uniform would have been nothing short of suicide.

Vice gave him a sidelong look—her eyes were brilliant blue flecked turquoise today. It seemed the colour looked different depending on the light. Curious.

She pursed her lips. "This isn't a jolly stroll along the promenade, Blackwood, this is *work*."

He cocked his head. "I didn't think *you* would consider work and pleasure mutually exclusive."

The corner of her mouth twitched, but she gave no reply, gaze fixed on the town stretching ahead.

She, too, wore light clothes—linen breeches, a sheer shirt cut low enough to draw attention, and a sea-blue waistcoat. With all the gold braid and brass buttons, it should have been garish. And yet the way she wore it with leather belts criss-crossed over waist and hips, holding three pistols and a battered sabre—somehow, she made it seem nonchalant. Topped with a tricorne hat to keep the sun from her eyes, there was no doubting she belonged here.

"Let's get this over and done with." Without waiting for him, she sauntered across the gangway and thanked the dock workers who'd manoeuvred it.

He sighed and strode after her. He was *trying*. He'd annoyed FitzRoy, that much was obvious. And Vice, too, but that seemed an easy task. However, he was attempting to integrate with their motley crew. They might be privateers, but he wasn't foolish enough to believe that meant their enmity towards him as a pirate hunter had disappeared the instant the ink on their agreement dried.

Walking at her side, he watched her out the corner of his eye. Now he was closer, he spotted silver hooped earrings glinting amongst the wild waves of her hair. As she moved, small, bright feathers hanging from the hoops gleamed in iridescent colours—bright blue, green, gold. He'd seen Saba wear similar feathers in her hair and as jewellery—perhaps the earrings had been a gift from her.

It wasn't a great leap of logic. Vice was clearly popular with the crew. In fact, although FitzRoy had told her to bring him along for his own ends, this spell on shore could work to his advantage. If he won Vice's approval, perhaps that would influence the rest of the crew.

Gods knew he didn't need people who were *meant* to be his allies, albeit temporary ones, attacking him. His hands tightened. Trapped on a ship full of enemies, under attack, there was no way he wouldn't lose control.

Getting them on-side, perhaps even befriending them, that was his only option.

He took a deep breath. He needed a distraction and to warm her to him: *let's get this over and done with* hadn't been an auspicious start.

"Why does FitzRoy send you to buy and sell supplies and cargo? Isn't it the quartermaster's job?"

She lifted her chin. "Fae charm gets good prices."

"Huh." Frowning, he examined her again. "So, you're gifted."

He almost said *too*, but he bit back the word. He could count on one hand the number of people who knew *he* was fae-touched. If the Navy knew, he'd be locked in sickbay working under a surgeon, rather than commanding his own ship, catching pirates.

They'd see him as just another commodity. Outside of the Navy, many others treated healers like chattel to be bought and sold—or stolen, especially on the high seas.

He narrowed his eyes at Vice—nothing about her appearance said she was fae-touched. No strangely symmetrical birthmark, pointed ears, sharp claws, or strange hair colour. "Oh, *your eyes*—that's your fae mark."

Gave him a sidelong look. "You noticed that, then?"

"The first time we met they were turquoise, the other day they were steel-blue, today they're more of a true blue, flecked green. I thought it was a trick of the light."

"They usually match the sea that day—at least that's what Perry says."

"I'd heard rumours the notorious Lady Vice was a sea witch, but I thought it was all exaggeration to make a good story."

She shrugged, eyes on the road ahead. "Some of it is. For example, I can't call down a bolt of lightning from a clear sky like this and strike you where you stand." She gave him a smirk. "Lucky for you."

Still annoyed at him, then.

Well, he had taken over her cabin, so that was probably fair. Though he'd done her the favour of tidying it. The first time he'd walked in, he'd thought the place had been ransacked in the fight. But when she hadn't commented on it, he'd realised she was just that messy. How did anyone think in such an environment?

The way she'd snatched that book from him, she wasn't going to thank him for making the place shipshape any time soon.

They hadn't walked much further in un-companionable silence before the looks started. Glowers from the shadows of a tavern door. Glinting eyes beneath a wide-brimmed hat. Even a sneer as one woman crossed their path.

Perhaps that was just how they treated newcomers in Nassau.

But then the whispers followed—a cluster of men and women in the mouth of an alleyway, a man too-casually leaning out a ground-floor window to mutter in his fellow's ear.

Damnation. Maybe they recognised him.

He kept his head high as if he hadn't noticed, but his arms and hands hung loose at his sides, ready to draw weapons at an instant's notice.

Wild Hunt—what a fool. He'd been so concerned about *The Morrigan's* crew attacking him that he hadn't even considered the pirates on shore and the land-dwellers who made their money from their trade.

"Blackwood," Vice muttered, leaning closer as they walked, "why is everyone looking at us like they're a few torches away from forming an angry mob?"

"I should imagine it's because I match the description of a well-known pirate hunter. Strangely enough."

"*Well-known?* Just how many ships have you taken?"

"Gods know—I stopped counting after the first couple of dozen."

A choked sound came from her, which she attempted to disguise as a cough. Thumping her chest, she cleared her throat. "Anyone I'd know?"

"Perhaps"—he shrugged—"Bonny Steed, Jack Shoals, Davy Davis and his son."

She missed a step, eyes widening. "Jack Shoal's been grabbed? When?"

"About four months ago."

"Bloody hells. You *have* been busy." She shook her head, gaze scanning the wide road. "Poor Jack."

"Poor Jack? No poor Bonny or Davis boys?"

"Jack was a good lad—helped me out of a sticky situation once, and we had a great night carousing after. Well, I say *night*—

more like a weekend." In the shadow of her tricorne, her eyes crinkled above a warm grin. The look soon soured. "Bonny, though—he was a prick. Deserved whatever he got. How'd you manage to take so many?"

He lifted one shoulder. "If I told you that, I'd be giving away all my secrets." Including the fact this is all a ploy. He swallowed. "Let's just say, I'll do whatever it takes to get the job done."

Eyes narrowed, she gave him a long look that would have made most men squirm. "Whatever it takes, huh? Come on." With a nod, she indicated an alley between timber buildings and split off in that direction.

A shortcut avoiding so many pirates, perhaps. Glancing up and down the street, he followed.

They ducked into the shadows and no sooner were they out of sight than she whirled to face him. "Right, let's sort this out."

She reached for him, and he flinched, catching her wrist on instinct.

He pulled her hand away. "What are you doing?" The last time she'd touched him—well, it had been in front of almost two-hundred people and yet had felt wildly improper. His blood had burned. It had taken every ounce of self-control to avoid making a damn fool of himself in front of his crew and *The Morrigan's*. Right now, her cool skin and throbbing pulse under his fingers were at once soothing and thrilling.

"I'm *trying* to keep you alive, though I'll be damned if I know why."

Mouth flat, he stared back, and when she tried to pull her wrist away, his grip tightened. "Glibness isn't a good enough answer."

Sighing, she rolled her eyes. "Calm down, Navy boy, I'm just trying to make you a bit less recognisable, so we don't get mobbed by angry pirates." She raised her eyebrows as if to ask whether he was going to let her get on with it.

He exhaled and released her. "Fine." Relief washed over him to no longer be in contact with her, immediately followed by longing —that cool hand on his forehead would be...

He clenched his fists and jaw. *For goodness sake, man, get a hold of yourself.*

"*Thank you,*" she said, an arch in her tone. With deft fingers, she began untying his cravat and snorted indelicately. "I can't believe you're wearing a cravat in this weather."

Thankfully she kept her gaze on her work rather than meeting his. It had been a mistake to make that challenging eye contact with her when he'd removed his weapons. He knew that now. At the time, fool that he was, he'd thought it would ruffle her.

To say it had backfired was an understatement.

He lifted his chin to avoid her fingers brushing his throat while she pulled the knot loose. The less physical contact between them, the better. Even this distance between them, a few inches, was too much to bear. Close enough to lean in. Close enough that he only needed to lift his hands and he'd be holding her waist.

He swallowed. A good couple of feet—that would feel much safer, but his back was already against the alley wall.

It was just physical attraction, nothing more, but, gods, was it insistent.

The cravat—focus on that. He cleared his throat. "I'd feel undressed without one."

The corner of her mouth twitched as she pulled away the length of linen. "Too used to hiding behind your uniform." Her gaze flicked to his face, narrow-eyed for a moment before she took a small step back. She looped the cravat around his waist and tied it at an angle, like the belts at her waist. "Better. This, though"—

she frowned at his face, lips pursed—"this might be a bit more difficult to disguise."

"What's wrong with my face?"

She laughed, breath sweet like coconut and banana. "Nothing. Nothing at all."

Her hands lifted as if she were about to cup his cheeks, and he forced himself still. He couldn't give in to this physical attraction any more than he could give in to the battle rage, but if she kissed him… Well, he might *tell* himself to pull away; whether his body would listen was a different matter entirely.

But instead of her fingers on his face, they plunged into his hair. He had to clench his jaw against a groan threatening deep in his chest.

Lips pursed, she frowned at a point above his left eyebrow. "*This* is the problem."

The white streak in his hair. His fae mark.

She combed and pushed it to one side. "Urgh, I can't even hide it. Your hair's so *thick*." She shook her head, attention all on his hairline. "I've never seen one so white and precise on someone so young before. No wonder they recognised you." She smoothed it flat as if trying to use the rest of his hair to hide the offending streak. He knew from his own attempts that it would only spring up as soon as she removed her hand. "What happened? A blow to the head?"

He'd been keeping his gift hidden from the Navy for long enough that the prepared line came easily: "I had a nasty shock."

Her head canted in query.

He took a long breath. Telling her the abbreviated version couldn't hurt. It might even get her to trust him and if he wanted to get the crew on his side…

"When I was twenty, my father passed away." Another long

breath. She didn't need to know how much he'd looked up to the man, seen him as a hero, wanted to be just like him.

"Oh." A crease between her brows, she nodded faintly. Disappointed?

"That wasn't the shock," he hurried to add. "I wish that was the only thing." He sighed softly. "After his passing, we discovered he'd racked up massive debts and..."

And he'd sold off parts of their land already, including an estate in the north, and various other items of value. All done without the rest of the family knowing. Then there was the discovery of a mistress and illegitimate son in Portsmouth.

That was more than she needed to know.

"Well," he went on, "add in an absconding fiancée and being forced from our home, and I think it's fair to say it was a difficult year."

The fiancée had left months before Father's death, and she hadn't exactly broken his heart. The betrothal to Lady Avice Ferrers had been arranged by Mother and Father. It struck him later that Father had intended to use her dowry to clear his debts. No romance, simply a matter of family duty.

How could there be any love? He'd only met the girl a few times, all when they'd been much younger. But including her made the story about his difficult year all the more compelling.

Brow creasing, Vice's expression softened, compassionate, almost sad.

Knigh's chest twisted. She felt sorry for him? The matter of his family's difficulties—surely to her it would just be a sign of how wealthy they'd been in the first place.

So perhaps it was the wayward fiancée that touched her. Hadn't she said at the ball that she was widowed? Something about how the story had come so quickly and a brief look that had crossed her face had made him wonder and now this... Maybe there was a vein of truth in it.

Who knew that the route to Vice's black heart would be through tragic tales of romance? It was almost enough to make him laugh.

He tried to soften his own expression, look like he genuinely was sad. He couldn't plumb his feelings towards Father—that was a dangerous box to open—but perhaps he could summon something from the distant memory of Lady Avice.

Although she hadn't broken his heart, the news she'd eloped with another man *had* been a slap in the face. In those few meetings, he'd clearly made a bad impression. Bad enough that she'd rather run away from her entire life and marry some penniless younger son of a baron than stay and marry him.

To think he'd been naïve enough to believe that would be the worst thing to happen that year.

Vice pursed her lips for a moment before she bowed her head and removed her tricorne. From the inside band, she pulled a folded piece of paper and tucked it in her pocket. "Disappointing fathers, eh?" She gave a sardonic smile, but there was something still sad in her eyes as she slid the hat onto his head. "That works," she murmured to herself and nodded. "What about your mother? How did the two of you manage?"

Knigh blinked. So it was the family that struck her more? *Disappointing fathers*—that sounded personal. Fine, he could follow that angle, as long as he didn't think too much about the man.

"*Four* of us—I have a brother and sister, too." He pushed the tricorne on more securely, angling until it felt comfortable. He could give a few details. It wasn't as if he were sharing naval secrets and he couldn't see any way she could use this against him. "We had to sell our whole estate, and I thought I might have to leave the Navy. I'd not long made Lieutenant and expenses rack up quickly when you're first promoted. Thankfully, my mother's sister was able to take us in, and she lent me the money to stay in the service."

Thank the gods for Aunt Tilda. When he'd needed to escape the Villiers name, it had made sense to borrow Blackwood from her. She had no children, and he owed her so much—it was the least he could do to continue the family line. It wasn't as if Father deserved to have his name live on.

Blinking, Vice started and backed away as though she hadn't realised she'd finished disguising him and had just been staring. "So talkative today. I believe this is the most words I've heard you string together at once."

He lifted one shoulder. "Well, we're serving on the same ship, now. It wouldn't do to be rude, especially to the woman whose cabin I've commandeered."

"Aye, best not to piss off a *notorious* pirate." She gestured to the street with a quick, stiff smile. "Shall we?"

ON FIRST NAME TERMS

When they emerged into the sun, no unwelcome attention lingered on them. As they continued up the road, he eyed her sidelong. Somehow, he'd managed to get her to speak to him civilly. Perhaps if he gave more, she'd share more.

"Of course," he said, scanning ahead, "selling off everything we had of worth, together with the scandal, destroyed my marriage prospects."

"I'm sure there are plenty of young ladies out there just waiting for their heads to be turned by a dashing young captain in uniform." She flashed him a grin and winked.

He scoffed at that reference to their first meeting. "Or rich young widows."

Her grin faded, and her eyes snapped away.

Damn it, he hadn't even asked a probing question, and he'd managed to make her shut down. He cleared his throat. "Still, the Na—my *work* means I can look after my family. And I wish to provide my sister with a good dowry."

"Such a dependable brother," she said, brows together. But the look was more thoughtful or confused than angry. "It sounds like you're working hard to turn your family's fortunes around."

"It's steadily paying off." His chest warmed with pride. He *had* worked bloody hard, but it was nice to hear it acknowledged, particularly by... Well, technically she was an enemy even if it didn't feel like it right now. "I reimbursed my aunt two years ago, and I should be able to provide my sister with a good dowry by the end of the year."

Her eyebrows rose, and she veered them into a left turn at the next intersection. "Pirate hunting pays well."

Inwardly he winced. Yes, the thousand guineas on her head was a handsome sum.

"In which case," she went on, "why are you helping us rather than turning us in? I heard my bounty had gone up—surely that would help your family a great deal."

Because my 'help' is just a way of getting you back to Albion without you realising and escaping.

He kept his face flat, calm, but the reminder jolted through him, cold as steel. This mild flirtation was one thing, and if it kept her on his side, it was an active, useful part of his plan, but he shouldn't be enjoying it.

The feeling twisted, like a dagger to the belly. Was that *guilt?* Gods, he shouldn't be feeling guilty about his plans for her. She was a pirate. He was a pirate hunter, and he'd been perfectly honest about the fact from their first meeting. She should know better than to trust him.

Hells, after what he'd done, *everyone* should know better than to trust him.

He took a deep breath. "You assume the bounty is only for your capture or death. Imagine the reward for bringing such an infamous pirate into the fold, for making her the crown's tame privateer."

She shot him a look, teeth bared for a second. "I may be a privateer, but I'll never be *tame*." Her shoulders were squared, her breaths deep. "I am my own, no one else's."

Blinking, he surveyed her again. He'd touched another nerve. He didn't expect someone who seemed so open and carefree to *have* hidden nerves to touch. "Sensible," he said with a nod. "It's probably best not to trust too easily."

It's probably best not to trust me.

She laughed, its volume not out of place here in the bustling streets of Nassau as it had been in Governor deLacy's ballroom. "Sensible! That's the first time I've ever been called that."

Grinning, he shook his head. "I can imagine."

Her eyes widened, and she grabbed his arm, angling them towards each other. "My word, have I cracked a smile on the face of the dread pirate hunter Blackwood?"

Damnation, she *had*. And he hadn't even intended to do it as part of his efforts to win her over—it had just happened. He straightened his expression. "It was only a mild grin, don't get too excited."

She clapped him on the shoulder, smiling as they strode on. "I'll still take it as progress. We'll make a pirate of you yet, Knigh."

"Knigh?" He'd been promoted to first names now?

"Blackwood's too many syllables." She shrugged. "Plus, I probably shouldn't say it around here, since you have such an *appalling* reputation."

"Fine, *Vee*."

"Vee?"

He gave a tilt of his head designed to look nonchalant, but his heart hammered. Giving her a nickname was meant to help her relax and prevent him having to call her by such a ridiculous word. But now he'd said it and she was looking at him like that, it felt... intimate. "I told you I wasn't going to call you Vice and since you won't tell me your actual name, this will have to do. Unless you've changed your mind on revealing your real—"

She stopped and raised her hand. "Never going to happen. Vee works fine. Now"—she gestured at the grocer's they'd stopped by—"here's our first stop."

They ducked into that store and several more over the next few hours, making arrangements to take on food, water, canvas, timber, gunpowder, and shot. Every shopkeeper greeted Vee warmly with smiles and hugs. They kissed her cheeks as if she were a beloved niece, and it looked genuine. They didn't have the stiff manner of someone who needed to keep an enemy happy or who was working under the weight of threats.

Their smiles, just as welcoming, even extended to Knigh. "A friend of Vice's is a friend of mine," one said, clapping him on the shoulder.

And it was a good thing he was used to schooling his expression because the deals she got were startlingly good. Fae charm did indeed get excellent prices.

He wasn't the only one to think so. It turned out the paper she'd slipped in her pocket was a list of personal purchases for the crew that she agreed to pick up in order to get them the best deals. Those store visits took up as much time as the ones for *The Morrigan*.

As the afternoon wore on, Knigh tapped the slip of paper in her hand. "And you always run these errands?"

She shrugged, mouthing 'done' repeatedly as she read down the list. "When we stop in a port long enough. Why?"

"It takes up a lot of your time—aren't the rest of the crew on shore leave, enjoying themselves?"

She blinked at him, a frown on her face followed by a slow

smile. “I can help them get more for their money. Why wouldn’t I?” She shook her head as if genuinely confused. “And it’s only time. I have however much of it the gods have given me—either I’ll still be alive to go drinking tonight or I won’t. Nothing I can do about it. Doesn’t hurt to help my crew in the meantime.”

He gave her a long look. The notorious Lady Vice ran errands for her crewmates *because it was a nice thing to do*. And she let the ship’s cat sleep on her bed, despite the fact the creature liked to tuck herself behind his knees or under his chin, taking up far more space than her small size warranted. From how affectionate Barnacle was, frequently demanding chin scratches and treats, it was obvious Vee doted on the little thing.

It was months ago that he’d received the offer from a member of *The Morrigan’s* crew to hand over Vice in exchange for pardons, land, and an eye-watering amount of money. The Admiralty had chosen Knigh to negotiate and carry out the arrest. But he’d come up with the plan to stop her sneaking or charming her way out of custody: make her believe herself a privateer, then she’d openly sail for Albion, ready for arrest.

He’d known she was cunning enough to evade capture or to escape if he’d tried to take her in the usual way, and the stories painted her as charismatic enough to talk her way out of chains.

He’d accounted for all that, but *this*...

“Well”—she squinted up at the sky—“we have one more stop, then I’d say we still have plenty of time for drinking.”

She set off at a brisk pace, and he had no choice but to shove down his confusion about her, about this plan, and follow.

When they stopped, his eyes widened. “A book shop?” He looked from the packed display window to her. “What happened to ‘let’s get this over and done with’?”

“This stop’s for me, and I’m not going to miss my chance, just because I'm playing nanny to you." She gave an exaggerated shrug. "Of course, if you'd rather get back to *The Morrigan*..."

Back with FitzRoy's resentment and the vague threat of any crew left on board. He lifted his hands. "Oh, no. I'm not in any rush." He opened the door and inclined his head. "Madam."

As she strode in, her chuckle blended with the chiming bell overhead.

The elderly shopkeeper gave her the same warm greeting the others had. His blue eyes twinkled, lively even though he had to be in his seventies. "Still driving a hard bargain, Vice?"

She picked up a book from one of the many shelves and flicked through it. "That depends, Waters—are you still trying to rip me off?"

He blinked slowly. "Would I?"

"Well, you try"—she returned the book to the shelf—"but luckily I lift something every five visits, so I figure that evens things out."

He scoffed. "And you wonder why I have to charge so much."

She chuckled and rounded the shelves out of sight.

Either Waters didn't care if she stole or he thought she was only joking, because he didn't make any move to keep an eye on her. He just waved Knigh towards the shelves and returned to the book he'd been reading when they arrived.

The shop was as well-stocked as any he'd seen, although some books had wrinkled pages and bleached covers from saltwater, and they were all coated in a fine layer of dust as if they'd been here a long time.

When he rounded the corner, Vee was bent over a book, features drawn together in focus. One finger traced over the page. What held her so rapt?

He craned to see. "You speak Latium?"

She jumped, and her gaze shot up to him—she really had been

so absorbed she hadn't noticed him approach. Blinking, she huffed. "What, you're surprised that a woman who swears with the best of them can also do so in Latium?"

The corner of his mouth quirked. "I suppose I shouldn't be since you seem to—"

The entry bell rang.

"Ho, Waters," a man's voice said as a single set of footsteps entered.

Vee's eyes widened and shot towards the door, but bookcases blocked it from sight.

Knigh frowned. "What's—"

She launched herself against him, hand over his mouth.

He only avoided slamming into the bookcase thanks to his quick reactions and the strength built through years of drills and hard work. Still, he had to catch her around the waist to keep them both steady.

But that only pulled her closer. Again, her hand was cool but the rest of her body, flush against his, was invitingly warm, pliant, a pleasing combination of angled muscles and feminine curves.

Gods damn it, this was even worse than when she'd searched him on deck. With her height and musculature, she fit against him far, far too well.

She smelled of rain on earth and sweet vanilla pods. That had been the scent in her cabin when he'd first walked in, and he'd had to open the window to blast it away. Now there was no escaping it. It filled his nose, addled his brain, seemed to even seep into his veins, throbbing through his body.

Her gaze was still towards the door, and she breathed hard and deep as if surprised but trying to stay quiet. Each one of those breaths pushed her breasts into his chest, and his traitorous fingers cupped her waist.

Swallowing, he released his grip and shook her hand away, trying to ignore his own heavy breaths. Control.

"Sorry," she mouthed and lifted a finger to her lips. As if he hadn't taken the hint!

"Mr Vane," Waters said, his tone stiff, "how can I help you this afternoon?"

Yes, focus on the conversation. That would be a welcome distraction.

"Seen *The Morrigan's* in town," Vane replied. "I know Vice comes in here. Just looking for her."

Vee bit her lip, eyes screwed up in a wince.

What had she done to anger this Vane character? He frowned, but she ignored the unspoken question, gaze towards the door.

"What a shame," Waters said, "you've missed her. She came shortly after lunch. When she left, she said something about going out with a hunting party this afternoon."

"Hunting? Blasted hells. Fine"—the doorbell rang again as the door opened and a breeze flowed in—"but if she comes back, don't tell her you've seen me, right?"

"I wouldn't dream of it, Mr Vane."

The footsteps faded, the door closed, and Vee sagged against him with a relieved sigh.

She took a long breath and grinned. But the smile quickly faded as her eyes met his.

They stood frozen in place. Somehow his arm had circled her waist again. His fingers dug into her body, attempting to remind him that this was what a woman felt like.

Her fingers flexed against his chest, and her lips parted. If he bent his head, his mouth would cover hers perfectly. He'd taste her, discover if she was sweet like the mango they'd eaten at lunchtime or nutty like the snacks she kept in her pockets. Lords, he'd learned far too much about her in this short time aboard *The Morrigan*.

The fae-touched were meant to be immune to fae charm—even the Duke of Mercia hadn't been able to use that magic on Knigh, and he was fae-*blooded*. But maybe there was some way Vee's still affected him. That had to be it.

Clenching his jaw, he forced his arms to his side.

She shook her head slightly and huffed a soft laugh, backing away until she knocked into the bookcase opposite. "Let's—um—"

"Yes, dinner." He nodded and sidled to the exit. Back to the crew, away from quiet alleyways and bookstores. Away from anywhere that left the two of them alone in a confined space.

Away from temptation.

A WARNING

That evening, Vee went carousing with the rest of the crew, and Knigh stuck to his cabin. He largely managed to avoid her all the next day, too, and as they left Nassau. He only emerged when he judged it safe—any temptation thoroughly quashed with cold water from the washstand.

He strode out of his cabin in full uniform. Much better—uniform, cleanliness, order. He could think straight again. His interest in Vee was purely professional.

Although it had raised an uncomfortable question.

Who the hells was this woman?

Was she the bloodthirsty murderer from the Naval reports, the villain who'd looked ready to cut him down on the deck of *The Morrigan* less than two weeks ago? Or was she the woman who looked after the ship's cat, did favours for her crewmates, and was greeted with warmth and open arms by every trader in Nassau?

There was no way she could be both.

The stories about Lady Vice had started over two years ago, when he was on the Duke's flagship, so *The Morrigan's* crew had to know her well. So far, he'd spoken to Wynn and Effie, the sisters he'd shown some knots to, but they'd only sung Vee's praises. He detected some hero-worship there.

Perhaps one of the men would give him a more neutral account.

In fact, Aedan, the man from Vee's boarding party, worked several feet away. His brawny arms strained against the mainmast's lines as he pulled them taut and tied a knot before coiling the ends. Tattoos across his knuckles read that common sailor phrase—*HOLD FAST.* He could've been any able seaman on a naval vessel. Between his work, he kept glancing over the side with a small smile.

Knigh slipped in beside him, working another line. "Good morning," he said with that same casual nod he'd seen the rest of the crew use with each other.

Aedan grinned. "A *very* good morning." He jerked his chin towards the water.

Frowning, Knigh peered over.

The crew had rigged a sail over the side, forming a shallow pool for bathing. Naval vessels did the same in the warmer tropical waters. It kept anyone who couldn't swim safe from drowning and stopped sharks reaching the bathers.

Half a dozen naked men ducked and scrubbed. Perhaps he would take a—

A woman rose from under the water, back to him, long, dark hair unmistakable. Nakedness unmistakable.

The breath caught in Knigh's throat, and his heart took up a quick beat.

Despite the men around her, Vee shook the water off, reaching back to squeeze out her hair. He could only see her arms, that near-black hair, the curve of her back, and the two dimples just above her rear, which itself disappeared below the water. The other men, though, they'd be getting a full view.

And she didn't seem to care.

"What's got your tongue?" Aedan leant close. They were the same height, so he could easily follow Knigh's gaze before he tore it away. "Ah." Aedan chuckled and rubbed his chin, blue eyes staying on Vee. "I suppose the lasses you mix with don't parade about like ours, eh? Vice especially doesn't give a damn, so get used to seeing her naked."

"So I see," Knigh said, voice coming out hoarse.

Aedan gave an appreciate smile over the side before looking at Knigh. "Don't mistake it for an invite, neither—she's just cleaning up, same as the men. And much as it's a lovely view, keep your hands to yourself." He sighed, clapping Knigh on the shoulder. "If the Captain sees a man touching her, the poor sod won't live to do it a second time."

Knigh swallowed. That explained the look FitzRoy had given them both after the weapons check. He cleared his throat. "Are they... involved?"

Aedan's face darkened like the sky before a storm. "Not for a while, no." His easy smile, so like Vee's, returned with a sour edge. "You've been in his cabin," he went on softly, "you've seen the *gold*. He's a mite covetous of his belongings, and he sees Vice as very much *his*." He lifted his muscular shoulders. "She might see it differently, but she's on his ship, so she doesn't have much choice in the matter." A quick breath left his lips as his gaze drifted over the side again. "Unfortunately."

Knigh narrowed his eyes. "That regret seems personal."

Aedan gave him a lopsided smile, then lifted his chin and pointed to a thin pink scar on his throat. "Very." Rubbing his jaw, he looked over the side again. "Once with her wasn't enough, but the Captain persuaded me there wouldn't be a repeat performance."

Once with her—so before the Captain found out, they'd managed to... Knigh's jaw popped at the thought of Aedan's big tattooed hands on her, his fingers resting in those dimples. Had he—

"Gods," Aedan went on, "I'm only alive because she found us, pulled a pistol and held it to *her* head. Said she'd shoot herself if he killed me. She knew exactly how to get him to let me go."

Knigh's mouth twisted with tension. "How romantic."

Aedan snorted. "Romantic? There's no love or romance with Vice. Fun? Yes." He nodded, eyes widening, brows raised. "A *lot.* But death is too high a price even for that much fun."

That expression. It said more than Knigh wanted to know. He blew out a long breath in an attempt to rid himself of the vision of Vee and Aedan. Or Vee and FitzRoy. "Well, I have..." He tried to keep his voice light, but it came out worryingly close to a growl. "I have... I'll see you later." With a sweep of his arms and twist of the wrist, he finished off the line he'd been fiddling with and secured it in place before stalking away.

"You're welcome for the warning," Aedan called after him.

"I didn't need it." He squared his shoulders.

Speaking to a male member of the crew had been a mistake—*that* one especially. It made sense—Aedan was their age, good-looking. Knigh had seen Saba and the other young women in the crew *looking* at him.

And Vee hadn't been shy about approaching Knigh at the Governor's ball before she realised who he was. He shouldn't be surprised that she'd had a liaison with someone like Aedan.

He'd learned something, though. And not just that she was *a lot of fun.* She'd saved Aedan's life, threatening her own in the process. Even if she'd only been bluffing to make FitzRoy stand down, there was always a risk of a loaded pistol misfiring, but she'd still held one to her head.

Still, Aedan's revelations had set his muscles solid. He shook his hands, trying to rid them of the tension.

"Been working too hard?" Perry appeared at his side, a bar of soap in one hand, a towel in the other.

"Perry," he breathed, relief colouring the word. She'd given him sound advice about what to wear in Nassau, and she'd listened to his suggestions about hammock stowage and had even thanked him for it. She was wise and fair—she'd be able to help him build a picture of the *real* Lady Vice.

She cocked her head at him, green eyes soft. "You sound like a drowning man who's spotted a lifeboat. What's wrong?"

"Can I ask you—"

"Of course. Anything." She gave him a gentle smile and scanned the deck. "Here's quiet." She led him to the bow and leant against the rail.

"I don't know how much Vice has told you about when we met—"

Perry scoffed. "Vice tells me everything—well, everything she's willing to talk about." She sighed. "Which isn't always as much as I'd like and is sometimes more than I want to hear, but there you go." With a shrug and an apologetic smile, she waved her hand. "Sorry, go on."

Did that mean she'd told Perry about the times they'd come too close for comfort? And about his family?

He crossed his arms and leant back against the rail opposite. "Well, she introduced herself as a young widow that night. The way she said it and one or two things I've heard since made me think that wasn't a lie."

"You picked up on that, then?" Perry nodded slowly. She wrapped the towel around the soap and tucked them under her folded arms. "Well, yes, she is a widow. They came to us three or four years ago, already married, but it was only a week or so after the ceremony. Very sweet, she was. Young love and all that." She waved a hand, gaze drifting to the horizon.

"Young love?" Knigh shook his head. "I can't imagine Vee being soft enough to cuddle up to any man and be *sweet*."

Perry's eyes shot to his. "*Vee* is it?" She gave him a pointed look. "And asking about her marital status. Someone's showing a lot of *personal* interest in my friend."

Keeping his face still, Knigh breathed slowly and fought against the discomfort tickling the back of his neck. Scratching it would give away how close to the mark she was.

When he didn't reply, Perry sighed and shook her head. "*Vee* can be *very* affectionate, she just... Look, I can't tell you much, but I love that girl, and maybe this will help you understand her. She's a lot of bluster, you know?" She spread her hands along the rail and leant back. "She and her husband wanted to stay on board, but FitzRoy wasn't convinced he'd be any use in the crew and Vice's gift hadn't manifested yet. As far as FitzRoy was concerned, they were paying passengers and nothing more unless and until the husband proved himself as one of the crew."

Knigh's brows twitched. So, it was her husband who was meant to become the pirate. "What happened?"

Eyebrows raised, Perry sighed. "The first battle came. His big chance. And... he died. Neck broke on the deck, right in front of her." She fixed Knigh with her green eyes. "She was only eighteen —she wasn't the woman you see now. She hadn't even hurt a person before that day, never mind killed, but she stood over his body and defended it. And"—Perry ran her hands over her face— "and he was all she had—she'd left her family, wealth, *everything* behind for him. She was alone and—"

"So she *is* from money. The aristocracy or—"

"That's enough." Perry straightened and waved the soap and towel parcel. "I told you she talks to me, but she never speaks of this. I only know about it because I was there. I shouldn't even have told you this much, but I wanted you to understand. Do you?"

He held her stare. Vee wasn't everything she appeared. The stories didn't even come close. Her comments about how short life was made sense now. Gods, maybe her whole flippant attitude and recklessness were just because she half-expected to die tomorrow. He'd seen her kill in battle, defending her own life. But when they'd taken the *Veritas*, fewer members of the crew had died than he'd expected, most of them leaders. He'd heard how she'd lead the boarding. Had she deliberately directed them to focus on the men in charge to get the others to stand down?

Raking a hand through his hair, he shook his head. It pounded with all these conflicting ideas about her. "I don't know. It's complicated. I need to... process. But thank you for telling me."

Perry nodded. "Woe betide anyone who mentions it within her earshot, so whatever you do, don't say a bloody word about it."

"Of course, I—"

"Sails!" The call came from aloft, shrill. "Starboard, sails!"

Was that panic in the sailor's voice? Knigh and Perry exchanged looks, the lines between her brows saying she wondered the same.

"Men-o'-war! Three!"

There was a beat of stillness, then the deck erupted in movement.

FRIEND OR FOE?

"Three Albionic Navy men-o'-war." Vice lowered the spyglass and wheeled on Knigh. "I thought we were legit now. Why are *your friends* attacking us?" Was this a trick? Had he fooled them all along?

Despite his usual mask, his gaze kept flicking to the approaching sails and a line formed between his brows. No, he had no part in this. And if even he couldn't hide his worry, they were definitely in trouble.

He wasn't the only one—the crew hurried across the decks and up the shrouds, eyes and hands on their tasks, but their faces were creased in concern, and they only spoke to pass on an order.

Knigh licked his lips and glanced at FitzRoy, Perry, then Vice. "I—I don't know. We're flying the right flag."

The Albionic jack quartered on a red field fluttered overhead. The flag of marque announced them as Albionic privateers—or at least it was *supposed* to. They'd raised it as soon as they'd identified the warships, but it had made no difference.

FitzRoy folded his arms. "And they're still on an intercept course."

"An *attack* course, more like," Vice ground out.

"Vice," Perry said, eyes fixed on the growing sails and the men and women working aloft, "can you—"

"No." She sighed. She'd been pushing *The Morrigan* on since the cry went up ten minutes ago, but the Navy was still gaining on them. "As light as we are, even with just two masts, we should be able to keep pace with a man-o'-war, but"—she squinted at the trio of ships—"they're *fast*. Maybe they have a sea witch of their own?"

"We have to stand down, then." Perry tore her gaze from the approaching sails and turned on FitzRoy. "We must raise the white."

FitzRoy glowered into the distance.

"Captain?" Perry lifted her hand as if to shake his shoulder, but she stopped short of touching him.

"No."

Vice's heart dropped at the word. She was all for throwing caution to the wind, for challenging the odds, but...

She shook her head. This wasn't a merchantman with a handful of cannons. They were facing three warships built solely to destroy. *The Morrigan* could fit inside a man-o'-war four times over and still rattle around. Hells, a first-rate like that probably carried fifteen cannons on the port side of just *one* of their three gun decks.

The Morrigan carried sixteen cannons. Total.

"FitzRoy," Perry hissed, "we'll—"

"They'll destroy you," Knigh said, voice flat, expression mastered again. "They're first-rates. Do you have any idea of the firepower of just *one* first-rate ship of the line? They could sneeze and obliterate *The Morrigan*."

FitzRoy lifted his chin, giving Knigh a cool look. "They'll destroy *us*, don't you mean?"

"No," Vice growled, "he said *you*. He isn't one of us and he—he's done this." She rounded on him again, neck knotted, and shook a finger in his face. "You've tricked us, or you've pissed your own people off so much that they've turned on you. Either way—you're going to get us all killed."

His cheek twitched, but he gave no other response.

"Fitz," she muttered, "we were fools to listen to him, to—"

"It was my decision to take his offer," Fitz replied, voice soft, "are you calling me a fool?"

"Enough." Perry stepped between them, her blond braid whipping in the wind. "Fault doesn't matter right now. Survival does. What do we do?"

Fitz's jaw rippled with tension. "We flee," he ground out, "then we deal with *him*. Vice—do what you can. When they fire, evade. We're twenty miles south of Inagua—we can lose them there if we reach it, their draught's got to be four times ours. They'll never be able to cross the shoals."

An excellent idea, but twenty miles? Even with her gift, it would take an hour and three quarters, maybe an hour and a half. She drew a long breath and glanced back at the warships, their Albionic flags now clear to the naked eye—they'd gained throughout this conversation. Getting to Inagua before they caught up would be... *Urgh*, she hated the word, but it would be impossible.

She swallowed and nodded. "Fine." They were already light, having sold their cargo at Nassau. "Can we offload the fresh water, lighten us up a bit?"

Jaw clenched, Perry nodded and made for the main hatch. "I'll see what we can jettison." She called over half a dozen men and women before disappearing belowdecks.

"I need the wheel." Vice looked to Fitz.

He waved a hand. "Do whatever you need to."

With a nod, she started for the helm, chest pounding.

To get the best speed possible and to, eventually, turn tightly and evade the inevitable shots, she needed to coordinate the ship's rudder with her gift working on the currents. But her focus and strength would be split between the sea and the wheel—she needed a firm hand to assist. "Aedan," she called, searching for him. "Aedan?"

"He's belowdecks checking the supplies are properly stowed," Knigh said, close behind her.

"Proper stowage?" She scoffed without warmth. "Thought that would be more your cup of tea."

With a tight smile, she relieved Bricus at the helm. When she turned, Knigh was still there.

"How can I help?"

"Find Aedan," she snapped, gripping the wheel's handles and expanding her awareness.

"That'll take too long. I'm here"—he lifted his hands and indicated himself—"I can help. I can do whatever you needed him for."

"I thought you were only here to observe."

"I can't fight for you, no, but this is sailing. *This* I can do." He gave a single, solid nod.

She huffed. "Fine. Hold her steady." She stepped back, keeping one hand on the wheel. "I'll be here, but I'll also be..." Waving her hand to starboard, she gave a half shrug.

He took the helm, grip sure. "You need all my attention here."

"And your strength—just follow my lead to ride the currents."

Her awareness faded from the deck, away from her crewmates hurrying, passing along orders, away from her damp hair blowing in the breeze, from her chilly skin where she hadn't had time to dry off...

It all faded away, leaving just her fingers on the polished handle.

Below, the sea already bent to her desire, channelling them north. Above, the wind was—ah, that could be better. She shifted its direction, a touch there, combined with a shift on the wheel, but—

She blinked and shook her head at Knigh. "No, too hard. Like this." She put her hand on his, so he'd feel the subtleties in her shifting movement.

"Ah. Yes, I see," he said, nodding and shifting his course to match her pressure and direction.

"Perfect." She flashed him a smile before drifting away again.

The currents pushed them on and she spread further—open water around them, a little shallower ahead, behind...

Her fingers twitched, and Knigh's hand under hers tensed in response.

Behind was...

Waves, natural currents and eddies, the tail end of the one she bent towards Inagua, but then—

A wall.

Her usual sensation of the ocean's vastness, the constant movement, it all cut off abruptly. It felt like a cliff stood behind them, blocking the sea and her gift, except there was no surge of waves against rock, and...

She blinked, coming back to herself and looking to stern, part of her awareness still pushing them on. No, there was no cliff, only the sea and the gaining warships.

"Vee?" Frowning, Knigh lifted his gaze from scanning the seas ahead to her. "What's wrong?"

"Something's"—she shook her head—"there's something

behind us that I can't..." She sighed and shook her head again. "It's fine, I can keep pushing us on our course." She smiled and squeezed his hand.

Onward.

But as hard as she pushed *The Morrigan*, the men-o'-war still gained, as did that blank wall. One ship split off to port, another to starboard, and the third kept on their tail.

Damn it, they'd be surrounded within minutes—and they were still almost half an hour from Inagua.

If she angled *The Morrigan* to stop the two closing in on either side, the one off their stern would catch up. All she could do was keep focusing on speed. Sweat broke on her brow and chilled her back. Her muscles burned.

"Gunports opening," the call went up.

Vice's heart thundered, and she gave Knigh a long look. "This is..."

Jaw set, he nodded. "I know. I'll be your hands—just direct me." His grey eyes were dark and strong as steel—maybe that was what made his level gaze reassuring even as they faced imminent fire from three warships.

Hard to starboard, sudden. Timbers groaned.

An instant later, the first ship opened fire with a dozen deafening *booms*. The shots sent water spouting high, splashing *The Morrigan's* decks and crew. But it was only water —a miss.

They hadn't expected such an unnaturally sharp turn. A ship couldn't move like this without a sea witch who could turn the currents *and* keep their sails full to prevent them being caught aback with the change in direction. A ship taken aback risked losing a mast or worse.

Thank the Lords and Ladies, and especially that unknown fae father for her gift.

She blew out a long breath. She squinted at the gunports of the second ship, now ahead of *The Morrigan*.

The deck shook as her crewmates returned fire with the chase cannons. Knigh bellowed some command about the sails.

She squeezed his hand. "Ready starboard cannons—double shot—tell them." Then she plunged back into the water, pushing them hard at the second ship. To strike their side would be suicide—it was the strongest part of the hull—but it just might make the other crew panic, and the speed would help her next manoeuvre.

At the last second, she veered to port, the warship passing just feet away to starboard, its hull towering thirty feet above *The Morrigan's* deck.

Its gunports flashed, spurted white smoke, and cannonballs skimmed the waves. But again, they hit the water harmlessly.

Vice nodded to herself and wiped her brow with her cuff.

The warships that had drawn up either side couldn't afford to fire too high unless they were positive they'd hit their prey. A stray shot could fly past *The Morrigan* and strike their companion.

The Morrigan ran parallel with the second ship now—this would be the perfect moment to—

The deck below her feet trembled as *The Morrigan* returned fire. This close, every double shot hit, splintering against the warship's hull close to the waterline.

Her legs trembled as if she'd climbed up and down the shrouds a dozen times in a storm. But the fae and the gods really must be on their side, because *The Morrigan* still hadn't taken a single hit. Catching her breath, she looked up at Knigh.

He was smiling.

Not that twitch at the corner of his mouth. Not a sardonic smirk. Not the cool smile he levelled at FitzRoy when he was trying to be civil. A real smile—mouth, eyes, cheeks all lifted and bright, transformed. He watched the waters ahead, so he must not have realised she was looking. Maybe he'd have been more guarded if he had.

Maybe he thought they'd make it to the shoals and escape.

She huffed a quick laugh and squeezed his hand again before dipping back into the deep.

A few more turns, more abrupt and twisting than any ship could usually manage, and they were still untouched except for a tear to their flying jib. Vice slowed them to fall behind the sweep of the first ship's broadside.

The Morrigan shuddered, and Vice stumbled. Splinters burst into the air. Someone screamed.

A hit to starboard.

Knigh twitched, smile gone. Wincing, Vice swallowed. But a team was already running towards their injured mates, and she had to concentrate.

And slowing had placed them closer to the third ship, still running a central course. *The Morrigan's* vulnerable stern was directly in the path of their chase cannons.

"Bollocks." She stared up at the three gun decks looming behind them.

In the periphery of her vision, something long and thin moved in the water, serpent-like, just below the surface. But when she looked, there was nothing there. Must've been a trick of the light on their wake.

"What is"—Knigh looked over his shoulder—"gods, they're... Wait... That's the *Sovereign*... Mercia?" His tanned skin turned ashen, and his hold slackened on the wheel.

"Mercia?" Vice steadied his hand. What was *Mercia?*

A shout went up from the *Sovereign*—she couldn't tell what they said, but it seemed to come from a tall man at the bow who looked down upon them. Whatever it was, the order rippled across the deck and flags rose. One was a pennant with a blue octopus. The Navy signalled with flags, but she'd never bothered to learn what they meant. "What are they saying?"

Knigh still stared, chest heaving. "Cease fire."

She gasped and whipped her head towards the *Sovereign*. Were they giving up? But they weren't slowing or peeling off from pursuit. Had they somehow—

"Crew of *The Morrigan*," the tall man at the bow called through a speaking-trumpet, his accent crisp as fresh canvas, "set anchor and prepare to be boarded for a visit by His Royal Highness the Duke of Mercia, Prince of Albion."

"What?" Vice's weakened legs buckled, and she only stayed upright thanks to her grip on the wheel. "Knigh, do you—"

He spun on his heel. His jaw was solid, his eyes bulged, every muscle and sinew of his neck stood out, rigid. Without sparing a glance for her, he strode fore.

"Anchor," bellowed FitzRoy, approaching the helm. He gave Knigh a look as he passed, one eyebrow raised, then arrived at Vice's side. "I suppose we'd better prepare for a royal visit."

HALF AN HOUR LATER, all four ships sat at anchor, and a longboat from the *Sovereign* approached *The Morrigan*.

Vice squinted against the sun glistening on the sea. As Avice Ferrers, she'd met the queen many times, but never her son. Like the rest of the royal family, and like her, he was fae-blooded, making him tall. Ah, *his gift*.

Perhaps his gift was for the sea, too, and that had been the blankness she'd felt in the ocean—an area he controlled or his awareness stopping her own. She'd never met another sea witch —maybe they experienced it as she did and maybe one sea witch's power blocked another's?

She sighed softly—there was so much she didn't know. But aside from the fact Avice Ferrers was dead, if she ever did return to Albion to seek answers to her magic, she'd be pressed into service for the Royal Navy. They'd force her to serve on a ship or at one of their coastal forts. A dull life of orders and obedience. She wouldn't last ten minutes.

As long as she wasn't caught setting foot on Albionic soil, she was safe.

Knigh stood to attention beside her, face a near-perfect mask. But his jaw was knotted, and tension flowed off him, as tangible as a gale.

Aedan and a handful of crew hauled the longboat up on the davits, and a dozen uniforms rose into view. The nape of Vice's neck prickled, and a chill trickled down her back.

The biggest plume in his hat, the tallest man there with the smuggest smile—even without the crimson hair, Vice would have known *he* was the Duke. His brown eyes, so like his mother's, sparked, settling on Knigh and staying there.

With a smooth stride, he set foot on *The Morrigan* and approached. His fae blood showed not only in that unnatural hair colour—instead of nails, pointed claws tipped each finger.

"Well, well, well," he murmured, paying no heed to his entourage forming a human wall on either side. "Knighton Villiers, as I live and breathe."

She blinked. Did he just say...

Knighton Villiers?

Her ears roared. Her chest tightened. She turned, the movement feeling sluggish, breaths loud in her ears.

The grey eyes, the nondescript brown hair—the boy she'd last seen a decade ago had that colouring, true. But... he'd been an arrogant coward. Too self-important to speak to her, but too fearful to swim to the island in her family's lake. That boy couldn't command a crew or take all those pirate ships. And his pasty, plain face hadn't held any hint of one day looking like *that*.

She swallowed and shook her head.

It couldn't be. The Duke had to be mistaken.

Although, hadn't Mama said he'd passed his Lieutenant's exam with 'full numbers' not long before she and Father had struck the deal? Knigh *was* the sort of man who'd get full marks in an exam.

But—no, Knigh couldn't be Knighton Villiers.

Not possible.

She stared at him. He had to correct the Duke, tell him he was Captain Knigh Blackwood. *Go on, tell him.*

"Your Highness," Knigh bowed, stiff and curt, "I don't go by that name anymore."

"Ah, yes"—the Duke's eyes glittered—"of course. Not since *the incident*. Blackwood, isn't it?"

It wasn't a mistake, he was...

A disbelieving snort burst from her.

Knigh was Knighton Villiers, the fiancé she'd fled three years ago.

A ROYAL VISIT

Knigh's body was so rigid, it was a wonder he could bow. He was more a puppet being bent by habit than a man choosing the action himself.

"Dear Captain Villiers," Mercia drawled, "you *must* allow me to apologise." The way the corner of his mouth rose looked anything but sorry. "When we saw your flag of marque, I believed it some pirate trick. It was only when I saw you at the helm with—with..." His dark eyes went to Vee, and his eyes widened slowly. "My, a dark-haired beauty aboard *The Morrigan*—could this be the infamous Lady Vice?"

"Guilty on that count, Your Highness," Vee said, her address and the bow that followed, near-perfect. Whoever she'd been in her previous life, she could summon that aristocratic manner when needed.

"And here I thought it would be my day to finally capture the notorious pirate."

"Alas, I hate to disappoint Your Highness, but I'm a privateer now, pardoned by the Queen herself—isn't that right, Knigh?"

"Knigh, is it?" Mercia raised his eyebrows.

Damn it, Vee. Did she not understand that would lead to questions?

"Indeed, madam, your charm more than makes up for any disappointment."

She flashed a bold grin. "So good of you to notice."

At Mercia's urging, she made the introductions to FitzRoy, Perry, and Bricus.

Watching it all in impotent silence, Knigh bit the inside of his cheek. His hands clenched against the desire to warn Vee, to step between her and Mercia.

Did she not understand who she was dealing with?

Yes, her manner was just about acceptable for a prince of the realm. While rather casual, she wasn't breaching too many rules of etiquette with the way she addressed him. Her introductions were flawless, in fact.

But Mercia wasn't just the Prince of Albion. He was so much more dangerous than that. The man was...

The breaths in Knigh's chest sped. Just seeing Mercia's face dragged him back to *that day*.

The air cold. A low mist over the sea. The rushing wall of water Mercia had used to divide their enemy's ships. The tang of copper and sulphur in the air. Their enemies' weapons on the deck. Blood on Knigh's blade. Mercia's wild laugh.

"Captain," Mercia said, "it's such a *marvellous* coincidence that I should run into you of all people—look who I have with me."

Knigh shook away the spectres and canted his head at Mercia. Gods, please not someone else from that day. Another face to send him back. Another set of eyes that had seen what he'd done. Someone else who knew what atrocity he'd been so close to.

A thin smile on his lips, Mercia stepped to one side and indicated a well-dressed young man behind him.

For a moment, all Knigh saw were the diamond shoe buckles, peacock-coloured coat, the emerald oak-leaf cravat pin twinkling. But when he looked past that to the man beneath, his world tilted. It was all he could do to stay upright.

Hair the same colour as his own. Hazel eyes that had looked up at him for the past twenty years watched him now above a broad smile. His brother.

"George?"

"Knigh," George said, shaking his head as he approached, "what the hells are you doing on a pirate boat?" He laughed and wrapped his arms around Knigh, clapping him on the back.

Heart pounding, Knigh stiffened before returning the embrace. His eyes stayed on Mercia, who watched with that cool, calculating smile.

What the hells was his brother doing on a ship of the line with that man? He wasn't in uniform, so he hadn't joined the Royal Navy in Knigh's absence. No, he'd have been too old to join now, anyway—Knigh had been twelve when he'd begun his studies.

That left only one answer. Knigh's stomach dropped. George had to be part of Mercia's entourage. The hangers-on who followed him everywhere into whatever depravities, whatever cruelties he indulged in or encouraged. Mercia's fae charm could push a man past his own conscience and certainly past the law.

Mercia's smile. That glint in his eyes. Wild Hunt take him, George was no coincidence. Mercia had chosen him precisely because they were brothers.

Knigh's heart twisted like it was going to burst, but he controlled his face and muscles. He must maintain a façade of indifference. If Mercia knew his friendship with George had him ruffled, he'd only dig his claws in deeper.

Smiling, Knigh patted his brother on the back and pulled away. There had to be some way he could catch him alone and warn him, tell him to put in at the next port and get home on the quickest ship he could find.

"Oh, Knigh"—George's eyes shone—"I've so much to tell you —*such* adventures we've had." He looked at Mercia with wide eyes, an unguarded smile.

It was a look Knigh recognised only too well. Adoration. Gods, how long had Mercia been working on him?

Even FitzRoy stared at him, a ghost of that look in his eye. Fae charm was heady magic on its own, and men like FitzRoy were drawn to gold and riches like moths to bonfires.

"What a touching reunion." Mercia's eyes glittered as he watched them, head cocked. He snapped his fingers. "And—oh, yes! It can continue this evening. You'll accompany us to a ball at Cubanakan."

"Oh yes, Knigh, say you can come!" George clapped, smile even brighter.

As if he had a choice. Such an invitation from the Duke of Mercia was *not* a request.

"Of course he'll come," Mercia said with a decisive nod. "Mr FitzRoy, the charming Lady Vice, you too. We were on our way there when we spotted your sails. We mustn't tarry any longer, in fact. Follow closely, and we'll see you safely into port—no more misunderstandings."

FitzRoy blinked as if coming to himself, then nodded and waved the crew to their tasks to get *The Morrigan* ready to set sail south-west.

Mercia leant close to Knigh, smile not reaching his eyes. "You can give me your report then—I'm most curious to hear how you ended up on a pirate ship with *her*."

Then the Admiral of the Fleet hadn't judged Mercia's knowledge of Knigh's mission necessary. *That* would put the Duke in an excellent mood.

Knigh inclined his head. “Of course, Your Highness.”

“Very good, Captain.” With a brisk nod, Mercia took his leave.

A knot in his belly, Knigh watched the Duke and his entourage return to their longboat, lower into the water, and row back to *HMS Sovereign*.

POOR ETIQUETTE

Chandeliers glittered, couples danced, and Knigh's blood simmered. He nodded and smiled stiffly, picking his way through the crowd, Vee and FitzRoy close behind.

Vee passed through with ease, glaring people out of the way when necessary. The wealth on display—those crystal chandeliers, the diamond jewellery, the gem-encrusted walking sticks—none of it seemed to impress her or make her stare after it with longing.

Knigh frowned. Again, not what he'd have expected from a pirate.

FitzRoy's reaction was more like it. His lifted chin, shoulders back, pride written across his features—it all added to his swagger as if he wanted to proclaim *I belong*.

But his eyes gave him away. They lingered on the riches, bright and covetous. Knigh had already warned the lieutenants he'd met to keep an eye on Vee and FitzRoy at the ball to ensure they didn't overstep any bounds.

Knigh had enough to worry about keeping himself in check. Long, deep breaths had helped so far. And he'd pushed his shoulders down and back—walking at attention was still tense, but it felt more controlled than having them hunched around his ears. Just knowing Mercia was here was bad enough, but if he could avoid the man, then—

"Captain Villiers," Mercia said, voice carrying from the centre of his crowd of hangers-on, "here." He dismissed them with a flick of his fingers. There was no sign of George.

Well, that had been a foolish hope. Knigh bit back a sigh as his pulse jumped and he angled their course towards the Duke.

They exchanged niceties. Again, Vee acquitted herself with an admirable nod to etiquette, despite her dips into humour that were perhaps a little too casual for a prince of the realm.

At least until the subject of the Queen arose. With far more enthusiasm than Knigh would have expected from an outlaw, Vee explained to FitzRoy. Thanks to the change in law some years ago, the Duke didn't stand to inherit the throne over his elder sister simply by virtue of being male.

"... if Your Highness will forgive me pointing out," she added, flashing him a disarming smile. "But it is quite a momentous shift for Albionic law—women having equal inheritance rights with men. I believe Queen Elizabeth I tried to pass a similar bill, but parliament blocked her." She raised her glass. "It's a law centuries in the making."

"Indeed," Mercia said, mouth rising in what might have been a smile except that his eyes glittered as bright and hard as the chandeliers overhead. "Madam appears to know a great deal more about Albionic law than one would expect from a *pirate.*"

Knigh gripped his glass, white-knuckled, torn between pleasure at seeing Mercia's irritation and horror at Vee for causing it. No doubt she thought it didn't matter, that this was just casual talk at a ball, but Mercia was not a casual man. Not when it came to his pride.

She cocked her head, teasing. "*Former* pirate, remember, Your Highness. Please, you must allow me this small celebration for the benefit of my sex."

Mercia's nostrils flared. "I suppose I must, though I cannot honestly say I can put much heart behind it, madam. I've heard the arguments for equality between the sexes. And my mother has indeed ruled a *very* long while, during which Albion has indeed prospered. However, on this occasion, I believe her vanity has clouded her judgment."

Vee's jaw knotted, every inch of her bristling as if he'd paid her a personal insult. "*Vanity,* Your Highness?"

"Of course"—he waved his hand dismissively—"you won't have seen my sister or Her Majesty the Queen. However, rest assured my sister is the very image of our mother. Choosing her to succeed is choosing to see herself upon the throne once again, even in death."

A chill coursed down Knigh's back and the silence in their group yawned on. Even FitzRoy stared from Vee to Mercia and back again. He shook his head and gulped the last of his drink.

Vee arched an eyebrow, an icy smile inching into place. "Her Majesty is a wise ruler. I'm sure she made her decision with a mind towards Your Highness's strengths and those of your royal sister."

Mercia stiffened, eyes narrowing slowly.

Bloody hells.

Vee's defence of the Queen was admirable, if surprising, but didn't she know not to contradict royalty? From the rest of her behaviour, he'd say that had to be something she *did* know but was choosing to ignore.

Mercia was not a man to be questioned—not only as royalty

but also as an admiral and human being. Loyalty and obedience, unwavering.

The look in Vee's eyes, sharp and bold, said nothing good could come of her thoughts. Not here, not with Mercia. He was so much more dangerous than his manners and charm suggested.

"In fact," she went on, raising her glass, pointing at Mercia, "I'd say—"

"Madam!" Knigh lurched forward. "I see your captain's glass is empty"—he smiled at FitzRoy then at her, unblinking—"perhaps you can show him the best way to pour punch without spilling it."

She'd joked about the woman at Governor deLacy's ball right before she'd been surrounded by Naval officers and forced to run—please, gods, let her take the hint.

Danger. Flee.

She cocked her head at him, a momentary frown tightening her features.

He fought to keep his breaths even, but he allowed his eyes to widen at her.

She inhaled sharply, eyes narrow. She wasn't going to take the hint—or, rather, she was choosing to ignore it.

No, don't. He touched her elbow. *Please.*

Her brows rose, and she sighed. "So it is. Come along, Captain." She nodded at FitzRoy and excused them before stalking away through the crowd.

Watching them leave, Knigh kept his body taut, so Mercia didn't see his relief at getting her away from his menace.

Mercia cleared his throat, eyes narrow on Vee's back. "Well done for getting rid of them." Despite the praise, he didn't smile. "Alone at last."

Knigh swallowed. At least this was the better of two evils. Who knew what Vee might say in front of the Duke?

Mercia lifted his chin and lowered his voice. "My uncle told me you had an unusual assignment but didn't explain anything more than that in his letter. I can understand him not wanting to commit anything to writing, but now you're here in person, you can tell me about your mission. Report."

With a deep breath, Knigh rebalanced his weight between his feet, straightened his back, lifted his chin.

This was just an officer reporting to his senior—he could do that calmly. There didn't need to be any reminders of *that day*.

He cleared his throat. "The Admiralty received an offer some months ago from a member of *The Morrigan's* crew," he said softly enough that only Mercia would hear. "The man was working with FitzRoy and said that in exchange for a pardon, land, and a sum of money, they would help deliver Lady Vice to the authorities."

Mercia chuckled, a cruel light in his eyes as they turned back towards Vee. "So, he's betraying her, and she doesn't even know? Oh, that's simply delicious." He sipped his wine. "And your involvement?"

Knigh swallowed the lump in his throat. That Mercia loved this idea only added to the doubts that had needled the back of his mind since he'd joined *The Morrigan*. "I worked with the Admiral of the Fleet to draw up a plan to secure her capture and ensure she'd stand trial in Albion without any chance of escape."

Mercia nodded slowly, thumb resting in the dimple on his chin. "Indeed, I've heard she's a cunning one."

"Your Highness heard correctly." On that front, anyway. The rest of the reports on Vee...

Well, the way the Navy had described her, he'd expected Lady Vice to be a monster like l'Olonnais or Ned Low. They delighted in torture and cruelty and employed those strategies liberally to fill their victims with fear and their own holds with riches.

Vee, though? The battle on the *Veritas*, the way the ordinary folk of Nassau loved her, even the way she'd helped him in the town and with FitzRoy... None of it sounded like the work of the notorious Lady Vice. Certainly not the work of a senseless killer.

Hells, taking that slave ship, freeing the people, and marooning the surviving crew was more the sort of thing the heroic Pirate Queen of the song would do.

Mercia raised his eyebrows.

Damnation, Knigh had been quiet too long. He cleared his throat. "Although FitzRoy and one other are in on the plan, the rest of the crew, Vice included, believe they are privateers working for Her Majesty. I'm travelling with them to ensure compliance on their end as well as to take her in to Portsmouth myself and ensure all proceeds according to plan once there."

At least that was the current plan. And although her guilt was printed in black and white on the arrest warrant folded in his breast pocket, black and white didn't feel so certain as it had a couple of weeks ago.

"Portsmouth?"

"Once they've taken a decent prize, they'll return to Albion—ostensibly to present it to the Queen. However, upon arrival in Portsmouth, Vice will be arrested to stand trial immediately."

Unless... What if he were to put in a request to the Admiralty to issue a pardon for Vee's crimes? Would they make her a privateer with all sincerity, rather than as part of his ploy?

"And the noose will be ready for her." The narrow smile returned to Mercia's mouth as he nodded. "Most cunning, Villiers. That woman has been a thorn in the side of civilised society too long—the songs and stories swell with each month that passes. She's in danger of becoming a folk hero—you can't walk through Lunden now without hearing *The Song of the Pirate Queen,* you know." His jaw tightened and the corner of his eye twitched. "I'm sure I don't need to remind you that the crown is expecting a great deal from this mission."

Wincing, Knigh inclined his head. Perhaps turning his plan in a new direction wouldn't be as easy as he hoped. But at least it sounded like they were edging towards the end of this conversation.

"However"—Mercia leant in with a meaningful look—"don't let her charms distract you from your duty."

Knigh froze, blinked, took a shallow breath. How had Mercia picked up on his troublesome feelings for Vee? They'd barely been in front of him for ten minutes across the whole day, and Knigh had maintained excellent control, even when Mercia hadn't been there.

But Vee *had* called him 'Knigh' back on *The Morrigan*. And he'd touched her elbow just now. Lifting one shoulder, Knigh scoffed. "She's a pretty chit, but it takes more than that to tempt me."

"Ah, yes"—Mercia's eyes narrowed—"Knighton Villiers, the Un-Temptable. Such a crying shame you weren't always so in possession of your self-control, isn't it?"

Knigh's heart stuttered in his chest, raising the hairs on the back of his neck.

The salty wind. Veins on fire with pure white rage. Hacking and hacking, more animal than trained warrior. Copper and sweat and gun smoke in his nose. His shirt more red than white. Blinking and looking down at his blade coated in thick blood. Only then seeing the men with weapons at their feet, staring at him wide-eyed, open-mouthed. The white flag of surrender. The spray of blood from—

"Poor Hopper," Mercia murmured. "Tell me, how does he manage with just one hand?"

Bile bit the back of Knigh's throat as his stomach spasmed.

The deck *that day* faded from his mind, leaving only the sounds that had finally hit him through the haze of battle lust—Billy's screams and Mercia goading him on.

Knigh's throat clenched. He couldn't show a response. He couldn't. Not in front of Mercia.

But Knigh had almost killed men who'd surrendered, and when his friend Billy had stepped in, he'd cut the poor man's hand clean off.

And Mercia, their commanding officer, had urged him on. *Go on, Villiers—show them some Albionic spirit. We'll feed them to my beast.* The laugh echoed in his ears.

Mercia had actually laughed.

Now he wore a cruel smile, dark eyes glinting. "Well, I'm sure he's muddling along with his disability and the generous pension. No harm, no foul, eh?" He waved a hand, and his smile brightened. "Good show, though, Villiers. Thanks ever so much for the reminder. Now, I must give my compliments to our host. Your brother's here somewhere—I'm sure he has *so much* to tell you."

With that, he breezed away, leaving Knigh frozen to the spot.

If he moved, he would vomit.

Lords and Ladies, if he moved, he might break—every part of him vibrated with such tension, like a glass humming under a high note.

What he'd done... And that Mercia had laughed and still found it so damn amusing...

His eyes misted, and he shut them, sucking in long breaths. The air was hot and stuffy, thick with perfume, more choking than soothing.

And the fact George was trailing Mercia around like a puppy...

Gods, he had to find his brother and tell him what kind of man he was mixing with.

Another long breath in, then out. Better. He clenched his hands, swallowed back the threat of nausea and strode into the crowd.

STOLEN TIME

Down the corridor from the ballroom, Vice circled an empty drawing room. FitzRoy was still impressed by rich people and fancy clothes. She'd grown up surrounded by all that, and it had lost its sheen a long time ago, so she'd snuck away, leaving him to rub shoulders with the so-called great and the good.

In here, silver boxes, porcelain sabrecats, a gold carriage clock—expensive trinkets covered every available surface. If something were to mysteriously disappear, they wouldn't miss it.

For a change, she'd been invited, rather than having to sneak into such a ball, and, really, it would be a shame *not* to grab something small and valuable while she was here.

The question was, *what?*

She rubbed her fingertips together. Maybe something Perry would like? She circled back to the bookcase by the door—there had been a little silver model of a fiddle on one of the shelves, and Perry played hers so joyously...

Then again, if she were to sneak upstairs, she might find something more expensive, like a sapphire necklace.

"You don't know what he's like, George."

Vice froze. Was that Knigh? And his voice *raised?* Mr Control only ever raised his voice to shout orders across deck.

Swallowing, she crept to the door.

"As if you really know what he's like, Knigh," a higher voice said, his brother's. "If he's that bad, tell me one thing he's done."

Who were they talking about? Vice narrowed her eyes, straining to listen.

There was a long pause.

"Just trust me on this," Knigh growled. "You must get off his ship—gods, stay here, I'm sure the Grays will be pleased to have you for a few weeks while you wait for the next ship home."

His ship? The Duke's?

"Oh, *must* I? You're not Father, you know. You can't—"

"No, I'm not—I didn't gamble and drink away our fortune. I didn't get myself a mistress and a bastard son in Portsmouth. I didn't die, leaving us destitute." Knigh's voice shook, and there was a soft sound of footsteps. "I had to clear all that up, and I risk my life every damn day to provide for you, so *yes*, I *can* tell you what to do. You are going home."

"Poor Knigh. It looks like you have ever such a tough life with that pirate whore of yours."

In the gaping silence, Vice pursed her lips. Funny how Knigh wasn't the whore if George really thought they were sleeping together. The hypocritical little—

A smash echoed through the corridor. She gasped.

Eyes wide, she covered her mouth, heart pounding. Hopefully, they hadn't heard. If Knigh realised she was listening to this, he'd be mortified. Much as she enjoyed mocking him, he didn't deserve that—he'd helped her today.

"What's the matter, Knigh?" His brother gave a short laugh. "Is she not spreading—"

"You *dare* complete that sentence, George." Knigh's voice was such a low growl, she barely heard it. Even through the door, she could feel the tension thickening the air.

"How about I leave you and your lover alone, and you leave me be?"

No response.

"Well, it's been a pleasure speaking to you, brother," George went on. "When I write to Isabel and Mama, I'll be sure to pass on your warmest regards. Good evening, Knigh."

One pair of clipped footsteps faded away. There was no other sound—Knigh had to still be outside the door.

Poor thing, he'd been tense ever since the moment he'd seen the Duke of Mercia. She'd put it down to the presence of such a high-ranking officer, but there was clearly so much more to it. What had the Duke done to make Knigh hate him so much? And why couldn't he tell his brother? Surely that would make him leave the man if he was really that bad.

Frowning, she rubbed her jaw. Poor Knigh. *Ha*—she never thought she'd put those two words together.

The way he'd raised his voice and broken something in the hall and had utterly shattered his usual restraint—the Duke must have done something awful. There was no way Knigh could face him again tonight. Lords, he might not even have the self-control to make it through the rest of this ball.

Frankly, she couldn't blame him. The stiff rules and even stiffer shoulders. The false smiles and the cruel whispers that came after. The pretence of civilisation when any one of them would sell out their daughter for wealth or an alliance with the right family like they were cattle to be sold or sent to slaughter.

Drawing a long breath, she shook her head.

Still no sound from outside. He'd probably had enough time to pull together some degree of calm.

She crept further into the room, then turned and stomped towards the door—he'd hear her approach and be warned. Pausing, she grabbed the silver violin and shoved it into her pocket for Perry. Then she threw open the door, eyebrows already rising to pretend surprise at the sight of him.

She didn't need to pretend.

His face was red, his hair a ragged mess as if he'd raked his hands through it a dozen times. His jaw, neck, shoulders, arms all stood as taut as lines straining against sails too full.

Wild Hunt, he looked a state.

"Knigh," she said in a high-pitched attempt to sound surprised but casual.

He stiffened, blinked, and turned to her slowly. His chest rose and fell in a measured rhythm.

"What an insufferably dull evening," she went on, rolling her eyes. "The crew will have a bonfire down on the beach—drinking, dancing, singing crude songs. Much more fun than"—she waved her hand towards the ballroom and the staid music drifting out—*"this.* I was just about to get out of here and join them if you'd like to accompany me?"

Clenching his hands, he watched the ballroom, eyes hard. Another long breath heaved through him, and his shoulders sagged. Without saying anything, he nodded.

"Excellent." She put her arm through his and started forward as if this were a jolly stroll rather than a rescue mission. Her shoe crunched on shards of porcelain. "Really, some people are so careless." She shrugged and smiled at him, then led the way out.

It took half an hour to walk down to the cove neighbouring the docks. The further they got from the mansion, the more Knigh's arm relaxed beneath her hand. A large bonfire pinpointed the location of *The Morrigan's* crew. Their songs and shouts reached across the beach, calling to her.

That was more like it. The sound of people—raucous, fun, unrestrained. *Real.* She tugged Knigh along.

His breathing was steady again, his expression calm, controlled as usual.

Once they left the cobbled street, her dainty heels sank into the white sand, forcing her to pause and slip them off. Perry was playing her fiddle, the high sound snaking towards them on the breeze. Excellent—she knew the best tunes to dance to, and Saba's beat on the drum was the perfect complement.

Knigh watched her dusting off her shoes and shoving them into a pocket. He huffed out a long breath and nodded. "Thank you." His first words since they'd left the ball.

Hitching up her skirts to free her legs, she canted her head at him. "For?"

"I think"—his brows twitched in a way that made her want to smooth her thumbs over the troubled expression—"I think you realise I was somewhat... agitated earlier. Mercia..." His chest heaved as if summoning the words was a battle.

What had the Duke done to cause the most unflappable man in Albion such torment?

"You don't have to explain." She gave him a half-smile. Gods, she itched to know, but... "I'm not so cruel that I'd—look, just come and dance with me and I'll call it even."

He shook his head. "I don't dance."

"Oh, well." She shrugged. His tension had faded, so she'd take that as a victory. "You can watch me, then. Just keep Rogers away—he gets a bit handsy, and I'd rather not spoil the fun by breaking his nose again."

He cocked his head, eyes narrowed as if he were trying to work out whether or not she was joking. Scoffing, he offered his arm.

"Very well, *madam*, I'll be your escort. Not that I think your modesty needs protecting—you clearly have that covered."

She grinned and slid her hand into the crook of his elbow as they set off across the sand. "You already know me so well." Her heart faltered as the words came out. He was Navy. A pirate hunter. And yet...

She swallowed. And yet he was warm and handsome and actually wasn't as much of an arse as she'd expected. Even with his military stiffness, he managed to make her laugh at times. True, some of those times were *at* him, but not all of them.

He'd even helped her at the wheel this morning. And, not that she'd ever admit it if asked, she had enjoyed herself when they'd walked through Nassau together. Plus, he'd been kind to Barnacle —she'd spotted him giving the cat scraps from his plate.

Shaking her head, Vice snorted softly. Best not to think too hard about the surprising aspects of Captain Knigh Blackwood... of *Knighton Villiers*. Lords, that was—how was *he* Knighton Villiers?

"Vice is here," Saba called over her drumming, smile bright, eyes wide. At her side, Perry grinned, fingers and bow dancing over her fiddle's strings.

A cry of greeting rose, and half a dozen dancers peeled off from the group by the bonfire, swallowing up Vice and Knigh.

Aedan came close. "Bored of the snobs?" He grabbed her free hand. "I'll show you some *real* dancing."

Laughing, Vice released Knigh and let Aedan pull her into a wild spin, sea breeze tugging at her hair, stars and moon circling above. Her heart woke, throbbing hard, and her breaths came fast from his pace. "I need more drink first."

"Here." Wynn thrust a bottle in her path. "Not too much, though—you're going to tell us a story later."

Vice pulled out of Aedan's grasp, stumbling to a halt. "Am I now?" She grabbed the bottle, taking a long swig of sweet, burning rum.

"Go on." Wynn bumped her hip into Vice's.

"Don't give us that"—Effie slung her arm around Wynn's shoulder—"you always do."

"Maybe." Vice shrugged and took another draught.

Just beyond Effie, Knigh watched her, eyes golden in the firelight, a small crease between his eyebrows. There was something to his look that made her pause. Want?

"Hmm?" She held the bottle out.

He shook his head.

"Go on, Captain," Effie said, cocking her head at him, a flirtatious smile lighting her eyes.

"Leave him alone." Vice withdrew the bottle, frowning at Effie. "If he doesn't want to drink, he doesn't have to. *I*, however, do." She took another gulp, and it swirled flame in her belly, making her feet itch to move. Eyes squeezed shut for a second, she held out the bottle for anyone who wanted it. "Phew, that stuff's strong."

Knigh pursed his lips before he grabbed the bottle from her, upended it and took three long draughts.

What was he—? She shook her head and shrugged.

He thrust the bottle at Effie, eyes back on Vice now he'd finished drinking. There was still that odd look she couldn't quite place—something like longing? Or maybe the look of someone staring at a knot they couldn't untie.

Wynn and Effie stumbled back into the dancers, laughing and singing along, leaving Vice and Knigh a few feet apart, stillness in the middle of the chaotic wheeling.

Vice cocked her head at him. "Are you—"

He lurched closer, now only a few inches away, warmth radiating off him. "How do you do that?"

She frowned and glanced at the bottle of rum being passed around, now in Aedan's large hands. He couldn't mean that—she'd barely had more than him, certainly not enough to be impressive. "Do what?"

His hand waved up and down. "Be *this*."

She scoffed, eyes narrow as she shook her head. What was he getting at? "I'm just *me*."

His brows contracted, the area around his eyes tensing. On anyone else, it would have been an unremarkable twitch, but on him, it felt more like seeing his expression break. *"Exactly."* He shook his head, again just a small movement, but something about it felt far truer than his usual studied gestures. "How are you so relaxed about it—about *everything?"*

Vice's heart clenched, painful for a second. Bloody hells—he *envied* her.

The poor man was wound tighter than cable around the capstan. And not just now, *always*. His shoulders, his arms, his jaw, neck, chest, all so stiff, they'd almost withstand a gale right up until the moment they snapped.

And his eyes, they were full of such intensity that when she looked up from her survey and met his gaze, it was like a physical strike. Every single thing he did was so controlled, calculated, no wonder he looked at her like that. What had the Navy done to make him like this?

She sighed softly. Damn him, but he'd helped her today. Maybe she could help him with this. Then they'd be even.

"Well"—she snatched the rum from Wynn as she scampered past, arm-in-arm with Aedan—"if you're out of practice, I find a bit more of this helps." To illustrate, she took a long glug, then offered it to Knigh.

He nodded slowly and took it, drinking long and deep. When

he'd finished, he licked his lips and raised his hands as if asking what next.

"Jacket off, too."

He gave her the bottle and obeyed, folding it carefully in half.

She snorted and shook her head, then grabbed it and threw it on a nearby rock.

Chest rising, he opened his mouth as if to argue, but instead, he just exhaled and nodded. "Anything else?"

Grinning, she thrust the bottle at Aedan as he passed. "And dancing—always dancing." She offered Knigh her hand, one eyebrow raised.

His lips tightened. Sparks flew off the fire as his gaze lowered to her palm where the silvery scar shaped like a padlock gleamed —the evidence of iron's cruelty to the fae-blooded.

A long swallow constricted his throat, and finally, he nodded and put his hand into hers. Rough knots of calluses scraped her skin.

"Don't worry," she murmured, "I'll take good care of you." With that, she winked and pulled him into the fray.

SHELL & SHIPWRECK

Almost a week later, *The Morrigan* was careened in a quiet cove on a nameless little island. Vice watched her crewmates climbing up scaffolds and ladders, scraping the hull clean. She crossed her arms—no sign of Saba.

Behind, raised voices approached. "... gave you the route of an *unguarded* Hesperian treasure ship—" That was Knigh.

"Yes," FitzRoy said, "but do you think we'll capture her without *The Morrigan* being in good order?"

Vice turned. Just the person—Fitz would know where Saba was.

"Look at the state of her," Fitz went on, waving a hand at the ship pitched over to one side. His brows were lowered as usual when he was dealing with Knigh. "Getting rid of the weed and barnacles will speed us by at least three knots."

She winced. They weren't *still* arguing about this were they? The morning after the ball, Knigh had received a tip about the course of a treasure ship. Even better, the officer told him it was posing as a merchant due to a lack of guard and gunship support.

Since Albion and Hesperia weren't *technically* at war, the Navy couldn't attack directly. A privateer sailing under black sails could. Knigh had wasted no time in telling FitzRoy, but instead of being eager, Fitz had insisted they pursue his own lead.

Someone else had tipped him off that Drake had visited a cave on this little island and possibly left clues to his treasure. Fitz had also insisted that *The Morrigan* needed careening before chasing any treasure ship.

But the cave would still be there in a week, and they'd careened the ship less than two months ago.

Looking at her now, yes, Vice couldn't deny the green slime and weed clinging to her hull or the barnacles studding the bow. But it was only a light coating of each, not enough to slow the ship significantly. Especially not with her gift helping them speed through the water.

FitzRoy's jaw clenched, nostrils flaring, and he angled towards Knigh, hands on hips.

That was the problem. Two captains on the ship and Fitz refused to give an inch. And careening gave him an excuse that made it look like he was acting in his crew's best interests rather than indulging a personal power struggle with Knigh.

She sighed. If anyone else had brought news of the treasure ship to Fitz, they'd be on course towards it right now, full sail.

"Look," Knigh said, voice curt as he mirrored FitzRoy's pose, "you're being—"

Oh, gods, no. *Don't complete that sentence.*

"Captain," Vice blurted. Whatever Knigh had been about to say, it couldn't end well. She smiled at the pair of them as they tore their gazes apart, blinking at her. "When I was walking around the island this morning, I spotted a wreck not far from shore a couple of coves away. Thought I'd investigate. I was looking for Saba but can't see any sign of her. Do you know where she is?"

Fitz shrugged. "I sent her with one of the foraging parties. You'll have to find someone else to take with you."

Vice huffed—foraging? She'd be gone all day. Precious few of the crew could swim. "She's the only one who's a strong enough swimmer to dive a wreck. I'll go on my own, then." She turned away and started north towards the other cove.

"You're *not* going alone," Fitz said.

In the same moment, Knigh said, "I can swim."

Vice spun on her heel in time to see them blinking at each other.

Fitz's mouth lifted in a sharp smile. *"Here,* you have your help. Blackwood, I'm sure you won't mind accompanying Vice. I suspect the pair of you will be gone the rest of the day—we'll manage without you."

He was offloading Knigh on to her again. Well, if it meant the two of them didn't tear chunks out of each other in this stupid power struggle, then *fine*. "Come on, Knigh."

Jaw tense, he watched Fitz a few seconds longer. "Very well." Moving stiffly, he tore himself away from Fitz and followed her.

They fetched a couple of net bags that they slung across their bodies together with a canteen of water and headed north.

"That story you've been telling the crew," he said as they skirted the border between rainforest and beach, careful to avoid manchineel trees. "It sounds a lot like *The Baron of Monté Alba."*

"You recognised that then?" Scoffing, she stepped over a trailing root. "I never claimed the stories were original. Many of the crew can't read—would you deny them a ripping yarn simply because of that?" She gave him a sardonic smile. "Not everyone grows up with the privilege of a gentleman's education, Lord Villiers."

His gaze snapped to her, and his lips tightened for a second. "And what about a *lady's* education?"

Touché. She snorted and pushed on until her breaths were too heavy for talk.

By the time they reached the cove, she was bathed in sweat. She stopped at a fallen log at the edge of the beach and took a long draught of water before offering Knigh the canteen.

"I'd normally do this with no clothes," she said, dumping her belt and weapons by the log, "but I don't want you keeling over, so I'll keep my shirt on, even if it drags in the water." She flashed him a grin, then kicked off her boots, unbuttoned her breeches and slipped them off. The hem of her shirt reached mid-thigh, so he couldn't complain that she looked too indecent.

He scoffed as he placed the canteen with her belongings. "Your concern for my wellbeing is noted."

"Knighton, was that a *joke?*"

He shrugged. "Almost." Looking out to sea, he tugged his shirt off.

Muscle corded his shoulders and arms, rippled across his stomach, and curved over his chest, taut and—

Well, that wasn't fair. Her mouth went dry, and her heartbeat sped.

"It's rude to stare, you know." The corner of his mouth twitched.

Blinking, she rubbed her nose and turned away. Well, it was rude to be quite *that*... She swallowed. Delicious-looking? Tempting? Off-limits? Yes, *all* of those.

She cleared her throat, grabbed a net bag, and started towards the surf lapping on the shore.

Her hands clenched at her sides. She couldn't think about how he'd feel under her touch. That wouldn't help anything because he was forbidden.

Or *was* he? Technically, they were on the same side now... And if he were willing, would a little tumble really be so bad? It was just bodies meeting and enjoying each other.

With Knigh being Navy, FitzRoy would leave him alone—he couldn't risk his pardon by killing an officer of the Queen's Navy. Knigh would be safe, unlike poor Aedan.

It was the *willing* bit that was the problem. She'd managed to get a physical reaction from him, yes, but getting his stiff mind to relax—that was never going to happen. Staid, straight-laced Knighton Blackwood wouldn't succumb, however tempted.

So, no, she shouldn't think about how firm that chest had been through his clothes when she'd searched him or in Waters' book shop. Nor how it would feel without the barrier of shirt and waistcoat, with the friction of flesh on flesh. She definitely wasn't going to think about sliding her hands up the perfect angle slanting from his waist to his powerful shoulders. Or those bulging arms wrapping around her, lifting her—

Wild bloody Hunt, she needed to get into that water.

She glanced over her shoulder, just enough to check he followed. He was a couple of feet away, within arm's length. She adjusted the bag crossing her body to keep her hands from any temptation to reach across that small distance.

"So"—she cleared her throat—"we're going to swim out over the reef. It's a couple of hundred feet, I think. The wreck is out there—you can just about see one of the masts at low tide." Squinting into the sun, she pointed. "Have you ever dived a coral reef before?"

"Not a reef, no, but I've helped recover wrecks."

"You're in for a treat, then—keep your eyes out for..." If he hadn't seen a reef, it would spoil the surprise to tell him about all the colour, the fish, the sponges, and shells, and her description wouldn't do it justice. "For *everything*. Come on." She waded into the sea, breathing a sigh as it washed away the heat and sweat and tugged on her gift, wanting her attention.

Once the water reached their waists, they swam out. Knigh's stroke was sure and swift—thank the gods for that, he hadn't lied about being a strong swimmer.

As they swam, she got a good view of his broad back, too. It was not a disappointment. Though she did raise her eyebrows at the black lines etched upon his skin. Tattoos on sailors were common, but she hadn't expected that to stretch to the officers. Across Knigh's back was a family crest showing a moon and two stars, surrounded by swirling stylised waves. Not the Villiers' crest—she vaguely remembered that involved shells. Maybe the Blackwoods, then.

Whoever's crest it was, the tattoo surged with his movements, its expertly wrought lines highlighting those damn muscles of his.

So tempting.

She clenched her jaw. Focus on the swim.

The sea bed dropped away gently. The water stretched on clear and blue in this sheltered cove. Within a few minutes, the sand gave way to rock, and on those rocks, the reef began.

She gestured to him to follow her lead and shifted to a breaststroke that left her face in the water.

Purple, pink, and chartreuse corals and sponges coated the jagged rocks. Crimson, green, and brown weeds wafted like the trees inland in the breeze. And amongst it all, fish darted in more colours than she had names for and a hundred different shapes and sizes.

Saba came from one of Arawaké's islands and had told her the names of some of the species here. Butterflyfish with large black dots near their tails. Hot orange squirrelfish with spiky dorsal fins. A pair of electric blue chromis darted through the reef, their iridescent bodies outlined with black fins and tails.

Vice opened her awareness. In all directions, movement, shifting light, a complex web of life. The sea sang with it, a symphony that she couldn't hope to understand with all its intricate, interlocking parts and players, but it filled her, warmed her, held her.

This was rightness.

Pausing to tread water and catch her breath, Vice glanced back at Knigh surfacing beside her. His eyes were wide, and his chest heaved.

"It—did you see?" He glanced down as if he expected it all to disappear. "So many colours—I've never..." He shook his head, a soft laugh huffing from his lips.

So it had hit him, too. "I told you." Grinning, she sculled away. "This is only the start—wait until you see..." Sharks, turtles, rays—there was still so much more they might encounter if they were lucky. "I don't want to spoil it. Come on, follow me—let's take a closer look."

She drew a long breath and dived, long kicks carrying her deep and further from shore. A glance over her shoulder revealed Knigh following, eyes bright.

They passed between two columns of coral, Vice spinning as she'd seen dolphins do and smiling when she saw Knigh follow her lead by not touching anything. Beautiful as the reef was, there were dangers too, including spines, poisons, and sharp teeth.

They took their time working their way towards the wreck, diving, coming up for breath and laughing with wonder at what they'd seen before diving again. She brought up an abalone shell just over an inch long. Its oval shape was rough and unremarkable on the outside; inside it gleamed in a hundred mother-of-pearl colours.

"Small but perfectly formed," Knigh said when she showed him.

She laughed and pressed it into his hand. "Perfect, eh? You'd better keep it then."

After he tucked it away in his pocket, they continued exploring. They swam with a loggerhead turtle almost as long as Vice was tall, its large form made graceful by the weightlessness underwater. Its scaled flippers swept slowly, propelling it above the reef with ease.

Knigh's eyes widened at the sharks and rays. When they surfaced and caught their breath, Vice reassured him that they were only small blacknose sharks, and although stingrays had a deadly reputation, they were safe. "Don't bother them, and they won't bother you."

They went on that way for almost an hour before she led him to the wreck. She narrowed her eyes at the weed-coated hulk.

The sorry-looking thing sat on a rocky outcrop of the reef as if it had run aground. From the size and remaining sections of two masts, it looked like a brig-sloop, the same as *The Morrigan*.

With the tide in, the water over the reef was around ten feet deep—enough for the draught of such a ship to pass over if it wasn't fully laden. Maybe a storm had blown it in, dashed it against these rocks.

But the bowsprit pointed out to open sea. Perhaps they'd been ashore and had attempted to leave on a low tide while fully laden. This edge of the reef was a few feet shallower than the southern side of the cove. If they'd anchored in the deeper water, the crew might not have realised the need to be so careful when leaving. And although a low tide here only changed the depth by a few feet, it was enough to make the difference between these rocks being harmless or ship-killers.

She surfaced to take a breath.

Knigh canted his head. "The rocks?"

"That's what I thought. Look, I've practised this—don't try

and match how long I stay under. Come up for breath when *you* need to."

"Good thing you warned me—I was planning on drowning."

She snorted. "Two jokes in one day? You *are* loosening up."

"Don't get used to it. Must be sunstroke."

"And here I thought I was just a bad influence on you." She flashed him a grin, then drew a deep breath and dived.

A natural swimmer, this deeper diving was near-effortless for her. Still, Knigh managed to keep up, his muscles apparently useful as well as easy on the eye, even if he did have to surface for breath more often.

Clusters of barnacles studded the wreck's broken hull, and seaweed waved, but it wasn't much thicker than the coating on *The Morrigan*—this ship couldn't have been here much more than two or three months. Perhaps it hadn't been picked over yet.

They swam across the main deck at its listing angle, identifying at least a dozen cannons. The others could have fallen away, sinking into the depths off the edge of the reef. Belowdecks, barrels and crates littered the hold, some scattered as if they'd fallen, others floating against the highest parts of the hull.

No exciting chests, full of treasure. And no bodies yet, either—the crew must have abandoned ship and made their way to shore.

After surfacing again for breath, they dived for the captain's cabin. Together, they wrenched the swollen door open and sculled inside.

Dim, rippling light illuminated a table, chairs, candelabra, a wide bunk. If not for everything loose lying scattered in one corner of the room and weed choking the cabinet and staining an ornate mirror frame green, this could have been FitzRoy's cabin.

They navigated the room by pulling their way along the algae-slimed furniture. Vice went astern towards a desk, while Knigh made for the bed and a low shape that could only be a sea chest.

Nothing in the desk drawers but stationery, but behind the desk, a blocky shape stuck out, as if something had fallen back there and become wedged between it and the wall. Gritting her teeth, she scrabbled down the back, fingers closing around —a box?

A knock vibrated along the wall. When she looked over her shoulder, Knigh waited by the door, pointing up. She nodded and waved for him to surface. Her lungs didn't burn yet, and this might be something interesting.

Now she'd disturbed the fine layer of silt, the top of the box gleamed—some sort of pretty, varnished wood. Decent quality. It was a foot long and less than half that wide. And it was firmly wedged in place.

The desk had been nailed to the deck, so she couldn't move it to free the box. Instead, she floated above it, braced her feet on the leather writing surface and heaved.

At first, nothing, just the strain of her muscles, warming, then a creak and she shot up, back slamming against the ceiling, blasting the air from her in a stream of bubbles.

Bollocks, that bloody hurt and now her lungs *did* burn, but she had the box. She pushed off the desk towards the door, shoving her prize into the net bag. With a quick twist, she was out the door and kicking for the surface.

They caught their breaths, and she showed him the box. It was locked, but they'd be able to open it back at camp. Later, they could bring helpers and the ship's boat back with ropes to haul up the sea chest and perhaps some of the cannons. Those could be cleaned up and sold off for a tidy profit.

"Now"—she glanced at the sun, still high in the sky—"I'd say we still have some time to explore the reef if you like?"

His teeth flashed in a smile. "Oh, yes, there must still be more you can show me."

She chuckled. "Oh, the things I could show you, Knigh." She winked and swam away from the wreck towards a part of the reef they hadn't yet explored.

He followed and as they dived again, something massive cut through the water, pulling on her awareness. She blinked out towards the open sea. A huge dark shape glided along the deep water just beyond the shallows, its course running parallel to the reef, coming closer.

WONDER

Vice squinted into the depths—if it was an archelon turtle, they'd be fine. If it was a bony-headed dunkleosteus or a tylo...

She swallowed, ears popping.

Beyond the reef's shelter, a powerful current ran south, sweeping out to sea. Whatever this creature was, it was strong enough to swim against the current.

She held up a hand of warning to Knigh. Perhaps they could take shelter in the reef, between the rocks. The wreck was probably too far away. The shore certainly was.

Slow-moving. That was a good start.

The creature drew closer. A wide, spotted head. The mouth opened, toothless, and some sixty feet further back, an upright, V-shaped tail swept side to side slowly.

A whale shark.

She released a relieved breath that bubbled to the surface. Smiling, she turned, but Knigh had already spotted it, his eyes wide, an uncertain crease between his brows. If she hadn't known whale sharks weren't carnivorous, she'd probably be wearing the same expression.

She nodded reassurance and pointed up—best they refill their lungs now, then dive again to get a full view of it swimming past.

"A whale shark," she told him once they surfaced. "I've only seen one before, and that was a juvenile, not yet fully grown. It was trapped in a fisherman's net. Saba and I cut it free."

"So, not a man-eater?"

She grinned and shook her head. "Come on, let's take a closer look—this is probably the biggest sea-creature it's safe to get close to."

They dived together, and once they were at the whale shark's depth, she tugged on his hand, taking them closer to the precipice. Her gift told her they were still several feet from the treacherous current.

Releasing him, she kicked right to the edge of the reef, and as the whale shark approached, its great, flat head came just a few feet away. Her heart hammered to be so close to such a giant.

Twisting, she watched the creature pass, the great sweep of its tail propelling it against the current with deceptive ease.

As it faded into the blue distance, Vice grinned and kicked up to the surface.

There were rare magical moments in life, and this had been one of them. And of all the people in the world, she'd shared it with a pirate hunter.

Laughing, she looked over her shoulder. "Wasn't that—Knigh?"

No sign of him.

"Knigh?" She turned in all directions, but he hadn't surfaced. Her stomach dropped. He couldn't hold his breath longer than her—they'd established that in the other dives. He had to be reaching his limit if he was still under.

She inhaled, then ducked her face, searching for—

Movement—out past the edge of the reef, Knigh's arms and legs pumped against the current dragging him away.

Bollocks, he must have drifted out too far while she'd been watching the whale shark.

Swallowing, she dived, pushing her awareness into that swift stream of water. With one arm stretched towards the current, she focused on just that. Gods, it was strong—how had the whale shark made it look so easy to swim against?

Knigh was now a dark, shrinking shape.

Her hand flexed into a fist, tension solidifying every muscle in her arm. With her mind, she pulled. The energy burned through her, arms and legs soon aching as if she'd been in an hour-long fight. Her heart thundered, the sound of her pulse pressing on her ears.

He wasn't getting any smaller, but he hadn't come any closer either.

Bugger. It was too strong, she couldn't reverse the whole current—there was too much water moving far too quickly. She could angle the flow where she needed and push tides to rise a little earlier, but this...

Her arm trembled, muscles shrieking, but she couldn't just let him go. If he was pushing that hard, he had to be close to running out of breath... if he hadn't already. The thought engulfed her, cold as the Albionic seas in winter—his face still, pale, eyes lifeless, staring on and on, just like...

She shook her head. *Come on, Vice, you can do this.*

She couldn't counter the whole current, no, but maybe she could take a small section of it.

Teeth gritted, she narrowed her awareness on a thin trickle centred on that dark shape.

The rushing current pushed past but that one little stream—that held still under her gift. Better. She nodded.

Now to draw him closer.

Frowning so hard her brow hurt, she squeezed her other hand into a fist and pulled. Her muscles groaned, and her joints popped but—yes, he was a little larger, a few yards closer. He wasn't moving. Her throat tightened.

Come on. More.

She willed and willed and willed, and her body shrieked, pain lancing through her limbs, bones creaking as if they were about to break. Her eyes stung—perhaps tears leaked from them and mingled with the salty sea, she couldn't be sure.

Lungs burning for breath, she angled Knigh towards the reef. Just a few feet more.

Maybe he realised he was moving against the flow, escaping its pull, because he kicked once, twice, and then he was over the reef, out of the current, and swimming to the surface.

A last burst of air bubbling from her lips, Vice let go and the stream of water she'd held onto whipped away like a plummeting anchor rope. For a moment, all she could do was hang there, muscles scorched with exertion. But she needed to breathe, too. With a couple of feeble kicks, she drifted up, legs complaining all the while.

And then the air broke over her head, and she gulped it in greedily, its freshness so searing it made her whimper.

Knigh trod water a dozen feet away, gasping. His eyes and face were red—he must have been close to...

She swallowed and shook her head, pushing away the thought. He didn't die. He was alive.

She scrubbed the stinging water from her eyes.

This wasn't like Evered. She hadn't led him to his death.

The breaths pumped through her, sharp and loud and a chill

engulfed her.

It was fine. He was fine. Just a close call. Nodding, she flopped back and let herself float, staring at the clear sky.

That cold settled into her bones. She'd used too much energy.

"Vee?" he said, close. "Are you—"

"I'm fine." But her voice came out soft and water splashed in her mouth. Spluttering, she righted herself, muscles sluggish and weak, the bag across her body dragging. "It's this"—she coughed—"bloody box."

Brow etched with concern, he caught her arm, grip strong and sure. "Here." He unhooked the bag and looped it over his shoulder. "Will you be all right to swim in?"

"I'm fine."

"Yes," he huffed, "you keep saying that."

"Well, I am." Her attempt to push him away was, admittedly, feeble. Still, he released her anyway, and she began swimming back to shore, pace painfully slow.

When they reached the shallows, she tried to stand, but her legs gave out, and she splashed into the surf, knees hitting the sandy floor.

"Vee." He hurried over and grabbed her arm, pulling her to her feet.

He was so close, his body heat spilled into her, and she had to bite back a moan at how welcome that was against the chills shaking through her. His arm looped around her waist.

She shook her head, teeth chattering. "Knighton, if you try and pick me up, I'll cut out your—"

"—tongue with my own dagger. Got it." He snorted but didn't try to lift her, only pulled her to her feet.

Still, she leant heavily against him as they stumbled through the lapping wavelets and onto the warm, dry sand.

"Wild Hunt," he muttered, "you're freezing."

She huffed. "You're telling me."

Once they were above the level of the waves, he lowered her into the sand. "There, that'll warm you up."

She flopped in the sunlight, eyes shut, chest pounding.

A minute later, he stood over her, blocking out the sun—except the sun was lower and she wasn't dripping wet anymore. "What?" Despite her wobbly arms, she managed to sit up, frowning.

"Bloody hells, Vee." Shaking his head, he sank to his knees and held out a banana. "You've been unconscious for almost an hour."

"Huh." She grabbed the fruit, tearing off the skin. When the sweetness touched her tongue, she moaned. She made short work of it, the powerful flavour and sugar cutting through her exhaustion.

She blinked, looking around. Her breeches and boots sat beside her, and he was fully dressed again, both net bags across his body.

He frowned, an odd tension around his eyes. "Are you back in the land of the living?"

Nodding, she grabbed her breeches and wriggled into them. "Just about, I think."

"Come on, let's get you back to *The Morrigan*." He held out a hand and helped her up.

Her legs complained at the soft sand and the effort it took to walk through, but she managed a smile as they set off. "You've got to admit it."

"What?"

"That was all pretty exciting."

Head cocked, he narrowed his eyes at her. "Are you..." Shaking his head, he snorted. "You're unbelievable."

Pushing through the sand, she arched an eyebrow. "You have no idea."

TREASURE

A few days later, Vice stood at the stern of *The Morrigan*, watching the nameless island shrink on the horizon. Frowning at the green smear of rainforest, she broke pieces off a banana and threw them into her mouth as Barnacle rubbed up against her ankles.

Knigh stepped into her peripheral vision and leant on the rail. The cat broke off and graced him with the same attention. "That's a deep frown."

She scoffed and waved the remaining banana towards the island. "A deep frown for a wasted trip."

He glanced fore and up into the shrouds where hands worked on lines and sails. "I'd say the rest of the crew don't share your sentiment—they're well-fed, rested, and the hold is stocked with fresh food."

"Yes, but we got no treasure from the detour—even that chest we went back for was just full of old clothes, ruined by the sea." She sighed at the wake frothing up behind them, rippling out into ever-smaller waves.

If she was going to become a captain, she needed to satisfy FitzRoy's desire for gold and this trip had done nothing towards that. She checked he wasn't nearby, then leant towards Knigh. "The food will spoil or get eaten, the water will get drunk. In a couple of weeks, it'll be like this trip never happened." She finished the last of her banana and tossed the peel into the water. "You were right, we should have gone straight after that treasure ship. This whole thing was a waste of time."

His fingertips tapped on the rail, and he smiled into the distance, perhaps at the last glimpse of the island, now just a dark spot. "Even if we didn't find any treasure or the key to Drake's fabled hoard"—he snorted, but a soft smile lurked at the corner of his mouth—"you seemed to enjoy yourself and—well, I know I did." Drawing a long breath, he turned to her, folding his arms across his chest. The tight gesture looked like an attempt to protect himself, to block others off, but it only served to emphasise the lines of his muscles under his shirt.

Vice blinked and raised her eyebrows, leaning one hand on the rail and resting the other on her hip—as open as he was closed. "You enjoyed yourself? On an island full of pirates?"

He lifted his chin. "I had the chance to swim around that incredible reef, to see that whale shark"—he sighed, shaking his head—"those are things I'm going to carry with me forever." His grey eyes glinted, almost blue under the clear sky.

He had to be playing with her. His face was poker-straight, though.

She frowned and shook her head, then gave him a playful shove, laughing.

"I'm serious." He lifted his hands. "It may be news to the great Lady Vice, but there are other treasures in life than gold."

"You've been spending too much time with Perry—you sound just like her."

"I'll take that as a compliment—she's very wise."

"I didn't mean it as one." She rolled her eyes but softened it with a grin. "Although, speaking of treasure, what happened to that box we took from the wreck?"

"FitzRoy took it while you were—*ahem*—replenishing energy."

"Stuffing my face, you mean."

He lifted one shoulder, a smirk teasing at the edge of his lips. "I'd never speak of a lady in such a manner."

Lords and Ladies, she'd never have believed it a few weeks ago, but the dread pirate hunter Blackwood was actually loosening up. Wonders would truly never cease.

A slight frown darkened his expression as he glanced fore. "So, you haven't looked in the box yet?"

"I haven't seen it since we got back that day. Why? What's in it?"

"I don't know. I haven't seen it either."

She narrowed her eyes. FitzRoy had spent a lot of time alone in his tent on shore and now was in his cabin. She'd assumed he was sulking about having to cut his nose off to spite his face by refusing to pursue the Hesperian treasure ship but...

"Maybe it contained something interesting." She pursed her lips and glanced down—they were immediately above FitzRoy's cabin. Swallowing, she lowered her voice. "If it were just gold or jewels, he wouldn't hide that—as much as he loves riches, he shares it with the crew, it would go to Perry to be accounted for and divided, but..." She looked aft, but the island had disappeared, only the horizon's sweeping curve remained. "But we found no clues to Drake's treasure on that island. What if that wreck had already made landfall, investigated the caves and found something? Saba said the ground had been disturbed."

Knigh watched her, edge of his mouth quirking. "Vee, do you —are you seriously saying you believe in that old wives' tale?"

"You mean, you don't?" She leant in. "Come on, what else would be important enough to keep locked in a box, if not gold and jewels?"

He stroked his cheek, fingers rasping against the stubble he'd let grow. "Government secrets? Naval orders? A map of troop stations and movements?" He cocked his head. "Details of a treasure ship's movements? Which my colleagues took a lot of time and risk to gather and yet we're only just picking up the trail now, over a week late because..." He took a long breath and shook his head, jaw and shoulders hard. He understood exactly why FitzRoy had delayed following the treasure ship.

She rolled her eyes, no interest in the pair of captains competing over the contents of their breeches. "Look, Drake was the greatest Albionic privateer who ever sailed the high seas. He sacked treasure ships and Hesperian towns dozens of times over. Where did it all go?"

"His descendants are still wealthy now—*that's* where it went. It's in some vault on the Drake estate."

She sighed and leant across the rail, staring out over the waves. No hidden treasure. What a dull way to see the world. "You really think he brought it all back with him?"

He mirrored her pose, forearms resting on the rail beside hers. "What else would he have done with it?"

"You know—hidden it somewhere. Buried treasure, like the stash Flint found up the coast from Nombres de Dioses—the silver was too much for them to carry and—"

"And their ships had left, thinking them dead—yes, I know the stories. Just because someone found *some* silver that *might* be from that raid, doesn't mean all the mad tales sailors spew are true."

"No, but—"

"Sails ahead!"

Vice's eyes widened, and she hurried to the fore rail of the quarterdeck, squinting into the distance. Not visible at this height yet, but the call came from the main top where they could see miles further than from deck.

Knigh stood at her side, jaw clenched. "Where are we?" He frowned back towards the island they'd left. "No, he can't have—"

"The *Covadonga,*" the shout came from aloft.

Knigh huffed. "He *did.* The wily bastard."

Her heart leapt. FitzRoy had timed their trip to place them along the treasure ship's path. There was still the chance of treasure after all.

Below their feet, the door to FitzRoy's cabin burst open. "Full sail," he bellowed. "Vice?"

"On it, Captain." Grinning at Knigh, she released her awareness and cast around for a nearby current she could bend to thrust them towards the prize.

Over the hour it took them to approach, *The Morrigan's* crew busied themselves with the usual preparations on deck. They sprinkled sand, readied sails, doled out weapons, and loaded rifles, pistols, and cannon. With all the noise, Barnacle sloped off to Perry's cabin.

When they raised the black flag, the *Covadonga* refused to strike her Hesperian colours. Instead, with a puff of smoke and a flash, they fired stern chasers, splashing far wide of *The Morrigan.*

From the fore rail of the quarterdeck, Fitz smiled coldly. "It's like that, then, is it?" He nodded to Bricus and Perry. "Rake her stern."

Rubbing her hands together, Vice grinned at Knigh on the wheel and helped *The Morrigan* speed closer. "Decided to help after all, then?"

He cocked his head, gaze fixed on their course. "Still just sailing." With a practiced hand, he leant into the wheel, turning the ship smoothly.

The deck thundered with cannon fire as they unleashed a full broadside, splintering against the *Covadonga's* stern. Cries and screams drifted across the sea.

The next volley took the Hesperians' mizzenmast.

At the front of the quarterdeck, Fitz drew a pair of pistols. "Prepare to board!"

Half her attention on turning *The Morrigan* to bring her alongside, Vice drew her rifle from the quarterdeck's gun rack and flicked open the breach block—loaded and ready.

"Hooks! Cover!"

Her team hurried over, ducking against the rail.

Grappling hooks thunked over the *Covadonga's* rails, and *The Morrigan's* crew hauled on the lines, drawing the ships closer.

She flashed Knigh a grin. "I'll see you on the other side." *When we have that treasure.* She turned to join her team, but he caught her arm, spinning her to face him.

His look alone would have been enough to make her pause—eyes dark below lowered brows, nostrils flaring, jaw knotted. He opened his mouth and closed it again, his breaths loud and fast. He swallowed. "Be careful."

She laughed. "Oh, you don't know me *at all.*"

He leant closer, his soap and cinnamon scent cutting through the sulphurous smoke. "I say that because I do."

His hand tightened on her arm, his eyes intense, and for a moment, all she could do was stare back. What did it matter to him if she was careful or not? Unless he *cared*...

She scoffed, but it came out as a half-hearted effort. She lifted one shoulder in a shrug and cocked her head, forcing a grin in place. "You worry about this ship, I'll sort out that one."

"Vee—"

Gunshot whistled overhead, and they both flinched. A puff of splinters rained from the spar.

He released her and steadied the wheel as they pulled up alongside. "Please?"

That look, the lines creasing between his eyebrows—she'd seen them on Perry plenty of times. Concern.

He *did* care.

Why the hells did a pirate hunter care about *her?*

Wild Hunt damn him, this was *not* the place or time to puzzle over his own personal brand of insanity.

Winking, she clapped him on the shoulder. "Try not to get shot."

Rifle in hand, she crouched beside her team as another shot flew overhead. It missed Knigh by only a foot, making him duck. She peered over the rail—who the bloody hells was aiming at the helm?

There, a tall man behind the *Covadonga's* mizzen, loading a gun, not entirely hidden by the remaining stump of mast.

"Cover," she ordered her team, levelling her rifle and cocking it. With a long, deep breath, she aimed.

Shots rattled left and right, smoke drifting in the breeze, as Saba, Effie, Wynn, Lizzy, and Aedan obeyed.

Vice exhaled, sights lining up with the rifleman's ducked head while he concentrated more on reloading than staying out of view. She squeezed the trigger.

A flash, a crack, a haze of smoke, and the distant spray of crimson, then he fell.

As she ducked and reloaded, the spent cartridge burning her fingertips, she smiled at Knigh. He was now safe and busy shouting an order aloft.

She fired off another shot before the ships bumped together

and she led her team in a leap across the gap, rifles left behind.

Pistol in one hand, sabre in the other, she shot and sliced out space for more of *The Morrigan's* crew to board. Other teams did the same further fore.

As they forged a path towards a knot of officers she guessed were gathered around their captain, there was a clatter and a cry.

"Vice," Saba shouted, blocking a blow from a black-haired man.

Vice followed her wide-eyed nod.

Every hatch on the *Covadonga* was open. A wave of royal blue edged with scarlet poured out. Dozens of Hesperian marines.

"Bollocks." Vice kicked away her enemy. This was far, *far* more men than they'd bargained for. "Fall back."

"Slight problem with that," Aedan said at her shoulder.

Their way to *The Morrigan* was blocked by Hesperian sailors, marines rapidly adding to their number.

The breath huffed from Vice's chest. "Surrounded."

THE OBSERVER

The sick knot in Knigh's belly tightened as he lost sight of Vee behind a sea of Hesperian marines. He paced the quarterdeck, peering through the smoke into the fray.

Clashing steel. Cries of fear, pain, and death. And beneath it all, the constant whisper of the sea—indifferent to the struggle playing out on the *Covadonga's* deck.

Knigh clenched his fists so tight his knuckles popped.

Damnation—there weren't supposed to be so many guards, certainly not a whole detachment of marines. That was why this treasure ship was worth pursuing—the lack of warships and servicemen available to guard it meant it was posing as a simple merchant to maintain a low profile.

Forty marines—that was *not* a low profile.

He swore.

He'd helped *The Morrigan's* crew sail, yes, but fighting was a different matter entirely. Killing outside of state-sanctioned war, that was worlds apart from...

But *was* it really so different from the Navy?

Grunting, he punched the mizzenmast. His blood burned.

Yes, it was different. It *was*.

The pirates had formed knots of fierce fighting, teeth bared, eyes wild, sabres and axes slashing and battering against their opponents.

One man fell. Then another, his high yell piercing the smoky-salty air.

Knigh's heart hammered. His stomach roiled. He couldn't...

He'd eaten with these people, drunk with them, hells, even danced with them and he *never* danced. And now they were on a Hesperian ship dying while he stood here and did nothing.

Observe only. Those were his orders, and he had to follow them.

Fighting for the Royal Navy was nothing like what these pirates did. Nothing at all. He only fought those who stood in battle, other military men who knew what they were getting into. Pirates, though, they attacked *civilian* ships.

But they gave the chance to surrender, didn't they? And if they refused to surrender to pirates, didn't they too know what they were getting into? Weren't they choosing to stand and fight? He'd only ever seen *The Morrigan's* crew, Vee included, kill armed men who didn't surrender, who considered their belongings worth fighting and dying for.

Hadn't he killed men who considered their country worth dying for? Were the two things so different?

Of course, a country was a more noble cause than money. Vee only attacked to—

Oh, damnation, who was he fooling? He fought for money, the same as she did. Didn't he target the pirates with the highest bounties? And before that, he'd followed orders, killing those deemed 'enemy' to Albion, because his family needed the wage.

The only difference was he killed under the banner of war and country, and that made it legal.

He massaged his buzzing temples, staring into the drifting gun smoke. Where was Vee? It was an age since she'd disappeared behind that wall of royal blue and scarlet. He paced the quarter-deck, hands clenching and unclenching.

There was nothing he could do.

It tore at him, jangling along his nerves, leaving them raw and ragged.

"Come on, Vee." He stared into the fray, thumb tracing the edge of the little abalone shell she'd brought up from the reef.

She'd been so sure of success, so driven to take this ship, just like he was when approaching a bounty with the promise of victory sweet on his tongue. It was unthinkable that she wouldn't survive and take her prize.

Fingers raking through his hair, he growled. This was impossible.

Then the marines parted—a crimson coat flashed in the gap. Knigh's breath caught. Her teeth were bared and bloody, her fore-head and down one side of her face covered in red, too. He'd never seen those lines on her brow before.

The back of his neck prickled. That look—it... If he didn't know better, he'd have called it desperation.

Then Vee moved, and he understood—her left arm was looped around Wynn's waist, straining to keep her upright. Wynn's shirt was red rather than off-white, and her head kept dipping as if she fought to remain conscious.

The line of marines closed, and he lost sight of Vee.

He stood at the rail, gripping it with white knuckles, but there was no more sign of a crimson coat.

A marine at the back of the group surrounding Vee pulled a powder flask from his bandolier and began loading his pistol.

Once he finished, all he'd need to do was instruct his colleagues to part, and he'd be able to shoot her at almost point-blank range.

Knigh's stomach turned, and bile coated the back of his throat.

"No." He couldn't...

But the alternative...

His pistol was in his hand. He stared down—hadn't even meant to...

Chest heaving, he paced away from the rail.

He couldn't. But maybe...

As long as he kept control. That would be safe. And *she* would be safe.

And whether she was the notorious Lady Vice or the heroic Pirate Queen—because he'd be damned if he knew which—at least he'd feel like he'd done the right thing.

Besides, if the pirates lost, the Hesperians would board *The Morrigan*, and he'd be forced to fight anyway. And outnumbered like that, losing control was inevitable. This way...

Turning, he cocked his pistol and levelled it at the marine. As soon as the royal blue uniform edged with scarlet was in his sights, he pulled the trigger.

With a flick of recoil and a *crack*, the gun fired and the marine staggered towards the *Covadonga's* rail. A dark stain spread across his jacket. Pistol and powder flask dropped from his hands as he turned. He looked down at the wound in his chest, stared up at Knigh, then fell.

Knigh huffed out a shaking breath. Decision made.

Muscles surging, he ran, leapt onto *The Morrigan's* rail and across the gap between the two ships.

Before his feet even hit the *Covadonga's* deck, he swung his sabre, slicing through flesh, jarring on bone.

He had to get to Vee. If she was still alive.

Another slash and blood sprayed his hand. The marine gurgled and thudded to the deck. The others nearest started to turn, eyes wide when they found themselves flanked.

Gritting his teeth, Knigh's muscles burned with fae-touched strength, and he easily cut through one man's defences and another's.

Copper and salt coated his tongue, eggy sulphur and smoke filled his nose. In every direction, red and royal blue.

With a grunt, he parried a thrust from a wild-eyed marine. Knigh turned his blade and swept across the man's belly.

You let us down.

His ears buzzed, and the only other thing he could hear were his breaths, harsh and heavy. Pulse throbbing, his body hummed, pushing his limbs harder, faster. Each blow vibrated through his arm.

A wild cry sounded, and it was only the way it tore his throat that told him it was his. Two more bodies landed. Somewhere distant, there was pain, but it didn't matter.

You lied.

Crimson—a coat, not blood. Arched brows rose in surprise, and Vee blew a relieved breath.

"So nice of you to join us." Her voice was strained, but she was alive.

Nostrils flaring, he nodded and blocked a blow aimed at her. Thank the gods, yes, she was alive. He drew a deep breath, cooling fractionally.

Ducking swiftly, she lowered Wynn behind him, the rest of the team forming a barrier around her. Vee wiped the blood from her eyes before taking up a place at his shoulder. She took out one marine with a low slash and Knigh reached past to thrust his sabre into the man behind.

"Come on, you bastards," she huffed between attacks, "just surrender." Then she said *surrender* again in Hesperian.

But the *Covadonga* didn't strike her flag or raise the white.

Together, he and Vee blocked blade after blade as wave upon wave of marines broke upon them.

Sweat and blood bathed every inch of his body, and the fallen men made the deck treacherous underfoot. His muscles burned, tensing and loosing into practised drills, catching one blow than another and another.

You ruined us.

His racing pulse thundered in his ears until he could barely hear Vee, even though she was close enough that her shoulder brushed his. He gritted his teeth as his vision blurred.

You were never the man I thought.

Breathe, parry, fist clubbing across a face.

You left us with nothing.

Hack, slash, red.

I was a fool to believe in you.

Cut and cut and cut.

The clang of steel on timber.

"Knigh?"

His breath, his hands, his arms shook.

Smiling—someone was smiling. People, pirates, mouths open, happy, but he couldn't hear them.

A cool touch on his blistering skin.

He wheeled, grabbing something, raising his sword.

"Knighton Villiers."

He stopped. He knew that voice, that name.

Slate blue eyes stared up at him.

He blinked. He knew those eyes, even if they weren't always that colour.

"Knighton," she murmured, and he stared at her lips as they

moved so slowly in comparison to the rushing of his blood, "they've surrendered."

Vee. Stillness. Eyes on them. The silence of held breaths. Hesperian swords on the deck. His ears popped and it all rushed back in.

Chest heaving, he stared at his sabre, the blade inches above Vee's shoulder. He held her wrist so tight his hand trembled.

"Knighton, come back."

He blinked and shook his head. Gods, what had he—

Dropping her wrist, he let his sword fall to the deck with a clang. "No, I"—he shook his head—"I didn't—did I?" He raked his fingers through his hair, gaze scanning her, but he couldn't spot any more injuries than she'd had earlier.

With a tight smile, she turned to the other pirates and waved a hand. "We've got ourselves a treasure ship, ladies and gents."

They stared from her to him and back again.

Gods, had they seen what he'd been so close to? What he'd almost done without realising?

She chuckled. "Celebrate, then!"

They released a collective breath, the sound a low murmur on the wind, and turned to each other with relieved laughs, grins, hugs, slapped shoulders.

Once the attention was off her, Vee's smile softened, and she nodded to Knigh, pulling him into a hug and clapping him on the back as if joining the celebrations. "We're safe, Knigh," she murmured, "all is well."

He exhaled, a shudder rocking through him as he let his head rest on her shoulder. "I'm sorry," he whispered, squeezing her. "Did I—"

"No." Her breath tickled his ear as she stroked his back. "You didn't hurt me. All is well."

"I'm sorry, I—"

Holding his shoulders, she pulled back, still close enough that the blood and sweat on her filled his nostrils, metallic and sharp and tinged with something uniquely her. Eyes softer than he'd ever seen them, she looked up at him and nodded once. "You saved my life—*our* lives is what you did."

"But—"

"Knighton Villiers—Blackwood—whoever you are. You saved my life. We have a treasure ship. These are things to celebrate. Understood?"

He stared back at her. He'd almost—Lords knew what he'd almost done. Again.

Her eyebrows rose.

All is well, she'd said. He'd *almost*, but he hadn't. She must have seen the rage coursing through him, burning away his self-control—burning away his *self*, Wild Hunt damn it. She'd seen it, and she'd brought him back before he'd hurt anyone outside of battle.

Licking his lips, he nodded. "Thank you."

Lords, Ladies, gods, he'd never meant anything as much as those two words.

CELEBRATION

Late that afternoon, Vice smiled to herself, strolling across the white sand of a nearby island as she watched her crewmates build a bonfire. They'd put the surviving men of the *Covadonga* ashore on another island with the supplies from their hold, and now it and *The Morrigan* sat at anchor in the sheltered bay. There hadn't been as much silver as they'd expected. That, coupled with the presence of marines, suggested the Navy had been fed information as a trap.

But it was more money than they'd had yesterday and a prize ship to present to the Queen.

Rubbing her face, she shook her head.

It had been a tough fight, and they'd lost good people. But they'd survived.

The sand was soft beneath her bare feet, the breeze fresh, and the sun warm. Yes, definitely alive.

Thanks, in large part, to Knigh.

She blew out a long breath, wincing as it pulled at the thin cut on her side. In the periphery of her own battle, she'd noticed him taking down marine after marine, brutal in his efficiency, over-powering in his strength. It was only once they'd surrendered that she'd had a moment to turn and really see him.

That look on his face... It was like he didn't see anything, hear anything—like he wasn't there at all.

She'd known the moment he'd come back—he'd blinked as if waking, and horror had flashed through his wide eyes. The way he'd stared at her—he'd feared he'd hurt her. She'd heard of berserkers before, but she'd thought they were just stories from the far north of Albion and the tribes of Noreg.

Pausing, she shielded her eyes from the dipping sun. In fact, that tall figure emerging from the rainforest ahead could only be Knigh. He'd been quiet since the battle and had disappeared as soon as they landed.

What he needed was to forget his fears.

Lucky for him, rum helped with that.

Smiling, she waved and started towards him. "Knigh."

He paused at the edge of the forest, watching her approach, a gentle crease between his brows.

She glanced past him into the green gloom beneath the trees. "Been exploring?"

"I needed to be alone for a while."

"Battle does that to some people."

His frown deepened. "Not—I shouldn't have"—he shook his head—"I wasn't meant to fight. The things I could have done..."

Lords, he really did need to forget.

"But you didn't. Gods, if I felt bad about everything I *could* have done..." She cocked her head. "Well, life wouldn't be much fun."

He sighed. "You don't understand, Vee. I *have* done things... In the past..." His gaze dropped, and his mouth formed a thin line.

What was it that haunted him? She chewed the inside of her

cheek. Something that made him ashamed. Curious as she was, she couldn't tear that from him—that would be too cruel.

"Knigh," she murmured, "the past is done. It doesn't matter anymore. What matters is the decision you made today—you helped turn the tide of battle."

She ran a hand through her hair, now clean of blood and sweat, and peered from the lengthening shadows towards the beach. Her crewmates delivered armfuls of wood to the burgeoning bonfire—their cries and laughter drifted across in the breeze. How many of them would be dead if Knigh hadn't boarded the *Covadonga?*

Swallowing, she shook her head. Wynn had almost ended up among that number, wrapped in canvas and given to the sea. But Lizzy had reassured her that now the wound was stitched up, as long as she had good food, plenty of rest, and her smelly poultices to keep infection at bay, she would be fine.

Her heart squeezed. On the deck of the *Covadonga*, it had felt close, though. She'd feared for Wynn. Wild Hunt, she'd even feared it was her own time, that she'd failed her team.

But she hadn't.

The battle was over now, and this was *after*. This was the time to celebrate and let relief wash over them and wish farewell to those lost.

Knigh needed reminding of that.

"Look at them." She jerked her chin at the gathered men and women as a waft of smoke touched her nostrils. "We were in a bad way when those marines came out. If you hadn't joined us... I'm not sure how many would have survived."

He watched the crew, lips pursed.

Who knew what vastness was going on behind that small expression? After seeing his rage today, the idea of him as an emotionless automaton felt ridiculous. He wore a mask of control, perhaps over emotions as deep and powerful as a riptide.

His chest rose and fell in a long, slow breath.

She touched his shoulder, and it was warm as always, despite the forest's shadows. "What matters is that we're here, we're alive for now, and we have treasure to celebrate."

His brows rose slowly and, blinking, he turned his grey eyes to her. The corner of his mouth twitched. "Why, Vee, that's almost philosophical."

She laughed and started towards the bonfire, tugging at his arm. "Well don't get too used to it, because I intend to spend the rest of the evening *getting philosophical* with a bottle of rum."

Across the cove, Saba, Lizzy, and Aedan emerged from the tree line, carrying round clay jars.

"Ooh." Vice's eyes widened. Those jars meant one thing. "Hold the rum, I think Saba's made palm wine." Mouth watering, she bit her lip and gave him a sidelong look. "Have you ever had it before?"

"No, it's expressly forbidden in the Navy, though I've heard of its"—he cleared his throat—"*formidable* reputation."

She scoffed. "My dear Captain Blackwood, you are in for a treat."

Sweet and strong, palm wine fermented quickly. Saba must have started the batch this afternoon. Tonight, Knigh would definitely forget about his fears.

Tonight, they would celebrate.

THE PALM WINE was just as sweet as she remembered, the songs were raucous, and the dancing stomped through the sand, wild as only people who'd stared death in the face could be.

From her perch on a fallen log, Vice grinned at her crewmates and gulped from a hollowed-out coconut shell. The damn slice across her ribs hurt too much for dancing and when she'd checked the bandage, it was already spotted with blood. No sense opening the thing up even more. At least the drink dulled the pain, warmed her cheeks, and frayed her edges like old sails.

Saba's rowdy song about a handsome shipwrecked sailor and a mermaid drew to an end with Aedan silencing his drum and Perry bowing a last high note on her fiddle.

Laughing, Vice raised her cup and clapped her free hand against her thigh. "More," she cried, "more!"

Knigh appeared from the cluster of dancers, his cheeks pink in the sunset. He crouched beside her, catching his breath and held his hand out.

She cocked her head. "What?"

He nodded at her cup.

Chuckling, she handed him the palm wine. "Got a taste for the stuff, eh?"

He scoffed. "Something like that." He took a sip, the lean lines of his throat rippling as he swallowed.

She shouldn't stare at that movement or the way his forearms gleamed where he'd rolled up his shirt sleeves. But, damn, they were nice to look at.

"What do they call it?" He thrust the cup back into her hand. "Dietsch courage?" He flashed her a smile close to that true, unguarded smile he'd worn as they'd fled the *Sovereign*.

Lords, her stomach flipped. Was she a sixteen-year-old girl at her first ball again?

She shook her head as he strode over to Perry and Aedan. They had a brief conversation, and Perry produced the guitar they'd found on the *Covadonga*. Knigh nodded and took it before settling on a barrel.

Vice frowned and rubbed her eyes. Maybe she'd had more palm wine than she'd realised. The stuff did keep fermenting, so it could have grown stronger over the past couple of hours.

"Can you believe it," Saba said, coming and sitting beside her, "straight-laced Captain Blackwood is going to *sing?*"

Vice shook her head. "I thought you'd slipped something in my drink and I was seeing things."

Laughing, Saba took the cup and gulped from it. "No, see? No special additions." She winked. "But you do need a top-up, I'll—"

A cascade of notes drifted across the sand, sending a shiver across Vice's shoulders.

Saba raised her eyebrows. "Wow, maybe he actually knows how to play that thing."

From the way he frowned, adjusting the tuning keys before strumming and nodding, Vice would've bet her cut of the *Covadonga's* prize that he knew *exactly* how to play that thing.

"Well," she breathed, "wonders will never cease."

Even the crowd who'd been dancing and had continued stomping into the silence, clapping their own beats, fell quiet, throwing curious looks at Knigh.

With a tight smile, he nodded at Aedan and Perry, then passed his fingers over the guitar's strings. At first, he played alone, the guitar murmuring a steady melody that lifted the hairs on Vice's arms.

Then his chest rose, and he began to sing.

Low, almost mournful at first, his voice crept across the sand, painful in its beauty.

He sang about lost sleep, dreaming of possibilities, and praying to the gods, the fae, anyone who'd listen that those dreams might come true. His fingers picked across the strings, pitch and timing perfect.

It was an old Albionic song, but one she hadn't heard in a long time. When, with a nod to Perry and Aedan, he sped into the second part, a solid, toe-tapping tune, it almost took her by surprise.

Aedan took up that beat, foot stamping into the sand as he pounded the drum. Perry's fiddle rose and dipped around Knigh's steady strum.

His voice, the sound warmed by a smile, lifted, optimistic as he sang about counting stars, seeking experience, finding riches beyond money.

Saba ducked by her. "Did you know he could—"

Vice shook her head. She'd been so absorbed in the music, so taken aback by his voice, she'd forgotten there were others here.

Saba's dark eyes were fixed on Knigh, glinting in the light of the streaked sunset overhead and the licking fire before them. The dancers wheeled, arms interlocking before they spun off to new partners, kicking up sand in their wake.

And Knigh? He stared into the fire, his teeth flashing against his tanned skin as he sang. His fingers upon the strings moved with effortless speed. His toes tapped.

The music throbbed through Vice, reverberating in her chest, making her feet move even though she couldn't get up and dance.

Lords, his song was infectious—his smile, too.

Shaking her head, she pressed the rim of the cup against her lower lip and blew out a long breath. Her lungs suddenly felt too small, as though she'd forgotten to breathe the whole time he'd been singing.

The tempo whipped up, accompanied by whoops from the dancers, and then with a last chorus and plucks on the strings, it was over.

The evening was cool and quiet, left with only the crackling fire and distant sigh of surf.

Knigh turned his gaze from the fire to her, the look loaded.

Or maybe it was just the music still reverberating through her that made her think that.

The crew erupted into cries and applause, and Knigh blinked as though surprised. Rising, he returned the guitar to its case and worked his way past half a dozen of the crew, who slapped his shoulders and offered bottles of rum and jugs of palm wine.

Saba leant in and grinned. "He's good with his hands." She nodded slowly. "Good to know."

Vice couldn't even summon a laugh or a smirk at that.

"Blackwood," Saba said when he arrived at their makeshift seats. "That was—well, I reckon every woman here has found a new and *deep* appreciation for music after that." She gulped her drink, eyeing him over the rim of her cup. "Half the men, too, I bet."

Knigh scoffed. "Thank you—I *think.*" He topped up Saba's raised cup with the jug of palm wine that had been thrust into his hands. He raised it at Vice in question.

Yes. Oh gods, yes—more drink. She nodded and lifted her cup for him to fill.

He sank onto the log beside her, arm brushing hers as he looked into the fire. "You didn't dance," he said softly as Perry struck up a fresh tune. "You always dance. Was it that bad?" He gave her a lopsided smile.

"In case you hadn't noticed, I haven't danced at all—our Hesperian friends saw to that." Wincing, she waved at her side.

His eyes widened, drifting down to her torso. "You're injured? Is it bad? I thought—"

"Ah, I'm fine. I'm more annoyed they tore my shirt." She shrugged. "Besides, you got hurt, but you seem to be managing." Thin cuts had crisscrossed his arms and the back of his hand by the time the Hesperians had surrendered. "You even serenaded us with an injured hand." She frowned. No bandages. "Hold on, didn't you have a cut there?" She pressed her fingertip into the skin just above his knuckles—skin that was whole.

He flinched, gaze darting around, but Saba must have decided to leave them to it, as her seat was now empty. His mouth twisted to one side, and he leant close. "Can you keep a secret?"

She scoffed. Funny question for him of all people to be asking her. *I'm Lady Avice Ferrers, your former betrothed.* "I think so."

He squinted and gave her an odd look, then glanced around. "Come on then." He rose and started away from the fire.

"Come on then, where?" She hurried after him.

"I mean it," he said when she caught up, "you can't breathe a word of this to anyone."

"Even if I knew what *this* was, I swear, I wouldn't." She glanced back towards the fire. "But, seriously, where are we going?"

"I don't want them to see the glow." Frowning, he glanced down at her side again. "Is it bad?"

"Glow? What glow?"

"You'll see. I found a cave when I was wandering this afternoon. It's not far."

They followed a stream into the rainforest, near where she'd found him earlier. The fading daylight barely penetrated the sighing leafy canopy. Still, it was enough to follow the path even without her fae-blooded sight. Within ten minutes, a rocky cliff rose ahead, and the stream disappeared into a shadowy cave.

"Is all this really necessary?" Looking back, the only sign of their camp was the pillar of smoke rising into the pink and orange sky.

He said nothing, just led inside.

What the hells was so secret? And *what glow?*

Shaking her head, she followed. Once she was inside, it wasn't as dark as it had first appeared. In fact, where the cave doglegged left, a dim golden light came from around the corner.

When she followed him around that corner, she gasped.

The last of the sun poured in through a hole in the roof. Its shafting light reflected in a still pool and scintillated off the walls and ceiling.

The cave's surface—she frowned and ran her fingertips over the nearest wall—it was covered in rough, glittering rock, almost like salt crystals left by the sea.

Knigh stared at the stalactites hanging from the ceiling, lips parted.

"Is this what you wanted to show me?" With that clear blue pool, the sparkling crystals, and soft sandy floor, this cave was undoubtedly beautiful, but it didn't seem to warrant his concerns about secrecy.

He blinked and shook his head. "No, I—it wasn't like this earlier, it must be the angle of the setting sun." He turned that disarming smile of his upon her. "*This* is an unexpected bonus. Now, show me this injury that's bothering you. We can't have you unable to dance all evening."

"Huh?" Her hand went to the spot where bandages looped inexpertly around her torso. Wild Hunt, the drink was wearing off—the cut throbbed, making her stomach turn.

"You asked about this"—he stepped closer, touching his shock of white hair—"afraid I lied about it being a nasty surprise." He raised his hands defensively. "Not about my father—that part wasn't a lie, just where this came from. It's my fae mark."

A fae mark. No wonder it was so bright and precise.

He cocked his head. "You're not the only one around here who's fae-touched."

Fae-touched. His strength, his charm—yes, it made sense.

Of course he'd assume she was *touched* rather than *blooded.* So few people outside the royal family were descended from fae, it was a natural assumption. Most people who had magic had been blessed by the fae for their own mysterious reasons. Like he had.

She glanced at his white streak again and snorted, shaking her head. "Well, aren't you just full of surprises tonight?"

Grinning, he lifted one shoulder. "Hopefully this one will impress you more than my singing. But, I need to touch the wound to heal you, so, show me."

Great. Alone with Knigh in a breathtakingly beautiful cave with his hand on her bare flesh. There was definitely no way this could escalate.

She swallowed, throat suddenly tight, and lifted the hem of her shirt until it revealed the bandages covering her from belly-button to breasts.

For a second, he just stared—perhaps he'd realised the same thing about this situation—then he blinked and nodded. "Do you mind if I...?" He pointed at the bandages.

"Mmm-hmm."

He stepped into her space, just as she'd done to him during the weapons check, and again his scent touched her nostrils—soap, worn leather, and cinnamon.

She had to stop that—his smell wasn't important. His closeness wasn't important. He was only doing this to heal her with his gift. That was all.

She held her breath as he unwrapped the bandages. A low growl sounded from his throat as the layers grew redder.

Closing her eyes, she braced a hand on his shoulder as he peeled the last layer from the wound. As careful as he was, her stomach roiled with the tugging motion and spreading pain.

"Sorry," he murmured, then ducked to look more closely.

"Wild Hunt take you, Vee—this is far worse than you let on." Scowling, he shook his head. "You've eaten since the battle, yes?"

Teeth gritted, she nodded. If she opened her mouth, she'd only end up whimpering, and no way would she make such a pathetic sound.

"Good. My gift will consume some of your energy as well as mine. Now, this will hurt a bit, but then it'll be gone—I promise."

"Just hurry up." With the bandage freshly peeled away, the wound throbbed, making her knees weak.

His warm palm pressed over the streak of red, lighting up the pain, and she gasped, fingers knotting into the hem of her shirt. But it was bearable.

He closed his eyes, a frown of concentration lining his brow.

A warm, golden glow lit up his hand, glistening off the cave walls. It sparkled and refracted from floor to ceiling, glittering and throwing flashes of light onto the pool's surface. The sight distracted her for a few seconds before agony lanced through her torso.

She flinched, but his free hand caught her waist, holding her in place.

"Wild Hunt damn you, bloody bastard, you—"

She clamped a hand over her mouth, gritting her teeth.

A thousand hot needles jabbed through her flesh, and a moan still escaped her grip, echoing around the cavern.

Closing her eyes, she bit on her knuckles and held her breath. It couldn't go on much longer. It would be over soon.

But the needles lit up fresh pain, as bright and pinpointed as the glittering walls, for one, two, three seconds... Four... Sweat beaded her brow... Five... Deeper darkness pushed at her...

Then it faded, and warmth bloomed in its place, as welcome and glorious as the sun on a wintry Albionic day. Sighing, she sagged, catching herself on his shoulder.

Then the warmth, too, faded, leaving just his hot skin upon hers.

When she opened her eyes, his chest was heaving in long, deep breaths, and the way he watched her, eyes at once dark and hot, made her heart stutter.

His fingers flexed on her skin, firm, strong, sending her pulse surging, and his gaze fell to her mouth.

She gave a brittle laugh. “Captain Blackwood...” Somehow formality felt safer, but damn it, did she want to be safe? “If I didn’t know better, I’d say you’re looking at me like you want to kiss me.”

His fingers twitched against her. “I do.”

THE CAVE

Pulse far too loud in her ears, Vice swallowed. This was… he was a pirate hunter and she a pirate… but after all that had happened today, the argument fell flat.

He was her betrothed, though—or had been. That could complicate things.

Lords and Ladies, did it matter? He didn't know who she was, and she didn't care who he was. He could just be a body fulfilling her body's need, and she could be the same for him. Gods knew he needed to let off steam after today's fight.

Besides, cool, restrained Knighton Blackwood wasn't some foolish boy to lose his heart after a kiss… or more.

She lifted her chin, an invitation. His breath brushed her lips.

"Then," she said, "why don't you?" All he had to do was lower his face a few inches.

"Because," he replied, voice husky, "if I start, I don't know where it'll stop."

So he felt it too. The tension that had been building since that first time they'd met, humming like one of Perry's high notes on her fiddle. When it broke, it wouldn't just be a brief kiss in a cave. Her body throbbed, calling for it, for him. Irresistible.

"Maybe you should start and find out."

Two beats, a slow blink, then his fingers plunged into her hair, and he pressed his mouth to hers.

Warmth surged through her at his touch, highlighting every sensation. The cave's chilly air on her hands and face. The solidity of his shoulder under her hand. The rough linen of her shirt still gripped in the other. His hand at her waist, fingertips of the other trailing across her scalp.

All that from a lingering union of lips.

They parted an inch, and when she opened her eyes, their gazes collided, as staggering as a pistol shot. She blew out a shaky laugh. A shiver raced through him, lifting goosebumps on his forearms.

Just one kiss. Definitely not enough.

In unison, she tiptoed back to his lips, and his arm circled her waist, crushing her against him.

Lords, he was firm and strong, and his pulse pounded under her fingertips as her hands slid over his shoulders and around his neck.

That pulse—he was alive, she was alive. They'd *survived*. And this was the reward they'd earned.

With bodies flush together, the heat coursing through her built, pushing her mouth open and inviting his eager response, tongue brushing hers.

At that touch, a boundary crossed, the kiss grew raw, hungry, frantic, his skin burning under her hands, their breaths mingling and echoing through the cave.

This was what she needed. Gods, this was exactly what she needed. She threaded her fingers into his hair, pulling him closer, deeper, and a groan rumbled in his chest—the louder cousin of the sound she'd felt when she'd checked him for weapons.

Maybe this was what he needed, too.

His hands sank to her backside, kneading, pressing, and with a surge of muscles, he lifted her from the floor, bringing their faces level.

She huffed a soft laugh—damn it, she didn't need encouragement, not in this. Pirate hunter or not, this was what she'd wanted to do that first time she'd seen him in deLacy's ballroom, all tall and broad in his uniform. And the want had only built the more he irritated her, the more he flirted and teased, and the more he was simply in her presence.

It didn't mean anything, only that she wanted him. That was all.

Trusting in his hold, she wrapped her legs around him, creating an unbearably perfect angle between his hardness and her core, sending pleasure streaking through her.

Too many damned clothes, though, but... what if he didn't want this? Not really. The last thing she wanted was his regret, his awkwardness tomorrow back on *The Morrigan*.

Bodies were just bodies to her, but not to everyone.

She wouldn't take advantage of him.

Hands on his shoulders, she pulled away, leaving her lips tingling.

A frown flickered on his brow, and he cocked his head, panting.

She caught her breath and swallowed in an effort to make her voice box remember how to work. "Do you—do you want to?"

Teeth flashing, he scoffed and nodded, his eyes wide. "Do you?"

"Oh, yes. Gods, yes."

His chest heaved in a long breath, then their lips crashed back together, all tongues and gasping and a nip to her lower lip that wreaked havoc with her spine.

In that case, they needed to do something about these pesky clothes. She scrabbled at his shirt, tugging it up until she was forced to break off their kiss to pull it over his head.

When she threw it to the floor, he went to continue, but she pressed her fingers to his lips, grinning. "Just a second," she murmured and let her gaze rove over him at leisure as she hadn't been able to at the coral reef.

Hells and damnation, it was far worse than she'd feared. His taut muscles gleamed in the dying light that glinted through the cave's crystals and flickered upon the pool. She ran her fingers across those broad shoulders she'd so admired in deLacy's ballroom, then along the line of his collarbones. She planed her palms down over his firm chest, precisely over the route she'd taken during the weapons check. Except now there was no uniform in the way and no battle of who could turn the other on more without succumbing.

This was exactly about succumbing and damn well enjoying it.

He watched her, breathing hard, as her touch lowered, and she finally let her thumbs and the heels of her hands explore the rippling muscles of his stomach.

She bit her lip. With him looking like this, it was more a surprise this had taken so long to happen.

Smiling, she lifted her hands to his face, tracing her fingers over the high cheekbones. "You are gorgeous, you know that, right?"

He blinked. "I—I—thank you?"

She chuckled and pulled his mouth back to hers. Clearly, not enough women had said that. A travesty. Men told women they were beautiful all the time and yet women so seldom repaid the compliment.

There was the dim sense of movement, then her bottom landed on something cold and hard, such a stark contrast with the pounding heat surging through their paired bodies it made her gasp.

With a grin, he palmed her thighs and pulled away just far enough to slide his hands to the hem of her shirt. His eyes widened in question.

"Bloody get on with it, Knigh."

A low chuckle rumbled from his throat, and he tugged off the offending garment, then dropped it to the floor.

She looked down, touching the place she'd been injured in this morning's fight. "Not even a scar."

He scoffed and pulled her hand away. "That wasn't where I was looking." One eyebrow raised, his lust-darkened gaze raked over her exposed flesh.

Shoulders back, she lifted her chin and watched his survey. Some felt ashamed of their bodies or hid them or compared them to others —too big, too small, too fleshy, too muscular for a woman, not enough curves. Not her. Just like the reef, bodies came in hundreds, thousands of different forms, and she'd never seen one that wasn't beautiful. Her body, like his, was not something for modesty.

The pad of his thumb circled the silver scar on her shoulder, and he nodded with a frown of understanding—he could tell it was a pistol wound. Dipping his head, he kissed it, confirming what she already knew.

It wasn't a flaw, an imperfection on her tanned, smooth skin.

It was something she'd survived. It said she was tough—she wouldn't break.

With a shuddering breath, his hand went to the spot where

he'd healed her, where there was no scar, and skittered up to palm her breast.

Her breath caught, and she arched her back, pushing into his touch, seeking still more.

As if goaded by her response, he gripped her thigh and bent, catching her nipple between his lips.

She gasped, closing her eyes and letting her head hang back. Even bolder than she'd anticipated. He really had fooled her with that mask of control and restraint, hadn't he?

His thumb grazed her other nipple just before he nipped the first playfully, pleasure-pain striking through her like a lightning bolt and making her jerk upright, legs tight around him.

He looked up at her with a wicked grin and licked the spot he'd bitten, soothing the hurt in a way that made her squirm. "What?" He raised an eyebrow again. "Did you think just because I was in the Navy, I hadn't learned anything useful beyond sailing?"

She swallowed, breath quaking, body burning in anticipation. "Clearly, I misjudged you."

Smirking, he kissed his way up her chest, hands fiddling with the buttons of her breeches. "Clearly. Let's see just how far..."

As his mouth landed on hers again, he tugged off her boots, then her breeches.

Gods, she really *had* misjudged him, hadn't she? Knighton Villiers was not the gentle lay she'd expected.

Cool air caressed her skin, a relief from the overpowering heat coursing through her veins, making her sigh against his lips.

With a firm hand, he pushed her back against the flat stone he'd propped her on. His fingertips glided across the tattoo that decorated the side of her hip and down her thigh, giving it an appreciative look before lowering to his knees.

"What"—she half sat up, but his palm on her solar plexus stopped further movement—"what are you doing?"

"I thought the Pirate Queen would appreciate a man kneeling for her." With a flash of a grin, he nudged her thighs apart and, Wild Hunt, she was not about to stop him.

Scoffing, she lay back, heart pounding in her ears. *"Badly* misjudged."

"You have no idea," he murmured before his tongue laved against her.

She gasped, back arching out of her control, now responding only to his sweet torment, his ravenous touch. Eyes closed, she focused on each point of contact—his grip on her thighs, his smooth strokes against her, the scrape of his stubble.

A low moan rumbled through him and into her core, saying he enjoyed this, too. As his tongue worked on her sensitive pearl, his finger circled her entrance with teasing pressure.

She writhed, and a pathetic sound echoed through the cave—that was her, near-begging. She needed more, craved more, wanted *more*. But her voice wouldn't cooperate to ask for it, to demand it. Instead, she bucked her hips and whimpered.

With a chuckle he obeyed her wordless command, dragging her into a sea of sublime pleasure from his silken touch.

It was unbearable... delicious... surging... incredible...

It was rapture.

Wave upon wave consumed her, building, building, building, each cresting higher than the last. With fingers and tongue, he strummed her, playing her as expertly as he'd played that guitar at the bonfire.

Lights sparked across the inside of her eyelids, and at last, the highest wave rose. It lifted her, carrying her away and crashing her upon some unknown shore in a thousand incandescent droplets.

He held her through the cries and the ebbing waves until she gasped for breath and fell limp against the rock.

Lords, Ladies, gods, whoever was listening—she had needed that. So badly. And bloody hells had he delivered.

Half-sitting, she pushed the hair from her face and blinked into the cave's gloom.

Except that while the last of the sun had almost disappeared, motes of blue light dotted the walls, fresh ones glowing into existence even as she stared.

She'd peaked plenty of times but never had a partner made her see actual lights before.

With a smile that wouldn't have been out of place on a sabrecat, Knigh rose, his body gleaming, all shadows edged with light. "Glow-worms," he murmured and bent over her, pulling her into a long, slow kiss that tasted of salt and herself.

She cupped his face, scraping her teeth against the fullness of his lower lip.

He pulled away, expression suddenly serious. "Are you sure you—"

"Wild Hunt, Knigh, if you make me wait any longer I might explode."

A small smile tugged at the corner of his mouth, but he made no move to act.

"Let me illustrate," she said and flicked open the first button of his breeches, "just how sure I am."

His breath hitched as her hands brushed against the hardness straining at the fabric. She couldn't help but smirk at holding that influence upon him when he'd just exercised such devastating power over her.

Enough anticipation, now was the time for speed. She'd done this enough times that the buttons were all undone within a matter of seconds. Then with a manoeuvre over that sizeable bulge at the front, she slid the breeches down his thighs.

He certainly wasn't at half-mast.

Huffing out a quick breath, he nodded. "Message received and understood." He kicked off his boots and let the breeches fall the rest of the way to the floor.

Heels hooked around the backs of his legs, she pulled him closer, biting back a moan when his hardness glided over her. Pleasure throbbed in her belly and tightened her thighs.

This was it—the point of no return. She wanted it—she'd been sure the moment she'd invited him to kiss her.

But him... Earlier, she'd doubted his resolution but after what he'd just done—no, that wasn't the action of a man purely letting his desire lead the way. He'd made the decision to do this.

With a hungry kiss, she guided him to her entrance, but the blasted man just paused there, tucked against her. His hands glided down her back until they gripped her hips, then his tongue plunged into her mouth, and he entered her slow inch by slow inch.

This was—she shook her head—unbearable. She grabbed his arse and tugged him the rest of the way with a groan. Stars burst across the black of her eyelids, forcing her eyes open—she wanted to see him, to watch that magnificent body of his.

Shuddering, he paused there, filling her. So gloriously full.

As if he sensed her watching, his eyes flashed open, gaze roving over her face, and he swallowed, throat bobbing hard. "My word, Vee," he breathed.

She nodded and looped her arms around his neck, pulling him in for another kiss, tinged with a low moan—it could have been hers or his or both. Who knew anymore?

Then he withdrew, almost leaving her entirely. The emptiness was shocking for a moment before he thrust back inside in one swift movement, forcing a cry from deep in her chest.

So badly misjudged. She shook, heartbeat roaring in her ears. His fingers dug into her flesh as if clinging on to control as, again, he paused there.

He inhaled slowly, then exhaled. "I should have"—his voice cracked, and he cleared his throat—"I should have asked earlier about… precautions."

Gods damn it, was he trying to drive her insane with this stop-start? "The preventative." He didn't have to worry about withdrawing before the end. "Now… *please…*" It sounded far too much like begging, but damn the man, he'd given her a taste, and she wanted more. She arched her back—that had to be a clear enough instruction.

He scoffed and pulled out again, pausing at her entrance. "Impatient."

"Damn right, I am—I've been waiting weeks for this."

One eyebrow arched. "Oh, *really?*"

The insufferable arrogance. The delicious arrogance. Gods, if this was just the start, the *well-earned* arrogance.

But his grin faded as she hooked her feet around his back and pulled him in, winning his hiss of pleasure.

Breaths heavy, he drove into her, strokes assured, smooth, powerful, urging the waves through her once more. As if that wasn't enough, he slid a hand between them until his thumb circled her pearl, stoking her cries, building the pressure to breaking point.

Too much. Far too much. She couldn't… Her chest—hells, her whole body was going to burst.

Biting her lip, she lifted her weight onto her thighs, still wrapped around his waist. A low breath huffed from him as he squeezed her arse with near-bruising intensity and took her weight as if it were nothing, lifting her from the rock.

Hips now free, she rode him, chasing those building waves. It only seemed to fuel his desire, sending his movements wild, powerful, demanding, more like the man she'd fought beside than the one she'd followed into this cave.

Their lips met, parted, fell upon each other's necks, kissed, sucked. He tasted of palm wine and salt. They licked and bit and cried each other's names until the waves broke over her, carrying speech, carrying everything away, leaving only pleasure so intense, so staggering it was almost pain.

On instinct, she rocked against him. Her breaths heaved, blown out by his pounding, urgent rhythm. The muscles in his arms and neck corded and a frown creased between his brows. He was close.

Swallowing, she drove harder and harder, but in chasing his last peak of pleasure, her own rose once more, intense and bright and building. Their sweat-slicked bodies glided over each other, a shockingly good fit, until the sparking light claimed her again, forcing breathless cries from her lips. Seconds later, a harsh moan sounded in his throat, and his whole body tensed, shuddered, and contracted, arms locked around her.

With a trembling sigh, he sank to his knees, still holding her close. His eyes opened and fixed on her, something profound, powerful in that look. He lowered her to the soft sand, and they lay that way for many breaths, the air between them heavy.

If that had been almost unbearable in intensity, this—his look—was too much to take. He—did he see too much? No. No, it was fine, she was just... so much had happened today...

To escape his gaze, she planted a kiss on his mouth, loosening her legs from around his hips. With a low sigh, he rolled onto his back, forearm over his eyes.

They panted, breaths loud in the sudden stillness of the cave. Only the dim blue lights of the glow-worms glistened on the crystalline walls and glinted on the pool. The sky through the hole in the roof was a deep violet-blue now, all traces of sunset erased by darkening twilight.

Her limbs splayed, loose and heavy. She shook her head. To think she'd expected him to be nothing more than a warm firm body and a welcoming mouth, a fleeting comfort after today's brush with death. After all, wasn't that what she and Fitz had been for almost three years?

Well, this...

A low chuckle shook through her. "Well, you were certainly more than I bargained for, Captain Blackwood."

He scoffed, and his arm dropped from his face. "Likewise, Pirate Queen. Bloody likewise."

CHANGING COURSE

The next morning, Knigh woke in his tent, warm and... and *relaxed?* Is that what the heavy feeling in his limbs was? And the one responsible...

Vee lay beside him, back against his chest, breaths slow with sleep. Her hair fell across the pillow in a messy halo of waves, locks touching his cheek, scented with that damn intoxicating smell of vanilla and petrichor.

He inhaled slowly, deeply, savouring it, her, this still moment when the familiar, simmering tension of deep-set anger and hurt didn't thrum in his veins. His hand on her hip flexed, drawing his fingertips against the lines of her tattoo. A compass rose surrounded by hibiscus flowers perfectly emphasised the curves of her hip and rear. He shook his head, a laugh lacing his exhalation.

Yesterday, his nerves had been ragged after losing control on the *Covadonga*. The palm wine had been as sweet and strong as she'd promised. And when he'd healed her, joining their energies, it had been heady beyond endurance—her body too close, the cave too private, her ease too seductive. Of course he'd been too weak to resist.

Lords, who was he fooling? He hadn't wanted to resist anymore. Attraction had sparked between them since their first meeting, had fizzled in the air like black powder every time they were alone and sometimes when they weren't. And yesterday she'd talked him down from his madness, she'd been kind and reassured him, albeit in her own irreverent way.

Smiling, he peered down her back and shifted his light grip until his thumb rested in one of the dimples above her rear that he'd so admired as she'd bathed. He nodded to himself. What had been unthinkable just weeks ago now felt achingly right. The pad of his thumb circled the little indentation, and a small hum of appreciation rumbled in his chest.

Everything had changed. And not just because of last night. It had begun much earlier than that.

Vee wasn't the monster the Navy painted a picture of in their reports. She was... Well, he wasn't entirely sure *what* she was, but she wasn't what they said—even he could see that. Everything he'd observed of her... No, there was no sign of her being a senseless murderer, a vicious beast, the notorious Lady Vice. And she might not be the noble, heroic Pirate Queen of the songs, but she seemed closer to that than the Navy's villain.

Even without desire clouding his reason, his assessment of people's trustworthiness wasn't the best—hadn't he believed in Father and the Duke? But he wasn't the only one who saw her this way. As far as he'd seen, Perry's judgement had been nothing but sound and she, in her own words, loved Vee.

Perhaps he was safe in this.

Purely from a naval standpoint, from the way she operated, privateering suited her. She preferred surrender over battle, targeted leaders when she had to kill, and rejected torture, unlike the most notorious pirates. She could be a great asset to the crown.

Although right now, eyes closed, no raised eyebrow, sharp grin, or flippant comment, chest rising and falling slowly, she looked soft, vulnerable, a beautiful woman rather than a naval asset.

He'd warned her not to trust him and she shouldn't. Gods, he didn't even trust himself, not after what he'd done to Billy, but here, in this tent, with just her... He wanted it. He wanted it so much, it ached in his chest. He didn't just want her to trust him, he wanted to be *worthy* of her trust. He'd already disobeyed orders to keep her alive, and he'd do the same again.

He exhaled, shaky. What *wouldn't* he do for—

A sharp rap on the front tent post made him flinch.

Vee tensed, frowning. "Mmm?" She rubbed her eyes and wriggled against him as if that would mean she wasn't awake yet.

"Blackwood?" Bricus called from outside.

Knigh's chest hammered. Wild Hunt and damnation, Bricus couldn't find her here. He tugged the blankets up from where they'd pooled at their thighs, even if it only gave the illusion of protection. "What is it?"

"Captain wants to speak to you in his tent."

Lords and Ladies, there was only one thing he'd want to talk about.

Vee's arrest.

Buggeration. He needed a way out of that plot. It was one thing to hand her over when he thought she was a monster, but the person he'd met, the woman who'd found her way into his arms was no such thing. To trick her into returning to Albion, to serve her to the authorities on a platter would be nothing short of betrayal.

Nothing short of wrong.

Gods, what had he tangled himself up in?

His arm tightened around Vee's waist and he ducked his face to her hair and its sweet smell of vanilla and fresh rain.

No, it was fine. He could fix this. He'd speak to FitzRoy now, play along, then he'd sit down and formulate a way out of this plan.

Once he put his report in, contradicting the patently false accusations about Vee and giving an accurate picture, the Admiralty would surely grant her a real letter of marque. She could become a legitimate privateer, and with her fame and gift, they might even fit her out a ship to captain, perhaps with Perry at her side. Her levelling influence just might keep Vee out of too much trouble.

"Blackwood? Have you gone back to sleep?"

Vee shook with a soft giggle.

He clapped a hand over her mouth. "I'll be right there."

"Right, well, don't keep him waiting—*he's* the captain."

Footsteps thudded away across the sand, and Knigh sighed, dropping his hand from her face. He took a long breath, then sighed it out. It was fine. He'd decided not to betray her, and he wouldn't. Hells, he should take a leaf out of her book—she wouldn't worry, she'd just solve the problem.

He would work it out.

She stretched, long limbs cat-like with their lean musculature. Grumbling, she turned to him, a sleepy smile on her face. She slipped an arm around his waist. "You don't have to go *right away,* do you?" Her hand found its way to his rear and gave a squeeze.

He scoffed, pushing her onto her back and rolling on top of her, weight on his arms. "I'm afraid I do." He cupped her breast, smiling at the way it filled his hand so perfectly. Her back arched, just a little, but in unmistakable response to his touch.

And damn it, despite his intentions to get to FitzRoy, he responded in turn, blood heating, heart speeding, body stirring against her. He cleared his throat. "Or at least I have to go soon and"—he dipped his head and caught her nipple between his lips, giving it a quick suck and making her breath catch—"for what I plan to do to you next, I intend to take my time." Next time, he would be languorous, savouring her in slow seduction, watching that blissful look on her face again and again. And again. He had the patience to make her beg—to say those words, rather than just *please* as she had last night and, gods, just the thought of that...

"Do you, now? And who am I to get in the way of your plans?" A slow smile claimed her mouth before she stretched, breasts lifting until he couldn't help but capture them each in turn, grazing his teeth against her hardened nipples.

He gave a low groan. Damn the woman, despite making love twice last night, she'd got him at full attention again. Shaking his head, he pulled away, kneeling and grabbing his shirt with a snort. "Oh, well played, madam, well played."

She grinned, eyes glinting in the dim light seeping through the tent's canvas. "What?" The fingertips of one hand traced a line above her breasts, ending at her collarbone.

With a soft growl, he turned away and pulled on his shirt. "I'm not looking."

"Spoilsport."

"Not so much that," he said, pulling on his breeches, "I just enjoy teasing you a great deal."

"Is that what that was? Bastard."

He chuckled and combed his fingers through his hair—that would do for speaking to FitzRoy. "I'd apologise, but I'm not even the slightest bit sorry." He crouched beside her and planted a lingering kiss on her lips. "Hearing you practically beg me to take you in that cave..." He shook his head, his traitorous hand gliding down to her breast. "Well, I never thought I'd hear the notorious Lady Vice beg for anything."

The notorious Lady Vice. He kept the teasing smile fixed in place even though his heart squeezed painfully.

She adjusted his hair, touch gentle. "I don't beg, I'm just not afraid to ask for what I want."

He bit the inside of his cheek. She wasn't the *notorious Lady Vice* at all. And he had to fix the awful plan he'd put in place. With a stiff nod, he rose, ignoring her protests, and ducked out of the tent.

WEAKNESS

The sea was wide and glimmering, the air fresh, and the wind with them, all without Vice having to use her gift at all. The *Covadonga* trailed in their wake as it had for the past few weeks, sailed by a skeleton crew, the silver safely split between it and *The Morrigan*. Breeze snagging her hair and tugging at her shirt, Vice strode fore.

What a bloody glorious day to be alive.

Speaking of glorious...

Walking the other way, deep in conversation with Aedan, came Knigh. He'd shed all traces of the uniform, now in breeches and loose shirt that the air blew against his torso. Again, the weather's cooperation was nothing to do with her gift.

His gaze hit hers, making her internal organs dance a jig.

To the casual observer, he gave no reaction. But she'd learned his little tells—the poor man would be a fool to play poker with her now. The fractional move of his eyebrows, the crackling spark in his eyes so much like lightning in grey clouds, she could almost feel it with her gift, and the sudden, hard breath raising his chest.

Both continued in their strides, eyes locked upon each other. Every fibre in her hummed the closer he came, and she had to hook her thumbs in her belt to keep her hands from the temptation to swat his arse when he drew level, as she so often did when they were alone.

Their eye contact only broke at the very last moment. Then he was past, and she gave a slow, shaking exhalation.

Ooh, just you wait until later, Knighton Blackwood.

"What's got you so cheerful, I wonder?" Perry watched her from the bow.

Cheerful? Vice blinked. Gods, she was grinning like a loon, wasn't she? She massaged her cheeks to get rid of the ridiculous expression and went to lean on the rail with Perry. Barnacle sprung to the gunwale, then to Vice's shoulder with a chirrup of greeting.

Vice obeyed the cat's unspoken command and stroked her. "I'm not cheerful. I'm just normal. This is normal me."

Perry narrowed her eyes, trailing them over Vice's face before shaking her head. *"Nooo,* you're definitely glowing. *And* I've seen you sneaking out of your old quarters when FitzRoy's not looking." She twisted her mouth to one side and tapped her chin with her forefinger. "What could possibly be the link between these two things?"

Scoffing, Vice folded her arms. "It's just sex. And he's good at it." She shrugged, ignoring Barnacle's miaow of complaint at the movement. "I'm always cheerful after a good lay." All true.

"Yes, but I've seen you after FitzRoy, Aedan, that delicious young man at Kayracou, those women at Kaiman, but never have I seen you like *this.*"

The back of Vice's neck prickled, the sensation creeping across her shoulders and down her back. That wasn't...

She'd just been smiling. She did that. A lot. Small wonder, after all, since Knigh had kept her well-satisfied over the past few weeks. And yet she still desired his nearness, his touch, the sound of his voice much of the time they were apart. How strange to be gratified and craving at the same time. Was that even possible?

Perry was still looking at her with that smug smile and cocked head. Like she was right.

"What do you mean *like this*, anyway?"

"Well, I don't think I've seen you snap at anyone in weeks... except when you're pretending to make Blackwood help you find something in his cabin—very convincing, by the way, well done."

Vice rolled her eyes. "Thank you for the excellent review of my performance—I hope you'll send it to all the newspapers in Lunden." She scanned the clear sky, the rolling sea, let the spray dust her face. "The weather's good without me having to put any energy into it. We have a Hesperian treasure ship. We have silver. And we are the Queen's own privateers. What's not to be cheerful about?"

One eyebrow raised, Perry nodded. "Mmm-hmm."

Wild Hunt take her.

Irritation needled across Vice's scalp. Perry was bloody insufferable. Just because she'd told her Knigh had called her *wise* and, yes, Perry did sometimes get things right, but right now she was acting like she was the fae's own seer who knew some great secret the rest of the world, especially Vice, was blind to.

Cheeks hot, Vice's nostrils flared. "Why are you looking at me like that?"

"I told you." Perry raised her hands with an exaggerated shrug. "Because you've had *just sex* with plenty of others, but I've never seen you have this reaction to it. At least not since—"

"Don't."

It was exactly as though she'd been plunged into a pool of ice. Every inch of her body tensed. The hairs on the back of her neck stood on end. Her stomach felt like a solid block of frozen rock. It was obvious where Perry had been about to go with that ill-conceived sentence. *Not since Evered.*

The foolish girl she'd been had loved him. She'd placed herself and her trust in his hands and he'd dropped it all to shatter upon the deck. They'd been excited for the adventure, the thrill of it all. But he'd stayed in their cabin the whole trip even once his seasickness had worn off, abandoning her so she'd been forced to earn a place here alone.

And beneath that layer… As her husband, he'd had control of her money, and he'd frittered it away on a poor deal with FitzRoy.

And the next… She'd trusted her body to him, too, but he'd hurt her, marked her when she'd challenged him, and outright refused to even acknowledge a woman could enjoy sex.

But she might have fixed it. Given time. Given a chance to adapt to this new place, he might have accepted it and gone back to being the dashing, charming man she'd married.

The man who'd abandoned her the moment he'd set food on *The Morrigan's* deck.

The only thing worse was what she'd done. She'd brought him here with her silly dreams. And he'd died because of it.

No surprise that foolish girl had fallen apart. The sea—the *world* was no place for dreamers or romance or love or any of it. Her only option had been to become Lady Vice. Who was strong. Who didn't rely on anybody. Who didn't love and so didn't grieve and would not break.

She shivered, arms wrapped around herself. This was why she skirted thoughts of him. It was too much. Too big a mistake. Too much hurt. It left her weak and hollow.

"I just found the correlation interesting," Perry went on, voice light. "Caring for someone is—"

"It's sex." The words somehow ground from between her teeth. "If you're doing it right, sex makes you smile. It doesn't mean I care for him. It doesn't *mean* anything."

It couldn't mean anything. That would be dangerous. That would lay her bare, ready to be destroyed the moment he inevitably let her down, just as Evered had.

Perry pushed a lock of hair from Vice's face, hooking it behind her ear. Vice kept stock-still as Perry pressed a warm hand to her cheek. "You just seem content," she said, gentle, low, like distant memories of a mother. "And that's—well, it's a lovely thing to see. I'm happy for you."

Drawing a fortifying breath, Vice jerked away from Perry's touch. She was *not* content. Well, no more so than usual—she was always content because she was happy with herself, with who she was. It was everyone else that was the problem: it was only a matter of time before they let you down.

And Knigh was no exception.

With a stiff smile, she backed away. "You're wrong."

Her chest heaved as she strode aft, ducking beneath the lines her crewmates manned to adjust the sails and gritting her teeth as Barnacle dug her claws in to stay in place.

Best not to rely on anyone too much, certainly not for her own happiness. She'd made that mistake before, and she wouldn't do it again. She was past needing anybody.

Perry might know some things, but on this occasion, she was so very wrong.

Sharp little claws dug into her shoulder again, and Barnacle jumped from her shoulder.

Vice flinched, blinking back to attention. She stood outside FitzRoy's door. She hadn't known where she was going when she walked away from the bow, but now she was here—yes, it made perfect sense. Her instincts knew exactly what she needed.

She would prove Perry wrong *and* rid herself of this pathetic yearning for Knighton Blackwood.

And it *was* pathetic. Just this morning she'd found herself thinking foolish, *foolish* thoughts. Lying against him in the afterglow of sex, she'd laughed to herself. *If this is what being with Knigh's like, maybe marrying Knighton Villiers wouldn't have been so bad.*

Urgh. No. *No!*

Being with him had clouded her mind. Made her weak. Made her think *feelings* were happening. All wrong. This was just physical.

It was something physical that she liked. That she wanted. That was warm and felt good and right and...

No. Just sex. Just bodies.

All she needed was someone else's touch to remind her that he wasn't anything special.

Lords, even just thinking it felt so much better—her breaths calmed, the warmth trickled back through her like ice-melt in Albion's early spring.

Her stomach twisted, yes, but...

She stood with her hand on the door to FitzRoy's cabin, the timber reassuringly solid. Her feet didn't want to step back to allow her to open it. Her hand refused to lower and grip the handle.

I don't want this.

It was a quiet voice right at the very back of her mind, the same place that tickled when something was wrong, when danger was near. Even now, the hairs on the nape of her neck prickled.

Such a quiet voice. Soft.

Weak.

She didn't want Fitz. Hadn't for a long time. But he'd been safe —she didn't need him. He couldn't destroy her.

Blackwood... Knigh...

He made her grin like a loon. He soothed the snarling beast inside her that bristled at kindness or pity and kept her jokes hard, her tongue sharp. He could get close like Perry and Saba did, maybe even closer—his touch did that. Something about his warmth or the intimacy of shared breath and quiet conversations in the dark softened her and let him edge through.

It was dangerous. That's what the hairs on the back of her neck were telling her.

She trusted her friendship and physical safety to Saba, Aedan, Lizzy, Wynn, and Effie, but only that. To Perry she entrusted the few feelings she allowed herself, but that was all.

She'd only intended to entrust her body to Knigh, but somehow it had gone further. The way she'd been unable to resist him... The way his taut control and discomfort had eaten at her... The way his distress after berserking had been unbearable and driven her to try and comfort him...

Damn it, even before she'd given him her body, she should've realised it had gone past that.

Trusting one thing to a person was safe. Trusting her all to someone? No. She'd done that with Evered and he'd broken the trust, himself, and what had been left of her.

Not again. Never again.

Even if she didn't want Fitz, he was a necessity. She had to endure it—a bitter antidote to the sweet poison that was Knigh Blackwood.

"I must do this."

Nodding, she pulled her necklace from under her shirt, letting it rest noticeably over her chest. Fitz had given it to her back when he'd first made her his. She'd never really cared for the design—

bright yellow gold with a massive garnet in the centre. Far too gaudy. But she'd got rid of all Avice's jewellery, except for Evered's ring, and this was the first thing anyone had given Vice.

Like a magpie with a shiny object, it wouldn't fail to catch FitzRoy's attention.

CINNAMON & SOAP

Head up, shoulders back, she entered FitzRoy's cabin.

"Vice?" FitzRoy looked up from the papers in his hands. "I'm busy."

Stomach twisting, she closed the door behind her, leaning on it. She kicked back that soft, weak voice, closing it behind a door in her mind and leant on that, too.

I don't want this.

"My darling Fitz, surely you're not too busy for me?" Smiling, she cocked her head and stalked around the table towards him, every movement mechanical. "You shut yourself in here all the time nowadays—aren't you lonely?"

His mouth flattened, but his hazel eyes grew dark, watching her. "I don't get lonely."

She perched on the table, knees brushing his. "But it's been a long time, hasn't it?"

"I've been busy."

Was 'busy' going to be his answer to everything?

It meant she could go. She didn't have to do this. She could...

No. Knigh had too much of her. Was too dangerous. He would let her down soon enough, and she needed to do this to... to...

Why?

Because I must.

Because Knigh wasn't special. Because it was just sex, which meant she could have *just sex* with anyone.

Because FitzRoy meant nothing. He was safe. And if she threw her body at him, it meant she didn't need Knigh, wasn't relying on him, and thus wouldn't hurt when he let her down.

With a ragged breath, she shoved her hair back over her shoulder. She let the necklace catch the sunlight spilling through the stern windows.

Predictably, FitzRoy's gaze fell to the glimmering gold, and his eyes lit up, breaths deepening.

"You've been too busy for too long," she purred. "And so troubled. I thought"—she placed her foot on the edge of his chair, brushing his thigh—"perhaps I could help take your mind off whatever it is."

"Vice," he breathed, "damn you, but you're a hard woman to resist."

Then he was tempted. Excellent. Exactly what she wanted. Precisely why she was here. Perfect.

Her stomach twisted again.

Yes, this was absolutely as planned. Physical reactions. Just bodies doing what bodies wanted to do.

Safe and under her control. No feelings involved.

With half a smile, she rose from the table and slid into his lap, across the chair, legs hooked over its arm. "Why resist?" She placed a stiff hand on his chest, thumb brushing a leather pouch hanging from a cord around his neck. That was new. And surprisingly plain for him.

His jaw knotted, but the pulse below it jumped, and his hand slipped up her back. "I suppose just a short distraction," he murmured, face inches from hers. His fingers sank into her hair, and he pulled her head back.

She gritted her teeth as he kissed her throat. The manoeuvre had played havoc with her three years ago. She'd been a girl then, easily impressed by how *masterful* he was. Then, she hadn't minded submitting, had even found it thrilling.

But now... Now his arm wrapped around her too tightly and his grip on her hair was more the gesture of someone baring a victim's throat for cutting. This was nothing more than a powerful man taking pleasure in exerting—in *proving* his dominance over her. And his tobacco and musk scent was... wrong.

Not cinnamon and soap, that traitorous corner of her mind whispered.

Shut up.

Squeezing her eyes shut, she forced her breaths deep, trying to calm her heartbeat, which raced but not with desire.

No, no, this *was* desire, just... just different from what she felt with Knigh. She wanted this.

No I don't.

With a groan, he yanked her head back, other hand flicking open the top button of her shirt.

No, no, no. That hurt and not in the way Knigh teased her with pleasure-pain. She squirmed, body fighting to back away even as she tried to leash herself.

When Fitz tugged open the neck of her shirt and squeezed her breast, it was covetous, greedy, not coaxing or even considering her pleasure.

She felt nothing but sickness threatening at the back of her throat.

The nails raking her breast said *mine*. The hardness poking her behind pulsed, sending a wave of nausea through her. Another yank at her hair didn't play with power—it didn't give and take, allowing her the chance to have the upper hand, before seizing it back again.

It only took.

When she opened her eyes, her view of the ceiling was blurred, her temples wet.

She didn't want this. Didn't want him. This had been a terrible idea.

"No," she gasped.

But he only kissed his way down her throat and pulled her shirt off her shoulder, mouth seeking the way to her breast.

"No," she said, stronger this time. "Fitz, no."

He twitched, the grip on her hair loosening. "Hmm?"

Chest and stomach heaving, she leapt to her feet. "I—no, sorry, I changed my mind." She shook her head, backing away until she banged into the table. Something clattered to the floor at her feet, making her jump. The box from the wreck—open. Empty.

Frowning, he cocked his head and adjusted his trousers over the obvious bulge at his crotch, but made no move to stop her. "You came to me. You started this."

"I know." She nodded slowly. "I know. And I'm finishing it." She edged around the table, not turning her back to him.

His eyes narrowed, then his mouth broke into a laugh. "Oh, dear, Vice. Something's got into you, hasn't it?" He waved his hand. "Run along and work it out, little Avice, and stop bothering me."

Stomach calming, she strode out, slamming the door shut and pulling her shirt back over her shoulder.

Fresh, clean air. Thank the gods for that. Just the smell of sea, no tobacco or musk. She gulped it down as greedily the day she'd saved Knigh from that current off the reef.

The crew went about their business, no one looking twice at her. Good.

Damn FitzRoy, though, he was right about one thing. Something had got into her.

Knighton bloody Villiers.

He'd ruined her for other men. That was all.

Shit. Shit!

Leaning against the door to Fitz's cabin, she dashed the tears from the corners of her eyes and gave a brittle laugh.

Maybe Fitz was just the wrong person to cure her of Knigh—she'd outgrown Fitz and his sexual preferences. Funny, these past six months, she'd put the end of their physical relationship down to his jealousy about *The Song of the Pirate Queen*. But hadn't she also resisted his control in bed around the same time?

Hands raking through her hair, she sighed. If Aedan wasn't off-limits, he would have been a much better choice, but she didn't want to get the poor man killed by Fitz. And did she really want Aedan?

No.

Shut up.

Teeth gritted, she fastened her top button. She'd just have to stay away from Knigh and—

"Vee?"

Blinking, she turned towards the door of her cabin—*former* cabin.

Knigh stared back at her, gaze passing over her fingers on that top button, her undoubtedly messy hair, her chest that still heaved too quickly. "Are you—did he just—"

"No." It burst from her, more a breath than a word. "No, he didn't..." His mind went there first, that Fitz had tried something she didn't want, not that she...

He cocked his head, confusion lining his brow. "Then..."

She swallowed, throat suddenly so tight it was a wonder she could breathe. Saying to him that she'd gone in there to seduce Fitz was impossible. Not that it should matter. It wasn't as though she and Knigh were anything to each other. She could sleep with whoever she wished. So could he.

And yet it felt like it *did* matter.

How could she explain this without him looking at her in disappointment and disgust?

Without hurting him.

Because apparently that was something she cared about now. Oh, gods. This was bad.

Boots clomped down the stairs from the quarterdeck, passing behind Knigh. "I think I know what's happened here." Perry looked from Vice to him and back again. "And I fear it was my fault. Blackwood, could we?" She gestured to his cabin.

He blinked, and the expressionless mask slid into place, driving a dagger of ice into Vice's chest. "Yes, of course." He opened the door and strode inside, not looking at her once.

She grabbed Perry's arm as she passed. "What are you doing?"

Perry raised her eyebrows, green eyes soft. "Fixing your foolish mistake," she murmured. "Will you let me? Or would you prefer to let the man who's made you so cheerful slip away because of your panic at—gods forbid—feeling some sort of emotion for someone?"

It wasn't panic. And she only felt desire for Knigh. That was all. Her jaw clenched. "Depends. What're you going to tell him?"

"The truth."

Not the truth. Anything but that. Stomach flipping, she shook her head. "No, no, that isn't—"

"Relax. I don't mean *all* the truth. Just that I teased you earlier and should've known better because this response was inevitable. What happened in there? How far did—"

"No—we didn't. I planned to. I sat in his lap, he touched me, kissed my neck, but no clothes came off. I didn't even kiss him..." She grimaced, the wrongness creeping across her scalp, a slithering echo of FitzRoy's touch. "I couldn't go through with any of it."

Perry nodded slowly, exhaling. "That's... good... I'll speak to him, pave the way, then you two can talk"—she grabbed Vice's shoulders, grip as strong as when she hauled rope, and shook her until their eyes met—"about your *feelings,* Vice. Understand?"

Her stomach turned, but she nodded anyway. She had no feelings worth talking about. She was fine. She didn't need help, she didn't need anyone.

And yet, she didn't want Knigh to block her out with that empty mask either. Nor was she ready for things between them to be over.

But she didn't have the words to explain. Even in so few sentences, Perry had summed it up far better than she ever could. Maybe she had panicked. Maybe her attraction to Knigh, the unbearable compatibility of their bodies, had just shaken her with its intensity.

"Thank you, Perry," she murmured, gaze dropping.

Perry sighed and squeezed an arm around her. "Oh, Vice, what am I going to do with you?"

"Keep picking up the pieces of the things I break?"

Chuckling, she gently pushed Vice towards the quarterdeck stairs. "Wait up there. Let's see if we can glue this together and get you back into those fine arms of his."

WORDSMITH

Vee paused in the doorway, the sight of her making Knigh's pulse skip as it always did. Her mouth twisted to one side and her gaze was slow to meet his.

Well, Wild Hunt take him if she wasn't *uncertain*. The Pirate Queen, always so bold, so sure, so comfortable and relaxed in herself—and here she stood in his doorway, tentative.

The chair creaked as Perry adjusted her position. She watched Vee with eyebrows raised.

When Perry had first started explaining Vee's behaviour, he'd been sceptical. But as she'd continued, the parts had slotted into place, connecting with other pieces of the puzzle he already had. With the tragic death of her husband. With her bluster and bluff glibness. With the moments of kindness and gentleness he'd seen. With the way she twisted away from certain topics with a joke.

Considering it all, of course Vee kept people away, men especially. Arm's length was safer than holding someone close, leaning on them, only for them to disappear.

It made a horrible kind of sense.

She closed the door behind her but stayed against it as if ready for a swift exit. Her jaw set, solid, and her mouth carved a straight line. Deep creases furrowed her brow.

It was like watching a battle. He cocked his head.

Eventually, she drew a deep breath and met his gaze. "I'm sorry, Knigh," she murmured. "I—I shouldn't have let Perry's teasing affect me. I was stupid to react like that."

He mastered his expression before his eyebrows rose, but—Wild Hunt. Vee, *apologising*. And admitting that she'd been ruffled. She was so close to talking about her feelings—precisely the thing she so often joked to avoid. The thing Perry had confirmed she refused to speak of.

For her, this was a huge step. He wouldn't make her feel even more uncomfortable by showing surprise or by teasing.

He nodded slowly. "I understand." Only thanks to Perry.

It didn't help that Vee was too stubbornly committed to her tough, frivolous façade to admit the truth. How much her husband's death had hurt. How much she feared loss and breaking. How much she shielded herself because of all that.

But yes, he understood.

A slow swallow rippled through her throat. "And, it didn't go—"

"I know what happened—or, really, what *didn't.*" He gave a slight smile he hoped was reassuring.

Much as Perry telling him what had gone on in FitzRoy's cabin had made him grip the edge of his bunk until it groaned, not a great deal had actually happened. Vee had retreated before that.

Even if she hadn't, they weren't beholden to each other. In private, they had one mind-blowing sexual encounter after another, with soft-voiced talks in the dark after. In public they flirted, teased, and even manufactured a few arguments to throw the crew off the scent, eyes smouldering at each other all the while.

But they hadn't discussed what this was between them. They hadn't made any commitment to each other or declaration of feeling or intent.

Realistically, what could they even have? His stomach twisted.

His assignment here was temporary until... Well, under the old plan, it was until Vee was arrested. But that wasn't going to happen anymore. Not that FitzRoy knew yet—telling him required the opportune moment. And there never seemed to be an opportune moment with the prickly FitzRoy. Still, Knigh had written the new report and just needed to send it back to Albion when they stopped at a suitable port.

Under the *new* plan, he wasn't sure how any of it would turn out. It all depended on whether the Admiralty would still give FitzRoy and Bricus their rewards. If they didn't, that could be a problem and an uncertain future for *The Morrigan*.

If they did, Knigh would likely be here until the Navy was satisfied the new captain, whoever that was, would continue working under the terms of the letter of marque. Then he'd return to the *Venatrix*, hunting the next pirate bounty, pulling himself back together after the cannon blast that was Vee.

So although seeing her walk out of FitzRoy's cabin had rocked through him like a punch in the gut, he had no right to expect nor ask for anything more than they'd already given each other. For whatever time they had left, that would have to be enough.

Let this be a pleasant break in his usual work—a hospitable island with laughter and pleasure and moments of welcome rest in her bright sun, before returning to the sea and its endless battles and the constant need to maintain control over his slumbering rage.

"Even if"—he cleared his throat—"more had happened, I'd

have no right to be angry with you. It's not as though we're married or engaged."

An odd strangled half-laugh burst from her and she covered her mouth. Such a strange gesture for her when she so often spoke her mind.

Perry glanced from him to Vee and back again. "So, am I safe to leave you two to talk alone? No more good counsel needed?"

They both scoffed, the tension in the room whooshing out with their breaths. "No," he said, meeting Vee's gaze, which was dark and unreadable today. "I think we have it from here."

Lips sucked in, she nodded. "Thank you, Perry."

"Excellent. I do love—er—well, I take a lot of pride in a job well done." She brushed her hands off as if she'd been working lines on deck. "Enjoy your chat"—she opened the door, a waft of air blowing through the room—"then *really* enjoy making up." She flashed a grin as brazen as any of Vee's, then disappeared, closing the door softly in her wake.

He gestured for Vee to sit. Perry's chair was empty now, but with a little luck, she'd choose the space on the bunk beside him. Maybe he shouldn't, but he wanted her close. Her cool hands on his brow, the reassurance of her touch, however temporary that had to be.

She watched him, then her gaze fell to the spot beside him. For once there was no hint of humour in her eyes, edging her lips. "I—I *am* sorry." Brows drawn together, she nodded. "It was a mistake."

Vee. Apologising. Again.

He snorted softly and nodded, smiling. "I know. In case it wasn't clear, you're completely forgiven—not that you wronged me. As I said"—he lifted his hands, palms towards her—"no right. No demands."

A sharp sigh blew from her, then the corner of her mouth rose, and she came to sit on the bunk.

Trying to hide his smile, he leant back on his elbows. Perry had said to talk, but what to say? About their *feelings*... Vee did not invite that kind of deep discussion.

And it looked like she wasn't about to start it. Fine. He would.

He cocked his head at her. "So, the great Pirate Queen Vice isn't as tough and unfeeling as she tries to appear."

Vee's shoulders tensed. "I am exactly as tough as I appear." She twisted to look back at him, bristling. "And I don't pretend to be unfeeling, I'm just immune to the silly, *soft* emotions. I feel joy, anger, excitement, humour, and desire very well." She huffed a long breath. "I'm not sure any of the others are worth it."

So she could pick and choose what emotions to feel? That would be a useful trick if it were possible. "What are these *soft* emotions, then?"

Snorting, she tossed her hair and flopped back beside him, jostling the bunk. "Love, sorrow, caring, grief..." She shrugged.

He rolled on his side to face her, propping his head up with hand and elbow. "I wouldn't say love seems very soft... nor grief. And I'd say caring for someone might be one of the fiercest feelings going." Wasn't that what had driven him to disobey orders and risk losing control by boarding the *Covadonga*?

A sardonic smile twisted her mouth as she stared at the sea-blue drapes over the bunk. "And how many times have you been in love, exactly?"

He cleared his throat. "Much as I'm ashamed to admit it, the Navy has left me little time to pursue that particular emotion."

Her chest rose and fell quickly. "Then, as someone who was once stupid enough to believe herself in love, allow me to educate you." Her tone was light like she was discussing how to cheat at cards or what was cooking in the galley. But her gaze was dark, heavy, like the sea before a storm. "Love is weakness. Love makes you soft. Love is a fool's game—it'll only destroy you. Stick to the Navy and other ways to spend your time. Lust, desire, sex—they have all the enjoyment and none of the risk. It's all just bodies."

He opened his mouth but couldn't give a reply. He couldn't refute it because he'd never experienced it. It wasn't as though he could hold up Mother and Father as an exemplar of romantic bliss.

Father. He gritted his teeth against a hot wave blasting over him. He hadn't thought of the man in days.

Vee swallowed then smiled brightly. "I avoid attachment for similar reasons."

Oh, Vee. What an absurd lie. One he could refute. "You seem very attached to Perry."

"Perry's an exception. I... I'd miss her if she went away."

"And what about me?" He hadn't meant to say it, but at least the words had the good grace to come out quietly. He did want to know, though. Perry had said Vee cared for him, that was the reason for her response. Was she right?

A war waged on Vee's face. A frown, then flared nostrils, then her lips pursed. Her eyes widened for a moment, perhaps in fear.

Guilt twisted in his belly. Maybe he shouldn't have asked.

Her hand slid across the sheets and her fingers interlocked with his, the grip as sure as someone hauling a man who'd fallen overboard back on deck.

He bit back a sigh at her cool touch. If he made a sound, he might break this spell upon her that edged so close to honesty, scant inches from vulnerability.

"That day," she whispered, barely above a breath, "at the reef..."

His chest tightened. When they'd dived to see the whale shark and he'd strayed into a powerful current...

Wild Hunt, he'd thought he was for Davy Jones' locker that day. And she'd poured so much of her gift, so much of her energy into bringing him back that she'd barely been able to swim to shore and she was an unnaturally strong swimmer. She'd lain on the beach unconscious, pale, shivering for almost an hour.

Because she'd miss him if he *went away?* He didn't dare voice the question.

Her gaze was still on the drapes.

His ears strained, ready for her to say something more in that quiet breath of a voice.

She inhaled, and he mirrored the action in anticipation.

She blinked, and all the heaviness disappeared from her eyes. Slowly, she smiled. "I'd miss your warmth," she said, voice low and velvety, no longer that tiny secret whisper. She turned his hand and let her finger circle the palm. "You're always *so* warm"—she rolled to face him, only a few inches away, gaze following the motion of her fingertip, thoughtful—"I wonder if it's part of your gift."

And the walls were back up.

He swallowed a sigh of disappointment. For Vee, she'd said a lot. This was the most they'd spoken about feelings in—well, the whole time they'd known each other. And she'd mentioned the reef in that odd, soft moment. It wasn't much of an answer, but maybe it meant she—in her own chipped way—cared for him.

She stroked his knuckles, pulling them to her lips. "And, these hands," she said against his skin, the air tickling, tingling. "I'd be sad to see them go." Eyes on him, she kissed each finger.

His body hummed with the low vibration of her words, the way her touches skimmed, teasing. He breathed a soft laugh and raised his eyebrows to ask what else she'd miss.

Her thumb rasped against the stubble on his jawline, making

him blink and draw a hitching breath. When her fingers whispered into his hair, he shuddered, pulse pounding.

"And I'd miss this really quite breathtaking face," she murmured.

"Hmm?" Now she'd released his hand, he was free to pull her close, press her body against his, her yielding curves and strong muscles such a sweet contradiction.

"Oh yes." She nodded, hand trailing down his neck, over his shoulder, and planing across his chest, leaving fire in its wake, "and this glorious body." Her hand slipped to his back, leaving nothing between them but thin layers of shirts and breeches.

Eyes dark, she smiled lazily, but her chest heaved against his, and her breaths fanned across his face, heavy and full. "And, of course, this mouth."

With the barest tilt, her lips feathered against his and it took every inch of his self-control not to surge against her but to wait.

"How could I forget?" Her words brushed against his sensitive skin, streaking sparks through him, stoking fire low in his belly.

It wasn't an explicit admission of how much she cared, but her touch on each part of him and her praise felt like playful worship. The kind of worship on Calan Mai's feast days, with its floral crowns and the chasing dance through the forest at night, full of laughter and lovers and quiet clearings. She didn't *say* the exact words, but her attention said he was special all the same.

At last, she angled her mouth to his in a thorough, delving kiss that made him groan and loop his other arm around her, wringing out every inch of contact he possibly could. Legs, stomachs, chests, arms, hands, mouths, tongues... It still wasn't enough.

He grabbed her thigh, pulling it around his hips, bringing her deliciously against him.

She made a soft sound into his mouth, following his momentum and rolling on top, hands planted on his chest, fingers flexed against him. Panting, she drew away an inch. "And yes, that tongue"—she bit her lip, gaze flicking to his mouth—"so very skilful. It would be a shame if that went anywhere."

Pride glowed through him. She certainly did enjoy his tongue. He'd given her a pillow to scream the evidence of that into on several occasions.

Grinning, he canted his head. "I didn't realise you thought I was such a great wordsmith."

She chuckled and lowered herself against him, the gentle pressure teasing. "That wasn't the angle I was going for."

"Ah"—he grabbed her rear and wrenched her hard against him, his breath catching—"then—then it's my singing?"

Cheeks a glorious shade of pink, more hot setting sun than delicate rose, she shook her head. "No, no, no." With each word she ground against him, wrenching a groan from his throat. "I meant—"

"I know *exactly* what you meant." He chuckled against her lips before the kiss grew urgent, and he gripped her backside, flipping their positions. With a last, hard drive against her—he'd finish *that* later—he yanked her hips to the edge of the bunk and knelt. "Allow me to demonstrate."

With a shaky laugh, she watched him trail kisses down her body, his gaze staying upon hers, even as he pulled off her boots and breeches and palmed her thighs apart. As he paused there, her chest heaved, mouth open in a way that made him want to lose himself against it.

"Now," he murmured, gaze still locked on hers, the scent of her filling his breaths, "I believe it was something along these lines..."

NASSAU NOW, NASSAU THEN

It was almost seven weeks since they'd last been in Nassau, but it might as well have been a lifetime. Perhaps several. Hadn't Knigh sworn off the temptation of Vee that day in the bookshop? And yet here they were, walking through the streets side-by-side, having thoroughly succumbed.

They took the same route as last time, snaking up towards the grocer's first. Again, he wore her tricorn hat and civilian clothes. He hadn't worn his uniform in weeks.

He wanted to offer his arm and walk the town with her hand tucked in the crook of his elbow, but she kept several inches between them, veering away every time he came closer. The way she lifted her chin and strode with such purpose didn't welcome interference from anyone else—him included.

This morning, he'd woken to find her still in his bunk where usually she crept out in the night, returning to the hammock she'd slung in Perry's cabin.

Face peaceful, she'd cuddled against him, arm draped over his waist. He hadn't had the heart to wake or move her, so he'd lain there until a sudden deeper breath, and the fluttering of her eyelids said she was awake. In that first moment, she'd burrowed against him with a soft sound of contentment—all gentle, affectionate, no note of seduction in her movements.

Then her eyes had sprung open, and she'd frozen. With a muttered oath, she'd stared at the bright light spilling through the stern windows and had rolled away and dressed, swearing about the time.

She'd been tetchy ever since.

Naturally, she was concerned she might have been spotted leaving his cabin. Someone must've worked out what was going on, but no one had said anything, except Perry. Aedan had taken to giving Knigh a broad grin whenever they were near Vee, but that was all. He understood the possible danger from FitzRoy well enough to keep quiet.

And even if word *had* reached FitzRoy, he was either past caring or was sensible enough to not threaten the Queen's representative.

That was still one problem he needed to deal with. He'd prepared a report to send back to the Admiralty, recommending they make Vee a privateer rather than arrest her. That was a start, and the contact who'd delivered FitzRoy's original message was here in Nassau, ready to take the report back to Albion. The contact was due to leave first thing in the morning. They were scheduled to arrive in Albion before *The Morrigan*, in plenty of time to warn the Admiralty to be ready.

But Knigh still hadn't had the talk with FitzRoy. There was no more delaying it—they'd be leaving for Albion within the week, once they'd stocked up for the voyage. He had to speak to the man tonight.

He sighed. That would be fun.

Vee glanced over at him. "Something wrong?"

Shaking his head, he scoffed. She was the one who'd spent the morning festering on the idea of her crewmates knowing she'd spent the night in his cabin. "Not with me, no, but you've been as tetchy as a sabrecat with toothache."

She blinked, gaze drifting away. "Hmm, I suppose I have, haven't I?"

"Just a touch."

Laughing, she shook her head and nudged him with her elbow. "Sometimes I think I preferred it when you were Mr Control and didn't make any jokes."

"I can bring him back if you like? Of course, he doesn't tend to entertain women in his cabin—that's far too wanton behaviour."

Her mouth twisted to one side and she cocked her head, narrowed eyes looking up thoughtfully. "Hmm... On second thoughts, I think I can put up with your sarcasm, even when it is at my expense." She grinned and closed the gap she'd kept between them, her arm against his as they strolled on.

Making her laugh at herself—and at him—seemed to have done the trick, because by the time they reached the grocer's they were chatting, teasing, flirting, laughing as usual, her easy smile back in place.

They went from shop to shop, stocking *The Morrigan* ready for the voyage back to Albion, as well as picking up personal items at a much-reduced rate for the crew. Again, the storekeeps had warm welcomes for them both—hugs for Vee and shoulder-slapping handshakes for Knigh when they recognised him from last time.

"Back again," the brawny timber merchant near the edge of town said when they walked in. Once he'd given the usual greeting, wrapping Vee in a bear-hug, he looked from her to Knigh and back again. "You know what, Vice? I always secretly thought you'd end up with me, but"—he gave an exaggerated shake of his head, lifting one shoulder—"I don't mind losing out when the two of you make such a bloody handsome couple."

Knigh scoffed, but the words spread warmth through him. His gaze slid to Vee.

Face frozen in a wide-eyed look, she took a step back. Blinking as if waking, she shook her head and snorted. "We're not—"

"No," Knigh said softly, "we're not." This was and could only ever be a temporary arrangement.

The merchant just laughed, folding his arms. "Don't look at me like that—I might not be fae-touched, but I can see when two people are shagging just as clearly as if it was a gift."

"Heh, well"—Vee planted her hands on her hips—"a broken gift, perhaps. Besides, *shagging* doesn't make a couple now, does it?"

Knigh's heart clenched, but he kept his face still. Was that all this was? But, no, it was weeks ago that she'd fled to FitzRoy's cabin and Perry had explained Vee's feelings. She'd even, in her own way, admitted to caring for him. Hells, she'd risked her life to save his.

He took a slow breath. She cared, she just wasn't about to advertise it to a Nassau timber merchant when she couldn't even say it out loud. After all, didn't she have a reputation to maintain?

The merchant's dark eyes narrowed, passing from her to Knigh again, the look making Knigh shift—far too penetrating. "If that was all I saw, then no, but you—"

"But we," she said, smile bright, eyes sharp, "are here to do business." Her hand thudded on the merchant's table, leaving a crinkled list of supplies behind.

They did just that, negotiating yet another rate favourable to *The Morrigan*. Still, Vee's usual ease carried a stiffness that was so out of place on her, it made Knigh ache. Excellent, just as he'd managed to cheer her up, this timber merchant had sent her closed and prickly again.

When they left, she squinted at the sky and backed away, steps crunching on the sand-strewn cobbles. "I—I have some private business to attend to." With a brittle smile, she nodded. "I'll see you later."

Knigh opened his mouth to argue, but her back was already turned, long legs carrying her away. What use would it do, anyway? He sighed and shook his head. Perhaps it was best to leave her alone for a while, anyway.

Rubbing the back of his neck, he watched her disappear around a corner. Frustrating woman.

Still, he could use this as a chance to explore Nassau for himself, discover some corner her usual route didn't cover. He set off in the opposite direction, letting his feet wander where they wished.

As his first visit had suggested, Nassau was a lot like the other trading towns settlers had built in the parcels of lands the local nations had granted. Perhaps a few more taverns and brothels than Port Royal or maybe it was that these were open about their trades rather than hiding behind more respectable façades.

In his wanderings, an earring in a shop window caught his eye. The earring's front was shaped like a dagger hilt and decorated with twinkling black gems. The back had been crafted to look like a blade. When worn, it would look as though a tiny dagger had been plunged through the earlobe.

I'll cut out your tongue with your own dagger.

He chuckled. How could he walk past that? No, just like he couldn't resist her, he couldn't resist this. It would suit her beautifully, the silver shining bright against her dark hair. Within minutes, he emerged from the shop, the dagger earring in his breast pocket.

As the day wore on, the sun beat down more and more mercilessly making him grateful for Vee's tricorn hat shielding his eyes. And when an astonishingly buxom woman leant from a window, beckoning him closer, he was also thankful for it as a tool to duck behind.

For the past couple of years, ever since he'd lost control and hurt Billy, he'd strived to avoid giving in to any emotion. He'd shouldered the constant fear it would unleash all his feelings in one terrible tidal wave. Now he'd well and truly caved beneath the weight of his terrible, wonderful attraction to Vee and yet...

He glanced back at the *professional*, and she smiled. With blond hair and pale pinkish skin, she was indeed pretty, but his body gave no response. Not even the slightest thrum of temptation.

A happy huff burst from his mouth, and he carried on his way.

He'd let his gentler, hungrier emotions for Vee show. He'd even acted upon them, and yet they hadn't consumed him with unbridled lust or opened the door for other, darker feelings to destroy him.

That woman held no allure for him whatsoever for one simple reason.

She wasn't Vee.

Which was glorious. But also awful.

A temporary arrangement.

Gaze on the floor, his mouth twisted. Maybe that was what she'd realised, too, when she'd reacted to the timber merchant's teasing. They couldn't *be* a couple because soon enough they'd be on separate ships, perhaps even on opposite sides of the ocean depending on where his next assignment sent him. Although he'd cut a swathe through the pirates of Arawaké over the past couple of years, they marauded the waters beyond this scattering of tropical islands, and he could be sent anywhere in the world to hunt them.

He sighed and when he looked up, he found himself outside Waters' bookshop. His subconscious must have led him here, seeking Vee. It wouldn't hurt to have a quick look.

The bell rang bright as the bells of the fair folk back in Albion when they rode past in the night, unseen, but heard.

Waters looked up, blinking. "Ah, Knigh, wasn't it?" He smiled, blue eyes twinkling. "Well, come in then, no need to hover at the door."

Knigh cleared his throat and obeyed, nodding as he entered. "Mr Waters."

The older man chuckled. "Just Waters—no Mr required in Nassau, young man."

"But didn't I hear you call someone Mr Vane last time I was here?"

Waters' eyes widened. "Observant fellow, aren't you? Well, Mr Vane is something of an exception. An exception I'd rather stay on the right side of. So, yes, he's *Mr* Vane, at least to the likes of me." His angled his head, a sardonic smile quirking his mouth.

Knigh glanced along the lines of bookcases as he approached the counter. Good, they were the only two here, so he was free to ask. "You protected Vee from him that day, though, didn't you?"

Eyes narrowing, Waters gave a deep sigh. "A little *too* observant, it seems."

"I'd apologise if I felt sorry about it." Knigh lifted one shoulder in a half-shrug.

Waters chuckled, shaking his head. "You almost sound like Vice." He glanced at the door. "Is she not with you?"

"No. I was hoping I might find her here, truth be told."

"As you can see"—Waters lifted his hand, indicating their only company was leather and paper—"no Vice here—save what's in some of the spicier books." He gave a wink. "I haven't seen her today—I only knew *The Morrigan* had returned when I saw you, in fact. Assuming you're still with them?"

Knigh nodded.

"Of course you are." Waters' eyebrows rose, and his eyes glinted above a warm smile. "Speaking of our favourite Pirate Queen..."

He reached under the counter, and Knigh couldn't help but tense thanks to all the years of combat training. But when he only produced a book bound in salt-stained blue leather, Knigh released the tension with a breath.

"This came to me some time ago with a large shipment of old books from"—he waved his hand—"*somewhere* on the mainland. I don't ask too many questions."

No doubt because his stock was mostly stolen from ships or towns or looted from wrecks. "Understandable."

"I've only just had the chance to go through them all, and I found this." He slid the book over the counter.

Knigh ran his fingers over the embossed shape of a dragon picked out in copper leaf, gleaming fire-bright like the sheathed hull of the *Venatrix*.

"I can't make head nor tail of the contents," Waters went on, "but I know she likes anything dragon-related thanks to her love of *el Draco,* so I thought I'd better keep it aside for her."

El Draco—that was what the Hesperians had called Ser Francis Drake. There were a few books about him on the shelves in her cabin. "Her 'love' of Drake?"

"As long as I've known her—anything I have on Drake, she buys."

Knigh scoffed. "Because of the treasure."

Waters' brow furrowed, and his fingers splayed over the countertop as he looked at the book. "I don't think it's just that.

Someone after that would be interested in the biographies and the mad theories scrawled by men convinced they know the key to finding his buried silver. But she buys the adventure stories, the epic poems written about his journeys, and books of his own poetry with just as much enthusiasm as the research material."

He tilted his head, gaze returning to Knigh. "Lady Vice might be a terror on the seas, a wily trickster, and, so I hear, a wanton temptress"—he snorted—"but she loves a ripping yarn." He cleared his throat and bent closer, a conspiratorial edge to his smile. "I think that's what brought her to the pirate life, you know."

To avoid those clear blue eyes, Knigh flicked through the book. Hand-written, not printed. Yellowed pages—maybe vellum rather than rag paper. Lords and Ladies, this was *old*. And not Albionic. The symbols... a few looked familiar. Ancient Hellenic? No wonder Waters couldn't make sense of it.

It wasn't a language the Navy considered necessary even for officers, so he'd never learned, but some of the alphabet was the same as the modern form and occasionally used in inscriptions. These pages could be a nonsensical arrangement of letters for all he knew. But—no, there was something about the repetition of the symbols, the split of paragraphs that made it feel like it just might make sense if one only had the codex or language to decipher it.

Just like Vee. He bit back a laugh. Lured to the sea by too many tales of pirates and adventures? It sounded just as likely as any other reason he could think of for her to be here. Didn't she have a wall full of books in her cabin? And didn't she tell stories for the crew? She'd even said she didn't want to deprive those who couldn't read of the chance to hear great tales. The Pirate Queen they sang of, whom the Navy feared, had a soft spot for gripping yarns. Who'd have thought?

Treasure aside, Drake was certainly an exciting figure. Perhaps Vee's interest in him pre-dated her time on *The Morrigan* with FitzRoy. Maybe it was a glimpse of the young woman she'd been before...

"'It isn't that life ashore is distasteful to me,'" Waters intoned, chin lifted as if he were an actor on the stage, "'but life at sea is better.'"

Knigh blinked. "Pardon?"

"Drake's own words, I believe, quoted to me by an eighteen-year-old Vice." He chuckled, eyes warm. "So, you see, she's always been fascinated by the fellow."

Shaking his head, Knigh flipped the book shut. "Enough of your sales pitch, Waters. I can see why Vee curses you for the amount of money she spends here. How much for the book?"

Maybe it would cheer Vee up.

This thing between them, yes it was only temporary, but they could still enjoy it while it was there. He would undoubtedly treasure it, just as he'd treasure the memory of the coral reef and swimming so close to that whale shark.

Knowing she had this and the earring, just small gifts from him, might make it feel like there was still some connection threaded between them like a course plotted on a chart. No matter how many miles of ocean separated them.

LONG LIVE THE QUEEN

Vice folded her arms, staring at the rocking ceiling above her head. Perry was ashore, so she had the room to herself for a while. And it was much-needed after what Fitz had just told her.

After she'd left Knigh, she'd finished her errands and come back to find Fitz alone. When she'd first entered his cabin, he'd raised one eyebrow, an amused glint in his eye like he expected her to try to seduce him again.

When she'd asked him about the box from the wreck, his expression had closed. "I can't tell you yet," he'd said softly. "If Blackwood finds out what it is, it'll belong to the Queen." He'd inclined his head meaningfully. "And you and I both know we've been looking for *this* since long before he arrived with Her Majesty's letter of marque."

Her stomach had dipped. A clue to Drake's treasure. It had to be.

Even now, lying in her hammock, that was the only conclusion she could draw. At last, after all these years, they had a clue.

In FitzRoy's cabin, her blood had bubbled with questions until he'd gone on. "Once we've docked in Albion and Blackwood's off the ship, it'll be safe to tell you, and we can go after the *real* prize. But until then, I can't risk any word escaping. You understand, don't you?"

She'd nodded, but only five words had really registered: *once Blackwood's off the ship*. He was leaving when they returned to Albion.

And he hadn't said anything.

Her stomach twisted like someone wringing out their washing.

He was *leaving.*

Of course he was. She should've known. Hells, she *had* known. Hadn't she told herself he was dangerous precisely because he would let her down at some point?

Everyone did. It was inevitable.

Papa. Evered. Even Kat—she'd married and left young Avice with Papa and no buffer against his anger. Mama couldn't help—she'd had her own struggles.

Don't submit. Don't end up like me.

She'd stood up to him that one night. That one time.

And Vice still hadn't repaid her.

She doubled over, clutching her stomach as the twisting tightened to sharp pain.

Eyes screwed shut, she breathed through it. This wasn't about Mama. This wasn't about broken promises. This wasn't about Avice.

She was Vice. She was here on *The Morrigan*. And she was dealing with a troublesome pirate hunter.

She shoved everything else into a chest she kept so far down, it might as well have been at the bottom of the ocean, and slammed the lid shut.

With a long exhale, she straightened.

Knighton Blackwood. He was leaving. And he hadn't told her.

Frowning, she squeezed her arms. Not that she cared, but he clearly thought she'd—what? That she'd *break* at the knowledge he was leaving *The Morrigan* in five or six weeks' time?

"Don't flatter yourself, Blackwood," she muttered.

He was clearly so concerned at her reaction, he'd put off telling her. How pathetic did he think she was?

She ground her teeth, jaw aching.

They'd always known this was just a fling. That's all she wanted, all she needed—a physical thing to fulfil a purely physical need. Well, he'd delivered.

And now she was done.

It was for the best. A clean break, keeping him at arm's length where he should've been all along. Where he'd be no danger to her.

He hadn't told her. Hadn't mentioned it, not even in passing. He clearly thought himself *such* a danger to her.

Well she'd prove him wrong.

And she'd gladly spare him a tearful farewell at the docks like some good little Navy wife left at home. Is that what he was expecting?

Scoffing, she shook her head, arms going rigid at the thought and sending the hammock swinging wildly.

Idiot.

She'd do it before they left Nassau. That gave her a good few days, then she'd tell him *thank you* and *goodbye* and wish him well for the rest of the trip, but he could find someone else to warm his bunk, and she wouldn't give a damn.

Her throat tightened.

No, she wouldn't give a solitary damn.

A knock rapped at the door—*rap rap-rap*. Too quiet for most of the crew. Too rhythmic for the rest. Too uniform to be anyone other than—

"Vee?" Knigh's voice.

Of course. Speak of the very devil.

She took a long breath and swung from her hammock, landing lightly. Shoulders square, she yanked the door open.

Deciding she was ending whatever it was between them and facing the full force of Knighton Blackwood's handsome face, crooked smile, and towering physique were two very different things.

Breath stuck in her throat, she backed away, letting him in. She hadn't intended to let him over the threshold and yet...

Here he was, slipping in, one hand half-behind his back, the door closing after him. His presence was far too much for this cabin that was considerably smaller than her own, crowding the space with his body and clean scent. Crowding her mind, as well.

She backed away until she hit the wall, arms closed across her body.

Perhaps one last time wouldn't hurt.

"Did you attend to all your business?" He smiled, head tilting. The hand behind his back shifted, too, revealing a brown paper parcel.

Oh gods, had he bought her a present? What? To soften the blow of his leaving? Was he planning to tell her now?

"Vee?" He took a step closer, now within arm's reach.

"What?"

"You said you had—"

"Oh, yes, er, that. Right." She cleared her throat, nodded. "All dealt with."

If he thought he could come in here and break things off with a gift... What, did he think it best to catch her in private, so she could cry quietly into his arms? So she wouldn't make a scene?

The corner of her mouth twitched at how bloody ridiculous an idea that was. He could tell her in front of the whole damn crew for all she cared—he'd get no response from her but a shrug and a *nice while it lasted.*

She'd save him the job. And the present.

Wild Hunt, what did he think she was, a debutant he'd deflowered who needed a pretty keepsake to salve her wounded heart?

Lifting her chin, she gave him a tight smile. "Look, Knigh, we need to—"

The door burst open. "Vice," Perry said from the doorway, blinking at Knigh. "Ah, Blackwood, too... Er..." She peered past him to Vice, face screwing up. "Sorry to interrupt, I—"

"It's *your* cabin."

"Nothing to interrupt," Knigh said, shuffling to the side, that parcel behind his back again.

Perry still hovered in the doorway. "Have you heard the news?"

Knigh's brows rose. "News?"

"The Queen is dead."

Vice's mouth dropped open, a chill in her bones. The Queen...

A lifetime ago, little Avice had climbed an oak tree, avoiding preparations for the Queen's arrival at her family estate. The lone red-haired woman walking through the grounds had spotted her, laughed at her avoidance of 'the dull business going on indoors'. She'd asked the girl about her love of Drake and listened to how she'd rather be an explorer and adventurer like him than a lady forced to wear dresses and welcome the Queen. The lady had gifted the girl a pin—a drake like Ser Francis's sigil—and told her that it had been given to her ancestor by the man himself. Then she'd left with a reminder that everyone had to do their duty eventually.

And when little Avice Ferrers had been caught and scrubbed clean, dressed and presented to the Queen, she'd found herself face to face with that new friend.

Now she was gone. And she'd never known Avice Ferrers, who'd remained her friend, who'd met Evered Lyons at *her* Calan Mai celebrations, was still alive and had always stayed loyal. Or that she'd even worn the jewelled drake pin every single day.

Everyone leaves.

Vice's heart squeezed even as she murmured the words, "Long live the Queen." Knigh said it too, and they all bowed their heads.

"Well, I need to tell the rest of the crew." Perry nodded with a sad smile and closed the door.

Long live Queen Elizabeth V. No more Elizabeth IV.

"What's that?" Knigh caught her hand, and she flinched.

"What?" She blinked, fingertips lifting from the pin where it was hidden under her collar.

His brow creased, staring at it. "That pin—where did you get it?"

Avice Ferrers. A stupid little girl. On one level, she knew she shouldn't be annoyed. The Queen thought her young friend Avice had died three years ago and the Queen's death was no more an abandonment of that girl than the winter was an abandonment by the sun. And yet...

Her heart squeezed again. Another friend, another ally gone, albeit one from years ago. The Queen was the whole reason she'd even met Evered, it was at her Calan Mai celebrations that he'd crowned Avice his May Queen.

One more tether to her old life broke.

The loose ends snapped back in a sharp reminder. She was Vice. She was strong. She didn't need the Queen or Evered or Kat or any of them, and she didn't need to be remembered.

Heat prickled across her scalp and down her neck. Good

riddance to Avice Ferrers. She deserved to be forgotten, fool that she'd been.

"I got it from a girl who died a long time ago," she muttered, arms folding. Let him get a good look at the pin—maybe he recognised it after all these years.

She'd shown it to him one of those few times they'd met as children. In the face of his stand-offish arrogance, she'd been competitive, determined to prove herself worth speaking to, not the useless lady he so clearly thought she was. After all, *she* had a token from *the Queen herself.*

She'd even said it with a little toss of her head. Idiot girl.

Ha, maybe he even wondered about his former betrothed. Lords, did he mourn her? Maybe *he* was the fool. He'd barely known the girl and the few times they'd met, she'd been quite mean to him. The last time, she'd challenged him to swim out to the island in the middle of their lake. When he'd refused, she'd gone without him and spent the day exploring it alone. He'd run back to his parents.

Why would he mourn such a foolish girl?

"Died..." His gaze fell away, and he gave a soft sigh.

Good, he believed it. No danger of anyone coming to look for her.

Eventually, he nodded, brow creased. "What happened to her?"

She clenched her jaw and lifted her chin. If he was that concerned about some long-dead girl who'd left him, then fine. She'd dissuade him of any such idiocy *and* get rid of him. This would shove him far, far away.

Two birds. One stone. Genius.

She tossed her head, just like that day she'd shown him the pin. "I killed her."

STAY THE COURSE

"I killed her."

Knigh's breath, his blood, the room stilled.

She stared at him, level, unruffled.

I killed her.

His chest squeezed as if his heart suddenly remembered how to work and heaved into life.

Vee—*Vice* had killed Lady Avice Ferrers. And she admitted it so calmly.

Her face was smooth, composed, just a slight rise of her chin, challenging.

She had no sorrow, no remorse, no feeling of common decency at all.

Lady Avice had been a little childish, so sure of her own superiority compared to him, perhaps. And he hadn't loved her, no, but she'd also been vivacious, burning bright with excitement about the world. What was it she'd said when she'd dared him to swim across the lake with her? A verse from an old poem:

Disturb us, Ladies, to dare more boldly,
To venture on wilder seas
Where storms will show your mastery;
Where losing sight of land,
We shall find the stars.

And Vee had murdered someone that full of life. An eighteen-year-old girl. An *innocent.*

But wasn't that precisely the kind of behaviour he should've expected from the notorious Lady Vice?

Wild Hunt, he'd forgotten who she was.

His blood ran cold as Midwinter snow.

What a fool. A complete and utter fool, taken in by a beautiful face and that relaxed charm of hers.

As his stomach spasmed, threatening bile at the back of his throat, he fought to keep his face still. He'd been sleeping with not just a criminal and pirate, but a *murderer*. He'd disobeyed orders. He'd developed *feelings* for her. Troublesome feelings.

His traitorous body had led him on this course. He should have listened to his head, to the Navy and their black and white reports. Lords, even Mercia had warned him. *Don't let her charms distract you from your duty.*

It was a wretched day when the Duke of Mercia proved to have better insight than he'd displayed.

He should have known.

But, no, he'd caved to his feelings, believing it safe, and this is what it had brought him. He'd let emotion cloud his already poor judgement. His damn gut had led him so very wrong.

Hadn't he known he was broken? Of course, the woman he'd developed feelings for would turn out to be the one who'd murdered his former betrothed! It was as if the gods conspired to prove to him just how little he could trust himself.

He shook his head. Nothing could feel so right and actually *be* right. He always trusted the wrong people—Father, Mercia, Vice.

And most of all, himself.

He should have known.

Fingers twitching against the wrapped book and earring, making the brown paper scrunch, he drew a long, ragged breath. "I need to..."

"Yes," she said, voice colder than a January wind in Albion.

But his feet didn't carry him to the door. Surely, she had to feel something. He frowned, asking her. Maybe he was mistaken. Maybe he'd misunderstood. Maybe there was an explanation.

Vee wouldn't kill an innocent. Surely.

Her jaw knotted, and she swallowed, throat constricting a long while as if the action was difficult. She drew a quick breath.

Here it was—the explanation. The justification. Maybe it had been an accident, or she'd had no choice or Avice had attacked her or—

"What's that?" Eyes narrow, she nodded at the brown paper parcel in his hand.

"Don't you—"

Her eyebrows rose, the look almost bored.

His heart roared in his ears, pulse heavy. "You killed an innocent girl."

She exhaled through her nose, a parent losing patience with an irritating child. "That's what I said, isn't it?"

He stared at her, waiting, waiting, waiting.

But she gave no explanation, no defence, no side of the story that showed why she was Vee, the heroic Pirate Queen, and not the villain the Navy had sent him to hunt.

Throat so tight he could have choked, he swallowed and

straightened his back. Every inch of steel clapped back into place, cladding against feeling, against acting on it, against *her.*

Face smooth as a death mask, he lifted his chin. "Just something I picked up in Nassau."

Her shoulders squared, and she cocked her head. "For yourself?"

"Yes."

She nodded once, the gesture so final it snapped shut the padlock upon his steel hull. "Good."

"Excuse me," he muttered and strode from the room, steps far calmer than the stuttering pace of his heart.

Lords and Ladies, gods, Wild Hunt—all of them take him because he'd been a damned fool.

His hands shook, fire licking through his veins as he approached the companionway, the world a blur of doors and timber and the dark of belowdecks. He threw open the hatch, ran upstairs, and gasped air that seared his lungs with its freshness and salt tang.

The sun slanted through him, tipping the world, sending his stomach roiling and bile burning the back of his throat. He ran for the side and vomited, belly spasming, knuckles cracking on the rail.

She'd deceived him. With that easy smile, that sharp tongue, that seductive body, she'd made him believe...

He heaved again, sweat chilling his brow, his back, his arms.

It had been a trick at the Governor's ball and at Kayracou Port when she'd sabotaged his sails and again when she'd hidden on the *Veritas* and caught him by surprise.

It had *all* been a trick. Their sordid relationship included.

And he'd been so ready to believe that maybe he could trust himself, that he could trust anyone, that he wasn't broken. That maybe giving into feeling, just once, wouldn't be so bad. That relaxing might be better than the constant vigilance, the rigidity, the control he'd lived by these past two years.

Wrong on all counts.

So very wrong.

He swallowed the bitterness.

Well, she wasn't the only one with a trick up her sleeve.

Once he'd discovered the kind of person Mercia really was, he'd had no power to bring him to justice—a queen's son was untouchable, it seemed.

But *she* wasn't.

And hadn't it always been the plan?

Fool that he was, he'd stopped carrying her warrant weeks ago, but he still had it. Arresting her was the right thing to do. The warrant said so in black and white. True, the law might not be perfect, but it was made by better men than him.

Hands running over his face, he nodded. He would go to FitzRoy and Bricus, confirm their scheme, then send a message back to Albion. That swift ship was leaving on the morning's tide. Instead of the report asking them to grant Vice a genuine letter of marque and a vessel, he'd write a new report alerting the Admiralty to their departure date and to expect their arrival in Portsmouth approximately five to six weeks later.

He drew a long breath, fingers running through his hair, pushing it off his face. Yes, they'd be ready to capture her as soon as *The Morrigan* docked.

No chance to escape.

No more tricks.

Justice had come for Lady Vice at last, and he'd be the one to deliver it.

ALBION BOUND

Almost a week later, *The Morrigan* and the *Covadonga* were loaded with supplies, ready to set sail for Albion. Vice paced the deck, excitement buzzing through her veins.

Knigh had left her the hells alone after their talk in Perry's cabin. It had certainly been a clean break. So clean that Vice had spent the past few days carousing with her team, either drunk or hungover, both helping her to forget just how clean a break they'd made, just how empty her hammock was.

Excitement, not emptiness—that didn't matter. What mattered was Fitz, about to announce who'd take the *Covadonga* back to Albion under her captaincy. Life was pretty damn fantastic.

Even better, once she had the *Covadonga's* helm, she'd be far away from Knigh. She wouldn't have to see his mask-blank face and rigid shoulders on her deck or suffer his judgemental stares whenever they found themselves on the same part of the ship.

Then things would be just perfect.

Cheeks stiff, she smiled and pulled her crossed arms tighter across herself.

Just perfect.

She glanced over at the *Covadonga* where hands checked the sails and lines but with no direction. Soon it would be hers. And once she'd delivered the silver in its hold, the new Queen would undoubtedly grant her its captaincy on a permanent basis. That's what they'd done for Cress Newport when he'd taken in the *Jackdaw* and gifted its contents to the Crown.

The door to FitzRoy's cabin crept open.

Here we go. He was going to call her in, brief her on what crew she could take, and—

Perry walked out, scanning the deck. Her face creased when she spotted Vice.

Ah, Fitz had asked Perry to keep an eye on her. Not exactly surprising and she *wanted* Perry on her crew, so that had worked out well.

Grinning, Vice sidled up to Perry and caught her arm. "So, is he going to make a big announcement, or does he just want me to go in there and—"

"Vice," Perry said softly, gaze slipping away, "maybe we should go to—"

Fitz appeared at the door, mouth flat. "Peregrina," he barked, "you forgot your crew list." He thrust a piece of paper at her.

Vice blinked. *"Your crew..."* He was looking at Perry, not at her. Her stomach tightened into a ball of hopelessly knotted line.

No, he was just giving Perry the list, as she'd be Vice's quartermaster. He'd come out here to tell everyone that Vice was the *Covadonga's* new captain. She swallowed and smiled, cheeks burning.

His gaze paused on her for a second before he returned to his cabin, slamming the door after.

"Vice," Perry murmured, clutching her sleeve, "I'm sorry, I—that's what I was trying to tell you. I tried to argue with him, but you know it's useless. When he's made up his mind, it's made."

Vice tore her gaze from FitzRoy's cabin door. *Tried to argue... made up his mind...* This didn't make sense.

Perry was staring up at her, a wince wrinkling around her eyes. "It's only temporary until we get to Albion. I'm not a proper captain."

Throat closing, Vice jerked away a step. *Not a proper captain.* Well, she wasn't any kind of captain at all—proper or not. He'd made Perry captain of the *Covadonga*. She shook her head, skin on fire, pulse pounding. He'd promised.

She'd spent the past three years learning everything there was to know. She'd done everything he'd asked. Risked her life how many times? Saved this ship from storms, from hidden rocks, from larger, better-armed vessels—from ships of the line, damn it. She'd even given him his first and only real clue to Drake's treasure.

"Vice, I'm sorry, I didn't—"

"Congratulations," she bit out and stomped to FitzRoy's door. She would remind him of all that, make him—

The door opened, and Bricus strutted out, a twist to his usual smile. He raised his hands. "Oh! Vice!" He chuckled. "Didn't see you there." The twist vanished, and a different light entered his eyes as he smiled up at her.

Pity?

She gritted her teeth and backed away.

No. She wasn't going to debase herself by begging FitzRoy for the captaincy—for *anything*.

Chest heaving, she turned as Perry finished unfolding the sheet of paper. "Aedan," she called, "Lizzy, Saba, Wynn, Effie..."

The names went on, and Vice listened for hers.

It didn't come.

Her whole team was going with Perry, leaving her on *The Morrigan* with—

Urgh, and there he bloody was.

Knigh, above on the quarterdeck, face unreadable as he watched Perry gathering her new crew to take on the *Covadonga*. Barnacle sat on the rail beside him. Traitor.

Her heart crumpled. For the best. A clean break. All of that, it was true, it was...

In another world, one where people could be relied upon, one where she'd made a different choice, he might've comforted her now. Reminded her that there were other ships in the sea, other chances the become captain. His hand on her waist, his quiet voice in her ear.

But. No. She stiffened. She didn't want that. Because in this world, everyone let you down eventually. Fitz not declaring her captain being just another in a long list of examples. It was only disappointment making her weak, opening up the door she'd closed.

Knigh hated her. That door wasn't only closed—she'd blown it to smithereens.

It was for the best.

Starting with Saba, her boarding team came over, touching her shoulder or grabbing her for a brief hug, muttering how unfair it was, that they were sorry to leave her, that they'd see her soon. At least those were the parts that reached through the blood rushing in her ears.

"Try not to get in too much trouble," Aedan said as he hugged her, but when he pulled away, his grin lacked its usual glint.

"Ha!" She nodded to them, hands landing heavily on her hips. "You lot try not to get killed without me, more like." Joints knotted, she waved them off, achingly conscious of Knigh's gaze on her from the quarterdeck.

Smug bastard. He had to be loving this.

And below him, Fitz emerged from his cabin, arms crossed, a small smile at the corner of his mouth.

Yes. Excellent. She was left here with *two* men she wanted to murder.

Bloody brilliant.

If she made it to Albion without wringing both their necks, it would be a miracle.

THE WELCOME PARTY

"Albion, ho!" The cry broke out across *The Morrigan* as Land's End drifted into view, rocky and green, greeted with cheers.

Vice barely glanced up from her work checking the main shrouds. Without Perry, Saba, or the rest of her boarding team, there wasn't anyone to swap smiles with. Even Barnacle was off somewhere. Probably with *him*.

It was certainly bloody cold enough to be Albion. She hunched into her frock coat, breath misting in the wintry air.

Yes, Albion was beautiful and green. Nothing she'd found in Arawaké was quite a match for the scent of freshly picked hyacinth, dew still beading its waxy petals. But that was a spring flower.

Winter? She did *not* miss that and its damp coldness that seeped into bones and frosted windows.

The *Covadonga* trailed in their wake. No doubt they'd be shouting, too, slapping each other on the shoulders, grinning at surviving another swift crossing of the great ocean.

Perry or Saba would have written letters on behalf of those who couldn't write, ready to send to family and loved ones once they were in port. That was usually Vice's job, but with the crew split across the two ships, she couldn't do it for everyone. Few left on *The Morrigan* had come to her and asked for the favour.

Wrist flicking as she coiled a line, twisting with the rope's lay, she sighed and scanned the rolling green landscape passing to the north as they skirted the coast.

Nearly there. Once they were settled in port, Knigh— no, *Blackwood* would leave, and she'd never have to see him again.

No more of his self-righteous glare or uptight march across deck. He hadn't sung or played guitar in weeks, so at least she'd been spared that.

No more of his low, rumbling laughter or his warm hands on...

Her knuckles ached as she squeezed the rope.

He hated her. And she hated him. Laughter and warm touches were all firmly in the past where they belonged. She didn't want any of it, didn't want any of him, didn't have any regrets.

Dragging in a long breath of burning-cold air, she forced her hands to resume. Coil and twist, coil and twist, coil and twist.

No regrets. Indeed, she deserved a medal, really, since somehow, she'd made it all this way without murdering Knigh or Fitz. That was mostly because she'd taken on extra watches, working long, hard hours.

Lashing, tightening, splicing, coiling, and knotting lines. Checking water barrels. Mending sails. Keeping watch until late into the night. Taking Barnacle down into the hold to hunt rats. Any job that had come up, she'd taken on, pushing her body harder and harder until she could collapse into Perry's bunk and sleep the long and dreamless sleep of the exhausted.

As for her thoughts, well, she'd kept them occupied, too.

Twist, turn, loop, and pass the end through—she tied off the line, nodding to herself.

Perry would have called it stewing, but she called it planning.

She continued it as she blew warmth into her stiff fingers, then went on to the next line and the next.

Fitz had promised her a captaincy. He'd failed to deliver.

Was it any surprise? He'd been jealous of her for almost a year. It was clear he was never going to make good on his promise.

What a fool she'd been. She'd forgotten she didn't *need* him—or anyone—to *give* her anything. She didn't need him to make her captain. She was going to take it.

As soon as they returned to Arawaké, she would find the *Venatrix*, take her, and declare herself captain. She'd already crept aboard once to sabotage and steal—it had been *easy*. She could do it again.

Damn waiting for Fitz to choose her—she chose herself.

She finished the hitch on another line and straightened, stretching her back. "Huh." She frowned astern, rolling her shoulders. The *Covadonga* was peeling off to the north, but *The Morrigan* continued her course east.

Pulling her coat tighter, Vice peered along the coastline they'd been following. Low, grassland with bare trees gave way to a wide, natural harbour. To starboard, they passed Eddystone Lighthouse. Plymouth? Why was Perry docking there? And where were they going on to? Southampton, maybe?

No sign of Fitz to ask. He'd spent most of the voyage avoiding her as much as she avoided him, and he'd locked himself in his cabin all this morning. Whoever was on the helm would know.

Still watching Perry's ship sailing towards the harbour, she trotted down the steps. "Where are we—"

Knigh gripped the wheel, back stiff, knuckles white. He stared fore as if their course took them between jagged rocks that required all his attention.

She clenched her jaw and drew a quick breath. Damn it. She'd so nearly made it all the way back to Albion without speaking to him. But what did she care? He'd be gone soon with no fuss from her. Just like he wanted. And other than a pleasant distraction back in Arawaké, he meant nothing to her.

Nothing.

Lifting her chin, she cleared her throat. "Where are we going? And why isn't the *Covadonga* joining us?"

He didn't tear his gaze from the easy course over clear waters. His throat bobbed slowly. "We're docking in Portsmouth."

She frowned, glancing east where Southampton, then Portsmouth lay. The nape of her neck tickled. "A *naval* dockyard?"

"Do I need to remind you once more that you're privateers and"—he coughed softly—"and you have nothing to fear from the Royal Navy?"

It wasn't fear. She scratched the back of her head, smoothing the hairs. Idiot.

Bricus approached from fore, his smile cheerful. "We're keeping the two parts of the treasure separate." He stopped a pace in front of her, staring up at her. Lords, when had his smile grown so infuriating?

She rubbed her face. No, that was unfair, she was just irritable being stuck here with Blackwood and FitzRoy. Bricus was simply a cheerful first mate—a good counterpoint to his captain, which was what a first mate was meant to be. She gave him a strained smile.

"Er, yes," Blackwood said, nodding abruptly, "yes. The silver's safer that way—it can't all be stolen in one go."

"And," Bricus added, folding his arms, eyes still glinting up at her, "they'll refit the *Covadonga* at Plymouth."

Vice chuckled, glancing out to sea, but Perry's ship was out of sight now. "Who'd be stupid enough to steal the Queen's silver in her own country?"

"The criminal element will do anything," Knigh said softly. "There's been a spate of attacks by highwaymen."

Like her sister, Kat. Her heart clenched, and her gaze drifted over the limestone cliffs and green hills of Albion. Once upon a time, it had been home. Something in it still called to her blood, to the gift that sang in her veins and told her each movement of the sea beneath her feet. The fae lived here and here alone, including her unknown father if he still lived.

So too did her real family. Mama, gentle and downtrodden beneath Papa's stomping feet. Kat, who'd had to turn highway-woman because of her useless husband. Nanny Alder—not blood, but family all the same.

Vice took a long, shaking breath and shook her head. Those were Avice's concerns—Vice had treasure to deliver to her new Queen.

"If there are problems on the road, it'd make more sense to take it around the coast and sail directly into Lunden—keep it on the water." She snorted and tossed her head. "But what do I know? I'm not bloody captain."

Bricus gave a bark of a laugh. "No," he said, eyes mirthless, "you're not."

She frowned as he strode away. What had knotted his breeches? Maybe he was pissed off he hadn't been chosen to captain the *Covadonga*. She'd wager he'd been expecting it after he'd been invited into FitzRoy's discussions with Blackwood back when he'd first offered their letter of marque. Well, he wasn't as good a sailor as Perry and nowhere near as well-liked—she was by far the better choice.

Blackwood stayed quiet, and she gave him a sidelong look.

Grey eyes still fixated on their course. Face taut but unreadable. Shoulders ringing with tension that had her fingers clenching and unclenching. Back before, she'd rubbed that kind of tension away, thumbs working loose the knots that formed either side of his spine. Not anymore. Not now he hated her.

She found herself leaning towards him and yanked her hands back down to her sides.

She was meant to hate him, too. Smug. Self-righteous. Uptight. And so scared she'd make a scene when he left that he hadn't even told her.

Maybe that was what had his shoulders all hunched up again —the fear of what she'd do when he turned his back and walked away into the naval dockyard.

Balling her fists, she tightened every inch of herself, as if her muscles could form a hard wall to keep him out. She'd do nothing. She wouldn't even blink, just like he watched their course ahead, unblinking.

He couldn't wait to get home—back to the bosom of his beloved Navy.

With a stiff chuckle, she removed herself from his presence and found more work to while away the last hours of the journey. It wasn't difficult, a ship was a piece of machinery in constant flux, responding to its course, the sea's movements, the weather, and crew.

At last, they circled the white cliffs of the Isle of Wights, their ghostly presence making her shiver. That brought them into the Solent, the strip of sea between Portsmouth and the haunted island. The Solent was busy with fishing boats and so many naval ships it prickled the back of her neck. They were almost as bad as the island. She lent her gift to their course, slipping them between the wakes of larger vessels and slowing as they approached the Royal Dockyard.

She narrowed her eyes. Seemed they warranted a welcome party—dozens of men waited on the jetty they'd been directed to, clothing proclaiming them as Navy. At the centre stood a middle-aged man, his uniform far fancier than Blackwood's, like the one the Duke of Mercia had worn. An admiral, then.

Frowning, she wandered aft from the bow. Could they be here for Blackwood? Ha, maybe he was in trouble for going against his orders and fighting with them. Maybe they'd come to arrest him as soon as he came off the ship.

Her stomach turned, and she sighed. Much as she was irritated at him, *by* him, he didn't deserve to walk into such an unpleasant surprise. He'd been an arse, but it wouldn't hurt to warn him.

Except he wasn't at the wheel.

Half her mind on the sea, channelling them into a berth between two frigates, she glanced around for him.

The Morrigan glided into place, gently bumping against the jetty as the crew threw mooring lines to waiting workers. Helping slide the gangway in place, the dockers were so quiet, it set her teeth on edge. Perhaps that's how they worked in naval dockyards, unlike the lively chattering folk she joked with on civilian wharves. She shuddered. Damn the Royal Navy and their stiff restraint.

Speaking of which...

Still no sign of Blackwood. Maybe he was packing his belongings from *her* cabin. She pursed her lips. If this Admiral really was here for—

"Help!" The door to FitzRoy's cabin burst open. "Help," he cried, stumbling out clothed in—

Rags?

Vice gaped. FitzRoy never wore anything short of—

"Help me!" He staggered to the gangway, eyes wide and wild on the men gathered on the dock.

Heart leaping to life, her hand fastened on her sabre, and she searched fore and aft for danger, but...

Wait, were his wrists bound?

She started towards him. "FitzRoy, what—"

"Save me from *her.*" His finger rose to point unerringly at Vice.

ARRESTING WEATHER

Vice blinked, squeezing her sabre's hilt. What had he just—

Marines and sailors poured across the gangway. Unarmed, *The Morrigan's* crew withdrew, sharing wary looks.

What the hells was going on?

Backing away, she drew her sword. No sign of Blackwood. Typical—the Navy was confused and attacking them *again* and—

"My name is FitzRoy," he said in the voice he used for orders that carried without any need to shout. He fell to his knees. "I'm the rightful captain of this ship, and I've been captured—arrest that woman."

"What?" she spluttered, raising her sword defensively.

"I've been captured by the infamous pirate harlot, Lady Vice." He levelled shaking hands at her again, turning his wide eyes upon the Admiral. "She kept me in chains—forced me to be her sex slave—"

"Sex slave? *What?*"

"—while she captained *my* ship."

A ringing began in her ears, and she shook her head. "Sex slave?" Her laugh came out shaky as she backed away. "In your bloody dreams, FitzRoy."

What was he doing? What was this?

Marines hurried to him, cut away the rope around his wrists, helped him to his feet, all as if he were a victim.

Her crewmates exchanged looks, their uncertainty clear in their slow movement, the way they hedged between action and surrender. Most of the weapons were stowed—after all, what need had they for guns and blades as they readied the ship for docking in a *friendly* port?

She laughed, the sound bitter on her tongue.

Still, they had belaying pins close by, and she had her sword.

What Fitz was playing at, she couldn't fathom, but the rest of this had to be some strange misunderstanding. Maybe he'd lost his mind—too much time alone in that cabin, obsessing over Drake's treasure.

Sabre levelled between her and the marines edging their way across the deck, she lifted her chin. "Infamous, I may be," she called, gaze flicking between the uniformed men, "and harlot, *perhaps,* but I'm no pirate. The Queen herself..."

The Queen. That was it. Their pardons and letter of marque had been signed by Elizabeth IV. Now her daughter sat on the throne. There must have been a mix-up, some document that had been misplaced or misunderstood in the handover between one monarch and the next.

She cleared her throat. "We have pardons and a letter of marque from Queen Elizabeth IV." She gestured to FitzRoy's cabin. "You'll find it with the Captain's log."

At the Admiral's nod, a marine with fancy epaulettes waved two men into the cabin.

"Take this gentleman somewhere warm to recover from his ordeal," the Admiral said, at last, his voice cool and resonant.

"Gentleman? He's..."

But the men obeyed him and whisked FitzRoy away.

Placing her feet carefully, she backed away further, putting the rail at her back to prevent the marines from slipping behind her.

Wild Hunt, something was wrong. So very, *very* wrong.

Her pulse jumped in her temples and throat, so hard that her arm shook with it. Ice crept over her shoulders and up her neck. It balled in her stomach, solid and heavy. It set her teeth on edge and only clenching her jaw stopped them chattering.

The men emerged from FitzRoy's cabin and brought the letter of marque to the Admiral.

Tilting his head back, he peered at it. "A forgery."

A forgery.

Breaths burning in her lungs, she shook her head. "No, we—we..." Her chest crushed, a moment's sharp pain. But Knigh... "No. He gave us—he said—"

"Arrest them all," the Admiral said with a wave of his hand, before turning and marching onto the dock.

"No, wait!" Her sabre flashed as she kept it between herself and the marines closing in. "We're privateers," she yelled. "The Queen's privateers!"

This wasn't happening. Lords, she wanted to believe that. But just as sure as the air was thick with the taste of salt and seaweed, the deck thudded with the heavy footsteps of dozens of marines.

They levelled their rifles.

Unarmed, her crewmates had no choice. They raised their hands in surrender and knelt as they were ordered.

Only she remained standing.

Her chest heaved as she shifted her stance, ready to fight. One of the frigates was hard against the rail, leaving no space for her to leap over the side, and—*bollocks*, there were riflemen taking aim from its deck. Maybe she could hold them off long enough to get to the stern, jump overboard, and let the sea carry her away. They'd probably get off a few shots, but...

"It's over, Vice."

Knighton Blackwood. Close to her left shoulder, voice soft, pitched only for her.

She stared at him, breaths ragged.

His mask was in full force, no sign of even those little tells of his that she'd learned. No sign of humanity. No sign of anything.

"Surrender your weapon, and no one need die today." His voice, though—it wasn't as cold as the mask. A softness. A plea.

He really wanted her to give in.

And he wasn't surprised by any of this.

"You bastard." Her stomach clenched, and bile coated the back of her throat. "You knew... You planned this... All along..." A manic laugh burst from her. Had he been thinking about this all those times he'd taken her?

Oh gods, she'd thought herself the sly one, the one who deceived her way to victory.

What a fool she'd been.

"Wild Hunt take you, Knighton Villiers," she whispered. Hanging her head, she flung her sabre to the deck. It clanged as loud as any ship's bell, the sound heavy, rocking through her with such finality she thought she might die there and then.

But she didn't. Her lungs kept moving, her heart kept hammering against her ribs, and her eyes followed Blackwood as he stepped in close and wrapped rope around her wrists.

There was no dock, no sky, no ship. No marines or crew. No sun or wind. Only this caving feeling in her chest and the increasing pressure on her flesh, the hemp chafing her skin. And *him.*

His gaze stayed on the rope as he worked. "I did warn you not to trust me," he said softly, yanking the knot tight.

She stared at the twisted rope, unable to do anything but breathe and blink. He *had* warned her. The first time they'd stood together in her cabin, in fact.

And fool that she was, she thought she knew better.

She hadn't *meant* to trust him. Hells, if anyone had asked, she'd have told them she *didn't.* But somewhere along the way, in that walk around Nassau when he'd spun her such a fine tale about his disappointing father, in battles fighting side-by-side, in the quiet times when they'd talked in the dark, in those moments when he'd held her close... Somewhere in all that, she must have come to trust him in some small, stupid way.

Because if she hadn't trusted him, he would never have been able to do this.

And if she hadn't trusted him, her chest wouldn't feel like it had just taken a full broadside from the *Sovereign.*

"Well played, Blackwood," she said, voice ringing hollowly, "well played."

HOME & HEARTH

The fleeting shadows beneath the archway leading into Aunt Tilda's estate gave a welcome respite from the bright day. With a long sigh, Knigh paused there. It wasn't hot, it was downright cold compared to Arawaké, but today the sunlight stung his eyes.

He'd spent the days since Vice's arrest either in naval offices giving his debrief report and answering endless questions, or in the small set of rooms he'd been assigned. The apartment was comfortable. Hells, it was luxury compared to cramped life aboard *The Morrigan*—but the windows overlooked the dock, and he knew that ship's sail plan too well to keep his gaze from it.

And every time he saw it, he heard, *Well played, Blackwood, well played.*

He shook his head. He'd thought himself prepared.

What an idiot. Nothing could have prepared him for that.

It had been bad enough when she'd looked like she was going to fight. Some lingering protective instinct remained in him because the thought of her being gunned down by marines had turned his stomach. Instead of standing back as he'd planned, he'd stepped forward to force her surrender.

But then somehow what came after had been so much worse. It was as if the moment he'd bound her wrists, all her fight had gone. Quiet, almost meek.

And although Vice had murdered Avice Ferrers, when she'd said *well played* it had been a dagger to his kidneys.

Traitor. That's what her tone had said. Between the words, that grotesque accusation. She must have wondered it—*when you made love to me, did you mean it? Or was it part of this?*

His stomach turned. Skin burning, he gripped his sabrecat's reins until they creaked against his leather gloves.

He had meant it. At the time. But he'd thought she was someone different.

Wild Hunt damn her. *She'd* betrayed him first. Made out that she was the noble Pirate Queen, that she wasn't a monster. She'd made him believe she was a decent human being.

He'd done nothing wrong. He was only bringing a criminal to justice, making the world a better place, earning another bounty.

But it turned out being right didn't ease the heavy blanket of guilt that had engulfed him. So when the Admiralty's questions had ended, he'd petitioned for leave and had ridden for his aunt's as quickly as possible.

He hadn't seen his family in far too long, as evidenced by George's terrible decision to befriend Mercia, and they'd give him some comfort.

Mother would be as quiet as she'd always been since Father's death. His sister would probably ask too many questions that he'd have to evade. And Aunt Tilda would smile and occupy him with descriptions of all the single ladies she just *happened* to know. So, the visit wouldn't be without its own difficulties.

But at least it was far away from *The Morrigan* and Vice's trial, which would be the talk of Portsmouth.

Nodding, he urged his borrowed sabrecat back into the sun and sped to the sand-coloured house atop the hill.

Isabel's blond head appeared at a window as he turned onto the sweeping drive, her eyes wide before she disappeared inside.

Despite himself, he smiled. She'd always been alert and... yes, her warmth would be welcome, even if he couldn't confide in her all his terrible truths.

By the time he started up the steps to the front door, she was throwing it open with a laugh. "Captain Knighton Villiers, you didn't need to sneak up on us—you're not hunting pirates now." Blue eyes bright, she grabbed his hand and pulled him inside.

"Sorry," he muttered with a wince.

"Still can't take a joke, then?" She chuckled and flung her arms around his waist.

His body jolted. This was the first time anyone had touched him since...

"I've missed you, big brother." Smiling, she leant her head on his shoulder and gave him a squeeze.

His chest filled, bright as the day outside. She meant it.

"Oh, Isabel." He sighed out a long breath, tension inching away as he wrapped his arms around her and patted her shoulder.

With a shout from Is, Mother and Aunt Tilda emerged from the far end of the house, shortly followed by the butler with a tray of tea and cakes that he deposited in the drawing room.

As Mother poured tea, Isabel and Aunt Tilda bubbled with all the news. So-and-so had received an offer from an earl. Is had a new pianoforte. She and Mother planned to go to Lunden and take a townhouse for her first season.

Knigh raised his eyebrow at that and at the cakes, which were flavoured with vanilla and saffron. The vanilla tickled his nose, far too close to *her* scent, and he declined Isabel's offer of one.

But it wasn't just the reminiscent smell that caught his attention. Vanilla and saffron were *expensive*.

The hem of Isabel's gown wasn't tatty and bore no signs of being let down as she'd grown over the years. Ruffles of fine lace ran along the neckline *and* cuffs. He had no reason to buy the stuff himself, but he knew it didn't come cheap.

Even Mother's gown in sedate, plain black was smooth and cleanly tailored, with no pulls in the fabric or signs of being adjusted as she'd lost weight after Father's death.

The pianoforte couldn't have come cheap and the way she spoke, it sounded like it was hers rather than their aunt's. Then there was this talk of a townhouse in Lunden...

His brow twitched. He hadn't been able to send *that* much money back from his wages, and Aunt Tilda's accounts were enough to keep her modest estate and a roof over their heads. They weren't going to starve and lived comfortably, but new clothes and an additional house and all the staff that entailed?

"What a pleasant surprise this is," Mother said, smile gentle as she handed Aunt Tilda her tea, "both my boys here at the same time."

Knigh froze, cup halfway to his lips. "George is here?"

"Oh yes, he arrived a week ago with gifts for everyone." Is smoothed her hand over her sky-blue skirts. "Didn't he choose well?" She blinked at him, smiling. Yes, the colour matched her eyes.

So, he'd got away from Mercia. And at least that explained the clothes.

Knigh let out a soft breath and nodded. "And did he give you the pianoforte, too?"

Is cocked her head. "Not exactly..."

Mother placed her cup and saucer on the table. “Your brother has been sending us an allowance for some months now,” she murmured.

“A very *generous* allowance at that,” Aunt Tilda said with a nod. “Wish I knew where he was magicking it all from—I wouldn’t mind finding that pot of gold myself.” Her eyes glinted above a narrow smile before she sipped her tea.

The back of his neck prickled, and a chill traced his veins. Where *was* George getting money from? He didn’t have a career or land, and Father hadn’t left any sum for them to invest.

The rest of the afternoon passed in polite chit-chat, with Knigh pointedly avoiding any detail of his recent work in Arawaké. Thankfully, he had the excuse of ‘naval secrets.’

Just as the ladies were about to go and dress for dinner, boots stomped into the hallway.

Isabel’s eyes widened. “George,” she called, springing to her feet with a smile.

Knigh swallowed, throat dry.

“George,” Is called again, “through here! You’re never going to believe—”

“Knigh,” George said as he appeared in the doorway, clothes as bright as those he’d worn at the ball all those months ago. His tone was cool, face smooth as though he’d learned from Knigh. “I wasn’t expecting you home, or else I’d have brought you a gift, too.”

And where would the money for that gift have come from? There was only one place his brother could have got the sums he’d been sending their family...

Knigh bit his tongue and smiled stiffly. “I hadn’t planned to come, but I was awarded some additional leave.”

George nodded slowly, still hovering near the door.

“Well,” Aunt Tilda said, patting her knees and rising, “we’d best beautify ourselves for dinner and leave the men to catch up, hadn't we?" As she passed Knigh, she paused and placed her hand on his arm, raising her eyebrows.

He told her as little as he told anyone else in his family, but she *saw* far more. She must have picked up on their chilly greeting and, being Aunt Tilda, she understood they needed to be left alone. All without him having to say.

Thank the gods for her.

Squeezing her fingers, he nodded, gratitude a brief, warm flare in his chest.

When they were alone, he met George's eye. "Where did you get—"

"Where do you think?" George's chin rose in a challenge. One hand on his hip, head cocked, hip dropped: he was the picture of Mercia at his most off-hand.

That was where he'd got the money.

Knigh bit the inside of his cheek, counting three long breaths. "Is that why you joined his little entourage? Money? Because I can get us—"

"No, Knigh." He huffed and rolled his eyes. "It isn't about money. Wild Hunt bloody take you if you think that's all anyone else cares about. Just because you're obsessed with the stuff." His nostrils flared, and lips pursed.

Blinking, Knigh took half a step back. Was this how George really saw him?

"And," George went on, "you might only spend time with people because you're *paid* to, but the rest of us are capable of actually forming emotional attachments with other human beings."

Knigh flinched, crossing his arms to disguise the movement. But the words hit, unblocked by his defensive stance. He clenched his jaw. "This is what you think of me?"

"Since Father died, yes." George's mid-brown hair gleamed in the late afternoon sun as he tossed his head. "That's why I was surprised to see you with that pirate woman. She seemed—"

"Don't—not her." His voice wavered. "Please."

Brows knotting, George regarded him a long while. Eventually, he took a deep breath.

Oh Lords, he was going to ask about her, about...

"Look," Knigh said before he could, "I'm glad you've come home and left Mercia. He isn't—"

"Left him?" George scoffed. "I haven't *left* him. He's in Lunden for the coronation, and I've just taken the opportunity to visit our family. You know, like you never bother to do because you think money will do the job of a brother and son."

Bloody hells, George. He didn't want to make it easy to have a conversation, did he? Knigh gritted his teeth and forced a faint smile in place. "Never? I'm here now, aren't I?"

"Because that woman's—oh no, wait!" George's eyes went wide, and he covered his mouth, an incredulous smile on his face. "Oh dear. You've... Knigh..." He shook his head. "She was Lady Vice, wasn't she? And I hear she's just been captured by the Navy." He laughed, a high sound of disbelief. "And you did it, didn't you?"

Every inch of Knigh froze, solid and cold as ice. George was putting the pieces together far too well, just like Aunt Tilda. He'd seen something between him and Vice before they'd even acted upon it and now...

"You're sending your own lover to the gallows." That incredulous laugh again as he shook his head. "And you say Mercy is so awful? He'd never treat *me* like that. You're the monster, Knigh."

Heart battering against his ribs, Knigh stared at his brother. Did that mean... "You and Mercia?"

George lifted his chin. "Mercia and I, yes."

No wonder he'd been so generous with George's allowance. The Duke had particular favourites in his entourage. Some lasted years, others a few months. But, always, he lavished them with gifts, including land and titles.

In exchange, they provided adoration and loyalty, unending, unwavering, unquestioning.

"You can't—he's—"

"Knighton. You have just told me you've arrested your lover and handed her over to the authorities." George sighed, the affectation dropping from his stance as his arms fell to his sides. "I know you seem to think Mercy is a beast, but until and unless you're prepared to tell me something he's done that's worse, then you can kindly keep your nose out of my affairs. Green is *such* an ugly colour on you. Mercy told me how you had a soft spot for him and I'm sorry your feelings weren't—"

"What?" The word burst from Knigh with a laugh. "I had a—*what?*" Scoffing, he shook his head. Oh, Mercia would lie about that, wouldn't he?

"Obviously, envy is where your hostility towards him comes from, and it's perfectly understandable. And"—he approached, an apologetic smile in place—"I also understand the strain you've been under since Papa's death. You've taken it all on your shoulders—every penny, every responsibility, every decision for the family. Well, I can help now." He cocked his head as he placed a hand on Knigh's arm, the touch only dimly registering. "You can relax—no need to throw yourself into danger hunting pirates. Mercy will provide for us all."

A deeper, darker cold prickled from Knigh's scalp, down his neck, creeping all the way to his feet.

His stomach turned. Mercia was a monster, far worse than Vice. He'd happily oversee the murder of men who'd surrendered, laughing all the while.

But there was no way he could make George understand. Not without revealing his own dark secret.

George patted his shoulder and gave a smile that should have been comforting. "You'll see." He nodded and walked out, calling over his shoulder, "Time for dinner."

Knigh was rooted to the spot. George was in Mercia's power, just like that beast the Duke kept bound with his gift. His fae charm had done its work.

And with his endless supply of money, the whole family had been dragged in.

Isabel would debut in Lunden thanks to that townhouse they could now afford to rent. With her warmth and bright eyes and the decent dowry he'd topped up with Vice's bounty, she couldn't fail to marry well. Mother would be less reliant upon Aunt Tilda's kindness. Plus, she loved the opera and the theatre—a season in Lunden would agree with her. Perhaps she'd finally return to wearing colour. Maybe he'd even hear her sing again.

There was no way out of this. Mercia had a hold on them all.

THE SONG OF THE PIRATE QUEEN

When they trundled through the streets with Vice on full display in a cart, her wrists tied, the people sang *The Song of the Pirate Queen*. Vice grinned and let the song—*her* song wash over her.

From the glowers darkening their faces, the guards hadn't expected it to go like this. People usually threw rotten vegetables and hurled abuse at the criminals being paraded by. Hells, after the arrest, *she* hadn't expected this either.

Oh, Lords, they'd finished the song, and now they were cheering.

Cheering.

Laughing, she waved, and they smiled and waved back. Children trotted along with the cart, little legs pumping until they managed to touch the wheel or timber sides, then they dropped back and held out their hands to show their friends.

The poor, *poor* Navy—this had backfired, hadn't it?

Displaying her like this was probably meant to show the people that the foul scourge of Lady Vice was going to face the

Queen's justice. Well, from their smiles and well-wishes, it seemed they preferred her free and tweaking the noses of authority *and* the Hesperians.

In fact, it looked like the whole situation wasn't nearly as bad as she'd thought when they'd arrested her on *The Morrigan.* The rest of the crew had already had their hearings. The authorities had decided she needed a separate trial, maybe because of her odd status, being a woman and, according to FitzRoy's insane accusations, the ringleader. She'd heard through prisoners in adjoining cells that the judge had only sentenced the others to a day in the stocks.

That was *nothing.*

So it seemed the whole matter of the arrest was just the Navy's way of making an example of them. Poor Blackwood, did he know that or was he sitting smugly at home somewhere imagining that she was soon to hang?

Still, there was the puzzle of just what on earth FitzRoy had done that day. What was that mad business with pretending he'd been captured and held by her?

She shook her head. Unfathomable, that was what it was. And it didn't change what she now had to do.

In the week since her arrest, she'd attempted to get an audience with the Queen. She'd shown her drake and crown pin, but the bastards had taken it away, believing she'd stolen it.

So, of course, she'd tested every inch of her cell, but the damn thing was solid. With no tools, the iron bars were impossible for her to break. Although she used her coat cuffs as barriers between her hands and the metal, her fingers had slipped onto it. They'd burned in white-hot pain, leaving blisters.

Even her fae charm hadn't helped—she'd pretended to be ill, thinking to trick the guards into rushing into her cell, where she'd overpower them and run. They looked at her writhing on the floor, their brows creased. Wringing their hands, they told her they'd been instructed by the Captain to, under no circumstances, open her cell door.

That had to be Blackwood. The prick.

Which left only this course. She was going to have to get out of this the old-fashioned way and prove her innocence.

Maybe easier said than done when she wasn't actually innocent. But ever since Blackwood had offered that letter of marque, she'd acted in good faith. With her fae charm, the judge would see that and worst-case scenario, she'd end up with a spell in the stocks before being released and allowed to go on her way. Then she could get back to the ship and give Barnacle a good squeeze. At least with the rest of the crew being released after the stocks, someone would be looking after her.

Cat aside, Vice still owed Blackwood for his betrayal. He might have tricked her this time, but that wasn't the end of the story.

When the cart rolled to a stop outside the courts, Vice stood before the guards could grab her. Smiling, she turned and bowed deeply to the crowd. They'd gone to the trouble of coming here, best to give them a show.

"Ladies and gentlemen of Albion," she said in the carrying voice she used to give orders on deck. "Your Pirate Queen thanks you for your loyalty." She nodded solemnly, then winked and blew a kiss just as the guards closed their hands on her shoulders and bundled her from the cart.

Laughing at their frowns and mutters, she let them direct her through the corridors until at last they shoved her onto a bench in a courtroom.

So small? She scowled, looking around at the empty galleries. Disappointing. They'd shut the public—her adoring fans—out. Must have realised their error in the parade.

There was only her, a handful of stuffy-looking men in white legal wigs, the judge in his oversized chair, a blond man in naval uniform, and half a dozen guards stationed behind her with another two at the doors.

Oh well, it would have been nice to have more witnesses to this victory, but no doubt the story of her talking her way out of court would get around anyway.

With a rap of his gavel, the judge called the court to silence—not that there was much chatter with so few people here.

"In the matter of the Realm versus—*ahem*—Lady Vice." He peered down his nose at her. "What is your real name, girl?"

"Lady Vice, Your Honour." She smiled her most winning smile.

His gaze stayed on her, level, no warmth there despite her fae charm. The flesh around his eyes tensed for a second, then his lips parted in a slow, cool smile, revealing pointed canines.

Vice's blood ran even colder than his smile. Oddly pointed canines. Far too sharp, far too long, overlapping his bottom teeth like a cat's did. A fae mark.

Bollocks.

He was fae-touched, possibly blooded, and either way, immune to her unnatural charm.

Double bollocks.

With a dismissive blink, he turned his gaze to one of the wigged men, pale-skinned and decidedly average, and invited him to put forward the case against her. One of the other wigged men readied his pen, he had to be a clerk of some sort, and the blond naval officer stationed himself just behind his chair.

... Piracy... Theft and murder upon the high seas... Capture of several vessels, including Albionic ones... Trickery of good men, seducing them to do her bidding... A monstrous threat to civilisation itself... *blah, blah, blah.*

The story was predictable. She could have laughed at the seduction part—when had she forced anyone to do her bidding?

Smile fixed in place, she narrowed her eyes at the pale man. She could do her own bidding well enough, *thank you*.

Still, she would remain silent until asked. If she couldn't fall back on her fae charm, she'd play by their rules and beat them at their own game with the truth. That'd teach them.

When the pale man had finished, the judge asked whether she had anything to say in her defence.

"I do, in fact, thank you, Your Honour." She rose and bowed to him, the picture of lady-like elegance. Let that confuse them, show how terrible a threat to civilisation she was with her perfect etiquette.

She cleared her throat and began her side of the story.

They'd been offered pardons and a letter of marque by Captain Knighton Blackwood, formerly Villiers. It was an offer she'd gladly accepted as they were good and loyal subjects of Her late Majesty. The Naval officer kept ducking and whispering into the clerk's ear as she spoke, making her burn with irritation and frustrated curiosity. Still, she did her best to ignore him.

"We've been working for the Crown for three, nearly four months as *privateers*. Why else would we sail a Hesperian treasure ship and half its silver into Plymouth? Why would we, ourselves, put in at Portsmouth and its world-famous *Royal* Dockyard, with the other half of the silver? If we were still pirates, that would be suicide."

The judge stared back at her, and his eyebrows lifted in such a subtle expression Knigh would have been proud.

"But," she went on, "if we were privateers, as I've said we *are*, doesn't that explain our actions? As privateers, it was merely part of our work taking and delivering prizes for Her Majesty."

"Your Honour," the pale attorney said, rising with a sheaf of papers in his hand, "I'd humbly ask you to consider—"

"I know." The judge raised his fingers to silence the attorney. "I've seen the testimony." He pointed at Vice. "Show her."

She frowned as the attorney approached and placed the papers before her. Hands still bound, she grabbed them and scanned the pages.

... acting as privateers...

... forced to accept her leadership...

... threatened the—

"You might be aware that the other members of *The Morrigan's* crew have already been tried," he said, returning to his desk. "However, what you won't be aware of is the contents of those proceedings as they occurred in a closed court like this one." He gave a frigid smile. "I'm sure madam can read quite capably, but as a courtesy allow me to save you the time sifting through all those pages with your hands tied."

Vice's throat closed, but she kept reading as he spoke.

"They are not here today because they fear the notorious Lady Vice and her fae-touched magic and what she, a sea witch, might do to them should she become aware that they have spoken against her."

Against her. Wild Hunt take the bastards.

"They predicted your story exactly as you've told it today because it was the lie you told them."

"The lie, I—" She scoffed, hands shaking and crumpling the paper.

"Just close enough to the truth to make it all the more compelling, isn't that right?" The pale attorney tilted his head. "You forced them to accept your leadership and piracy by claiming they were acting as privateers for Her Majesty. When they dared to speak against you, you threatened the life of their beloved Captain FitzRoy, held captive in your cabin."

Her throat had closed so much, it was all she could do to push out a strangled laugh. Her fingertips tingled as she scanned the pages.

... Through means of a letter of marque forged by a Mr Waters of Nassau...

Heart battering against her ribcage as hard as a boot against a locked door, she shook her head. They meant to go after Waters, too. At least Nassau was beyond the Navy's reach... wasn't it?

"No, it didn't—that wasn't—"

The papers fell from her tied hands, leaving just the last page stuck to her sweaty fingers.

We the undersigned attest to the truth of this document... William North... Frederick Longe... Robert Bricus...

The names went on and on, not a friend among them.

No. Because her friends had all been sent with Perry. They were miles away. Maybe they'd been arrested, too. Even if they hadn't, they'd have no idea what was happening here.

Her heart plummeted. FitzRoy had set her up. All these men—they were the ones who'd never really warmed to her or who'd stayed neutral, except for Bricus, he...

What do I know? I'm not bloody Captain.

No, you're not.

And he'd worn that odd mirthless look when he'd said it, hadn't he?

All this time, had his cheerful smiles hidden hatred? But what reason could he—

The gavel hammered. "If *Lady Vice* has nothing further to add in her defence?"

She blinked at him. What could she say? FitzRoy, Blackwood, that damn officer leaning over the clerk's shoulder—they had it all sewn up, didn't they? As neat and final as a dead sailor sewn into his hammock ready to be tipped over the side.

Oh, well played indeed, Blackwood.

She shook her head.

"Very good," the judge said with a brief smile, "no sense in delaying the inevitable and wasting the Court's time." He nodded in approval. "Then it seems my verdict is a straightforward one. I find the accused guilty on all counts."

Guilty. Her skin crawled.

Well, he wasn't entirely wrong. Maybe this was just punishment for all those years before the letter of marque.

"And to the matter of sentencing, this too is straightforward. With no extenuating circumstances to consider, I sentence you, *Lady Vice,* or whoever you really are, to be taken in one week to Southsea beach. There you will be hanged by the neck until you are dead."

The blood roared in her ears. But, no, she'd heard him correctly. Hanged. But—but hadn't the others...

No. They'd blamed her for their actions. That explained their lenient sentences. She was the scapegoat, she had to hang to allow them to escape with only a spell in the stocks.

Bastards. Pricks. Wild Hunt take the lot of them and chase them for all time.

And with Perry possibly captured or else just ignorant of what was happening, there was no possibility of rescue.

Of course not. No sense in relying on anyone else to save her.

She could do this herself.

Seven days. She'd have to make a plan and escape by then. The weather—maybe there was a storm nearby she could call in. A lightning strike could cause a fire, a distraction, then—

"And until that time," the judge said, lifting his chin, "you're to be kept in a gibbet cage on Portsea Castle walls as an example to others who might follow in your heinous footsteps."

Something like nails dragging down the inside of her skin froze her.

A gibbet.

Made of iron.

It would block her gift and—

She looked at the silvery padlock scar on her palm, the little blisters where her fingers had slipped onto the bars of her cell.

And it would burn.

BLOODY REUNION

With rough hands, the guards bundled Vice out of the courtroom, down a winding staircase, to a small, dimly-lit cell beneath. She'd heard about these places. These were the rooms where the condemned awaited their sentences.

She was now one of the condemned.

It wasn't possible... And yet here she was.

Body a knot of tension, she twisted her wrists against the ropes. But they were just as tight and chafing as when Blackwood had tied them.

The guards paused at the cell door, holding it open.

"Thank you ever so much, gentlemen," an all-too bloody familiar voice said.

"FitzRoy?"

As she stared, mouth open, he swept into view, beautifully dressed in black and gold, hair clean and shining, rings on his fingers. Never had she been so glad to see so much gold.

"I won't need long," he told the guards as they locked the door behind him and skulked away down the corridor.

Shaking her head, she almost laughed. This was—*had* to be part of some ploy of his. He was going to spring her out.

"Bloody hells, Fitz, you have some interesting timing." Scoffing now the guards were out of earshot, she rubbed her face, whole body sagging. "For a second then, I thought I really was for it. I've got to give it to you, I can't work out what scheme you've concocted. I'm just glad it involves getting me out of here and, I assume, a large sum of money." Grinning up at him, she held out her wrists.

Hazel eyes trailing to her bindings, he smiled softly. "Oh, my dear Vice. You're partially right."

Shrugging, she huffed. "Well, just a small sum of money will do."

"Oh no." Eyes glinting, he shook his head. "No, this involves a very large sum, indeed. Lots of noughts. But I'm afraid you won't see any of it." His head cocked, and his gaze drifted up. "Well, I suppose you *might* see me ride past your gibbet in my shiny new carriage. Because, just to be clear, my *scheme* doesn't involve getting you out of here."

Her body had forgotten how to work. Her grin was frozen in place, and her eyes just stared at him. She couldn't even feel her heart beating heavily as it had in court, and it was only the fact she was standing that said her muscles and lungs still functioned.

She prized her teeth apart, swallowed, worked her tongue around her mouth. Gulping a long breath, she blinked. *"What?"*

"Oh, my lovely." Shaking his head, he approached, boots scuffing softly on the stone floor until he was only half a foot away, the front of his splendid coat brushing the backs of her fingers. "My dearest, most darling creature." He rubbed a lock of her hair between his thumb and fingertips, gaze on it like he was examining fine silk at the market. "You still don't understand, do you?"

Eyebrows raised, he looked at her face, eyes drifting over every feature slowly. "This was all part of the plan. Sorry, I should clarify—*my* plan. Bricus helped me make an offer to the Navy. We get pardons, land, and that large sum of money I mentioned and in exchange, they get you. When Blackwood came aboard and gave us the Queen's regards, that was the code to say the Navy and Crown had accepted our offer."

Her throat closed to something the size of a reed, and it took all her effort just to keep breathing. Every inch of her went stiff and cold as stone as his words sank in. *My plan.*

And Blackwood's involvement... from the very start...

To think, she'd believed his primary danger was to her *feelings*. When all along, he'd been playing a far more deadly game. Maybe it had been just sex, just bodies to him. A perk of hunting her down. An extra bit of smug satisfaction for him, knowing that he was screwing her and later would be screwing her over as she sailed right into his trap.

Chest aching, hollow, she shuddered. What an idiot she'd been. He was dangerous all right.

Hadn't she told herself there was something off about the whole offer? But, no, she'd just been happy that they were finally privateers like she'd always wanted.

What a damn fool.

Was he off somewhere celebrating? He was probably telling his friends about how good a lay she was, how she hadn't suspected a thing. The great Pirate Queen laid low by his scheming, his sexual prowess.

But he wasn't here. She'd have to satisfy herself with tearing Fitz to shreds with a few choice truths.

"You"—her voice rasped, forcing her to stop and swallow

again—"you couldn't stand it, could you? The stories, the songs, the wanted posters—all about *me*. Such a pathetic creature that you couldn't bear to be overshadowed by a woman." Face tight, trembling, she sneered at him.

"A pathetic creature?" He smiled, eyes narrow, cruel. "My darling, I'm not the one bound and locked in a cell." He sighed and traced his thumb over her cheek, the sensation crawling through her. "But you're, again, partially right. A *girl* shouldn't overshadow her captain." He snorted, shaking his head. "Bricus spent years telling me, I was just too blinded by you to see. You weren't even a quartermaster or first mate and, yet you strutted across my deck, through *my* ship like you owned the damn thing." His jaw knotted, and nostrils flared.

So Bricus *had* always been against her. Had he felt that her odd position in the crew gave her too much power, trod on his toes as first mate?

"But that wasn't all." Fitz lifted his chin, a tight smile on his mouth as his hand slid down over her jaw to her throat. His fingers rested there at the point between neck and shoulder, thumb on the hollow between her collarbones. The pressure grew a shade too heavy for comfort.

She would not back down. She would not flinch. Face as still as Blackwood's, she glared back at him.

"You see," he murmured, a sigh in his voice, "I'm tired. I've spent my entire adult life chasing Drake's treasure. And all I have to show for it is a scrap of paper." His other hand touched the leather pouch dangling from a cord around his neck. "Years. All for a piece of paper I don't even understand."

She ground her teeth. She'd have read it for him if he'd asked, just like the books about Drake written in Latium. No wonder he'd put off talking to her about this until 'after Blackwood was off the ship'—really it was to delay *ever* having to show her.

Treacherous prick.

"So, yes, your fame and popularity and those ridiculous stories about you stung, but I haven't done this only for my wounded pride." The pad of his thumb stroked her throat, again the pressure closer to choking than a caress. A threat.

Her chest heaved, but she stood fast. She was due to hang in a week, what the hells did she have to lose? She'd throw herself at the Wild Hunt before she'd let him frighten her.

"I'm done chasing a treasure that might not even exist," he said, smiling. Disappointment laced the expression. "This has given me a great fortune, which I'm going to take and retire in luxury. Who knows?" He cocked his head. "Maybe I'll even name my estate in your honour—Vice Hall has a ring to it, doesn't it? Sounds like the kind of place *I'd* want to—"

In one movement, she grabbed the front of his coat, the brass buttons biting into her fingers, and kneed him between the legs.

With a choked gasp, he keeled over, clutching his crotch and staggering away.

"You bastard." Body shaking, she stalked towards him. Blood on fire, muscles tense, there was no elegance to her movements. "You bloody bastard—Wild Hunt take you and chase you for the rest of your days."

He backed into the bars with a clang. When he looked up, his eyes widened. "Guards," he called, voice strained, breathless. "Guards!"

She was only a foot away. Her wrists were bound, but she could still throttle the life out of him like he'd threatened her with.

Stupid, angry tears misted the edge of her vision, and her pulse roared. "You treacherous bastard," she spat, fingers closing on his shirt front.

But the cell door flew open and guards surrounded her, pulling her away with bruising grips.

"No," she bellowed. She'd left that courtroom calmly, she'd be damned if they'd take her from here quietly, too. "No." She kicked, clawed, screamed, bit, thrashed, body burning.

Even through the stone of the courthouse, she could feel the sky overhead churning, as frantic as her pulse.

She twisted and snarled and braced her feet on the floor, pulling. But there were too many of them, and her hands were tied. They just gripped harder, biting into her flesh, grinding against bone, lifting her with ease. They carried her into the corridor.

Chest heaving, FitzRoy stared after her, finally unbending.

But he was soon gone from her sight, leaving just her useless struggle against half a dozen men.

When had he become such an enemy that he'd leave her to this? That he'd help *cause* this?

A wordless cry of rage tore from her, echoing through the stone hall.

When Evered died, she'd lost everything. Or at least she'd thought she had. Perry and FitzRoy had been there... the ship had been there... And thanks to her gift, she'd proven herself and earned a place there. A home.

Now...

It had never been love between them, but she'd cared for him in her own way. And just like Papa, just like Evered, now he'd let her down.

And Knigh had, too. He hated her, and that was her doing, her choice. That she could deal with. But this? This was beyond merely letting her down.

Well, damn the lot of them. She'd escape. Somehow. She had to.

The daylight seared her eyes when they carried her out, but dark clouds threatened to the south.

She could use those.

Come closer. Faster.

With a little agitation from her, the clouds built, charged, darkened into a burgeoning storm.

Lightning crackled along its leading edge, and a peal of thunder shook the air moments later.

She went limp in the guards' hold—resisting their grip was a waste of energy. She had a better way to use it.

Limbs slack, she let her awareness drift upwards. Their fingers on her, the cold air on her face, their voices—it all faded.

The sky thrummed. Perfect. The clouds—*her* clouds blew closer on an unnaturally sudden wind.

Her muscles seared as she drew it closer, closer, churned the electricity within to an overwhelming level, ready to discharge at her command.

Then she was screaming. Burning.

No more sky, no more storm, no more wind at her call. Just white-hot pain on her hands and hairline.

Twitching, she gasped a harsh breath and opened her eyes. Her stomach roiled, churning as hard as the storm she'd built.

To the right, black bands criss-crossed her view over the city. To the left, a grey stone wall stretched away.

The cage rocked as the door crashed shut.

An iron cage.

The unmistakable *clunk* of a key turning in a lock tolled through her.

Hunching in her coat to keep from touching the bars, she turned.

A young man in naval uniform pulled the key from the lock, face set in an expression far too grim for his smooth cheeks. At his nod, the cage lowered from the battlements, leaving her alone, dangling from the walls of Portsea Castle.

An example for everyone to see.

The sickness crept through her veins, seethed in her belly, silenced the hum of her gift that had been such a constant she'd stopped noticing it.

And she was alone. *Truly* alone this time. No Perry, no Barnacle, no ship. No feel of the sea breathing beneath her feet or at the end of a dock. She could feel nothing but the iron, the sickness, and the throbbing pain of her knuckles and forehead where she'd touched the vile stuff.

Hugging herself, she pulled her coat tight.

To the south, lightning cracked once, twice, and then the clouds dissipated.

THE NOTORIOUS LADY VICE

Knigh stood in the window of the drawing room, hand resting on the cool glass. Outside, a constant drizzle put a grey cast on the sky, the gardens, *everything*. The fingers of his other hand traced the smooth curve inside the shell he *still* kept in his pocket.

Idiot. He should throw it on the fire. He should have thrown it in the sea when he was still in Portsmouth. He should place it on the floor and stamp on it and crush it to a thousand shimmering pieces.

But he didn't. Frowning, he held it, pressed his thumb into its shallow cup. The purples and yellows of the reef. The blue light of the glow-worm cave. And the changing sea-colours of her eyes—green, turquoise, flecks of frothy pale blue, deep teal, clear cobalt...

Blinking away the ghost of those colours and images, he rubbed his eyes. He *would* put this behind him. He would forget her.

George was a fool to trust in Mercia, but he was right about one thing. Knigh *had* been under a great deal of strain since

Father's death. No wonder some silly part of his mind was reluctant to let go of something that had been a brief, bright comfort out at sea.

He scoffed. Or at least the lie had been. The truth was as comforting as a lightning strike.

"What's so amusing?" Isabel's voice chimed from the door, closely followed by the light tap of her footsteps.

Taking a deep breath and dropping the shell back in his pocket, Knigh turned. He only managed a half-hearted smile. "Nothing, really."

"Well, I've just heard the news from Portsmouth." The tilt her head was teasing. "You didn't tell us you'd captured such an *infamous* villain."

His heart gave a heavy thud. There was only one person she could mean. He cleared his throat and turned back to the window, leaning his elbow high on the frame. "You know I don't like to discuss work."

"Yes, I had noticed." She appeared beside him, peering outside as if she expected to find him occupied by something more exciting than Aunt Tilda's gardens and the endless drizzle. "I thought you'd want to hear the outcome of all your hard work."

It had been a week since he'd left Portsmouth. Enough time for—"The trial?" He barely got the words out before his throat closed.

"Guilty, of course."

"Of course." He should have felt nothing. Or the swell of pride at victory and a job well done. Instead, there was only cold. Over his scalp, in his chest, coating his fingertips, making his bones brittle, freezing his toes. "And"—despite his attempt to sound light, his voice cracked, forcing him to clear his throat—"and the sentence?"

"Hanging."

Exhaling, he pressed his forehead against his forearm and closed his eyes.

This was the plan. He'd known this would happen. He'd *made* it happen. And yet...

His stomach twisted, writhing like that barrel of eels, coating his throat with bile.

"Knigh?" Isabel's voice was as soft as her touch on his shoulder. "What's wrong?"

Blasting a harsh breath, he pulled away, arm dropping from the frame. *Get a hold of yourself.*

"Nothing is wrong. Nothing." But the heavy, heaving pit of his stomach said that was a lie.

"You know," Is said, frowning as she looked up at him, "I've noticed something in the past couple of years—since you started pirate hunting rather than serving with the regular Navy." Gentle lines creased her brow. "You've withdrawn from the family, and I don't think it's because of Father and what he left behind. It was after that. What have you seen out there?"

He clenched his hands at his sides as his stomach turned again. He didn't deserve her kindness. Didn't deserve her large blue eyes looking up at him so softly, with all the light of a sister looking up to her big brother and all the wisdom of Aunt Tilda.

"I've read books about wars and pirates," she went on, "and I know the things Father did—all of them. I may not have been out in the world and seen it all, but I'm not so innocent. You can tell me."

But he couldn't. He'd shatter that look, that admiration in her eyes if he told her what he'd done to Billy and what he'd nearly done to those men who'd surrendered. Swallowing, he shook his head.

"I've never seen you like this after an assignment, Knigh." Her voice was barely above a whisper. "What's eating you up about this particular capture? And what's the significance of that shell?"

He looked down—the damn thing was in his hand again. Scoffing, he held it up. The late morning sun gleamed upon it, painting a whorl of a hundred pale colours on its iridescent inner surface.

Perhaps he could talk about that—or at least some of it.

"She"—his voice rasped—"the woman—"

"Lady Vice?"

He nodded. "You've heard the stories—you know how cunning she is. I had to use unorthodox methods to ensure her safe delivery back here." They were formal terms, *safe* terms—this was almost like delivering a report. "I joined her ship for over three months, ostensibly to ensure they obeyed the terms of their letter of marque. In fact, it was to keep an eye on her and bring her to Albion for justice."

Is nodded, gaze passing between him and the shell.

"She was always going to ha—be ex—be *dealt with* in this way." He exhaled. *Hanged. Executed.* They were impossible words to get over his tongue, bristling in his throat like fish bones. How on earth could they apply to someone so full of life as *her?*

He shook his head. "But she wasn't what I expected. Or, rather, she hid her monstrous nature very well indeed..." He told Is about Barnacle and the shopkeepers of Nassau. About Perry's love of her and the way she spent hours shopping for the crew. About how she'd saved his life more than once. About how she brokered surrenders whenever she could and had eased his anger when tensions ran high. Those terms were suitably vague, protecting Is from the full knowledge of what he was capable of and hiding the true extent of his relationship with *her*.

"... Vee even makes chasing slavers a priority—not long before I joined the crew, they captured one. She persuaded her captain to give the proceeds of the ship's sale to the people who'd been enslaved, setting them all free."

"Vee." Isabel's eyebrows rose gently. "You keep calling her that."

He froze, heart skipping a beat. Gods, he had said that, hadn't he? Damn it, he was meant to be reciting all her crimes, reminding himself that she deserved her fate.

"You and she"—Is tilted her head, eyes wide with no hint of judgement—"there was more going on between you, wasn't there? She was your lover."

His throat closed, and he stared at her. But her look didn't waver. She gave an encouraging smile.

Exhaling through his nose, he nodded once.

"And this is why it's bothering you." She slipped her arms around his waist and stroked his back. "No wonder you've spent the whole time you've been home brooding."

One arm around her shoulders, he covered his eyes, squeezing them shut. What a bloody fool he was. "I was trying to remind myself of all the reasons it's good that she's been caught, and yet I still find myself lingering on the good things." He shook his head. He couldn't trust his judgment, especially when it was so effortlessly swayed by Vee's easy smile and warm flesh. He had to regain control.

Taking a deep breath, he disentangled himself from his sister. "Thank you," he murmured then drew himself to his full height. Shoulders back, chin high, stance at attention.

Still with that soft smile, which had now turned sad, Is looked up at him. "You say all the reasons it's good that she's been caught—I don't think you've told me a single thing she's done wrong. Could it be that the stories are exaggerated or even untrue? Perhaps she's the victim of a terrible—"

"She killed Lady Avice Ferrers." There. He'd almost forgotten.

Is flinched, eyes wide. "As in..."

He heaved a long breath and nodded. "As in my former betrothed. Is, she murdered a defenceless eighteen-year-old girl."

"How? When did you..." She shook her head, fingers pressed into her lips until they went white.

"After... after things had gone further than they should have. But as soon as I found out, I ended it." Another deep breath dragged through him like an anchor trailing through sand. "I don't owe her anything. I didn't betray her." He shook his head.

"No, you don't." Is pursed her lips and smoothed his hair. "But I don't think every part of you understands that. You—it sounds like things ended abruptly and now she's in Portsmouth awaiting execution following a trial you didn't attend. Maybe you need to speak to her, tell her why Lady Avice's death affected you directly."

Heat unfurled in his muscles and his cheeks. "But I don't owe her—"

"Again," she said, raising a hand, "no, you don't owe *her* an explanation. But I think you need to do it for yourself. Perhaps when you know you've told her everything, when you tell her she'll be paying for *all* her crimes, including the murder of Lady Avice Ferrers... Perhaps then your mind will be quiet, and you'll stop clutching at that shell when you think no one's looking." The corner of her mouth lifted.

He huffed out a long breath, shoulders sagging. She had a point. "When did you get so wise?" He ruffled her hair, and she ducked away, swatting him off before patting her coiffure back into place.

"I am nineteen, you know. Old enough to be married with a child of my own—I'm not a little girl anymore."

He sighed. "No, you're not, are you? You've grown up a lot since Father died."

"Well, that and I've spent far too much time around Aunt Tilda." She grinned and tugged on his waistcoat, starting for the door. "Come along, to Portsmouth with you."

Groaning, he raked his fingers through his hair, but he followed. "I have a horrible feeling you're right."

"Of course I am." She took his hand and patted it. "We'll soon have you mended, big brother. And then you can come to Lunden with me to help fight off all the rakes vying for my hand."

He snorted. "You're clever enough to run rings around them. I fear they might be the ones who need protecting from you."

Chatting about her plans for Lunden, Is led the way upstairs to help pack his bag. Although his tread on the stairs was heavy, his heart and limbs were far lighter than they'd been in weeks.

He'd return to Portsmouth, get the Admiralty to grant him a meeting with Vee—*Vice*. Then he'd get the closure some traitorous part of himself so badly needed.

Yes, he had a plan to rid his thoughts of the notorious Lady Vice. Soon he would be free of her once and for all.

INTERFERENCE

Scowling, Knigh stomped down the stairs of the Admiralty Offices. There was no reason for them to deny him a meeting with Vee unless *someone* had interfered.

And there was only one person likely to have done that.

FitzRoy was staying in an upmarket inn closer to the edge of town, and within a few minutes, Knigh was on the right road. Despite the chilly air misting his breaths, his cheeks burned. What had that bastard said to the Admiralty? Did he not understand he could ruin his career? No, this was FitzRoy—he knew exactly what he was doing.

Knigh paused at the inn's door and drew a long breath of chilly air. He'd quite happily wring FitzRoy's neck, but he was an officer of the Royal Navy and as such represented Queen and country. He would not enter an inn and start a brawl. He wasn't an animal.

Nodding, he clenched his jaw. That was far more the sort of behaviour he'd expect from a pirate like FitzRoy.

There was no sign of the man within, but after eyeing his

uniform, the innkeeper pointed him towards a private dining room. Even better—he'd catch him alone.

When he threw the door open, FitzRoy's dark eyebrows shot up over the rim of his wine glass. "Knighton Blackwood!"

Knigh stilled in the doorway, veins throbbing with an intense need to punch him in the nose. He swallowed and took a long breath, forcing his arms to his sides.

FitzRoy grinned and swept his glass to the side in an expansive gesture. "My old friend. I didn't expect to see you back here—I thought you'd be off enjoying your reward like I am."

His glass passed over the table covered in a dozen plates. Roast pheasant. Baked cod. Oysters covered in flecks of parsley. A golden pie oozing gravy where a quarter had been cut out. Crusty bread and a pat of golden butter. Cheeses from pale yellow cheddar to a veined green-blue Stilton. An array of vegetables, steam rising from their bowls.

Knigh stared at it all, the savoury smell turning his stomach. He shook his head.

FitzRoy gulped his wine. "Ah, but, don't tell me, you've come back to watch her hang? It's the first time I'll watch a woman I've bedded die, and while I must admit I'm curious what that will feel like, I wouldn't have ridden halfway across the country to see it." Laughing, he raised his glass. "I didn't have you down as such a sick bastard, Blackwood."

His words stole Knigh's breath, and it took a moment before he could gather the air to speak. "You—how can you talk about her like that?" He'd betrayed a member of his crew and clearly felt not even the slightest shadow of guilt. *He* was the monster.

"You're not going to join me, then?" He gestured at the chair opposite.

"Of course I'm not going to bloody join you."

Chuckling, FitzRoy put his glass on the table. "You're upset about the harlot's fate."

"Aren't you?" Knigh's nostrils flared. The man was unbelievable. What did Vee ever see in him? "And don't call her a harlot. You know she's more than that even to you."

FitzRoy snorted and broke off a morsel of cheese. "She wasn't my wife. *I* owed her nothing." He threw it in his mouth and chewed, unruffled.

But he *did* owe her. As a member of his crew, she'd placed her safety in his hands.

And as a lover, she'd placed herself in Knigh's hands, too.

Gritting his teeth, he shut out the thought. He pressed his hands into the varnished table, glaring at FitzRoy. *He* was the one in the wrong here. "At least I always told her not to trust me, but she trusted you, she was part of your crew for how many years?"

FitzRoy's amusement faded as he drew a long breath. He took his time wiping his hands on a napkin, then stood, lifting his chin. "Don't lecture me, Blackwood," he said, voice gravelly, "you were as much a part of this as I was."

"But you owed her, *I* didn't."

FitzRoy's mouth set in a straight line. "So you don't believe you owe a lady you let in your bed anything?"

Legs tense, Knigh almost took a step back, but years of practice kept the reaction in check.

FitzRoy couldn't know that—he was just digging for information. It was a guess. If he knew, he wouldn't have been able to keep his possessiveness in check. He wouldn't have attacked Knigh as he had Aedan, but he'd have said something or betrayed his envy. He was not a man who had mastery over his emotions.

Shaking his head, FitzRoy scoffed. "Of course I knew. Did you think the pair of you were subtle? Ha! Did you think you could even *be* subtle about that on a ship? Why do you think the Admiralty won't let you see her?"

Straightening, Knigh turned and strode to the fireplace, blood seething in his veins, forcing movement. He leant on the mantlepiece, back to FitzRoy so he wouldn't see the frown so tight on his brow it ached. The bastard knew the whole time.

And he'd told the Admiralty. They hadn't summoned Knigh yet, so his career might not be ruined, but this would be a mark against him. If he was lucky, they'd put it down to a man's loneliness at sea—just the needs of the flesh, nothing involving *feeling.*

"Poor boy," FitzRoy went on, "only now realising he's come here to push his own guilt on me." His laugh rang through the room, through Knigh's chest.

"Don't you"—but he couldn't finish the sentence.

Heat sparked in his veins, and he turned, covering the distance between him and FitzRoy in a few paces. Chest heaving, he managed to stop toe-to-toe with him. "You don't know what you're talking about."

Keep control.

Deep breaths.

FitzRoy didn't back off. A smirk tugged at one corner of his mouth, and his eyes glinted. "Don't I? You see, you've come here and made these accusations about how I should feel. About what I owed her. About how she trusted me. But I think you're really talking about yourself."

Fists balled so tightly they popped, Knigh's body burned with tension, with the threat of white rage. "No."

A cruel smile took over FitzRoy's face. "Oh *yes.* You've just come here to make yourself feel better, to soothe the guilt keeping you awake at night. To tell yourself you owed her nothing. To reassure yourself that she didn't trust you." His eyes narrowed.

"What I can't work out is why you went through with it in the end."

Knigh tore his gaze away from FitzRoy's. The bastard. How had he managed to turn this back on him?

Something red glinted on the front of his shirt, below the gleam of pearls. The scoundrel was wearing Lady Avice's pin. He must have taken it from Vice. Well, he didn't deserve it any more than she did. It had been a sign of loyalty for Lady Avice, and FitzRoy wasn't capable of that. It belonged with her family.

Maybe the gods had put it here to remind him.

He took a deep breath and met FitzRoy's gaze, veins cooling, calming. Whatever the twisting in his stomach said, he was right in this. He tore the pin from FitzRoy's shirt and held it up, the ruby eyes glinting. "She killed Avice Ferrers. I will not feel guilty about her facing the justice she deserves."

FitzRoy blinked once, twice, then he burst into laughter, taking a step back and doubling over.

Slipping the pin in his breast pocket, Knigh frowned, backing away. The man was addled—he'd be no help. Knigh threw open the door.

Still laughing, FitzRoy shook his head and wiped the corner of his eye. "If only you knew the truth about Avice Ferrers."

And now he was trying to twist her memory, too.

Teeth clenched, Knigh slammed the door and stormed away.

IRON & IRONY

The drink did no good.

He'd tried whisky. He'd tried rum. He'd tried stout. He'd even tried gin—good old mother's ruin.

And none of it made a damn bit of difference.

You've just come here to make yourself feel better, to soothe the guilt keeping you awake at night.

FitzRoy's words kept coming to him again and again.

She had killed—*murdered* an innocent girl. For all she played the roguish hero, Vice was a *murderer*.

But... *You've just come here to make yourself feel better, to soothe the guilt keeping you awake at night.*

Growling, Knigh shoved his hands in his pockets. The sharp edge of the shell bit into his fingertips.

Wild Hunt take the damn thing. He snatched his hands out and fisted them at his sides. He'd been walking through the streets so long, the fuzziness of the alcohol had started to wear off. Even the sparse lamplight was too bright, lining the city streets with far too much clarity.

The drink was supposed to help him forget. That's what Vice had recommended before, and it had helped back in Arawaké.

But here, now, it just left him hollow. Aching. Tired.

So damn tired.

Along the street, a lady sat in a window lit by a lamp, her gown cut scandalously low, a little too much rouge on her mouth. The sign above the door confirmed it: *Mrs Pettigrew's Parlour for Entertainments.* A brothel.

Being in Vice's arms had helped him forget before, had soothed his churning emotions, had even helped quieten the anger he carried for Father. Perhaps...

But looking at the lady as she caught his eye, cocked her head, smiled, beckoned, he couldn't summon the slightest wish to join her inside, even though it would have been warmer than out here in the cold night air.

He clenched his jaw and strode past. His damn body still only wanted *her.*

And maybe in a way it was right.

Isabel had said Vice might be the only one who could bring him closure. And although the Admiralty had denied him a visit, perhaps he didn't need their permission.

Every step feeling like doom, he let his feet carry him to the castle.

Its low grey hulk was mostly shadows punctuated by lamps, torches, and braziers. Still, he knew its battlements and square keep from his years studying at the naval college. He approached from the west, where one of its broad gun platforms loomed, covered in cannons, ready to fight off enemy ships that broke through Albion's sea witch defences. No one had done that in centuries but not for want of trying.

On the road ahead, before the castle walls, a small, grey shape sat beside a brazier, furry back to him, looking up, pointed ears alert. He blinked. "Barnacle?"

The little cat turned, revealing her white belly, almost glowing in the firelight. She gave a chirruping meow of greeting.

"What are you doing here?" He crouched and petted her, winning enthusiastic purrs.

Her muddy paws said she'd been away from the ship for a while. What had so drawn her attention?

His gaze trailed up the castle wall—up, up and...

"Oh gods."

A black cage hung from the walls, fifteen feet above the street. Inside, a dark shape huddled, nearby torches hinting at a deep red coat.

His stomach knotted. He'd come to find her but...

Even from this distance, that posture was wrong, so wrong for her. She didn't huddle. She wasn't small. She was...

A murderer. Remember that, you idiot.

Drawing a deep breath, he scratched Barnacle behind the ears, then stood. On the castle walls, flickering shadows and torchlight revealed the circuits of guards. But down here, he was alone.

The castle was meant to defend the coast from attack by sea, so as the city had grown, they'd filled in the moat on the landward side to create more space and allowed houses and shops to butt right up to the castle walls. That's what he'd spent too much of his early teens climbing and sneaking over with friends, escaping lessons, finding mischief.

If that boy had only known what was to come...

Still, that childhood play would make this easy. With a quick glance, he confirmed he was alone and clambered up a crumbled stretch of wall, across a low roof, and up its pitch. There was one tricky moment where his head spun, just the hint of alcohol's effects, but he caught a crumbling chimney and righted himself.

Edging across the remaining bricks of another long-abandoned building brought him to the castle walls and within arm's reach of the cage.

The iron made his skin prickle. The warmth of his gift shrank at its presence. How bad was it to be encased in the stuff?

It was cold up here, but the brazier below gave off a little heat. Of course—he shuddered—they didn't want her dying from the cold before her execution.

Biting his lip, he forced his eyes to her.

Coat pulled around herself, she was crumpled inside the gibbet cage—back braced against the far side, knees against this side, hands tucked up in her sleeves. Her eyes were closed below a deep frown. Her breaths weren't slow and deep as he'd seen them in proper sleep. She was only dozing. Even in this scant light, he could see her cheeks were hollow, and shadows ringed her eyes. Her usually tanned skin was pale and sallow.

She looked ill.

His stomach twisted so tight it stole his breath. Crouching on the wall, he rubbed his face. This had to be unbearable for someone fae-touched, tantamount to torture. Being executed was one thing, but this...

"Vee," he murmured. "Vee?"

With a sharp breath, her eyes opened, darting side to side. When they landed on him, they widened, and her mouth fell open. For a few seconds, she only stared.

Eventually, she shook her head, exhaling through her nose. "You've got a bloody nerve showing your face here." She pulled herself upright, face contorting in a wince. "If these bars didn't burn, I'd reach through and drag you off that damn wall."

He blinked, shook his head. "What?" *If these bars didn't burn...*

Oh Lords, Ladies, Wild Hunt. He had to catch himself against the cold stone of the castle wall as the world tipped. The iron didn't just block her gift. She wasn't fae-touched.

If it burned her, it meant...

Gods. She was fae-*blooded*. Part-fae. Not wholly human.

No wonder her gift was so strong. No wonder she looked ill.

Iron could kill a fae... Was this how it started? Sickness and burns, then a slow, painful decline, and finally death.

His stomach spasmed.

Wrong. This was wrong. His bones creaked with it, cold in the shadow of the iron cage.

He drew a long breath, gripped the stone wall.

No. He only thought it wrong because he'd allowed himself to be compromised by emotion. He'd been confused by her charm, her physicality, their connection.

Shoulders hunched, every angle of her turned inward to avoid touching the metal even through her clothes. She folded her arms and glared at him. "What do you want?"

Clenching his jaw, he steeled himself. "You hang the day after tomorrow. I needed to speak to you first."

Her nostrils flared. "Did you now? Well, I'm so glad I can be of help to *you*." Her body shook; her neck corded. In the dim light, her eyes glistened. "You traitorous bloody bastard."

He swallowed, braced like a man climbing the shrouds in a storm, waves lashing his face and trying to stop him from his work. Necessary work. If that man didn't get to the yards, he couldn't trim the sails, and the ship might lose a mast: they would all be doomed.

Traitorous. He'd told himself that word, had heard it in her tone when he'd arrested her, but that did nothing to soften the sound of it from her mouth.

But this was necessary, just like that desperate climb up the shrouds.

Isabel had told him. He had to face this woman before she died, and this was his last chance. He had to get out all the words clogging up his throat, wrapped around his heart, blocking his lungs.

Lifting his chin, he met her gaze levelly. "I told you not to trust me. It was always the plan to—"

"Oh, I know all about your plan." A tight smile paled her lips. "FitzRoy told me everything. Him"—her finger stabbed towards the city, the knuckles standing out against her bony hand—"I should have expected it from *him*, but you." Her throat rose and fell as she swallowed, shaking her head. "I thought we had an understanding. Damn fool that I was, I trusted you —*almost* trusted you. We worked well together, I thought we were..." Her words dissolved into heaving breaths.

He stared at her skinny fingers. They'd always been strong, but her body was wasting away locked in this iron.

"We made a good team," she growled and crossed her arms, tucking her hands away. "Or at least I *thought* we did. All the bloody while, you were just after what you could get before you arrested me. Did you laugh? Did you have a good time swapping notes with FitzRoy?" She chuckled bitterly, eyes bright.

Each word was a sabre driving through him. "I'd never—"

"You'd never what?" Her mouth twisted. "Never betray me?"

No. Damn her. He wasn't going to apologise—*she* was the traitor. She'd started this by fooling him into believing she was anything other than a monster. Heat flared in his veins, pumped through his heart.

He was right. She was wrong.

"Oh yes," she went on, "noble bloody Navy boy, he'd never screw a woman and then royally screw her over, would he? He'd never—"

"You're a murderer." He raised his eyebrows at her—let her dare to deny it. She'd said it herself.

She blinked. "What?"

Shaking his head, he scoffed. "Listening to you, anyone would think you're some poor, innocent victim in all this. But you're not." Let her hear the damn truth. "You like to pretend you're some noble pirate who frees the enslaved, maroons slavers, and only kills in battle when it's life or death. But you're a murderer. You killed my betrothed. She was eighteen years old, and I don't believe for a second she was a threat to your life. You killed Lady Avice Ferrers."

She blinked again. The corners of her lips twitched. She covered her mouth, and a breath burst out of her—almost a chuckle. Then she guffawed and shook her head.

Why was she—

Head tilting back, she laughed.

And laughed. And laughed.

ON WILDER SEAS

She sounded half-mad.

Stomach turning, Knigh clung to the castle wall to force himself to stay in place and not climb back down to the ground and leave her to her madness. She was as bad as Fitz-Roy, laughing at someone else's misfortune, laughing at her own terrible deed. But he had to stay here and face her. It was the only way to put an end to this.

Finally, it faded to a chuckle as she wiped her eyes. "Well, at least you've given me a good laugh before I go."

Every muscle thrumming with rage, he snarled, "You're disgusting. How can you murder someone and—"

"I didn't murder her, you idiot."

Denying it. Were all criminals the same? He scoffed, shaking his head, but when he met her eye, something about the flat look gave him pause. A thin thread of cold needled through him. "But you said—"

With an impatient sigh, she rolled her eyes. "I lied." Cocking her head, she smiled, but it only made her eyes glitter hard and cold like the stars overhead. "Or at least I was speaking *metaphorically*—really, I thought you were an educated gentleman. I no more murdered her than you murdered the arrogant little boy you once were. Remember?

Disturb us, Ladies, to dare more boldly,
To venture on wilder seas
Where storms will show Your mastery;
Where losing sight of land,
We shall find the stars."

The cold thread became twine, then thick footropes, then an anchor cable, grating on his bones, leaching away all the hot rage, all the warmth until he shivered. "That poem... How do you"—he shook his head.

Had Lady Avice told Vice the poem before she'd killed her?

But then the other things she said... That she hadn't killed her. That...

The 'arrogant boy' she spoke of wasn't dead, he'd just grown into someone very different, thanks to the Royal Navy. So, was Lady Avice Ferrers also alive and... just... someone very different?

His chest tightened. No. Not possible.

But she was still smirking back at him, amusement in her eyes, laced with bitterness.

"That poem," he breathed, voice feeling far away. "The pin... But she's—"

"Dead?" She said it too brightly, and her eyebrows rose like it was a joke he was too stupid to fathom. "Do you still not understand? Avice Ferrers is just as dead as Knighton Villiers."

Ba-DUM—his heart gave a hard, heavy squeeze. His fingers tingled, and cold sweat beaded on his brow.

He'd changed his name, hadn't he? After what he'd done to

Billy, he'd needed to put distance between himself and Knighton Villiers, and he'd wanted to escape the constant reminder of his father. So Knigh Blackwood had served the purpose.

And could she have done the same? No, when said out loud *Ay-viss* didn't sound like Vice, but when written down... Take off the *A* and *Avice* became *Vice*.

Lady Avice Ferrers had become Lady Vice.

Oh gods.

Hands shaking, they raked through his hair.

Oh gods. What had he done?

"You didn't kill her... you *are* her." He blinked. The voice didn't sound like his, but it came from his raw throat.

"Oh, well done." She clapped, then winced and gripped her hands together. Blisters and red burns covered her knuckles and fingers. The sight of each one made him crumble just a little more, like the old wall he stood on.

Wild Hunt take him, this was his fault.

"What happened? How did you—" He shook his head, throat closing.

She snorted. "You don't get to have that story."

No, of course not. Not after... Damnation. *What have I done?*

All this. Her trial. Her punishment. And what had he ever, really, seen her do wrong? She'd been a pirate for years, but she'd *wanted* to become a privateer, she'd told him that in their night-time talks. Even before the letter of marque, there were startlingly few reports of *The Morrigan* attacking Albionic ships.

He had no guilt about employing underhand tactics against pirates. To catch them, he had to think like them. His unorthodox methods were one thing when used to right a wrong, but to *execute* a wrong...

"Vee—Avice, I—"

"Don't call me that." All hint of amusement had vanished,

leaving her face cold, tired, and so sickly it made his stomach spasm.

He swallowed down the nausea, but every part of him roiled, churned, like an angry sea upon a shingle beach. He'd continuously fought his feelings for her, not trusting his emotions or gut instinct, and that was what led to this mistake. This gross mistake. He'd been far too eager to believe himself wrong, to believe the worst about her.

"Vee, I"—he shook his head—"I've been an idiot. I'm so sorry—and I know that doesn't fix anything, but I'm going to get you out of here."

He was. Gods knew how, but he'd said it, and he might not have thought it through first, and he might not have the slightest idea *how*, but he would do this thing. Somehow.

"Go away, Knighton." Her voice was flat, her eyes dark.

She had to believe in him. He would do whatever it took to right his wrong. "You won't be hanged. I promise you."

Snorting, she waved him off. "I'll believe it when I see it. It's not as if I'm going anywhere, is it?"

With a last look at her, he climbed down from the terrible iron cage without a single misstep. Stone cold sober.

Was it any wonder? This was...

Lords, it was beyond imagining. Beyond his worst nightmares or wildest dreams. The woman he'd travelled halfway across the globe to hunt was the girl his parents had arranged for him to marry. The woman he'd made love to, laughed with, held close as she'd slept was the young woman who'd eloped with another man. *Vee* was the same woman he and everyone else had thought dead for the past three years.

Once his feet were back on the ground, he rested his forehead against the wall's rough brick. Blessedly solid.

Did her family have the faintest idea? Her parents? Her sister?

Had she ever written to them? Maybe they knew and kept the secret.

If they didn't know, should he tell them? No—that was her decision, but what if she...

No. She wasn't going to be hanged. That was non-negotiable. Nothing else was important right now.

The problem—one of so very many—was that the Admiralty had refused him a meeting with her. There was no way they were going to free her on his say-so or even agree to a re-trial. As far as they were concerned, thanks to FitzRoy's sudden love of the truth, Knigh was just another young man who'd let his loins lead him on a merry dance to a beautiful woman's tune. Captain Knigh Blackwood had been hopelessly compromised by Lady Vice.

And, to them, she was the villain they'd always claimed. It didn't matter a bit whether she was Lady Avice Ferrers or whether she'd killed the girl three years ago. She was the notorious Lady Vice and they had her in chains to be hanged the day after tomorrow.

That meant the only way was to break her out. To break the *law*.

He took a heavy breath. In this, the law was wrong. A wrong that he'd helped cause with schemes and lies. He'd used those things against her, and now he would have to use them *for* her.

It would cost him... He winced—Wild Hunt it would cost him—his career, his family, his chance to set foot on Albion as a free, law-abiding man ever again...

His family would be safe, though. He'd just never be able to see them. At least he'd made Isabel's dowry, and George was bringing home money—albeit from a questionable source.

Even if their future didn't have that security, he might still make this same decision.

Because if he didn't, she would die and that would be on his head.

Forever.

It wouldn't be an *almost* wrong, like when he'd *almost* killed those men who'd surrendered. It would be a thing he'd done and had to live with, like Billy's hand. But this time it wouldn't only be a limb he was responsible for the loss of—it would be a life.

Eyes shut, he pressed his forehead into the wall until the brick almost broke the skin, a rough, low-level pain. It would be nothing compared to the pain of allowing this to happen to Vee.

"Focus," he whispered to himself. *This is what's at stake.*

Somehow, he needed to orchestrate a breakout from a public gibbet for the Navy's most prized captive. From the side of a castle. In the middle of a city that had built up around their biggest dockyard. And then he had to get her out of that city. Hells, out of Albion would be preferable.

A shape weaved around his ankles, rumbling in a low purr. He crouched and picked Barnacle up, holding her close, scratching under her chin.

In the east, the sky lightened, hazed with the golden threat of dawn.

And he had a day to do it all.

THE PLAN

The fresh morning air, the waves' lulling song, and the sight of ships soothed Knigh's churning stomach and mind a little. The gulls screaming overhead, though—he winced. They weren't helping the headache throbbing across his brow.

His palms were slick with sweat. This next task...

He grimaced. It was one he'd been putting off far too long and somehow, amid all this mess, it had found him. Shoulders squared, he brushed his hands down the front of his coat—civilian, not uniform—and strode along the wharves.

After speaking to Vee, he'd spent the remaining hour or so of darkness in his rooms. With his thoughts turning over and over, sleep was a distant impossibility. Instead, he brewed a strong pot of coffee and went through his belongings and made a mental audit of all resources available to him.

There weren't many.

FitzRoy wouldn't help and neither would Bricus—the way

he'd spoken about Vee, it was clear that behind his cheery smiles, he'd harboured resentment towards her for three long years.

No one in the Navy would help break the law and even if they would, he couldn't ask it of them. Besides, it would be too difficult to sneak a woman on a Naval vessel to escape.

He had weapons, but he'd prefer to do this without injuring anyone. Any guards at the castle were only doing their jobs. This mess wasn't their fault—it was well and truly his.

To break open the gibbet cage, he'd managed to gather a few basic tools. It wouldn't be an elegant job, but the poker from his rooms looked slender and robust enough that it would fit in the keyhole. Add his strength to one end and, Lords and Ladies willing, it would break. Surely the fae would give favour to his attempt to free one of their own.

As for getting to the cage—that would be the same as this morning. No one had seen him there under cover of darkness. With a bit of luck, no one would see him there tonight, either. Now he knew the lay of the land, he could even smother the brazier and any torches he came across. It would be harder for the guards to spot his work or Vee's escape.

By the time he'd finished all that, the Admiralty's offices had opened, and he was in full uniform. He was reasonably sure of the result, but he had to *try* this the legitimate way.

Vice Admiral Yorke, the man who'd helped arrest Vee, had agreed to see him, despite the lack of appointment. That was a positive start.

Unfortunately, it was the only positive note. As soon as he began outlining his argument, the grey-haired man smiled and steepled his fingers. He thought this a lover's regret or a heartsick young man. Maybe that was why he allowed Knigh to retrieve some of Vice's belongings from her sea chest in the Admiralty basement—keepsakes of a tragic romance.

Yorke even added a further stab of guilt as he saw Knigh from his offices.

"Now, continue your leave and return once this business is all taken care of and your mind is rested. You don't want to end up like your friend Billy Hopper, retired from the Navy far too soon, do you?"

The name twitched through him—the night's revelations had left him too exhausted to smother the reaction.

Yorke smiled and gestured to the door. "Go to the civilian docks if you want a reminder of that fate."

Billy was docked in Portsmouth.

It was the first time they'd been in the same place since he'd left the Navy and Knigh owed him a visit. Owed him a lot more, in fact.

So here he was, at the civilian wharves, south of the Royal Dockyard. After changing from his uniform, he'd found some familiar faces in one of the taverns preferred by Navy lads and a few questions had got him the name of Billy's vessel. The *Swallow*, a merchant barque that ran passengers and Albionic goods like lace and wool to Arawaké and returned with spices, tobacco, and other Arawakéan specialities.

He'd only planned to visit Billy to see if there was anything he needed, any way he could help. He hadn't expected to hear he was still sailing, never mind that he ran a route all the way to Arawaké. Perhaps he'd have space for two more passengers...

When he spotted the ship, he froze mid-step. What was he doing? He hadn't seen Billy since they'd landed in Albion after that fateful tour, and now he was darkening his door to ask a favour.

Closing his eyes, he pinched the bridge of his nose. He needed more coffee. And willow bark—that helped with headaches.

He had to do this. Running away wasn't an option. This might be the only way he could get Vee out of Portsmouth. If he could get her to Arawaké, she'd be out of the Navy's grasp, just another pirate on the seas. And this time she wouldn't have him hunting her.

Plus, he would pay for their passage. It didn't have to be a favour. Billy wouldn't be complicit—plausible deniability.

"Knigh?"

His spine straightened. He knew that voice. Gulping, he rubbed his eyelids before opening them.

With a broad grin, a tanned man hurried over the *Swallow's* gangway, dark eyes wide and shining. "It *is* you."

He'd grown a beard over the past two years, but there was no mistaking that smile, the round eyes—even his dimples were still visible through the neat facial hair.

Billy Hopper.

THE HONEYMOON

Knigh's stomach turned, and it took all his willpower not to run or vomit. Or both.

"Captain Knighton Villiers," Billy said, then snapped in a sharp salute. Grinning, he closed in and grabbed Knigh's shoulder, giving him a good, long look. "I heard you'd made Captain. And the youngest ever, too. Congratulations, my friend." He clapped Knigh's back. "Always knew you would."

My friend. Knigh blinked.

Lords, he was just staring at the poor man, wasn't he?

He cleared his throat. "Thank—thank you." His gaze skittered to the left cuff of Billy's coat where a hand should've been. Where it would have been, if not for him. He swallowed back bile. "How—how are you? This looks like a fine vessel."

If anything, Billy's smile grew broader, and he gestured at the *Swallow*. "She is, she is! And, as for me, I've never been better."

Knigh's chest ached. Billy didn't need to say that to make him feel better. But to say so would be pitying and cruel. Billy was the one who'd lost a hand, and it was his fault—Knigh wasn't the victim here. So he smiled like it was true and nodded.

But... with that tan, and those bright eyes, Billy *did* look healthy. Maybe even happy.

Knigh arched his eyebrows. "Never better?"

"A ship of my own—well, a share of it, anyway. The wind in my hair. And a damn sight fewer rules." He stroked his beard. "I've even been able to grow this without anyone court marshalling me."

Despite himself, Knigh snorted.

"Although," Billy said, eyeing him with raised brows, "from the state of you, I wonder if the rules have eased over the past couple of years."

Knigh rubbed his cheek, stubble rasping his fingertips. Unshaven, not in uniform. A *state* probably was the term for it.

Billy cocked his head. "That is, if you're still in the Navy?"

Not for much longer. He swallowed and nodded, the thought heavy, making his head pound harder. "I'm—I'm just on leave at the moment."

"You, *on leave?*" Billy chuckled. "Wonders will never cease."

His heart skipped. One of Vee's favourite phrases. He needed to make arrangements. With a little luck, Billy would be leaving soon. "I—ah—actually, I'm on honeymoon." Saying Vee was his wife seemed the most plausible way to explain them travelling together and would provide her an identity.

"Honeymoon?" Billy's eyes went wide again, and he grabbed Knigh into a fierce hug, slapping his back. "You sly dog you! I'd heard you'd made Captain, but not this! It seems we have a lot to celebrate. Come, have lunch with me."

"I—I can't possibly, I—" Knigh raised his hand, backing away. Billy's kindness was too much to bear. Not when all Knigh deserved was resentment, retribution, some sort of repayment for the disability he'd caused.

But, of course, Billy was too good a person to show the hatred he had to feel somewhere deep inside or to make Knigh uncomfortable.

Knigh winced. All the things he wasn't. Too good, too kind, too thoughtful.

"I insist," Billy said with a final nod. "But if it helps, I'll let you buy." He winked then called to an older sailor inspecting lines and let him know he'd be back soon. He promised to bring back some lunch then turned towards the buildings lining the seafront. "Come on, Knigh. You can catch me up on everything you've been up to, and I'll see if I can't persuade you to invest in my business." He flashed a bright grin and led the way.

Sighing, Knigh followed. He couldn't deny Billy anything. Not when he owed him so much.

It turned out Billy had used the lump sum he'd received from the Navy—topped up in secret by Knigh—to start a business with a family friend. They'd bought a ship, which Billy sailed with a few modifications for his hand and, of course, help from a skilled crew, most of whom were former Navy. They traded between Arawaké and Europa, mostly Albion, focusing on those commodities that were specialities of the respective areas. By all accounts, the business was successful and currently in the process of financing a third ship.

Billy somehow cajoled him into eating a little and to his surprise, his stomach kept the food down.

It seemed his friend genuinely was at least enjoying some prosperity. Maybe his life hadn't been completely ruined that day Knigh had cut his hand off.

All this time, Knigh had pictured him shut away, struggling, unhappy. That thought had coiled with the anger for Father, twisting and seething into an anchor cable too heavy to raise.

A half-smile in place, he listened to Billy talking about his latest trip and how there'd been some problems with a passenger attempting to seduce him. If he wasn't happy, he was at least not miserable.

"But here I am going on about my adventures," Billy said, shaking his head and setting his cutlery aside. "I haven't even asked you about your greatest one. Marriage, eh?" He chuckled and took a sip of his ale. "Tell me about the lady, then."

Knigh's belly flipped, threatening to bring the little he'd eaten back up. The clock on the mantlepiece said it was nearly one o'clock. "Unfortunately, I can't linger, but I wonder if you might have the chance to meet her soon."

Thankfully Billy had only arrived in Portsmouth the day before yesterday, so he wouldn't recognise Vee from the reports of her trial. Not that she was recognisable at the moment. His stomach twisted again.

He would make this right.

Licking his lips, his gaze slid to the gravy and picked-at slice of pie on his plate. "She arrives in town tonight, and I was actually at the docks to try and secure our transport to Arawaké."

He swallowed. He'd worked out the story as he'd taken stock this morning and had embellished it as he'd walked down to the docks. But saying it out loud, knowing he was lying to Billy, was a different matter entirely and the words coated his throat.

"I mean to settle her there, so she won't be far away when I'm working." Forcing his breaths slow and even, he chanced a look at his friend.

A slow smile spread across his lips. "Well, I never. Knighton Villiers is actually *in love.*" He chuckled, shaking his head. "You don't want her far away while you work? I thought you lived only for the Navy. When you said you'd married, I assumed it was a matter of family duty, not a love match." He leant over the table and patted his shoulder. "Well, for that I must apologise and wish you much more heart-felt congratulations than I did earlier." Brown eyes earnest, Billy held his eye contact and nodded. "Congratulations, my dear friend. I'm so happy for you."

Wild Hunt take me.

He didn't deserve this from Billy, especially not in response to a lie. But it was a necessary lie. A life-saving lie. If he could just make this plan work...

Clinging to that thought, he pushed his mouth into a smile. "I'm hoping you have space for two more passengers when you return to Arawaké."

"Ah"—Billy nodded—"I see. Well, I'm afraid we leave in the morning, I'm sure that's too—"

"It's perfect." Even better than he could have hoped, in fact. If they could get away on the early tide, they might even escape before the guards spotted Vee wasn't in that cruel cage. "She—my wife—she doesn't have much taste for Portsmouth, so she'll be glad to leave as soon as possible."

Frowning, Billy blinked. "Well, if you're sure, then, yes, I have the berth."

Knigh scratched his face to hide the relieved breath he exhaled. "Thank you, Billy. I can pay now, it's—"

"No, you can't." He shook his head, a laugh in his voice. "I won't hear of it."

Knigh clenched his jaw and rose. Billy might decline payment now, but he had a whole voyage to slip the money to him. "We'll see."

Billy just laughed and stood, pulling his coat on. "Get yourself out of here—it sounds like you have more preparations to make for this mysterious wife's arrival."

"You can say that again."

They said their goodbyes, and Knigh promised to bring some belongings to the *Swallow* later.

Knigh hurried further inland towards a reputable inn. He'd secured their passage, but he still needed to finalise other parts of his plan before the sun set.

From the look of her this morning, it was going to take some work to disguise the fact she was a fugitive. A lady's clothes, a wash, food, and, preferably, some time to rest before they slipped through the city to the docks and masqueraded as husband and wife.

He rubbed his face. Even then, with how ill she looked, someone might sense something off and look too closely. This kind of sickness—he wasn't even sure if he could heal it with his gift. It might just take time and care. Perhaps when he dropped his belongings off with Billy, he'd mention that she was unwell, and he was hoping Arawaké's climate would help her health. That way, he wouldn't be too shocked by her appearance. But then again, maybe she'd look better after a wash and some rest.

Glancing along the road confirmed no one followed him. Good—best if the Navy didn't know about this visit to the inn or the other errands he needed to run this afternoon.

He couldn't take Vee to his Navy suite—that would be leading her into the lions' den. First, he'd rent a room in the inn, explaining his ill wife was due to arrive late tonight and would need a bath and food.

Then he'd buy the best clothes he could find—there wasn't time to have something made for her, but pawn shops and second-hand clothes shops would have fine ladies' cast-offs.

Plenty of officer's wives only wore a gown once or twice, there would have to be a decent stock of such outfits in the city. Vee's height might be an issue, but she'd have to make do with what he could find.

Rubbing his hands together against the nip in the air, he clenched his jaw. What else?

His gaze crept over the shops and houses of the bustling street, then across to the distant castle towers. Gods, she'd be freezing up there today. His heart clenched. Please say they'd stoked that brazier.

He bit his lip. A warm cloak or coat. And she'd need comfort after the torture of that cage and—and what he'd done.

Goosebumps rose on his flesh, and his stomach turned again.

He swallowed. He didn't have time to dwell on his monumental mistake. If they got away, he'd have the whole journey to Arawaké to think about it.

Right now, though, he had to focus on tonight. This plan, its perfect planning and completion were all that mattered.

So. He nodded and huffed out a breath. What could he do to bring Vee some small comfort after all she'd been through?

Barnacle was in his rooms, ready to come on their trip, but maybe his budget would stretch to some little extras. He could make sure the undergarments were the softest he could find—they'd be gentle on her tender skin. Medicinal salts for her bath would help, too. Fruit, nuts, cake to help her regain energy. He also had the book—the dragon one he'd bought in Nassau. Yes, that was the kind of thing Vee would appreciate.

Sweet-smelling oils would be a kindness—a pointless luxury, but one that, hopefully, would say... would say he cared.

His throat clenched, and his fingers closed over the shell in his pocket. "I'm so sorry, Vee," he whispered. "Gods, Lords, Ladies, please help me help her and I'll spend the rest of my life trying to make up for this."

He pulled the shell out, his knuckles white, and pressed it to his lips. "Please."

THE DREAM

The sun was setting over Portsmouth, but if she closed her eyes, she could just about persuade herself she was on a ship. The sea was close enough to smell, all seaweed-salty, and to hear rushing against the castle's footings. Gulls called and, in the pretty image, wheeled above the *Venatrix's* sails. The rocking motion every time she moved was the shifting of waves against hull.

The constant movement she'd spoken to Knigh about that first time they'd met.

Frowning, she screwed her eyes closed tighter. Thinking about that took her too close to reality. Reality was where most of her body ached and the parts that didn't, seared with constant pain. Her hands and the burn on her forehead most of all.

In reality, her body had betrayed her, thanks to this damn iron. There was the pain, but also the trembling weakness and bone-deep exhaustion.

But worse, so very much worse, was that she was alone. Even Barnacle, who'd been circling below the cage for days, the sweet, silly thing—she'd gone. Vice hadn't seen her all day. It was probably just as well—staying here would get the cat nothing. Hopefully, she'd found somewhere warm and dry with someone kind who'd give her endless chin scratches.

Quaking, she buried her face in her hands and bit back a sob.

It was just the feebleness. Just the exhaustion. Just the gnawing hunger. That was all. They'd given her water, bread, and cheese, but she'd struggled to eat, sickened by the iron.

She wasn't crying. She wasn't upset. She wasn't weak.

Because sorrow was powerless. Sorrow got you nowhere. Sorrow had nearly drowned her when Evered had died. And she wasn't that person.

She was strong. She was tough. She was...

She was on the *Venatrix*, sailing through the broad, beautiful blue of Arawaké. She could almost feel the sun on her face, the sea below. If she reached out, she'd be able to take the wheel and steer their course somewhere new, somewhere...

"All is well." One of the guards above.

It was pretty, but it was a lie. She wasn't at sea, on the *Venatrix* or any ship. She was...

... Going to die alone.

Knigh wasn't coming. There would be no last-minute pardon or a rescue attempt. She was stuck in here. Even when they released her from this cage to take her to hang, she'd be too weak to use her gift to save herself.

Every child knew the stories about the fae-touched or fae-blooded who tried to use their gifts when they had no energy left to give, when their bodies were too weak.

They died.

But if she was going to be hanged anyway...

It had to be worth a try. As soon as she was clear of this iron, she'd call in a storm or fog or a gale or something—*anything* that might help her escape. A lightning bolt striking the gallows would be a good distraction. Mist could cover her escape.

Assuming she was still alive to run.

The sun shone through the clouds, glinting on the water on the sleek backs of dolphins following the ship, leaping and twisting through their wake. She laughed and pointed them out to Perry and Saba.

He wasn't coming.

She could have cried at the sight of him this morning, and her vision had blurred a couple of times as they'd talked. But, no, she hadn't given him the satisfaction of seeing her cry, of seeing her weak, of seeing how much just the hint of a friendly face had meant to her.

Pulling her dirty coat tighter, she folded her arms against the cold and screwed her eyes shut. That wasn't moisture coming from them.

It was the sea's refreshing spray. It glistened in the sun, arching a rainbow over the deck and saying the fae approved of their work, of her captaincy, of...

She must have dozed off because there was a sudden metallic clang, close-by, and when she jerked, eyes opening, it was full dark. Even the brazier below had gone out and the nearest torches and—

"Vee?"

With a sharp breath, she flinched and blinked into the darkness. Edged in moonlight, there he was, back at the top of that wall just as he had been this morning.

Eyes stinging, she sagged against the cage, the iron uncomfortably hot even through her layers of clothing.

"You came." Even to her ears, her voice sounded broken, but...

Did it matter?

He was here.

"I did," he murmured, voice thick as velvet, "and I'm going to get you out."

Hand covered with a handkerchief, he pulled something out of the lock—a poker? That must have been the sound that had woken her—him breaking the lock. He hooked it into his belt, like a sword at his side, and pulled the door open.

It was like a window had been opened in an unbearably hot room, and she gasped down the pleasant shock of untainted air.

"How?" She blinked at the impossibility of the open door.

But, no it wasn't real. This was one of her imaginings or a dream. She hugged herself and waited for it to pass.

"Vee, come on." The hands on her arms felt real enough—strong, firm, familiar.

And warm, so warm—the comforting kind, rather than the iron's scorching heat.

When she clung to those hands—yes, they still felt real. He helped her across the gap, slid an arm around her waist, gripping the castle wall with the other.

Still real.

Even if it wasn't, she could pretend. Closing her eyes, she buried her face against his chest. Yes, that smell was right—cinnamon, worn leather, fresh soap.

"Is this real?" His coat's braid brushed her lips when she spoke. That was an odd detail to imagine.

He squeezed her and pulled away, gaze finding hers. "This is real. I am here. You are free, and we're going to get away from this place."

Someone came for her. *He* came for her. He'd put her here, but now he was...

She shook her head as it began to throb. Too much. This was... And she was so tired. This was no time to focus on how she'd got here, what he'd done. He said she was free, but if they didn't get away, that freedom would be only temporary.

Lines of worry creased between his eyebrows. "Do you think you can climb down if I help?"

Clenching her jaw, she nodded. If it would get her out of here, she'd dance her way down the bloody wall.

One hand always on her, he helped her descend, steadying her when her legs trembled, lifting over one tricky spot until, at last, her feet were on the ground.

She'd never been so damn grateful for dry land, and a small moan burst from her lips at the feel. No iron. No burning, sucking, weakening iron. She sank against the alley wall and caught her breath.

Her legs trembled, but she managed to undress and quickly wash in a trough at the mouth of the alleyway, while Knigh kept watch. The frigid water barely registered on her already-cold skin. They returned to the alley's shadows, and he retrieved a duffle bag hidden in a doorway. Teeth chattering, she changed into the clothes he pulled out.

Chemise, stays, stockings, dainty shoes, and a plain gown in dark blue wool. A lady's clothes. Not an outfit anyone would associate with Lady Vice or any other prisoner.

He also passed her cheese and an apple, which she gobbled up as he laced the stays. The food, oh Lords, nothing had ever tasted so good as that salty cheese and the sweet, sweet apple. The sugar stopped the trembling and gave final confirmation: this was real.

She rubbed her eyes as if she'd just woken. "Wait"—she combed her hair with her fingers and started pinning it up—"you said *we* are going to get away."

Jaw knotted, he stuffed her coat and breeches into the duffle, gaze far too intent on such simple work—he didn't want to meet her eye. "I did."

"But if you leave with me now, you'll be—"

"I know." His chest rose and fell in a long breath. He tucked a shawl around her shoulders, then a thick winter cloak. It took him much longer than necessary to tie the cloak's cord before he finally made eye contact. "I'll be absent without leave. I'll—"

"Your career will be over. You'll be a fugitive from—"

"Vee." His nostrils flared, and a moment's anguish wrinkled the skin around his eyes. "I know. That's the decision I've made."

She swallowed, a chill settling even through all the layers. "But your family—"

"They're taken care of." But the flat line of his mouth said he wasn't happy about it. He swung the bag over his shoulder and turned to the alley entrance, offering his arm.

There was his sister's dowry and his mother and brother to take care of, too. From what he'd said about their financial position, it wasn't something to be solved as quickly and easily as a click of the fingers.

"How?"

"Mercia," he growled.

She winced and took his arm, leaning heavily on him. Not ideal. Maybe not permanent. There was *one* way his family's finances could be taken care of permanently, though. And her own. "Is FitzRoy still here?" she asked as they left the alley, pace slow to allow for her aching legs.

"In the city?" He frowned down at her before going back to scanning the road ahead. "Yes, why?"

"Where's he staying? I owe him a visit."

He squeezed her hand. "If you go after him, sword drawn, we'll—"

She scoffed and shook her head, though the motion sent dizziness spiralling through her. "Not revenge... at least not physical revenge. He has something I need."

"If it's your pin"—he reached into his breast pocket—"I have it already." He held out the red enamelled drake, rubies dark in the night. Only the pearl crown gleamed, pale and ghostly.

"Huh." The rush of familiarity made her head spin again as she took it—the shape her fingers knew so well.

"I took it from FitzRoy. I—I'd planned to take it to Av—to *your* parents so they could place it with whatever memorial they have for you."

"Thank you." She slipped it in her pocket—best if she wasn't seen wearing it here in Portsmouth, not while she was trying to parade as an anonymous lady. "But that wasn't what I had in mind. Where is he?"

"Vee, you—"

"If you're about to try and tell me I can't do something, I'm walking away right now." Pursing her lips, she gave him a side-long look. They both knew it would be a painfully slow stumble away, but she'd damn well do it. "I'm going to find him whether you help me or not. And it's in your interests to help me because if I get caught, they'll wonder how I got out."

With a deep sigh, Knigh changed course and took her to an upmarket inn a couple of streets away.

"We shouldn't stay on the road too long." He glanced left and right, a frown shadowing his eyes. "The longer we're out here, the more likely it is you'll be spotted and recognised."

"Warning noted and ignored." With a tight smile, she nodded and removed the cloak and shawl, thrusting them into his hands. "Wait here. I won't be long. And I won't kill him, but I need to borrow this." She slid his dagger from his belt and dropped it into her pocket, hilt-first so it wouldn't tear the fabric.

His jaw tightened, but he said nothing, only sank into a dark doorway to wait.

A VISIT

Drawing a deep breath, she smoothed her hair, arranged a lock of it over her shoulder, and adjusted her stays, making her cleavage heave at the neckline of her gown.

It was late, but the inn was bright with candlelight and felt full, even though only half a dozen officers sat at one end, bent over a game of cards. Swallowing, she angled away from them. On the way, Knigh had said her description had been in every newspaper along with reports on the trial. Back to the officers, she approached the bar. Behind it stood the innkeeper, watching Vice with narrowed eyes, smoothing hands down a scarlet gown.

Biting the inside of her cheek to avoid wincing, Vice bowed to the lady. Every muscle and tendon groaned at the movement, but she held in the grunt that threatened in her chest. "Madam, I've been sent by Mrs Pettigrew to provide entertainment to a Captain FitzRoy."

"Ah, one of Mrs Pettigrew's"—the innkeeper's pale eyes surveyed her—"you're a bit skinny, aren't you?"

Charming. Smile fixed in place, Vice tilted her head. "I've been ill."

"Hmm. I suppose some like them skinny." Lips pursed, the woman nodded to a back door, presumably leading to the staircase. "Room 3. Though you might have made a wasted journey—the state he was in when he went up, I'd wager he's already asleep."

Perfect. "I'm sure I'll be able to rouse him."

"I could use entertainment, if this FitzRoy's indisposed," one of the men called, his friends laughing and slamming their drinks on the table.

Not perfect. If they saw her face...

She laughed and called over her shoulder, "I'll get to you later." Hopefully, that would be enough. She raised her eyebrows at the innkeeper and sidled towards the door, scratching her forehead to hide her face from the rowdy officers.

Her heart pounded. Never had eight feet felt like such a distance to cross.

But then she was through the door and in a small hallway. Her knees shook, and her chest heaved as though she'd climbed a mountain, not just walked through an inn.

But she carried on, pausing for a break halfway up the stairs.

Unsurprisingly, the door to room 3 was locked. No light spilled through the crack underneath. No light was good—it meant he'd drunk himself into a stupor. But the lock...

Chewing her lip, she peered through the hole—the key blocked her view. That was a good start if she could just...

She glanced around and soon found an etching in a frame—perfect. In a moment, she had the frame open and the etching's thick paper in her hands.

With another check that no light came from his room, she slid the paper under the door below the handle.

Now to get the key out. If Knigh's dagger was slender enough... She drew it—yes, perfect. It just about slid into the keyhole, albeit with a scrape of metal on metal.

She winced at the *thunk* as the key dropped to the floor. Frozen, she listened.

Just the distant voices and laughter of the men downstairs and the tall clock ticking at the end of the landing.

Exhaling a shaky breath, she put the dagger away and slid the paper from under the door. The key dragged, rasping on the floor, but it was a quieter sound than when it had landed—if that hadn't woken him or anyone else, this wouldn't.

And there it was—dark metal. *Urgh*, iron.

The back of her neck crawled, and she pressed her hand to her mouth to stifle the gagging.

"It's fine," she whispered. "It's just a little key." It wasn't that cage.

Inhaling slowly, she used the hem of her skirts to protect her fingers and lifted the key. Through the fabric, it felt too hot, like sitting near a roaring fire. She shoved it into the lock and turned, sighing once she was finally able to release it.

Shaking her hand, she paused and listened again.

Still no sound.

She crept inside and closed the door before the light could disturb him.

It took a few seconds for her eyes to adjust to the dark, but her fae-blooded sight soon revealed the whole room. It was like a hundred other inn rooms—cabinet, fireplace, chair, dressing table, large four-poster bed.

Except that on this bed lay FitzRoy.

She clenched her jaw at the sight of him, sprawled on his back, head turned away, snoring softly.

The bloody bastard. While she'd been locked in an iron cage, he'd been here sleeping on a feather bed, enjoying his freedom, enjoying his *life*.

A few steps took her to him. He looked peaceful—dark eyelashes against his cheeks, chest rising and falling slowly and—

There. The pouch.

She smiled, baring her teeth. Well, if he'd given up on Drake's treasure, he didn't need it. And he certainly didn't deserve it.

There was no sign of the knot that held the cord in place and trying to pull it over his head could wake him. She drew the dagger.

Lords, Ladies, gods, and Wild Hunt, it was so tempting to put it to his chest, just below that pouch, slide it between his ribs and drive it through his stinking heart.

But he was asleep. This wasn't a fight. He wasn't even armed —his sabre sat on the dressing table. However much her fingers itched for revenge, it wouldn't be right.

And finding Drake's treasure without him—that would be an even better revenge, one he'd have to live through.

Nodding, she lifted the pouch and sliced through its cord. "I'll have that," she breathed. "*Thank* you."

Eyes narrowed, she watched him for a moment. There was something distinctly unsatisfying about leaving him here. For one thing, he wouldn't know what had happened to his precious clue.

Unless she left a calling card.

Oh yes, he'd wake up tomorrow, no pouch, then see... She squinted from the bed to the wall opposite—there hung a painting of the sea. *Ha,* perfect.

It took a minute to dip her fingers in the ash from the fire and smear a large V across the painting.

There. He'd know.

Smiling, she wiped off her hands on the curtain. She twitched it aside and peered out the window to check Knigh was still there.

No sign of him but four figures in red coats strode through the street, stopping at an alley a few buildings away. The gold braid of their uniforms glinted in the lamplight.

Marines. Shit.

Had Knigh spotted them and hidden? Although without her, he was safe—they wouldn't yet know what he'd done.

Wincing, she crept from the room, limbs complaining, begging her to just sink into the chair by FitzRoy's fireplace... just for a while...

But she resisted.

The landing was quiet. She had to pause halfway down the stairs, when a wave of dizziness swept over her, almost pitching her over.

Eyes closed, she clung to the wall, just breathing.

The world tipped and tilted beneath her feet, as wild as a deck in a storm.

Come on... She bit her lip, pressing her forehead to the wall. She didn't have time for this. If those marines *did* know she'd escaped and that Knigh had been the one to free her...

Sucking in a deep breath, she pulled herself upright and dragged herself downstairs.

She couldn't go out the front—the marines might recognise her, even in this outfit.

Maybe splitting up had been a bad idea.

Still, it was done now.

Biting her lip, she tried the other door at the bottom of the stairs. It led to a narrow corridor with a door on either side and an exit. Thank the gods for that.

When she took the exit, the cold night air hit her, staggering compared to the cosiness of the inn. Gods, she could use that shawl and cloak right now. Hugging herself, she started along the alley, away from the marines at the front of the inn.

Movement in the dark. She gasped, body too sluggish to respond before a warm hand clamped over her mouth.

They'd caught her. Wild Hunt. Gods. Lords. Ladies. This was it.

Her heart reared, clamouring against her chest, and she grunted against the palm, muscles screaming as they stiffened and ached. An arm wrapped around her waist, but she couldn't fight him off. She could barely summon a wriggle from her broken body.

"It's me." Knigh's voice, barely above a breath in her ear.

Thank the gods. She sagged, and he released her, hand staying at her waist as she wobbled. "Wild Hunt bloody take you, Knigh, I thought they—"

Her throat closed, and she shook her head. That they had her again, that she'd go back in that cage and hang tomorrow.

"I know," he said, handing her back the shawl and cloak. "There were marines—"

"Out the front"—she nodded and pulled it around her shoulders—"I saw them, that's why I came out this way."

"Half a dozen more on that road, too." He nodded at the other end of the alley, away from the front of the inn. "We're going to have to wait."

She shivered, tucking her hands under the cloak, blinking slowly. Lords, the wool was so soft, she could wrap it around herself and sleep.

"Vee?" He cupped her cheek, tilted her face up.

With a sharp breath, she flinched, eyes wide. They'd drifted shut. "I—I can't stay out here. I need..." Food, rest, sleep, warmth. Gods, she almost groaned at the thought.

Brow creased, Knigh bit his lip, gaze slipping away. "We could... I can..." He glanced up and down the alley, jaw clenched. "I don't know how we can slip past them. I'm—I'm sorry."

There was one way. The marines would never see them if she could gather the energy...

Swallowing, she lifted her chin. "I know." She took his hand and crept towards the back road. "Come on."

"Vee—"

"Shh." She paused several feet from the alley mouth, where the marines wouldn't see them in the shadows. "Never tell me that I can't. Just be ready to get us to this inn of yours." If she keeled over and he had to carry her, so be it.

Closing her eyes, she slowed her breaths.

It was hard—gods, it was so hard to forget her body and slip away when it ached and trembled. When the cold nipped at her fingers and cheeks. When the cloak, soft as it was, chafed the blisters on her hands, threatening to split them open.

Out there, in the moist air... In the dark, cold night... On the open sky...

She drew in a damp wind, blowing it up from the sea, over the shingle beach and through the streets.

Her body complained at the cold and somewhere warm hands fastened on her arms, keeping her upright.

The wind brought in fog, shrouding the city, drifting through lanes and up alleyways, blocking—

Then there was darkness.

FOG

"Wild Hunt take you, woman," Knigh muttered when her body went limp. He caught her, swearing again at how cold she was.

But the road was choked with fog—the marines wouldn't see them pass.

Clenching his jaw, he surveyed her still face. Warm breath touched his cheek. She was alive then. Thank the gods.

Though this holding her close was a kind of torture. His hands ached for the contact, to comfort her, to touch her. But he was the one responsible for her suffering.

He'd betrayed her. There it was—as bare and raw and horribly simple as that. He'd betrayed her. He didn't deserve to hold her, to touch her, to have what he wanted.

And yet he couldn't leave her in this alley.

So he held her against his body, pulling his coat around them both, trying to share what body heat he could, and kept his hold functional, gentle—what she needed, not what he wanted.

Heart aching, he set off into the shrouded streets. Every inch of him knotted—ears straining for any sound through the mist, eyes alert for the slightest movement, body taut and ready to dive into an alley. Anything to get her to the relative safety of his room.

Her cheek was like ice, tucked against his neck, and she weighed far too little. Her chest barely moved with shallow, slow breaths. She'd eaten a little but, if anything, she looked even worse than when he'd first taken her from the gibbet cage, cheeks hollow, lips pale.

"Vee, if you bloody die, I'll never forgive you..." *Or myself.*

He should never have let her go after FitzRoy. What had she needed from him? There was no sign of blood on her clothes or hands, so she must have stayed true to her word and not killed him.

If she had, would he have deserved it?

Because if FitzRoy deserved it, then so did he.

His throat clenched, making his breaths sharp as frost.

He should never have gone through with the stupid plan.

Cold cloaked him, as thick as the fog, tickling the back of his neck. Frowning, he paused and looked left and right—what was wrong?

No voices, no footsteps, no—

Not out there. Here. Her chest was still.

His heart squeezed like a fist had closed around it.

"Vee?" He tapped her cheek. "*Vee.* Vice? Avice?"

Her eyelids fluttered. "Don't call me that."

A heavy breath heaved from him, almost a laugh. "Well, don't bloody die, then."

"No plans to." Blinking slowly, she gave a half-smile.

"You could've fooled me. That mist—you risked too much—"

"I got us some cover, didn't I?"

He growled. "Only by nearly killing yourself."

"Well, it's done now, and I'm not dead. Considering my position at sunset, I'm taking this as a great victory."

"We're not out of the woods yet." Glaring into the gloom, he ducked down a side-street—the footsteps ahead might have been civilian rather than marine, but it was best not to chance it. "We still need to get you to the inn, bathed, and dressed properly."

"Dressed properly?"

"Yes. I've"—he cleared his throat, the words bristling—"I've got passage to Arawaké for myself and... my wife." She stiffened in his arms, and he stumbled on. "And—uh—of course, she needs proper attire."

She scoffed and tugged at his hand around her shoulder. "I think I can walk now."

Of course, she'd want to be away from his touch as soon as possible. He set her down carefully but offered his arm.

"So"—she raised an eyebrow, a faint glint in her eyes painfully like the Vee he knew—"you bought me clothes?"

"I did."

Chuckling, she took his arm, and they set off again, the pace so slow it set his teeth on edge.

"What're you laughing at?" He scowled into the darkness. Gods, they'd be spotted before they reached the inn at this rate. With all this mist, he wasn't even sure how far they were from the inn.

"The idea of the dread pirate hunter Blackwood out shopping for ladies' clothes." Her weak grip on his arm flexed the slightest amount. "Please tell me you bought me underwear, too."

Teeth gritted, he paused at the intersection, checking the road sign—thank the gods, they were only a couple of streets away. "I don't think you understand the seriousness of this situation, Vee. We're—"

"Oh, I understand." She gave a mirthless laugh and held up

her blistered hand. "I fully understand. But this is the only thing keeping me going. I can't just curl up in an alleyway and give in, which is what my body wants to do right now. Let me laugh and joke about this, and my legs will keep moving."

That's what her cavalier attitude was and always had been. A safety net. A shield. A lifeline.

And he'd just dismissed it as childish banter, a sign she didn't take things seriously. Well, maybe that last part was true, but there was so much more to it than that.

Sighing, he shook his head. "We're nearly there. The innkeeper thinks you've just arrived. I've told them you're ill in order to"—he bit his lip and looked away—"to—er—"

"Explain how awful I look?" She pursed her lips and nodded. "I've seen my hands—I can guess what the rest of me must look like. Bet you're glad you're not..." But she trailed off, nostrils flaring, gaze on the floor ahead.

They walked on in silence.

Turning right at the next road, golden lamplight dazzled him through the mist. He froze, staring into the fog.

Civilians wouldn't carry a lamp.

Military would.

IN HIDING

Blood roared in his ears as he looped an arm around Vee's waist and scooped her off her feet. No time for her complaints—they had to get off the road *now*. Perhaps she understood, because she made no sound except for a gasp, and as he hurried back the way they'd come, she kept watch behind, eyes wide.

"I don't think they saw us," she breathed.

He ducked into the next alley, only putting her down once he found a sheltered doorway to the left. He glanced further in—damnation, a dead end. They couldn't cut through to the next street.

Their breaths heaved as they both stared back the way they'd come.

Light cast the fog on the road golden.

Wild Hunt, had they heard his footsteps? Not wanting to draw attention, he hadn't quite broken into a run, but maybe they'd heard him anyway.

He forced his breaths slower, deeper, straining his ears to hear the slightest noise.

Eyes wide, pupils full, Vee bit her lip.

No way could she bring more mist to their aid this time.

Footsteps, out at the end of the alley.

Vee tensed against him. “Bollocks.”

An understatement. Corner of his mouth twitching, he nodded.

Hazy shadows moved in the mist, growing darker, larger, more distinct.

He swallowed. The marines he’d seen so far tonight had been checking alleys, and if this patrol came down here, he and Vee would have nowhere to go. He nudged her into the corner of the doorway. Flipping up the collar of his slate grey coat, he shielded her with his shoulders. If a marine lifted a lamp and glanced down the alley, he’d look like part of the shadows.

Hopefully.

Lips tight, she stared out past his shoulder, the creases between her eyebrows far too close to fear for his liking. She squashed herself back into the corner, whole body tense, trembling. The vein in her neck jumped.

The footsteps grew louder. Stopped. Scuffed, as if someone turned on the balls of their feet.

Heading this way—had to be.

She took a long, harsh breath, eyes bright and upon his.

Jaw clenched, he pressed her into the corner. The smaller they were, the better.

More footsteps. Golden light licked the fog, growing brighter.

Damnation, even nearer.

Her fingers knotted into the front of his coat. Breath held, he crushed her into the wall—other than staring back at her, it was all he could do.

The footsteps were so close he could hear not only their tap but also the faint crunch as they trod grit into the cobblestones a few feet away.

Vee flinched, eyes darting as if searching for an escape they both knew wasn't there.

He was going to find them.

Another tap and crunch.

All this. For nothing.

Knigh could barely swallow. Every hair on the back of his neck stood to attention. Vee closed her eyes, turned her face into the corner, teeth bared.

Another tap. Half the lamp came into view, glaring bright.

His ears rang.

"Conroy," a distant voice called, "over here."

The lamp rose and then slid from view as that turning-scuff sounded again. "What is it?" Conroy was so close, Knigh heard him inhale after the shout.

"Think I've found something."

A sigh, then the footsteps started again, growing quieter.

Knigh exhaled as quietly as he could, and Vee's eyes flashed wide in question. He nodded, then peered out from their doorway.

The lamp had disappeared around the corner, casting a haze of golden light through the fog to the left.

"Come on," he whispered. Holding her hand, he crept ahead.

Voices, light, footsteps, all to the left.

They turned back onto the road, feet whispering over the cobbles.

Lords, it was tempting to run, but that would be too noisy. Jaw clenched, he led her to the right-hand turn they'd tried to take before, glancing over his shoulder. The lamplight pooled in the mist, growing dimmer all the while.

It was only after they'd taken another two turns that his heart returned to normal speed. Vee's pinched expression faded, replaced by the slack look of someone beyond exhaustion.

They made it to the inn's back entrance without any more encounters. Vee paused at the door, raised her hood and squared her shoulders as though she wasn't ready to drop. Gods bless the woman. A fierce pride burned in his chest as she nodded for him to open the door.

They slipped past the innkeeper with a brief greeting. The woman bowed and went to check on the water the maid was preparing, as promised.

Vee shuddered, a soft breath falling from her lips as the innkeeper left.

He held out a hand to help her up the stairs. By the time they reached the top, he was carrying her.

"Nearly there"—he opened the door to his room—"and you can have a bath right away."

Eyelids drifting, she nodded, cheek rubbing against his chest.

No. No. No. He wasn't meant to be enjoying any part of this. Her touch was a matter of necessity, life and death. There was and could be no affection left between them. She was just exhausted and ill. Once she was back to herself, she'd want him far, far away.

As he shut the door, warmth brushed his ankles. Barnacle threaded around and between his feet. Damn cat—was she determined to trip him up?

Avoiding stepping on little paws, he made his way to the settee and lay Vee on it. "Rest here for a while. I'll get food and hot water."

She gave a tight smile and a nod, before pulling the cloak tighter and closing her eyes.

With a chirrup, Barnacle was on the settee, nose against her cheek.

Vee's eyes flicked open. "Barnacle?" She ran her hands over the cat's head, blinked. "It is... It's..."

A choking sound heaved from her and Knigh started forward, heart racing. Gods, she was so ill, was this—

But then her eyes screwed shut, and she gathered the cat close and buried her face in her fur. Her shoulders shook, and her breaths came sharp and fast.

She was crying.

Full sobs, wracking her body.

Covering his mouth, Knigh backed away. All that toughness, all that glibness. All for show. Even so bluntly saying she'd killed Avice—it was all a way of... of...

He shook his head, stomach clenching. A way of keeping people at a safe distance. Of keeping those 'soft' emotions she'd spoken about in his cabin at bay.

"You're really here," she whispered into Barnacle's fur as the cat nuzzled her way under her chin. "You're safe. My little love. My little goblin-beast."

Biting his lip, Knigh strode for the landing and down the stairs. It was too much.

He'd persuaded himself she was a monster. A murderer. And with how flippant she acted at times, how cool she could be, it had been so easy to persuade himself that she was unfeeling.

He raked his hands through his hair. What an idiot he'd been.

What a damn idiot.

He went to the kitchen and took a pail of hot water from the wide-eyed maid who'd been about to carry it upstairs. With a tremulous smile, he insisted he'd fill the bath as his wife wasn't well enough to be disturbed. And he needed to do something, anything to still the quaking of his hands and quiet his mind.

He was the monster. To do this to her. To condemn someone fae-blooded to an iron cage. To betray someone he'd...

A knot blocked his throat as he poured the first pail of water into the copper bath by the fire in their room.

Shaking his head, he swallowed and dared to look at her again. She'd fallen asleep on her side, Barnacle curled up against her chest with her eyes alert, watching his movements.

He didn't deserve any of it. To feel any way about Vee. To attempt to seek her forgiveness. To want to be worthy of her.

And after all this, she still might not make it safely away.

Once she was clean and dressed, they still had the journey to the *Swallow*. Then they had to leave port and hope no one raised the alarm. The Navy could easily blockade the Solent, prevent anyone departing, then they'd be stuck, and an escape over land would be far more difficult. Perhaps impossible.

Swallowing, he rose and nodded. He *would* help her escape. It was the only way to even begin to ease his heart and make what he'd done bearable.

More importantly, it was the only way she'd survive.

THE FULL EXTENT

By the time the bath was full and steaming with the heady scent of lavender and rosemary bath salts, Knigh had pulled himself together. It was simple. He'd get her out of Portsmouth, do anything she needed, be her willing servant. And, eventually, one day, maybe he'd be able to live with himself.

"Vee," he murmured, brushing hair from her face, "your bath is ready."

Her eyes remained shut, lashes dark against her cheeks. That burn above her temple was a startling, angry red against her horribly pale skin, but her lips had a little colour to them, and her skin didn't feel as cold as it had earlier.

Barnacle stretched and sat up, tucking her tail around her paws neatly before looking up at him with baleful green eyes.

She knew what he'd done.

Yes, she was a cat, but that look...

Frowning, he shook his head and touched his knuckles to Vee's cheek. "I know you probably don't want to move, but it'll warm you up, and we need to get you looking the part." *Of my wife.*

His stomach knotted. She hadn't commented on that earlier, only on the fact he'd gone shopping for clothes. But once she was back in full awareness, no longer exhausted and afraid, he couldn't picture her taking to the role gladly. They'd have to share a cabin and pose as happy newlyweds all the way to Arawaké.

Yes. Once she realised, she was going to kill him.

And he'd deserve it.

Wincing, he shook her shoulder gently. "Vee?"

Her lashes fluttered as she took a long breath—he'd seen her wake enough times to know she was conscious now. His stomach turned again.

"I don't think I can move." Her hand inched away from where it had balled up under her chin.

"The bath will help." He tried an encouraging smile, but gods only knew what the expression looked like with his face so tight. "I can... Your—your clothes... If you need help?"

Rubbing her face, she nodded and pushed herself to a half-sitting position. She groped at the ties of her cloak, but her hands shook too much to grasp them.

"Here." He knelt and pulled them for her.

Nodding, she closed her eyes.

With every garment, his stomach tightened. When she'd changed in the alley, it had been too dark for him to see much but now...

When he removed the gown, her arms were thin under her chemise, and she barely filled the stays even though they were laced as tightly as they'd go. The layers of petticoats had disguised how much her curves had sunk. Without them, she wasn't much more than flesh and bone. None of those powerful, lean muscles, none of that glorious, soft fat over her hips and rear.

A week in an iron cage had drained it all away.

There was no doubt, now: if she'd stayed there much longer, she'd have died even without the hangman's noose.

"Oh, Vee." He shook his head and pulled off the stockings that were far too loose on her legs. "I'm—I'm so—"

"Please don't," she murmured, eyes still shut. "Not right now. I need to focus on getting the hells out of here. Your apologies only remind me of..." Her throat rippled, and she shook her head. "Of how we got here. And if I get too wrapped up in—in hating you, I won't be able to let you help me." Jaw knotting, her nostrils flared. "And much as I'm loath to admit it, I can't do this on my own. So, save it until we're safe. Then I can threaten to cut out your tongue with your own dagger."

There it was. She was only this escape away from hating him. He shouldn't be surprised, but his heart still clenched, painful, too tight. She had every single damn right.

He rubbed his face, every hour of wakefulness suddenly falling upon his shoulders, dragging his limbs down.

Unable to meet her gaze, he lifted her upright and pulled off the chemise. It took every lesson in discipline, in self-control, in stillness not to react and curl in upon himself at the painful contrast between her now and all the other times he'd seen her glorious naked body.

She wasn't a shadow of herself, but something far less substantial—a spirit or an echo.

Wordlessly, he carried her to the bath and eased her into the steaming water. She sighed, eyes closing, expression momentarily so close to bliss, it twisted in his gut as sharp as a blade.

"Eat some more, and I'll be able to heal your burns," he murmured, placing a small table within her reach. Stew, bread, cheese, an apple, a slice of light lemon cake he'd bought this afternoon at a nearby bakery. He'd even splurged on a small bowl of almonds imported from Europa.

As she picked at the food, movements slow, clumsy, he took the sponge and the sweet-smelling soap he'd bought and set to work cleaning away the grime of imprisonment, so she'd pass as his wife.

CRUEL IRON

An hour later, she was dry and dressed in a new chemise, a little colour in her cheeks.

Biting his lip, keeping his fingers from curving around her too much, he set her on the bed. He propped her against the stacked pillows. "Do you think you—"

"I feel a lot better already." She nodded, blinking slowly. "I'm just—I can already feel the warmth leeching away." She smiled tightly and tugged on his hand. "Come on, heal me—maybe it'll warm me up."

Chest aching, he sat on the bed and sandwiched her raw, blistered hands between his. They weren't as cold and rough as they'd been earlier. That was progress.

With a wriggle, she brought herself closer, legs and body against him. She eyed him sidelong with a sardonic smirk. "Still warm, Blackwood. Still warm."

He couldn't help but snort at that echo of her usual self. Releasing her hands, he pulled the blankets over their laps, tucking her in.

She, of all things, rolled her eyes, which were deepest, darkest grey-blue tonight. “Thank you, Nurse Blackwood.”

It stung, but perhaps it was a sign she really was feeling better. If she’d made this much improvement already in just a few hours, maybe she’d make a full recovery at the same rate. That’s assuming she’d ever make a *full* recovery…

The thought jolted through him, forceful as a rifle shot.

Because the truth was, he didn’t know. There were stories about fae dying in iron but none about those who escaped and recovered. Who knew if they *could* recover or how long it might take? It was possible she’d be permanently weakened by this.

He scrubbed his face to dash away the dampness in his eyes before she saw it.

If—*if* that happened, then he’d serve her forever. Simple as that. Or as long as she could bear to look at him, at least. He could be the strength she’d lost.

Wild Hunt damn it, he’d willingly work himself to death for this.

He drew a long breath and took her hands again. “Tell me the instant you feel faint. I’ll try to keep as much energy expenditure on my end as possible, but it will still drain you. There’s nothing I can do to prevent that.” He frowned and ducked, forcing her to meet his eye. “Vee, this is important. Do you understand?”

Swallowing, she nodded. “I understand. Try not to kill me.” The corner of her mouth twitched, and she flexed her hands in his grip.

“Keep your eyes open, then I can see if you pass out.”

“Just get on with it.”

Gaze fixed on hers, he delved within, to that core of golden light that kept him warm, that had fled in the presence of the iron gibbet cage, that he brought out to heal.

The back of his neck tickled—he always closed his eyes when

he healed, seeing her as he did this private thing felt intimate, vulnerable.

A flicker of a frown crossed her face, but she kept her eyes on him and gave the smallest nod as if willing him on.

He slowed his breaths and dived to the centre of that light, where it blazed brightest. Where distant voices sang in a language he didn't understand but felt like he'd once known. When he went this deep, that soft song called to him, alluring, welcoming, promising a warm home and hearth and sincere, loving acceptance.

But he'd been told in no uncertain terms: to follow it was to die.

So, instead, he scooped up handfuls of the light and brought it from that place, carrying it here into reality. His hands shone in that familiar warm glow, and at once Vee let out a soft sound that was part-pleasure, part-relief. He knew from experience on the receiving end how wonderful it felt at this point.

But then came the next part.

Every muscle tense, he raised his eyebrows. Was she ready?

Her jaw knotted, and she nodded, hands trembling in his loose hold.

When he pushed the light into her, he gasped. The deficit—the lack in her… it was a yawning pit, cold, empty, dark.

The last time he'd healed her, when he'd closed his eyes and touched his magic to hers, she'd shone with crackling energy, incandescent, brilliant, powerful. Now, he could barely pick out a dim light in her, like one of their cave's glow-worms at a great distance.

She flinched, eyes screwing shut, hands pulling away and forcing him to tighten his grip. "Bastarding hells. Wild Hunt bloody"—jaw clenched, she threw her head back and exhaled.

And just as wonderful as the glow of his gift had been a few seconds ago, he also knew how agonising this part was. He could withdraw and end the healing having only taken away the worst pain of the burns. He could slow, which would lessen the pain but make it last longer. Or he could push all the harder, making the pain far worse but only for an instant.

Wincing, he slowed—she was too weak. She'd already endured enough. He'd end it for now, finish the rest another day.

Chest rising and falling rapidly, Vee opened her eyes and met his gaze again. "Don't stop." Her mouth set in a line and she nodded once, eyes blazing.

Of course she'd say that.

But if she was strong enough to urge him, maybe she was strong enough to take it.

Sighing a harsh breath, he gathered the golden light into a tight ball. This moment—this was the worst, but it would be over in an instant. Gritting his teeth, he channelled the energy, and it pulsed in ferocious white heat.

Her cry ripped through the night and then she fell limp.

Lords. Ladies. Bloody hells.

Damnation, he'd pushed too hard. "Vee?" He touched her cheek—it was warmer than it had been earlier. And her colour was better. Perhaps...

Brow beaded with sweat, she panted, then flexed her hand in his. "Don't panic." She gave a white-lipped smile. "I'm alive."

He sagged and snatched his fingers from her skin. *No taking comfort in her touch, remember?*

"Hopefully they'll think that was just us shagging." Swallowing, she shook her head and opened her eyes. "Wild Hunt take you, Knigh Blackwood, but you have the most painful bloody gift I've ever encountered." She examined her hands, turning them over. "Though it's effective—I'll give you that."

No more gnarled joints and dry skin. The burns had vanished, except for the old one on her palm. It made sense now—she must have touched an iron padlock, hard and for several seconds for it to leave such a detailed and lasting scar.

"Very effective," she breathed, clenching and unclenching her fists. A grin tugged at the corner of her mouth as she stared at the smooth, firm movement. "Almost good as new." She huffed a short laugh. "Thank you. I—I thought they might never work properly again."

A lump in his throat tightened his smile and prevented speech, but he nodded.

Perhaps he could heal her from all the iron's damage. Sickness was more complex to treat than an injury. Although, maybe the metal was technically a poison to her, rather than a disease. He'd never healed someone from poisoning. It wouldn't be easy, and it would take a great deal of energy from both of them, but it could be worth a try.

If they escaped on Billy's ship.

Theorising about healing iron-sickness for a fae-blooded fugitive was a task for another day.

He took a long breath, loosening the tightness of his throat. "I fear the pain isn't done for tonight." His gaze flicked to the angry red burn above her temple.

"Let's get it over and done with."

By the time he'd healed that burn, Vee could barely keep her eyes open and lay against the pillows. He managed to encourage her to eat a little more to help replace the energy spent before she burrowed down in the blankets, back to him.

Still sitting up in the bed, he craned over to peer at her face, check she didn't look in pain. Eyes closed, expression soft like this, it was a wonder he'd ever believed she could be a villain. He shook his head and sighed, snuffing out the candle on the bedside table, leaving just the light from the fireplace and a lamp on the mantlepiece.

He checked his pocket watch—three o'clock in the morning. They had maybe five hours before they'd set sail. The bed creaked as he sat up and swung his legs over the side. He should keep watch out the window, then he'd spot if—

"Knigh?"

It was so soft, he wasn't sure he'd heard it. He held his breath.

"Don't leave me, will you? To—tonight, I mean." Her shoulders heaved with a heavy breath, and she rolled over, one hand landing in the empty spot where he'd been sitting. She opened her eyes, and for a while, just looked at him.

He couldn't move. He couldn't go to the window, but he also couldn't slide back in place next to her. He wanted to pull her into his lap, keep her warm and close, and just let her sleep in his protection. But what damn protection was he to her when she had an entire country's Navy after her? When he'd been the one to hand her to them?

"I always said you were warm"—she scoffed—"and right now I need that warmth."

His heart twisted. He'd promised himself he'd give her whatever she needed tonight. If she needed this, then so be it.

Nodding, he returned to his spot.

She pursed her lips and tugged at his arm. "No. Here."

He almost laughed. It was so like her to ask for exactly what she wanted. He shuffled down in the bed until she nodded in approval and pulled his arm around her. She wriggled into place, head and one hand on his chest, body pressed against his. Then she sighed and closed her eyes.

Almost at once, her breaths slowed into the rhythm of sleep, and all tension slid from her.

Stomach a knot of guilt and longing, he pulled the blankets up around her shoulders, careful all the while to keep his other hand on her back, exactly where she'd placed it. He stared up at the bed's canopy and settled in for the wait until dawn.

He would listen for the castle's alarm bells. He would get her to that ship. And until then, he would keep her safe.

LIMPET & BARNACLE

Waking was like swimming to the surface from a great, great depth. Her arms and legs were heavy, but the pain had faded to a dull ache rather than the sharp agony of that damn iron cage.

Oh, but she was warm. So warm.

She stretched gingerly, experimenting with her weakened muscles. Everything still worked, just more slowly. She certainly wouldn't be able to lift anything heavy and climbing the shrouds wouldn't be possible for a while.

But she'd survived the night.

She took a long breath of cinnamon, leather, and sweet soap.

Oh Lords. That warm shape she'd limpeted onto was him, wasn't it?

As she'd drifted off, she'd asked him to stay in bed. She'd said it was for warmth.

A lie. It was for comfort. Familiarity. Reassurance that she was, in fact, alive.

Clinging on to the man who'd destroyed her.

Pathetic, weak woman.

Oh, but he *was* warm, and the air on her face was cold and couldn't she stay here just a little longer? If she pretended she was still—

"Vee?" He shifted and brushed her face, maybe pushing away hair.

She made a low grumble and buried her face between the blankets and his chest. "I'm asleep."

"We need to get going."

Sighing, she pulled herself out from the covers and forced her eyes open. "I know."

They still needed to get to the ship. There was a chance the Navy would blockade the entire Solent if they discovered her missing and thought she might try to flee on a boat. Considering she was a pirate and a sea witch, that would be a safe assumption.

She pursed her lips and dragged herself from bed, staggering when she first reached her feet. Holding the bedpost, she paused, legs trembling.

Weak muscles. Right. She had to remember that.

If they blockaded the port, she'd usually just sweep their ships away, but in this state? A little mist had made her pass out last night.

Scowling, she splashed herself clean and started dressing. Barnacle watched through one eye from her spot on the bed. Vice's heart melted just a touch at the sight of the little cat.

Knigh lurked by the window, peering out through a crack in the curtains. He still wore the same shirt and breeches that he'd worn all night, thoroughly rumpled.

But he didn't seem to care, attention fixed outside where it was still dark. When he turned to help lace her stays, his brows were knotted.

"What's the matter?" she asked as he tightened the cord far more gently than Perry ever did.

Her stomach twisted. Perry. Where was she? Had they been captured at Plymouth or had the plan only ever been for her?

Urgh, and she hadn't even asked Knigh. She rubbed her face. Once they were safely on his friend's ship, there'd be plenty of time to talk. "Knigh?"

"Those patrols we saw last night..."

"Right. What about them?"

He made a noisy exhalation, and she could picture his mouth in a straight line. "That's not normal. Not so many of them, anyway. I just saw another group pass—they checked the alley over the road."

"Just like that group last night did."

"Exactly. I'm—I have a theory, and I hope it isn't correct."

"Spit it out."

"Because they hadn't sounded an alarm, I thought your escape had gone unnoticed."

Cold seeped through her, almost as bad as the chill that iron cage had set deep in her bones. "You *thought?*"

"If I were Vice Admiral Yorke, I wouldn't want to publicise the fact my prized prisoner had got away. Especially not after crowing about such a great victory. I'd try to recapture you quickly and quietly, say with patrols of marines searching alleys, stables... maybe even houses and inns."

"Wild Hunt, you're a sneaky bastard, Knigh." She shook her head as he tied off the laces. "No wonder you caught Jack." *And me.* A shiver crept through her.

"I'm hoping Yorke isn't as sneaky. But I fear I'm right." He twitched the edge of the curtain and peered out again, shoulders squared, body tensed, as ready as a sabrecat on a hunt.

She clenched her jaw, gaze tracing over the muscles of his

back, visible where his shirt skimmed them. He was still whole, still strong. Her body had failed her, her muscles stripped away. She hadn't been able to look at herself naked as she'd bathed last night—that was the main reason she hadn't even tried to resist when he'd brought out the sponge and soap. His reaction when he'd undressed her had told her enough.

Horror. Disappointment. Pity.

She spun on her heel, ignoring the wave of dizziness that blanketed her, and snatched the petticoats he'd bought.

"We need to go." He abandoned the window and yanked on his coat. "Now."

His tone stilled the joke on her tongue.

Bollocks. He was serious. And worried.

And, the way he strode around the room, stuffing belongings into his duffle bag, he was on full alert.

She tugged on the petticoats, tied their ribbons all together in one bulky bow that would've made a lady's maid faint, then pulled on the gown and buttoned the front. The cat twisted around her legs, eyes flashing with agitation.

Knigh swept the cloak and shawl over her shoulders while she pulled on the silly pointed shoes. Running a hand through her hair, she patted her shoulder and called for Barnacle.

With a chirrup, the little cat jumped up and draped herself across the back of Vice's neck.

Sword and pistols at his side, Knigh already had the door open. He glanced up and down the landing, then with a nod, he signalled for her to come.

"No time for arguments, I'm afraid," he muttered.

Before she could ask what he meant, he'd picked her up. She gritted her teeth, both against the indignity and at Barnacle's claws digging into her shoulder. She wouldn't have admitted it if asked, but he did make short work of the stairs compared to how slowly she'd walked down the staircase at FitzRoy's inn last night.

"Fine," she growled when he set her down by the back door. She scratched Barnacle's head, and the claws retracted from her flesh, just gripping the thick woollen cloak. "What did you see out there?"

"A dozen marines on the front road. Whether they just happen to be in this part of town or they've connected me to your escape and then to this place—well, I suppose we'll find out when I open this door."

He pressed into her hand something hard, wooden, familiar.

She blinked, eyebrows raised. She didn't have to look at it to know a stag decorated the handle. Avice Ferrers' pistol, just like Kat's. She squeezed the perfectly shaped grip and nodded. Just the feel of it steadied her hand.

"Primed and loaded," he murmured.

"Thank you." Quite how he'd got hold of it would have to wait. As would a great many things. Like his betrayal. Her gratefulness soured, and she frowned as he opened the door, blocking the way with his broad shoulders.

Damn him, betraying her and then acting like *this*.

He was deliberately shielding her, in case marines waited outside. And he'd been so gentle last night, like a mother cat lifting kittens by the scruffs of their necks. It had always amazed her how they did that without injuring the little things with their sharp canines. Now here he was, the fearsome warrior, the berserker who'd bathed her and scrubbed behind her ears. Who'd massaged shampoo into her scalp. Who'd even combed her hair so carefully it had almost made her weep with gratitude.

She swallowed, trembling, but no shots rang out, and there was no clang of steel on steel.

His shoulders lowered an inch, and he slipped into the alley, offering his hand.

She looked at it. She could refuse. After what he'd done, did she really want to touch him?

But, damn it, yes, she did. At least for now. The sky was lightening, approaching dawn, but it was still dark, still cold. And although she'd never been afraid of the dark before, this night was different.

If the Navy had their way, it was the last night she'd see.

With a heavy breath out, she took his hand and walked into the darkness.

They slid between the shadows. Her own slowness pained her, but at least her step was as quiet as ever. Thank the fair folk for her fae blood. Maybe there was some truth in the old wives' tale that they could walk silently, even over a hall of shattered glass.

Her breath was too loud in her ears. And her heart—it roared in a fast, uneven beat, making her clutch her chest. But apparently, she was the only one who could hear it, because Knigh didn't turn and tell her to hush.

They swept west, then south, judging by the paler shade of blue behind, then turned left. He had to be leading them in a route to avoid all those marines.

Swallowing, she squeezed his hand. *If they find us...*

When they paused in the next alleyway, she caught her breath. That smell—was that...

She sniffed the air. Yes. A low groan slipped from her mouth. The sea. They were near. It called to her, said that if she just spread her awareness, it would cradle her, weightless, away from the pain, away from the blasted weakness shaking through her limbs.

Knigh glanced back the way they'd come as she released his hand and crept further into the alley.

Waves lapped at ships, smacking and splashing and rushing.

Lords, they were so close. She could taste the iodine and salt tang now, the odd seaweed flavour of ocean air in Albion, different from that of Arawaké.

She rounded a corner and there they were—the civilian docks. If she'd been well enough to, she'd have run.

But this wasn't a time for running. Taking a long breath, she peeked out from the alley. No sign of marines left, and—

Knigh yanked her back into cover, finger to his lips, brows in a furious knot, eyes glinting in the dimness.

Footsteps.

TO HIDE IN PLAIN SIGHT

Men's voices. Marines or dockers on their way to work?

She and Knigh stood inches apart, bodies rigid, breaths heaving in the same air. Barnacle hunched, stiff on her shoulders.

To come so close and be caught...

The thought tore at her. If the wall hadn't been at her back and Knigh at her front, she'd have fallen.

"Marines?" she mouthed.

He shifted the barest inch, eyes intent down the road. The way his jaw tensed said *yes*, but he nodded anyway.

Bollocks.

This was it.

Bollocks!

No.

She shook her head. They hadn't come this bloody far only to be caught.

They were looking for her—an escaped pirate in a flashy red

coat, dirty and dishevelled. With a little luck, they didn't know Knigh had helped her, either.

They could make this work.

A long breath. A nod. "Kiss me," she whispered.

His gaze snapped back from the road. "What?"

"When they come close, you'd better bloody kiss me."

A pained look creased over his face.

Of course, kissing her now she was all skin and bone wasn't exactly appealing. Well, it wasn't for his enjoyment.

Chin lifting in challenging invitation, she grabbed his shirt and slid her other hand into his hair, hiding that tell-tale white streak. Maybe they knew he was involved and had his description.

The footsteps, the voices grew louder.

Barnacle jumped off her shoulder and huddled against her ankles.

His chest heaved, once, twice, then his head bowed, and his lips were on hers.

Lords and Ladies, she'd missed them.

It was only meant to be a way of hiding in plain sight, a way to explain their presence in the alley. But somehow the tentativeness of his mouth, the gentle touch of his hands circling her waist, holding her upright... Wild Hunt damn it, it was far more devastating than all the hungry, passionate kisses they'd shared.

Her fingers threaded through his hair, so thick, so luxurious. His scent of cinnamon and soap mingled with her beloved sea air and crowded away thoughts of marines and escape until they were the mere distant concerns of mortals.

He stroked her cheek, smearing something wet up into her temple as his hand slid into her hair, and he angled her face for better access. Still slow, still gentle, their tongues brushed, the touch almost reverent.

Heart clamouring, painful, fast, she clung to him. This—no, it felt like goodbye. And she wasn't ready for that. Everyone else had left. He was the only one who'd come back. And the bastard had made her like him. Even if he had—

Laughter and catcalls yowled from the road. The marines. She twitched away, but Knigh's fingers flexed against her scalp, holding her mouth against his.

Hiding in plain sight. Right. That's all this was.

"Did you get a good look at her?" A deep voice pitched for the other marines, not her and Knigh.

Her skin prickled, ice cold. Buggeration. She was the only 'her' around. If they came closer...

Her chest tightened. Knigh's hand on her waist stiffened. Their breaths blew together, harsh. Should they break off and run or—

A set of footsteps approached.

They were nearly at the ship. Running would only take them further from that promised escape. She needed to get back to the sea, back to Arawaké and, hopefully, back to Perry.

Maybe if she gave them a good show, they wouldn't want to interrupt...

Groaning as if this were the most erotic experience of her life, she wrapped her legs around Knigh. He tensed, but took her weight, cradling her.

More laughter. "Ooh-hoo-hoo! Looks like they're getting frisky, lads. Better leave them to it, eh?"

The footsteps stopped.

"Come on—let's not spoil their fun."

The guffaws grew quieter as the main body of marines must've drifted away down the street. But that single set of footsteps that had come close didn't start up again. He had to be deciding what to do.

Piss off.

Knigh pressed her against the wall, hand running up her leg and pushing up her skirts. Good, he'd got the picture.

Her pulse pounded in her chest, her throat, her head. Never had she focused so hard on listening whilst kissing someone.

"Hmm." Footsteps again, but fading. "Give her one from me, mate!"

At last, they pulled apart with heavy breaths. Her heart was going to explode, it was beating so fast, part-fear, part something she couldn't place.

He lowered her to her feet before wiping his cheeks. Hers were wet too. Frowning, she knuckled it away. They were both just tired. So, so tired.

In silence, they stood there, not meeting each other's gazes while they waited for the marines' footsteps to disappear entirely.

Just hiding in plain sight. That was all.

Attempting to distract herself, she peered out from the alley in time to see the marines go around a corner.

Barnacle settled back on her shoulders, and with Vice's tight nod, they continued on their way in silence. Despite adjusting their course to avoid the patrols, Knigh had directed them well, because they emerged directly opposite the jetty where the *Swallow* was moored.

With a quiet greeting, Knigh hailed a tanned young man with round, dark eyes.

"You're early." From someone else, it might have been a rebuke, but the way he smiled so broad, so open, he clearly didn't mind. "Well, we can get underway—the tide's with us already."

He waved them aboard, and Knigh made brief introductions —thankfully setting sail prevented anything longer. Much as she was curious to meet a *friend* of Knigh Blackwood's and much as this Billy seemed warm, his joviality grated this morning.

It had been a long night.

And, she reminded herself with a glance at the distant grey castle, it wasn't over yet.

They still had to make good their escape.

IN THE END

Between giving orders to his crew, Billy waved Vice and Knigh aft, saying they'd get the best view and wouldn't be in the way up at the stern of the quarterdeck.

Holding hands, they went in silence. The only noises were the crew's voices as they worked and the sounds of a vessel—wind and canvas and wave. Barnacle jumped down from Vice's shoulders and began sniffing her way around the ship.

Vice's lips still tingled from that kiss. Their last. Ever.

Knigh's hand on hers was a death grip. Maybe he was still feeling the after-effects, too. Or maybe it was just the close call with the marines.

Once they pushed away from the jetty, the ship swayed, and she blew a long sigh. Movement, that was better. Just like she'd said to Knigh in deLacy's horrible still ballroom. That part of their conversation hadn't been a lie.

They reached the rail, and she leant partially against it and partially against Knigh. They looked astern, watching Portsmouth drift further away.

The wind tugged her hair as if it were glad to see her back. Although she could affect the weather over land, it was always easier at sea. Maybe something about the combination of her gifts or just some fae-blooded affinity with the sea. Who knew?

Without any help from her—she had too little energy left—that same wind filled the *Swallow's* sails and pushed them along.

Warm at her side, Knigh squeezed her hand as they watched the shops, taverns, and wharves on the seafront grow smaller...

Eyes aching, chest tight, she scanned the jetties. Marines could still appear. Their rifles could easily cover this distance. Something about the tension in Knigh's body against hers said he thought the same.

... Smaller...

Nothing yet. But their way could be blocked. Swallowing, she turned to check fore. Ahead was only sea—the gap that would lead them out from between Portsmouth and the Isle of Wights.

... Smaller...

The buildings on the seafront were just a dark line with the pinkish dawn starting behind.

No bells sounded an alarm. Maybe they hadn't found her empty cage yet. Maybe Knigh was right, and they were keeping it quiet. With a little luck, they'd stay quiet until she was out on the open ocean.

The tension in his arm ebbed, and his thumb stroked the back of her hand.

She nodded. She felt it too.

They were away.

She sighed the deepest sigh of her life.

"Thank you, Knigh."

But the words tasted bitter. And his hand under hers... The touch of his skin was warm, but it also prickled.

He'd come for her in that cage when no one else had. He'd

saved her life. And he'd given up so much to do it. His status as a law-abiding subject. His country. His career.

For him, it wasn't just a career. It was inextricably spliced with his identity, like two ends of rope neatly joined. Then there was his family's financial stability and independence from Mercia.

Knigh was now a fugitive fleeing Albion.

And he'd done it all for her.

But.

She clenched her jaw. She'd only needed saving because of his betrayal.

Who knew if her body would ever be right again? If this damage was permanent...

She shook, blood burning, skin cold, trapped between horror and anger.

If it was permanent, it would be his fault. She'd be weak and vulnerable forever, maybe not able to use her gift properly, and it would all be because of him.

Because he was too bloody stupid to understand she hadn't *actually* killed Avice Ferrers. Because he'd been too ready to believe she was the villain his beloved Navy claimed.

Because he'd done the inevitable: he'd let her down.

She should have known.

Wild Hunt, she *had* known.

People always let you down in the end.

And here was the perfect case in point, so bloody tempting with that gorgeous face, flawless body, and... and...

Breaths too fast, she squeezed his sodding hand.

Bastard.

Despite all that, his closeness was comforting.

Lords and Ladies, it would be easy to continue like this, especially since they were posing as husband and wife. But... It had been a comforting lie to get through last night. It had served its purpose, and now the desperation and fear of escape had faded. And she couldn't just forget what he'd done.

She swallowed it down—*stamped* it down, and slammed the lid shut. It was for the best. She didn't want him, didn't need him. Just bodies, that was all they'd ever been. She didn't care about him. He didn't mean anything to her except a route back to Arawaké where she belonged.

Nothing more.

Nodding, she pulled her hand from his grip. "Yes," she said, lifting her chin, smiling, "thank you so much for getting me out of the mess you got me into in the first place."

He stilled, turning towards her, brow creasing in an expression that, on him, was the equivalent of breaking. "Vee, don't—"

She scoffed, outrage bubbling in her veins. "Don't you dare tell me 'don't'. Not after what you did." For something to do with her hands and to keep them far, far away from him, she folded her arms. "I'm being reasonable. I'm coming with you now but purely out of convenience and because it's my only chance to escape."

Closing his eyes, he bowed his head. It shouldn't have, but his defeat pierced her.

They'd made such a good team. And...

Weak. You're being weak, Vice.

Eyes burning, she scowled at the distant shape of Portsmouth, its lights flickering in windows as the city awoke to the news that Lady Vice had escaped. That victory wasn't nearly as sweet as it should have been.

"I'm not leaving you..." He said it so softly it was almost lost in the sound of the *Swallow's* wake. "Until... until you're better, at least. Then you can tell me to throw myself under the Wild Hunt's hooves."

"Good." There was too much to do, and much as it set her teeth on edge, she couldn't do it all alone. Besides, the treasure would benefit him, too. She touched the neckline of her gown and smiled stiffly. "You have a family to provide for, and *I* have the means to help."

He blinked, then looked at her sidelong, maybe checking whether she'd lost her mind.

"You might have betrayed me, and I might hate you for it"—if she said it enough, it would be true—"but for now we're allies. As I've *tried* to tell you before, I'm not a monster." None of this was easy for her, no way was she going to make it easy on him.

She arched an eyebrow, keeping her expression all sharp edges, despite the deep exhaustion dragging on every muscle. "Even I can appreciate that you've lost everything tonight. But your family shouldn't have to suffer for it."

"You don't need to concern yourself with my family," he muttered, rigid as his mask glided into place.

"I don't need to, but I choose to. They've already been let down by your father, I'm not going to let you disappoint them, too."

Urgh, when had she started caring about people she hadn't even met? It was his fault. All of this was his fault.

She tore her gaze from him and watched Portsmouth's lights disappear behind the Isle of Wights. A relieved sigh huffed from her. It wasn't total safety, but they were that bit further away with no warships in pursuit.

"So." He cleared his throat. "What now?"

She tightened her arms and leant her hip against the rail. Her damn knees were already wobbling. "Well, assuming we survive this and make it all the way to Arawaké, I'm going to get my revenge on FitzRoy and everyone who's betrayed me." The thought was hot and bright like a brand—the only energy left in her—and it raised a smile.

"But he's back there, he's—"

"Retired, I know." She scoffed, shaking her head. "Really, Blackwood, how many times do I need to tell you? I'm not a murderer, whatever you might think. If I wanted to kill FitzRoy, I'd have done it already. I had the chance. I could have killed him in his sleep, with your dagger. Kind of fitting, eh? Considering you worked together to betray me."

She smiled cruelly, but the way he snatched his gaze away gave her no pleasure. He'd even taken the fun out of mocking him.

"No, don't worry yourself," she went on when he remained silent, "you haven't unleashed a monster on the world. I'm not going to murder anyone." She took a long, deep, cleansing breath of that sweet sea air. Somewhere in the world, Perry had to be breathing in the same air. If she was free, she'd return to Arawaké.

"I'm going to find Perry, get a ship, and take the thing FitzRoy wants most in all the world."

"Gold?"

She grinned, a proper, full grin. He might have predicted her behaviour well enough to capture her, but she could still surprise him, it seemed. "Better than that."

The skin around his eyes tightened, curious, calculating.

"This." She pulled FitzRoy's pouch from the front of her stays. "He hinted at what it was." A clue to Drake's treasure—a *real* clue. "I haven't even looked at it yet, but he was wearing it as he slept, so I'm inclined to believe him."

Knigh narrowed his eyes at the pouch, then he sucked in a sharp breath. "Oh. From the wreck? You think it's..." He shook his head, incredulity blatant in the rise of his eyebrows. He opened his mouth but snapped it shut again in silence.

She snorted and pushed the pouch back in place. No doubt he'd been about to say again how it was all a myth but thought better of it considering her current mood. Wise man.

"So," he said, at last, gaze drifting over the white foam kicked up behind them, "you're still going after it, then?"

The poor man hadn't realised, had he?

She let him squirm in the quiet as she scanned the cloudless sky, marking the fading stars—the same stars that would help guide them once they were back in Arawaké. Soon. And her strength would return over the trip. It *would.* It had to.

"No. I'm not." She smirked, watching him huff a soft breath, maybe of relief.

He nodded. "I mean, I can see how that would... *vex* him. *If* you managed it. But the whole thing is a—"

"Captain Blackwood," she said, lifting her chin, "you didn't let me finish."

If you managed it.

Ha! Foolish, foolish Knigh.

She scoffed and leant over the stern rail, cool salty spray dusting her skin, such a glorious relief after the stillness of land, the cruelty of iron.

"Your family needs money. Hells, *you* need money. I need revenge. And I wouldn't say no to the money either. So, no, *I'm* not going after Drake's treasure."

Head cocked, she flashed him a smile, all brash confidence.

"*We* are."

Vice & Knigh's adventures continue in
AGAINST DARK TIDES, out now.
Read on for the author's note with behind the scenes details and a sneak peek of *Against Dark Tides.*

If you enjoyed *Beneath Black Sails*, please leave a review on Amazon and/or Goodreads.

Desperate for a bit more Vice & Knigh together? Join my newsletter and as a thank you gift, you'll receive a copy of *Hissing Hellcats*, a short story set after *that* glow-worm cave.

AUTHOR NOTE

Caution: Here be Spoilers!

Read After *Beneath Black Sails*.

So, was that how you expected the first instalment to end? You knew Vice couldn't just fall into Knigh's arms and let things be smooth sailing (pun semi-intended) between them.

Don't worry, I have a happy ending planned for the characters/series, but you didn't think these two would find their way there in just one book, did you? No, they have a long way to go, but everything will be settled by the end of the fourth book, *Through Dark Storms*, I promise!

In the meantime, though, I do have a short story featuring Vice and Knigh (and Barnacle!) set during the period between them getting together and their breakup, *Hissing Hellcats*. I give it to my newsletter subscribers as a free gift here: https://www.claresager.com/bbsback/

They say you should write the book you want to read but can't find. That's definitely a good description of my author goals. I love stories that combine thrilling action, cunning intrigue, and a gut-wrenching romance. Some stories get it just right for me, while others get the adventure spot on but don't have any romance or give it a horrible tragic ending where one of the couple dies. I can enjoy those stories, but they're not my **favourites**. When I write, I always try to write the book I'd like to find on the shelf that blends action, intrigue, and romance.

This series is my take on the classic pirate adventure, heavy on the action and the romance, while my *Counterfeit Contessa* series leans more towards the intrigue and romance. (If you've read the CC books, you might even have spotted a little easter egg in there for the BBS series…)

I've always wanted to write about pirates—it's probably something to do with growing up watching films like *Cutthroat Island* and *Hook*. But, I have to admit, I always put it off because I was intimidated by ships. They're big, complicated beasts with weird, specific names for every little part and special rules, and I had no idea where to start writing about them convincingly. So I didn't.

Then Vice came along.

She started as an idea for a character for a roleplaying game that never ended up going ahead. When I was creating the character, this backstory hit and I found myself writing pages and pages about how she'd run away to sea, expecting a great, romantic adventure… only for her husband to die in his first battle in the most unheroic way possible. Definitely not a fairy tale ending to that relationship.

But then, I think happily ever afters depend on where you end the story, don't they? Vice's story didn't end with her husband's death, as you've seen. You can read more about her past in *Across Dark Seas,* the free full length prequel. https://books2read.com/across (If Amazon is showing a price for this book, please let me know! Sometimes they stop price-matching randomly.)

That first idea for the character of Vice was some years ago now, but I kept the notes ready to write about her *some day*.

After the second *Counterfeit Contessa* book, *A Sleuth & a Charlatan*, I wanted a bit of a break from that series—it's a mammoth-sized book (twice the length of BBS) and quite dark at times. I loved it, but I wanted to write something different—more light-hearted, shorter.

Guess who poked her head up out of the crow's nest and gave me a wave. (And a grin and a wink!)

Maybe it was watching Black Sails on TV or playing Assassin's Creed Black Flag some years earlier, but I had a real hankering to tell a pirate story.

And Vice was pretty insistent.

Now you've read BBS, you know how tenacious she is, how confident she is that things will work out as long as you give it a go.

And I could kind of see her point. I love reading and learning—I think that's part of what I love about writing stories, it's the perfect excuse to research new topics and keep learning. I didn't have to know every single thing about sailing a tallship—I wasn't writing an instruction manual. What I did need to know, I could learn.

Vice added that what I didn't know I could bluff. In Knigh's words: *That woman!*

So I bought a stack of books on pirates and sailing ships, I bookmarked gods know how many websites, and I drew myself little diagrams of different parts of ships and the names for directions as an aide memoir. And I let Vice have her way.

I'm glad I did.

I loved writing this book, which is, really, my homage to the pirate and sailing stories I grew up with and discovered later in my teens and 20s. Things like *Pirates of the Caribbean, The Mysterious Cities of Gold*, and, as I mentioned already, *Black Sails, Assassin's Creed Black Flag, Cutthroat Island*, and *Hook*. I've included a few Easter egg references to some of these stories in BBS (and later books in the series, so keep your eye open for those). Did you spot any?

I had so much fun, in fact, that I actually laughed evilly to myself while writing some scenes. (Particularly the weapons check scene, which is one of my favourites!) And I hope you enjoyed reading this book as much as I did writing it. If you do and you have a couple of minutes, it would really help me out if you were able to pop a really quick review on Amazon and/or Goodreads—it doesn't have to be long, just a sentence or two is fine. It's the number of reviews that seems to be most important in helping encourage Amazon to show the book to other readers.

At the time of writing (April 2020), we're about a week out from the book releasing, but I've been getting feedback and reviews on Goodreads from advance readers. The reviews have all been great (Yay!), but one or two people aren't keen on Vice or aren't sure of her yet.

And I'm not entirely surprised by that. She's flawed, she's prickly, and she makes some terrible decisions, as you've seen.

But she's also affectionate, determined, ferociously loyal to her friends, and, really, doing the best she can with her personal traumas. Isn't that what we all do in life?

I really wanted to write about an imperfect heroine—someone who's scarred (and sometimes scared), who uses humour and glibness as defence, and who has a lot of room for improvement. If you've read *Across Dark Seas*, you'll have seen how some of her less pleasant/more destructive behaviours are coping mechanisms.

So, yes, she's great at lying to herself (I think she's almost convinced herself that she doesn't have feelings for Knigh!), but I hope you can see that isn't the whole picture and that a path to growth lies ahead of her.

Also, like a lot of women in 2020, Vice has **had enough**. And she's definitely over following rules set by a man's world. So, she's not going to apologise for knowing what she wants and going after it.

On the subject of feedback, a few readers have commented that they'd like to get to know some of the secondary characters better. I've tried to keep this book quite focused to maintain the pace, but rest assured there'll be plenty of time to get to know various of Vice's pirate friends (and foes) in the future books. (And perhaps even in spin-off series…)

If you simply can't wait until then, you can meet Perry, Saba, Lizzy, and Fitz in *Across Dark Seas*, the short prequel novel to this series. (When I say 'short novel', it's about half the length of BBS, to give you an idea.)

Everyone who's read BBS is united on one thing, though: they **love** Barnacle. I mean, she's a cat, what's not to love? She's quite special to me, too, as she's a combination of two of our pets. Her personality is based on our cat Deedee (who's currently lying in the sun in the living room), and her appearance matches Ghost, the cat we had when I was a child. If you keep an eye on my Instagram feed (@claresager), you'll see photos of Deedee and her brother Dash.

[Edited January 2022: You can also get a free short story featuring Barnacle, Hissing Hellcats, as a free gift for joining my newsletter crew here: https://www.claresager.com/bbsback/]

Then we have Knigh. Ah, dear, cunning, damaged Knigh. Just like Vice, he's struggling with his own traumas and emotional wounds, but I'm looking forward to sharing his journey to wholeness with you.

Did you enjoy them both discovering their past connection? That's another scene that had me laughing wickedly as I wrote.

I knew from the start that I wanted Vice to butt heads with a man who was, in so many ways, her opposite. And I loved the delicious irony of him being her former betrothed, whom she was quite adamant she hated and would never marry.

As I wrote BBS, I was wondering what it is I love so much about enemies to lovers and opposite sides of the tracks/opposites attract pairings (the *Counterfeit Contessa* books are about a low-born thief who poses as an aristocrat in order to rob from the rich... She, of course, meets her match in one of her aristocratic targets. ;)).

Yes, the banter and arguments are fun, and the disagreements are a great source of tension and conflict. But, deep down, I think it's because of this central idea that is hugely important to me: **what connects us is greater that what divides us**.

I love it when characters look at each other, judging by what they see and think they know about X (pirates and pirate hunters in Vice and Knigh's case), and think 'We have nothing in common.' Then as they get to know each other, they discover the other one's positive traits, surprising deviations from their picture of what an X should be, and, finally, some common ground.

On the subject of romance... If you've read my other series, you might notice the love scenes in this book were rather more spicy! The *Counterfeit Contessa* books are the first I ever finished writing and I was very much conscious of people I know reading them, so I kept things a bit tamer than I might've.

I also hadn't discovered that there are all these other readers like me who also love the adventure *and* the romance, including the sexy times that can involve.

Nowadays, I know I'm not alone in that. In fact, I'm one of the admins over at Romantic Fantasy Shelf, a Facebook group for readers who love romantic fantasy, fantasy romance, and fantasy reverse harem. In the group, we are non-judgmental about heat levels and there are those who like it sweet as well as plenty who like it spicy. You could say, I've found my people! (If this sounds like your cup of tea, you can join us here: https://www.facebook.com/groups/romanticfantasyshelf/)

As for BBS... When I started writing, Vice really jumped off the page as quite a sexual person (and I think in general there's that angle to pirates—they live by a very different set of rules from the average person in their era).

I always knew that things between Vice and Knigh would simmer right from the start, with the tension building to boiling point... But with how opposite they are in a lot of ways, I also knew it wasn't going to be easy for Knigh to act on his feelings and desires. He isn't the sort to dive in for a quick kiss in an alleyway (or book shop) on a whim. (And Vice, tempted as she is, is too wrapped up in the fact he's a pirate hunter to make her move as early as she normally would.)

By the time I got to the battle on the *Covadonga*, I knew that when Knigh cracked, he would crack completely—kissing, sex, all of it at once.

But when I reached the glow-worm cave, I was really torn. I wasn't sure where to pitch it in terms of explicitness. Did I stick with the shorter scene with sensual terms and soft focus I'd already used in *A Thief & a Gentlewoman* and *A Sleuth & a Charlatan*?

I'm a believer that sex scenes are a great opportunity to reveal a lot about characters and their relationships, so I knew I didn't want to cut away (and I felt like I'd be cheating you guys after all that hot tension). Also, with the way things had bubbled between them for so long, fading to black would have been incongruous.

Eventually, I decided to just write the scene without worrying about it or thinking of anyone else, just letting the characters lead the way (And Knigh certainly took things in a direction I (and Vice) wasn't expecting! Naughty boy!). I figured that afterwards I could read and decide whether to tone it down, cut parts, etc.

In the end, I barely changed the scene and I actually think it's one of the best things I've ever written. I'm really proud of it. So much is shown between them and it is a fitting culmination of all that sexual tension in what I hope is a great pay-off, while still showing how far they have left to go. Plus, you know, I happen to think it's hot as hells. Phew!

Moving on to another issue where I had to make a call about what to show and what not to... I think it's fair to say that my pirates are a fantasy version of pirates—the reality was a lot dirtier, deadlier, and frequently a lot less noble. Their reigns on the high seas tended to be much shorter thanks to unglamorous ends caused by stray gunshots and nasty diseases. Many of them also engaged in slavery, though there were others who stood against it and freed the enslaved people they encountered. Many pirate crews included former enslaved people in their number. Sad to say it, but even Sir Francis Drake engaged in the slave trade in his early career.

Some of the pirates referenced in BBS are real figures, like Ned Low and François l'Olonnais. Those two committed terrible acts of torture and were pretty horrifying people, even by the standards of the day.

History is full of beauty and horror, just like the modern world. In writing this series, I made a call about how far I wanted to stray into the horror and where on the spectrum of cruelty and nobility I wanted my pirates to sit. Again, I was guided by the initial idea of keeping this series *fun* and more light-hearted.

If you want to learn more about real pirates, I highly recommend the Pirate History Podcast, which is as entertaining as it is educational.

Just as my pirates are like real pirates and not, the world I write in is like the real world circa the 17th/18th century but not. Both the *Beneath Black Sails* series and *Counterfeit Contessa* series take place in the Sabreverse. Yes, I named it after the real stars of the show—the sabrecats that most cultures ride (rather than horses).

The CC books play out in not-Constantinople (Arianople in the Sabreverse), inspired by my dual British and Turkish Cypriot heritage, while, as you've seen, the BBS books take place between not-Britain (Albion) and the not-Caribbean (Arawaké).

Some notable differences in Albion: how colonialism/empire played out, the fate of Boudicca and her fight against the Romans, Elizabeth I's life and how it interacted with the return of the fae.

I think there are plenty of hints throughout this book and the others in the series to give you an idea of what happened in my version of these events, but let me know if you'd like me to talk about that more in a blog post or future author notes. If you don't already get my newsletter, sign up here and then reply to the welcome email to let me know: https://www.claresager.com/bbsback (And remember, to thank you for signing up, you'll receive that free Vice, Knigh, and Barnacle short story.)

Some differences in the wider world that we've seen so far (there are other things that haven't appeared in any of my books so far... some day you'll get to see!). Numerous now-extinct creatures still exist, examples can be seen in the creatures Vice thinks of when she and Knigh swim the reef and she feels the whale shark approach. Sabrecats themselves are based on a mashup of various extinct species that tend to be grouped as 'sabretooth cats' with the more recently extinct Caspian tiger. I had the idea that they were domesticated much earlier than cats were in our world because if you're travelling in a world with dangerous, large megafauna, it's a benefit to ride a creature that can defend itself and you with claws and teeth.

Slavery is also different, as seen in the *CC* books: before the events of T&G, one of the central characters Derry was enslaved in Noreg (not-Norway) and transported to the not-Mediterranean. As the story of colonialism has played out differently, so too has the history and story of slavery. There's less of it, for one thing, and it's not focused on the trans-Atlantic slave trade, and much of it isn't based on the idea of people as property. I've tried to be sensitive and push the wheel of the Sabreverse's world towards social justice, but I know that intent doesn't mean I'm immune from writing things that may be problematic. My unreserved apologies if I have and I'd definitely appreciate an email to let me know.

On a more light-hearted note... The glow-worm cave is inspired by images I've seen of an amazing cave in New Zealand full of blue-green glow-worms. So, yes I'm aware that the glow-worms in the Americas don't tend to be that colour, but those photos were just so gorgeous, I had to try and recreate the place, and I bowed to the Rule of Cool on this occasion. If you'd like to see photos, I've saved some on my Lady Vice Pinterest board.

If you'd like to see that and some other fun stuff relating to the series, I'm adding bits and pieces like a playlist, the Pinterest board, and, soon, a map, to this page on my website: https://www.claresager.com/bbssecret

So, there you have it, a few of my thoughts and inspirations for this book. What did you think? Who was your favourite character? Vice? Knigh? Maybe you're a fan of Perry? Or perhaps you prefer a bad boy, like FitzRoy? Who would you like to see more of and get to know better? What moments had you cheering or ripping your hair out? Sign up and reply to the welcome email to let me know!

I tend to email my newsletter a couple of times a month, plus the occasional brief update when I have a new book out, so you're the first to know. I usually share photos from my travels and research, advance snippets of what I'm working on, fantasy book deals and new releases, plus cool giveaways. It's also the best place to get all the news about Vice and Knigh's adventures first. You can sign up here: https://www.claresager.com/bbsback

Thanks for picking up BBS and reading this—and well done for getting to the end of my author note! I'll catch you again at the end of *Against Dark Tides* where Vice and Knigh will have to deal with the aftermath of betrayal, a devious Duke, and a sea creature once thought the stuff of legends...

[Edited September 2020: Read on for your sneak peek of the opening chapters of ADT.]

For now, I'll just wish you happy reading!

All the very best,

Clare Sager, April 2020
x

AGAINST DARK TIDES – SNEAK PEEK

THE VISCOUNTESS VILLIERS

Vice smiled sweetly across the card table, the expression making her muscles ache. She'd used this smile so often over the past two weeks, she thought she might've grown accustomed to it by now, but no. Some things she'd never get used to.

Knigh Blackwood kept his gaze on the cards already revealed on the green baize. Cool, calm, and collected as ever. He'd re-perfected his mask over their voyage so far, and every blank expression made Vice's insides ache and itch until she had to fidget. How easily he shut her out.

From their seats either side of Vice, Lord and Lady Pevensey exchanged a glance before both raising their eyebrows at her. Vice fought the urge to give them a triumphant grin and instead cocked her head at Knigh.

"Darling," she said, voice over-bright, "remind me again, does a full house win?"

Does a full house win? She bit back a snort as she revealed her cards. Lady Pevensey had two of a kind, Knigh three of a kind, and Lord Pevensey had folded already. Obviously it won.

A flicker of a frown crossed Knigh's face and his lips flattened. He glanced at her cards, then back at her, his grey eyes narrowing a hair's breadth. For a man with such controlled expressions, he really should've been better at poker.

"Well, my *dearest* Verity, you appear to have won *again.*" But he didn't smile, and the way his eyebrows rose said he learned she'd cheated.

Of course she'd bloody cheated. She was a pirate. What did he expect?

It wasn't as though he was in any position to lecture her.

"Oh, you two," Lady Pevensey sighed. "Gazing adoringly at each other." She smiled and shook her head, hand resting on her chest. Another sigh. "Young love." She shared a meaningful look with her husband.

With her perfect plum-coloured gown and caramel-gold hair, Lucia Pevensey understood the importance of appearances. However, that understanding didn't extend to seeing what lay behind them. In the case of Viscount and Viscountess Villiers, it was less young love, more fake marriage of convenience between mortal enemies.

Vice gave Lucia a sweet smile, though, and scooped up her winnings. A few guineas. Some money of her own, and—

A warm grip, a little too hard, fastened around her hand, pressing the coins into her palm.

Knigh.

The hairs on her arms stood on end. She gritted her teeth. His touch had no effect on her. None whatsoever.

Urgh, why did I say he could help me find Drake's treasure? It had been a stupid, *stupid* moment of weakness, wanting to help his family... not wanting to say goodbye to him. The way he'd bathed her that night must've addled her brain—no one had treated her so gently since she was a child. After all the pain of the gibbet cage, was it any wonder it had messed with her mind and screwed up her judgement? Well, with any luck, he'd be only too happy to leave her to her own devices once they were back in Arawaké.

"Let me help you, *my love.*" He turned over her hand, exposing the spot up her sleeve where she'd been hiding cards all evening. As if it was a caress, he slipped his fingertips under the cuff and across the delicate skin of her inner wrist, no doubt checking for more illicit cards.

Well, he could check all he liked. She'd used the last one in that hand.

He gave her a pointed look.

So what if she'd cheated? It was his fault she had nothing of her own—or at least hadn't until she'd had such a mysteriously good run of luck at cards tonight. She couldn't keep relying on him and his money forever. Hells, he had so little of the stuff, she couldn't if she wanted to.

No way did she want to rely on Knigh Blackwood for anything.

Not after what he'd done.

Her chest tightened.

His hand was still on her, fingers on her pulse point. He'd gone very still. So had the room. His eyes were doing that thing again—saying sorry without any words.

Well, sorry wouldn't cut it. Not when he'd betrayed her, arrested her, and left her at the mercy of a naval court.

Yes, she was *technically* guilty of the crimes. But that wasn't the point.

The *point* was, he'd shared her bed and said such pretty, *pretty* words when all the time he'd plotted with FitzRoy to capture her and claim the bounty on her head.

And it was a very sharp point—a lot like a dagger in the back.

Oh, he'd tried to explain. During this trip, he must have made at least half a dozen attempts. But every time he started, rage bubbled up in her, burning and unbearable.

At least, that's what she thought it was. If it wasn't rage stinging her eyes and blocking her throat, then it was something far worse.

Something unacceptable. Something powerless and pathetic and broken. Something she *would not* succumb to.

Anger was stronger.

Lord Pevensey cleared his throat.

Knigh flinched as if he'd forgotten they had company. Vice blinked and snatched her hand away, skin burning where he'd touched it.

"Are we going to play another hand," Pevensey said, his voice teasing as he raised one black eyebrow, "give us a chance to win back our money, or are you two going to do this all evening?"

Vice smirked. Another hand meant another chance for her to win. She stacked her coins. "Well, if you—"

"I'm afraid not," Knigh said with a stiff smile. "My wife grows tired. She's on the mend, but we mustn't keep her from her sleep. Isn't that right, darling?"

Vice's skin prickled, and her hand squeezed around a golden guinea until it bit into her skin. She was still weak from the iron gibbet cage, and she'd spent the first few days of the voyage sleeping, but she'd put on weight and had much more energy now.

Last night, she'd burned another candle low trying to work out FitzRoy's damn clue. When she'd opened his pouch, she'd found a page torn from what was perhaps a handwritten journal with lines from Drake's poetry written on one side. Whoever had copied it had broken the lines in strange places, leaving half the page empty. On the back were a few jagged lines, like someone's pen had meandered across the page. Was that a clue or an accident?

One thing was for certain—it was bloody infuriating and she'd made no progress on working out what it meant, despite not dropping into bed until eleven o'clock.

Still, if she could manage that, she could stay up later than—she glanced at the clock on the wall—than *nine.*

This wasn't his concern about her health.

Jaw clenched, she unleashed a first-rate glare at him. How bloody dare he? If she cheated, it was none of his business. Besides, the Pevenseys could afford to lose it.

"Indeed, you seem much improved, Lady Villiers." Pevensey gave her a small, pitying smile that turned her stomach. His wife's opposite in looks and character—dark where she was fair, arch where she was gentle—the expression was all wrong on him. "Though I'm sure your health wasn't helped by that terrible fright you had on your way to Portsmouth."

"Oh," Lucia exclaimed and fanned her face. "Do not mention it, darling! I cannot bear to hear of it." Swallowing, she turned her wide blue eyes to Vice. "You poor thing! Attacked by a highwayman—I don't know how you survived. It must have been so frightening." She bit her lip. "Tell me about him again."

For someone who couldn't bear to hear of it, Lucia asked about the fabricated attack a lot—every night they'd dined together, in fact.

Knigh had made the story up to explain Vice's—or rather, Lady Villiers' lack of jewels and limited wardrobe. After all, the wife of a viscount should have rings and necklaces and new gowns for her trip.

But she wasn't his wife. Verity, Lady Villiers didn't exist. She was Lady Vice, wanted pirate, and here solely out of necessity. Perhaps Knigh had forgotten that.

Fine, if he wanted to usher her away like a good fake-wife, he could. But it wouldn't be without consequences.

"Frightening doesn't cover it, Lucia." Vice made her voice grave, her chest heave, as if terrified at the thought. "He's quite the most vicious beast I've ever encountered."

She shot Knigh a small, cruel smile.

Just desserts.

She widened her eyes, the perfect mirror of Lucia's expression. "I rather think he played upon my sympathies, telling me how desperate his family's situation was, plying me with pretty manners and even prettier words. Why, I nearly cared for him"—only *nearly*—"but then he took *everything.*"

Maybe Knigh hadn't taken it, exactly, but he'd made her lose it all and that was practically the same thing.

She raised an eyebrow at him, while Lucia gasped and fluttered about how terrible it was.

Knigh's face was a mask. Still. Solid. Only his chest moved, steady.

Then his nostrils flared, just once, the movement so small no one would have seen if they hadn't been paying attention.

But Vice *was* paying attention. And as far as Knigh Blackwood was concerned, that minuscule movement was a great victory.

"Now, darling," she drawled and rose, slipping the coins in her pocket, "let us retire, since I'm so *very* tired." She held out her hand as if she needed his help.

He had no one to blame but himself. She was only playing up to the role he'd made for her—the invalid wife who needed to get to bed so early. The poor weak thing.

Maybe it was cruel. But it wasn't as cruel as locking a fae-blooded woman in an iron cage. And it wasn't as cruel as sleeping with someone you planned to betray.

A breath later, Knigh rose and circled the table, his face a mask once more. "Of course," he murmured, offering his arm.

They wished the Pevenseys goodnight and left the cabin. No sign of Barnacle—probably off with the ship's tomcat again.

In silence, Vice and Knigh walked the corridor, gaits offsetting the ship's sway with ease.

She let out a long breath. That sway cooled her, pushed away the anger. Not so long ago, she thought she'd never feel it again.

The sea.

Her beloved sea. Immense. Ancient. Ever-moving. It whispered to her gift, called her, sang to her.

It would never let her down.

Unlike Knigh Blackwood.

KEEPING UP WITH THE PEVENSEYS

As soon as their cabin door closed, Vee rounded on him, cheeks flushed, eyebrows drawn low.

"How bloody dare you?"

Knigh held his face stiff against the desire to wince. Stopping her cheating *was* the right thing to do and yet...

After what he'd done, perhaps he should let her do whatever she wished. It certainly didn't feel right to deny her anything.

But, gods, this cabin—it was too small for both of them *and* her anger. A double bunk against the bulkhead with a chest at its foot, a tiny desk and a dressing table, then a strip of deck down the middle. That was it.

Chest heaving, she shook her head. "You do understand you're the reason I have no money, don't you? All I wanted was some of my own."

He stood stock-still, but inside, his stomach twisted and his heart faltered. A chill snaked through his bones.

It *was* his fault.

Just like her skinny body was his fault, and her wasted

muscles, too. She had put on weight but still didn't fill the clothes he'd bought her. Physically, she was a shadow of the woman he'd first met. And her gift wasn't in any better condition.

His fault.

His poor judgement. *Again.*

Bile touched the back of his throat.

Jaw clenched, he swallowed. "And how would we have explained it when they discovered you were cheating?"

"They wouldn't have found out." She huffed and turned her back on him, pacing as far away as she could in the cramped cabin. Scowling, she yanked pins from her hair, wincing and rubbing her scalp. She did that most nights—the weight of her hair coiled and pinned in place was yet another small torture he'd played a part in inflicting upon her.

She shot him a sharp glance and dropped the hair pins on the dressing table. "And there is no *we*. *I* could've explained it away just fine." She began to undress, shrugging off the top layer of her gown. "Thanks ever so much for your concern."

He sighed and untied his cravat. There was a *we* whether she liked it or not. It might have been necessity, but it was still there. If they were going to make it back to Arawaké safely, they needed the Pevenseys as well as Billy and his crew to believe that they were indeed husband and wife, rather than fugitives—she a pirate and he a Navy deserter.

Deserter.

He held still as his stomach twisted again. Deserters were cowards. They fled their duty to Queen, country, and comrades. Yes, he'd walked away from his post, but he'd done it out of a sense of duty to right the wrong he'd done Vee.

No matter how much he turned the thoughts around in his head, the two things didn't fit. Deserters were cowards.

He shook his head, running his hands over his face. However

hard it was to reconcile, the outcome was the same—he was a deserter and the punishment for that was death.

At least he and Vee had that in common.

All stiff, jerky movements, she finished undressing and threw her clothes into the chest at the end of the bed, leaving just a chemise skimming her body.

He winced, first at the careless way she stowed her clothing, then at the lack of curves for that chemise to glide over. The hips he'd held on to, the breasts he'd worshipped, both diminished thanks to the torture of an iron cage.

His fault.

Breaths heaving, he turned away and hung up his jacket. His chest was hollow, his heartbeat echoing against his ribs.

"The Viscountess Villiers," she muttered with a snort. "Well, at least Papa would be happy to hear that, albeit three years too late."

He scrubbed his face again. Such a tangled web. Pretending to be married to his former fiancée... Lying about her name—Verity was the first name he'd come up with, easy to explain away if he slipped and called her Vee.

Plus the fact they'd ended up on Billy's ship, of all places. Hopelessly tangled.

Stuck at sea with the two people he'd most wronged in his twenty-three years of life. Perhaps the gods were even more angry at him than Vee was, and this was their way of punishing him.

He'd caused this. He had to endure it.

With a long breath, he squared his shoulders and faced her.

She stood at the dressing table, shawl tugged around her shoulders. She was often cold since her ordeal.

Another stab of guilt in his gut. He clenched his jaw against it.

A small teapot sat on the dressing table, steam rising from the spout. The cabin boy must've brought it while they'd been playing cards.

Vee poured the hot water into a cup, then stirred in a spoonful of herbs. An open jar stood beside it, the green, brown, and purple herbs familiar.

Why would she have the preventative? And where from? He hadn't presumed to pick the stuff up when he'd bought her supplies ahead of their escape.

Maybe it was a different tea. He cleared his throat. "Is that—"

"Yes. It is. It helps with our moons." The teapot's lid clattered off when she slammed it on the table, her shoulders square, back to him. "Get over yourself. I'm not about to jump on you. It's not all about sex."

Knigh winced. Two words. That's all it took to set her off, like ill-treated gunpowder.

And he was the one who'd done the ill treatment.

It wasn't as though he expected her to want him. Not after betraying her so badly. He'd hurt her too much. They'd so nearly had something, but now all that was left was this mangled wreckage.

He smoothed away the wince. Helping her get back to Arawaké wouldn't repair things between them, but it was the only way he knew to even attempt to make amends. He had to endure this.

Stay the course.

With all the timing of a ship-killing wave in a storm, an all-too-familiar creaking began from the cabin next door. Rhythmic. A woman's cry. A muffled grunt.

"Do they never stop?" Vee hissed.

The Pevenseys. Very happily married, by the sounds of it. Every night. A noisy, insistent reminder of what was missing from this cabin. From his life.

The air thickened.

Just a few months ago, he would have taken those two paces towards Vee, pulled the shawl away and replaced it with his own warmth. He'd have traced the lines of her back with his hands, lifted her into his arms, covered her mouth with his, and taken her to that bunk. Their cries would have put the Pevenseys to shame.

Now, those two paces may as well have been two leagues of rough sea for all he could walk across it.

She spun on her heel, eyes wide.

He froze, face hot. She couldn't know his dangerous thoughts. Did she somehow want—

Then he heard it, too: a shout. "Help!"

From above deck.

"Man overboard!"

BENEATH THE SURFACE

Knigh's stomach dropped, and he threw open the door. Vee sprung after, tea forgotten.

Frowning, he called over his shoulder, "Vee, you can't—"

"What have I told you about telling me what I can't do?"

He huffed through his nose, running for the companionway. No time to argue, even if she was wrong.

If a sailor had fallen overboard, he'd be left behind in the darkness, floating on an endless ocean for cold or sea or creatures to snuff out. The only hope was to halt the ship as quickly as possible and send a swimmer or boat back.

But in the dark...

Legs pumping, Knigh took the steps two at a time.

Problem was, most sailors couldn't swim.

"Llyr!" The shouts were louder. Llyr was one of the younger apprentices, a cheerful boy of fifteen with a keen eye.

Other cabin doors thudded open. Vee's breaths huffed behind

him. She was too weakened for this. If she exhausted herself, she could get ill again.

To aft, men clustered on the quarterdeck with lanterns. To fore, there was movement and the scrape and squeak of wood and metal—they were launching the ship's boat.

"Heave!" Beyond the common room skylight, men braced the main mast, readying the ship to heave to.

Vee could halt it quicker, but...

He paused at the base of the quarterdeck steps and turned to the companionway as Vee emerged. Breaths heavy, she leant on the skylight.

"We need to stop." Just saying it tightened his throat. She hadn't been able to use her gift since Portsmouth, but if they didn't reach Llyr, the boy would die.

Taking a deep breath, she nodded and clenched her jaw. "I—I can do it." Another inhale and she closed her eyes, a frown running dark lines between her brows.

Something in the air changed. Maybe the pressure, maybe the wind, but it made his ears pop, like diving at the reef had.

The ship drew to a halt and shouts of surprise came from the men working the lines.

Face tense with concentration, Vee nodded. "I've got it."

Torn between running to the quarterdeck and keeping an eye on her, Knigh started up the steps, constantly glancing between her and the lanterns raised over the stern.

When they reached the crowd searching over the rail, his muscles were thrumming with pent-up energy and she had paled a few shades.

"Llyr!" The cry went over and over. No response.

The sea was black and glinting like spilt ink. The night sky was lighter, spattered with a spray of stars, twinkling and serene despite the calamity playing out on the *Swallow*.

Hands tight on the rail, Knigh scanned the ever-shifting waves. At his side, Vee did the same. Out on the water, movement flickered, and he sucked in a breath to shout that he'd seen Llyr, but then a gleam of cold moonlight followed. It was only the shadows playing tricks.

The crew discussed who could swim—not many of them. And it didn't sound like they were confident in their skill.

"I need to"—Vee pulled the shawl from her shoulders—"if I get in there, I can—"

"No." His stomach lurched, and he yanked the shawl back into place. "Vee, no."

"Don't you—"

"I'm not telling you what you can't do," he hissed. "Yes, you'd be the best person to go in any normal circumstances, but"—he pushed the soft wool onto her shoulder, letting his hand rest there just a moment—"but you're not well enough. You're freezing and I can see how much it's taking out of you to hold us still. That boy needs you to keep the wind in check."

Was she always going to be like this—weakened, because of his betrayal?

Her jaw knotted, and she glanced out across the waves, nostrils flaring. "Gods damn it, Blackwood. I hate it when you're right."

"Sorry." He winced.

She was right about one thing—someone needed to get in the water and find him. It was the only way.

How must it feel out there? Cold. Alone in the dark. Unable to swim.

Teeth clenched, Knigh nodded to Vee before turning and threading through the crowd to Billy.

He leant against the stern rail, hand clenched upon it, pale in the lantern light. His usually bright expression had vanished and his round eyes squinted out over the water. A balding sailor beside him held a coil of rope in one hand and its end in the other as if ready to throw it out to Llyr.

"Billy." Knigh clapped him on the shoulder. "I can swim. I'll go." He nodded to the sailor, who blinked once before handing over the rope. Eyes on the sea, Knigh tied one end around his waist.

There was movement behind him. "Knigh"—Vee grabbed his hand—"no. What are you doing?"

Knigh? She hadn't called him that since Portsmouth. It was always Blackwood.

When he looked up from the knot, her expression made his guts twist. Eyes wide. Brows knotted more tightly than the rope at his waist. She was afraid.

She shook her head. "If you go in there I—I can't pull you back in." She squeezed his hand, gaze beseeching. "Please, Knigh, don't."

Turning his hand, he caught her chilly fingers. "I have to."

Alone in the dark and the cold, unable to swim...

Knigh shuddered. The poor boy could be dead already.

He grazed his thumb over her knuckles, then finished the knot. "How do you think people manage when they don't have a sea witch on board?" He patted the rope and tried a reassuring smile.

She still wore the same stricken expression.

Seeing Vee afraid was frightening in itself. Seeing her afraid for him...

He shook his head and turned for the rail. No time to puzzle over that.

The soft hush of oars signalled the ship's boat was in the water. A moment later, it came into view, lanterns pooling across the sea's surface.

Beyond their light, the blackness stretched out, now punctuated by the occasional ripple reflecting golden light.

Nodding to Billy, Knigh climbed onto the rail, his balance effortless from a decade of working on ships. He threw the coil of rope to the burly bosun, Morholt, who piloted the ship's boat. An experienced sailor, he caught it deftly and nodded, understanding what Knigh meant to do.

Knigh took a long breath and dived.

Follow Knigh into the dark—read AGAINST DARK TIDES now.

ACKNOWLEDGMENTS

Writing might seem like a solitary pursuit, but getting a book out into the world is by no means a solo effort.

Huge thanks and adoration, then to my crit partners/author support life raft committee/all round awesome Team GLORF: Catharine, Beth, and Jennifer. I consider myself so lucky to have found you three. Thanks for all your feedback, support, and encouragement, especially in getting Vice's story out into the world.

Love and thanks to my author friends who are always ready with feedback on book descriptions or to share the latest thing they've learned. This includes but is not limited to the RFS crew, Carpe Fabulum, and all the amazing friends I've made through 20Books conferences, podcasts, and so on. I couldn't keep going without you wonderful folk.

A massive thank you to my amazing cover designers: Deranged Doctor Design. Daaaaaamn, you guys! You nail it every time. And huge thanks to Trif, who created the new text-based versions of the covers – aren't they stunning?

Infinite thanks to my Advance Team and ARC readers for their amazing hard work and kindness in reading and reviewing my work. I am humbled by your generosity.

Thank you to all my wonderful readers (yeah, you guys!) who join my newsletter, review my books, or send me emails/tweets/Facebook messages/pictures of them reading my books on Instagram. I always dreamed of having a book out in the world with my name on it. I didn't even think to dare hope I'd hear from readers but now I do and it is the best feeling ever. So, **thank you.**

And thanks, always, to my mum and sister for encouraging my love of books and to my husband for all his support.

ALSO BY CLARE SAGER – SET IN THE SABREVERSE

SHADOWS OF THE TENEBRIS COURT

Gut-wrenching romance full of deceit, desire, and dark secrets.

This series follows Vice's sister, Kat.

Book 1 – *A Kiss of Iron*

Book 2 – *A Touch of Poison*

Book 3 – Title TBA.

BOUND BY A FAE BARGAIN

Steamy fantasy romances featuring unwitting humans who make bargains with clever fae. Each book features a different couple. Interconnected standalones.

Stolen Threadwitch Bride

These Gentle Wolves

MORTAL ENEMIES TO MONSTER LOVERS

Five fantasy romances each by different authors, set in their own worlds. These enemies to lovers stories are united in their promise to deliver "I came to kill you" angst, scorching romances with inhuman, morally grey heroes, and happily ever afters.

Slaying the Shifter Prince, by Clare Sager – Set in Elfhame

Discover the full series here:

www.mortalenemiestomonsterlovers.com

ABOUT THE AUTHOR

Clare Sager writes fantasy adventures full of action, intrigue, and romance. She lives in Nottingham, Robin Hood country, so it's no surprise she writes about characters who don't always play by the rules.

You can find her online home at www.claresager.com or connect with her on social media at the links below or by email at clare@claresager.com.

instagram.com/claresager
tiktok.com/@claresager
bookbub.com/authors/clare-sager
facebook.com/claresagerauthor
amazon.com/author/claresager
twitter.com/ClareSAuthor

Made in United States
Orlando, FL
26 September 2023

37308968R00326